ONE MORE DANCE WITH DADDY

A NOVEL BY

CONSTANCE L. COOPER

©2023 by Constance L. Cooper
All rights reserved. No part of this book may be reproduced, stored in a retrieval system or transmitted in any form or by any means without the prior written permission of the publishers, except by a reviewer who may quote brief passages in a review to be printed in a newspaper, magazine or journal.

The author grants the final approval for this literary material.

First printing

This is a work of fiction. Names, characters, businesses, places, events, and incidents are either the products of the author's imagination or used in a fictitious manner. Any resemblance to actual persons, living or dead, or actual events is purely coincidental.

ISBN: ???

Printed in the United States of America

One More Dance with Daddy is printed in Calluna

Cover design and layout by KingsizeCreations, LLC
www.kingsizecreations.com

ONE MORE DANCE WITH DADDY

CONTENTS

PRELUDE - MARLENE	
CHAPTER 1 - CAROLINA AT KADENA	1
CHAPTER 2 - HOME AGAIN	15
CHAPTER 3 - A RING ON HER FINGER	38
CHAPTER 4 - BLINDSIDED	54
CHAPTER 5 - MASON	69
CHAPTER 6 - ILLUSIONS AND DISILLUSIONS	88
CHAPTER 7 - ENDINGS AND BEGINNINGS	104
CHAPTER 8 - MARK	122
CHAPTER 9 - CALLING IT QUITS	138
CHAPTER 10 - A NEW BEGINNING	153
CHAPTER 11 - JEFF	166
CHAPTER 12 - LOVE AND THE LOSS THEREOF	183
CHAPTER 13 - DADDY'S GONE	198
CHAPTER 14 - LIVING THE DREAM	214
CHAPTER 15 - CORPORATE WIFE, CORPORATE LIFE	229
CHAPTER 16 - AN ADDITION TO THE FAMILY	244
CHAPTER 17 - CALIFORNIA HERE WE COME	260
CHAPTER 18 - CALIFORNIA, THERE WE GO	276
CHAPTER 19 - KIRK	291
CHAPTER 20 - COMPLICATIONS	307
CHAPTER 21 - JORDYN	321
CHAPTER 22 - A COLD DAY IN HELL	337
CHAPTER 23 - THE END OF A ROAD	352
CHAPTER 24 - DALLAS IN THE REAR VIEW MIRROR	368
CHAPTER 25 - PRISON, FRAUD AND THE SHAPE OF THINGS TO COME	383
CHAPTER 26 - FLOOD	398
CHAPTER 27 - STARTING OVER	413
FINALE - THE ANNIVERSARY	423

PRELUDE
MARLENE

On a bright spring morning just after sunrise, the road west from San Antonio uncurled over the rising Hill Country like a dark gray ribbon of asphalt paving. The road slashed across meadows thickly strewn with wildflowers, some patches so thickly grown that they appeared as a solid patch of color – the dark blue tipped with white of bluebonnets, yellow coreopsis, yellow and red Indian blanket, and pale pink primroses. The azure sky was dotted with puffs of cotton-white cloud, moving as slowly as the occasional cow, sheep or goat grazing in their pastures. The girl in the passenger seat of the Oldsmobile sedan flipped her long dark brown hair back over her shoulder and stretched out her legs. The sun had risen at their back, sending long dark shadows racing ahead of the Olds, every time they came to a rise in the road. The two women had gotten an early start, in the early morning darkness for the day long drive.

"It was nice of your dad to loan you his car for the trip. It's twelve hours to get to El Paso – and it better be worth it to see that boyfriend of yours." Marlene commented.

"This old thing?" her good friend, Betty Ellison looked sidewise. "Daddy's buying a brand-new Ford for himself, so he said Mama and I could drive this car. It will be worth it all, Marlene. I simply can't bear it if Bud ships out to Korea without my seeing him before he leaves – I would simply die! I'm so glad that you could come with me; Daddy simply wouldn't allow me to drive all the way to El Paso alone. It's just not safe these days. What if I had a flat tire? And Mama wouldn't approve of Bud and I going out together without a girlfriend to chaperone." Betty giggled. "But since you're perfect, being an ol' married woman with a li'l boy and a lap-baby, Mama approved!"

"Not as old as that!" Marlene flared up with mild indignation. "I'm only twenty-two on my next birthday – it's not my fault that Gianni and I married so young, and he turned out to be a no-account cheating hound-dog. I was only fifteen, he was nineteen; everyone thought he was a good Italian boy, and we were perfect for each other, and there was a war on, too. No one knew how many more years the war would last and what might happen if his draft number came up, so my parents let us go ahead." The indignation faded. "I 'spose they feel a bit guilty about that now. That's why they were so nice about minding Frankie and Carolina this weekend. Anyway, Poppa Lew loves Frankie, and thinks the world of him. He's gonna pay for him to go to a good private school when he's old enough!"

"And Carolina's a real sweetie," Betty agreed. "I can't hardly wait until Bud and I get married and have babies of our own!"

"Just be certain in your own mind that Bud's the right guy for you," Marlene sighed. "Not only was Gianni Amato a no-good cheating hound, but he wasn't above hitting me, when he had too much to drink and his boss at the job was giving him fits. I couldn't take it anymore; I was afraid he might start beating on Frankie and the baby, so I left him a note one morning and took myself and the kids back to San Antonio on the train before he ever went that far."

"Does he ever come to see the kids?" Betty asked, sympathetically. The Olds topped another rise with an effortless surge of the powerful engine.

"No," Marlene answered, a frown cutting a severe line across an otherwise flawless brow. "He'd have to come all the way from Houston; he's such an awful father I purely don't want him to have anything to do with Frankie and Carolina. Me, I wish I could find a daddy for them as good a daddy as Poppa Lew is for Bobbie an' Jane and me."

"Well, Bud has lots of single pals," Betty consoled her friend. "Maybe one of them would suit."

"I just don't think so," Marlene sighed. "Trust me on this – there aren't many guys out there who want to take on a ready-made family and all. I'm almost resigned to being a grass widow."

"You?" Betty chortled outright. "You're gorgeous! You look like Dorothy Lamour, and you dance like Ginger Rogers! Wear that lovely slinky black cocktail dress that you packed, the one with sequins on it, when Bud takes us to the Officer Club for supper and dancing, and you'll have to borrow a baseball bat to beat all the lonely men off with! It's a big post, and surely most of them haven't promised to be faithful to the girl back home."

"I hope so," Marlene replied, sourly. "I've had enough of two-timing men and mean drunks for one lifetime!"

"All right then," Betty glanced down at the gas gage. "We're almost to Junction – let's trade off driving there. We have enough in the tank to get to Fort Stockton and gas up there. Maybe find a place for a bit of lunch. If we top up again in Van Horn and don't waste any time there, we'll be in El Paso by six o'clock. I'll call Bud from the Coral Motel and he'll come to get us for supper. We'll have a wonderful time, I promise!"

• • •

They reached El Paso just at sundown; the crest of the mountain range rising above the city like a slumbering lion was touched with a line of bright gold against a sky briefly tinted the color of oyster shell. Lights in the city began to twinkle, like fireflies in the shadow below. With gratitude, Marlene slid out from behind the wheel of the Olds, stretching her stiffened knee joints and flexing fingers cramped from a three-hour-long stint at the wheel, as Betty went into the motel office to check in, and to call Bud from the pay phone there. Marlene had little hope for this weekend, having agreed to the trip mostly to break up the routine, and to get away from her parents' big house, where she lived with her two children. She always felt a little guilty, asking her parents to babysit so that she could go out to a movie, or out dancing; it was a frivolous and unserious thing for a mother to do, and although her parents never voiced an unkind word on the rare occasions when she asked them for that favor, Marlene felt their unvoiced disapproval deeply.

Now Betty emerged from the motel office, swinging a key on a ring around her finger.

"Room ten!" she exclaimed merrily, "And I got ahold of Bud. He's coming to get us in half an hour! Can you be ready in that time? I call first dibs on the bathroom!"

"Only if you don't take more than ten minutes at it," Marlene replied. "I want to wash up, too, since we're all sweaty and sticky from the drive…"

"As for me, I value my personal daintiness," Betty snickered, and Marlene made as if to hold her nose.

"As if your boyfriend would seriously mind, if you were all sweaty and sticky," Marlene put the Olds into gear, and drove slowly into the motel grounds – a long 'U' shaped compound, of single-story rooms, with overhanging tile roofs which provided partial shelter for parking. The rooms all had doors painted in bright colors – coral, orange, turquoise and green. She parked the Olds in front of Unit 10, and Betty unlocked the door with a flourish.

"Last one in's a rotten egg!" Betty caroled, as Marlene fetched her suitcase from the Olds.

The two girls spent a frantic twenty-five minutes in bathing, dressing, and vying for space in front of the single bathroom mirror, applying makeup and doing their hair. Marlene put her dark brown hair up in a loose roll, allowing one long curl to drape artistically over her shoulder. Barely had she started applying dark red lipstick, then there was a quiet knock on the door.

Betty squealed, "He's here! Bud! How do I look, Marlene?"

"Like every lonely soldier's dream," Marlene answered, and went on carefully outlining her lips while Betty flew to the door. She counted to ten, and then to twenty, hearing the door open and shut, a male voice saying, "Hi, beautiful – it's so good to see you!" and Betty replied with incoherent expressions of endearment. Then Marlene emerged from the bathroom, slightly miscalculating how long the embrace between Bud and Betty would last.

"Oh, Bud," Betty gasped, as they sprang apart, somewhat guiltily. Betty was blushing furiously, and Bud had a smear of her red lipstick on his chin. "This is my friend Marlene – I wrote you about her, I think. We took turns driving. Marlene – this is Bud. Captain Gene Russell – just that everyone calls him Bud."

Bud was a husky, open-faced young officer, with an innocent face and short brush-cut brown hair; Marlene was absolutely certain he had gone out for football in high school or college – likely quarterback. He just had that look about him.

"I certainly hope this is Bud; otherwise, you would have a lot of explaining to do," Smiling, Marlene collected up her evening handbag from the bed, and the light wrap which went with the black sequined dress. "Pleased to make your acquaintance, Bud – Betty didn't stop talking about you all the way from San Antonio."

"She's quite a girl," Bud replied, proudly. "Are you two ladies ready for dinner? I'm gonna be the talk of the battalion, when I walk into the club with two gorgeous women on my arm."

"Tell them we're your harem," Marlene replied, and they all laughed.

• • •

Heads did indeed turn when Bud escorted Betty and Marlene into the Officer Club in time for supper. A quiet rustle of conversation throughout the elegantly appointed dining room momentarily died. In the brief silence, a waiter showed the three to a booth along the far wall and took their orders for a drink from the bar. Betty and Bud sat close together opposite, while Marlene took out a cigarette and lighted it. The lights in the crystal-hung chandeliers overhead were turned low, like yellow candlelight, reflecting on polished silver, crystal, and china. Each table was spread with crisp white linen tablecloths, set in the center with vases of fresh flowers, and white candles in silver holders. Most tables in the dining room were occupied – taken up by men, most of them young, some in uniform. Those few women, scattered among them were all well and tastefully dressed – and Marlene was reassured that she looked just as good as they did, and that her own black cocktail dress from Joske's department store in San Antonio was every bit as chic and fashionable.

This was all so elegant, Marlene thought wistfully. She would love to be regularly escorted to a nice high-class place like this for supper by a handsome young officer.

As the waiter appeared with their drinks and delivered a sheaf of menus along with them, Marlene noticed a young officer in a convivial group of men at another table staring fixedly at her. She looked away for a moment to tap the ash off her cigarette, but when she looked again in his direction, he was still staring at her. He was tall and fair-haired, with a square jaw – she thought he looked a bit like Steve Canyon the flier, who appeared every week in the Sunday comic pages.

Somewhat flustered by this, Marlene turned her attention towards the menu, assuming that if the young man at the other table was so interested in her that he must make as excuse to approach their table and strike up a conversation. Surely Bud must know who he was …

"What do you think I should order?" she asked Bud. "It all sounds terribly good, but I just can't make up my mind!"

"The trout almandine is good," Bud replied, "But I'm going for the prime rib special."

"Whatever you think would be best," Marlene replied, and closed the menu. "Since you're buying. Bud, who is that – the blond man with that group at the big table? He keeps looking over at me."

Bud glanced over at the table across the room from them. "Oh, Captain Visser, you mean? The guys call him Dutch. Dutch Visser; bit of a stick in the mud, though. He doesn't have a regular lady friend. Doesn't drink much so he's not much fun at parties, but he's as smart as a whip."

"He sounds nice," Betty chirped. "It would be perfect if he came to the dance with us – then you would have a date, too, Marlene…"

"It would," Marlene agreed, somewhat wistfully, but when she glanced over at the table where the blond officer had been sitting, he was not there. She glanced casually around the dining room but didn't spot the handsome Captain Visser anywhere. She felt a distinct pang of disappointment; a stick in the mud, an officer, and one who didn't drink. He would certainly be a change and a step up from her ex-husband in Houston. *Ah, well – plenty of fish in the sea, and plenty of handsome and unattached young men at Fort Bliss*, Marlene thought, philosophically as Bud caught the eye of their waiter and beckoned him over to take their order.

• • •

Saturday morning, the day that followed before the girls had to return to San Antonio, was to be spent at the big swimming pool that was part of the Officer Club complex. Bud came to the Coral Motel in his own car and gave them a brief tour of the historic part of the fort; the old cavalry barracks from the last century, a long avenue planted with many trees and lined with tile-roofed officer's houses, and the square mansion with galleries all the way around which once was the home of General Pershing. Bud pointed out the old main guardhouse and a range of long stone-built buildings which once housed the quartermaster stables, and wagon and wheelwright workshops. Betty was impressed, and Marlene politely pretended to be. The mountain ridge loomed over Fort Bliss like an enormous sleeping lion. The morning was cool, but the cloudless sky promised a warm afternoon. They spread out their towels on the soft green grass at the edge of the pool, while Bud and Betty dared each other to jump in first.

"It's too cold yet for me," Marlene insisted, and let them go. She was pulling on the rubber swimming cap on her head, trying not to pull too painfully on her long hair, as she tugged the edges flat. Concentrating on that task, she didn't realize another presence until a shadow fell over her, and a tentative male voice ventured a question.

"Hi … I saw you at the club last night, and I wanted to come over and introduce myself, but you were with friends and …"

Marlene squinted against the bright sunshine – the blond Captain Visser, looking even handsomer in broad daylight. He had blue eyes, as blue as the sky beyond his shoulders. He was wearing swim-trunks and a baggy shirt, half-unbuttoned – obviously he had planned to go for an early morning swim. Right at this moment, he looked uncertain. "Do you come here often…" he asked. "I've never noticed you before, and I think I would have …" His voice died away, and he looked most horribly embarrassed. Marlene found that curiously endearing; so handsome and accomplished, according to Bud – but the farthest thing from the masterful caveman male, about to overwhelm a woman with charm, assurance, and a big club.

"Marlene Stewart … and no, this is the first time. I came with my friend, Betty Ellison – she's dating Bud Russell."

"Adam Visser," he still looked tentative, but his face brightened when he noted the absence of rings on her hands.

"Can you sit down," Marlene suggested. "I'm getting a crick in my neck, looking up at you. Yes, I saw you too, last night in the Club. I thought you might come over and introduce yourself, but you didn't."

"I am now," Adam Visser crossed his legs and dropped to sit, Indian fashion on the grass next to Marlene's towel. "Pleased to make your acquaintance, Miss Stewart."

"It's actually Mrs. Amato," Marlene explained. If he was going to run like a scalded cat, she might as well give him every chance early on. "I was married for a while. But we divorced two years ago, and the kids and I haven't laid eyes on him since."

"Oh?" Adam's face brightened even more, which Marlene found to be reassuring. "Well then it's his loss, I'd say. And my own gain."

That was when Marlene first thought – *I could really come to love a guy like this.*

CHAPTER 1
CAROLINA AT KADENA

Carolina's first memory was of playing in the garden of one of the little houses built from concrete blocks in the officer housing neighborhood where she lived with her older brother Frankie, and their mother and father. All the houses looked alike, plain concrete block walls painted white with red tile roofs, a three-part picture window to the left of the front door, and three smaller windows to the right. Their house was almost brand new, but someone had planted a hibiscus bush with bright red flowers in front of the big window, which made it different from all the other identical houses. Mama made red curtains, to hang in the window, curtains that were the same red as the hibiscus blossoms. All the houses in the family housing area were brand new; there were very few trees, save a scattering of gnarled old ones which hadn't been in the way of building the houses. There was a hill, with a large boulder in it, behind the house, and many dips and hollows in the grassy hillside. Daddy explained once that they were the remains of Okinawan bunkers and trenches from the war. Just over the hill, and outside the base barrier fence, there was a Okinawan tea house, a quaint little place set in a garden with many little shelters under the trees. In the evenings, the music from the tea house floated on the evening air. Carolina listened to that music as she fell asleep in bed every night, the mosquito net over the bed stirring in the evening breeze as if it was dancing to the music.

Sometimes Mama and Daddy would take Carolina and her brother down to the seaside, to play on the white sand beach, build sandcastles, pile sand on top of each other, and see the little salt-water crabs who swiftly tunneled into the wet sand after a crystal-clear wave rolled in. They watched the fishermen going out in their boats; the fishermen were barefoot, but they wore round straw hats with a pointed top and a wide brim. They used big nets to catch fish, every day; flinging the circular nets with a weighted edge so that they seemed to hang in the air for a moment, before falling into the blue-green water and trapping schools of silvery fish. Stunted trees clung to the cliff edges overlooking the beach, hanging on by their roots against the wind and those occasional storms that swept in from the ocean. One of Carolina's vivid memories was of Daddy going through the house, closing, and battening down all the jalousie shutters which covered the windows, as a violent typhoon was about to blow in from the ocean. The house was very dark during that storm, since the lights flickered and went out at the height of it, as the wind howled against the outside walls and heavy raindrops battered against the jalousie shutters. She and Frankie and Mama and Daddy sheltered in the kitchen, the room on the inland side of the house, and Mama told them stories while a camp lantern fizzled and shed white light overhead. When the storm passed, the whole street was strewn with broken branches and leaves shredded from the scattered trees.

Carolina at three and a half years old, often played with one of her dolls strapped to her back with a long scarf, just like Kimi and Suki the Japanese maids had shown her how to do. Kimi and Suki wore colorful kimonos with trailing sleeves, and straw 'zori' sandals on their feet, with a bit that went between their big toes and all the other toes. They did a lot of cleaning and cooking for Mama, and it was very nice, although it seemed as if rice was part of every meal, even breakfast. Carolina liked rice, liked it a lot, and didn't mind eating it at all. Kimi and Suki always had time to play with Carolina; touching her wavy blond hair and saying admiring things to each other in Japanese about Carolina's fair hair and bright blue eyes. They called her Caro-san; it made her very happy when the maids played with her, but she was happiest of all when Daddy came home from work every day, and she ran out the front to meet him, and he swung Carolina up over his head.

"How's my best little girl!" he would say, while Carolina giggled. Then he would put her down on the ground, and turn to six-year-old Frankie, who had the same brown eyes and near-to-black hair as Mama. Frankie would solemnly render a proper military salute to Daddy, who would return the salute. "And my best little soldier!" Daddy would say, and Frankie replied, "Yes, sir!" Then Carolina and Frankie would have playtime with Daddy in the yard, as Mama and Kimi or Suki saw to fixing a supper for them all. Mama would be watching them play from the kitchen window, smiling at the three of them; Daddy tossing a baseball for Frankie and Carolina to catch, teaching Frankie how to ride the new bicycle that he had bought at the Base Exchange, or pulling the red toy Radio Flyer wagon with Carolina riding in it, up and down the yard. Daddy had even built a sandbox in the back yard, for Carolina and Frankie to play in, building roads and tunnels and sandcastles of the fine sea sand that the box was filled with. The sandbox was very popular with the children in other houses close by. Carolina couldn't imagine a happier life.

The only thing that she and Frankie hated was having to drink a big glass of milk made from powder, every evening after supper, while Mama and Daddy smoked their cigarettes. Mama made them drink the milk, saying that it was best for their health – and she and Frankie were not excused from the table until they had drunk every drop. It made Carolina and Frankie both gag until the tears came, although never so much that they threw up.

"I wish that we could get fresh milk, like we did at home!" Mama often said to Daddy, across the table. This puzzled Carolina, every time Mama said this; *weren't they at home?* One afternoon, as they waited for Daddy to come home from work, she asked her older brother for an explanation.

"Frankie, you know how Mama says that we could get nicer milk at home. Aren't we at home?"

Frankie looked scornful. "You're such a baby! You don't remember where we lived before? With Poppa Lew and Granny Margo?"

Carolina solemnly shook her head. "No, I don't. Tell me."

Frankie sighed, making a theatrical show of his exasperation. "You don't remember the big ship, and the ocean all around, and how Mama was so sick from the ship rolling all around. You were sick, too – but I wasn't," he added proudly.

"Tell me," Carolina begged. This was a new thing for her, as she absolutely could not remember any of it. Frankie sighed again.

"We lived in a big house, with Poppa Lew and Granny Margo. That was home, back in the States. From there, we went on a train, first," he said. "You and me, in our pajamas, and wrapped up in blankets, 'cause it was the middle of the night and everything was all dark. Poppa Lew drove us to the train station downtown in his car, with a big stack of our suitcases. There was a big man in a railway uniform, he loaded up all the suitcases into the baggage car and Mama tucked us into bed in a little room in the train. You and I went to sleep right away, 'cause it was that late. When we woke up, the train was out in the desert, jus' rolling along. Then the train came up to mountains, the tallest mountains you'd ever hope to see, going around bends in the track, so that you could look back and see the end of the train. The train tracks went so far up into the mountains that there was nothing but rocks and snow all round, and sometimes went through long dark tunnels made of wood before we came down on the other side of those mountains. Then we got to the city station, in San Francisco – that's a big city on a big ol'bay, on the coast of California. We didn't stay long in San Francisco, though. Mama got a taxi … and all of our suitcases got piled up and tied to the top and the driver took us to a big ol' fort on the other side of the city. Daddy told us afterwards that it was 'the port of embarkation.' An' all the sojurs and airmen shipped out from there, to Japan and the Far East."

"Then what happened?" Carolina asked, breathless with curiosity.

"We went down through the big sheds at the port of embarkation," Frankie explained. "And Mama showed all her papers and orders to a man at the gangway, who let us go onto the big ship. The sailors told me it was named *Breckenridge*, like the park back home, where Poppa Lew used to take me to the zoo and the 'musement park. We were on the ship for weeks. And it was boring and noisy all the time, and you and Mama were sick in our room most of the time, and Mama wouldn't let me go anywhere by myself. She said it was too dangerous, and too easy for me to fall off the ship without her holding on to my hand. But even when she stopped being sick, there was nothing much to look at, just the ocean an' the sky. There weren't even any birds, until we got to Okinawa. I was glad when we got here. Daddy met us and took us to our house. It was funny," Frankie cocked his head to one side, and added. "All the houses looked alike! Daddy said they had just been built, so that families had some place to live."

Carolina was mildly envious of Frankie, when he started the first grade at the elementary school on base for those children of the military, just a short walk away. Carolina envied him for being able to play every day on the school playground with his best friends, Danny Avery and Junior Babcock. Because of their last names, they all sat next to each other in the classroom, and when they lined up to go out to the playground, for fire or storm drills, or to go somewhere else, they were all three next to each other. Sometimes Mama drove Frankie to school, if she wanted to run errands afterwards, in the Hudson sedan that Daddy had bought for the family to use. Mama didn't really like the Hudson, as there was something the matter with it that couldn't ever seem to get fixed.

One day, the Hudson stalled out after a trip to the commissary, with Frankie and Carolina in the back with bags of groceries. This was on a busy road through the base, an uphill road, with a few cars behind them on the road, and many more coming the other way.

Suddenly the engine made a funny grinding sound, and Mama said a few bad words under her breath. The Hudson lurched to one side, the car behind them blared a horn, and Frankie asked,

"Mama, what's wrong?"

"This stupid car!" Mama snapped. "Of all the places to break down ... be quiet, Frankie – tell your sister to sit still!"

Carolina shrank into the corner, suddenly terrified, not so much by the sound the Hudson's engine and gears, other cars honking at them from behind, but by the sound of panic in Mama's voice. The car lurched, and a sack of groceries set on the back seat between them fell over, spilling oranges onto Carolina's lap, and onto the floor. She slid against the back door of the wildly lurching automobile, clutching two oranges. Mama was saying bad words in a low and frantic voice to the steering wheel of the swerving, halting car, while those car horns kept blaring away angrily, just behind them. Frankie reached across the tilting sacks of groceries and put his hand over hers.

"It's okay, Caro ... just be quiet."

Carolina sniffled, and began to cry, in panic – this was worse than a bad dream, Mama so angry at the car, the car that Daddy had bought for them. Frankie repeated, "Caro, don't cry..."

Frankie kept on holding Carolina's hand, even when the car stopped lurching; now the engine noise sounded perfectly regular, and it stopped that dreadful grinding and lurching. Carolina sniffled and wiped her face with the back of her hand. They were at the top of the hill, the hill full of the houses where they lived, just past the elementary school where Frankie went every weekday.

Mama parked the car by their house and began carrying the brown paper bags full of groceries into the house by the door into the kitchen. She was still muttering indignantly to herself, but

Carolina was happy and reassured by the fact that everything was normal again. Kimi had cooked a hot lunch for them, while they were away, and she came to help Mama bring in the groceries. Although that night after supper, when Mama and Daddy smoked their evening cigarettes and Frankie and Carolina struggled to drink their tall glasses of horrible, chalk-tasting milk, Mama mentioned the trouble with the car.

"Adam, that car stalled out today on the hill, coming up from the commissary. I won't drive it again with the children in it, until you can get the darned thing fixed! I can look to myself, if it breaks down again, but I won't risk getting stuck somewhere with Carolina and Frankie in that cranky old thing."

"Don't worry – I'll see what can be done," Daddy promised, and Mama seemed content with that.

But weeks went by, and Daddy kept saying that he would get the car fixed, but nothing ever was done about the problem with the starter or the clutch. Mama turned out to be adamant about not driving it anywhere with Carolina and Frankie in it, and since Daddy loved the children very much as well, he seemed to agree with Mama. Carolina didn't mind; but sitting in the back seat of the Hudson waiting while Mama shopped or ran errands was boring. She would rather have been at home playing with her dolls, or in the sandbox, while Kimi and Suki kept an eye on her as they cleaned the house.

One afternoon, when Mama was out with the car, Frankie said that he was going to go over and play at Junior's house.

"What are you going to do?" Carolina asked, out of idle curiosity. She supposed that they were going to play ball with some of the other boys, in the big vacant field out beyond the base housing where the Babcocks lived; she wasn't the least interested in that. The field ended at the test range, beyond which they were never supposed to go, not even to chase after a lost ball, because it was so dangerous, with the soldiers shooting their guns. Junior Babcock was Frankie's best friend from school, a husky boy who could already ride a two-wheeler bicycle without training wheels and pitch a baseball with surprising accuracy.

"We're going to explore the old tombs on the hill," Frankie whispered furtively, after looking around to see if there were any adults nearby. "Junior says they're haunted. You don't wanna see a ghost, do you?"

Carolina considered this carefully. If there were ghosts up on the hill, hanging around the crumbling, stone-built tombs, then they would be Okinawan ghosts. She liked Kimi and Suki, and the mama-sans in the little shops near the base who made much of her. So did the papa-sans who did work on the base. She decided that she would like their ghosts, too, if there even were any, in daytime. As Carolina had understood it, ghosts only appeared at night. Although maybe it was different for Okinawan ghosts. At any rate, she wasn't afraid of them, and now she had a strong desire to go with Frankie and Junior on their ghost-hunting expedition.

"I do. Take me too, Frankie. If you don't, I'll tell Mama on you, when she gets home."

Frankie looked as if he would refuse, but then he nodded. They told Suki that they were going to play at the Babcocks' house, and Carolina tied her biggest baby-doll to her back with a long scarf. Suki smiled and covered her lips to giggle. Junior Babcock and Danny Avery were waiting for them, sitting on the sidewalk in front of the housing unit. Their faces fell when they saw Carolina.

"I had to bring her, she would tell on me, otherwise," Frankie explained.

"I want to see an Okinawan ghost," Carolina insisted. "Or I'm telling."

The boys assented, with glum faces, and Junior said, "Follow me, then – there's a bunch of paths going every which way up the hill. My Dad said that the Okinawan families come every year on a certain day in the springtime to bring gifts an' things to their ancestors buried up there. Dad says it's sort of a family vault. Some of them have hundreds and hundreds of dead buried in them."

"Like skeletons?" Danny asked, hopefully, and Junior – whose father was one of the Protestant chaplains and therefore knowledgeable about such things – shook his head.

"No ... only ashes in big jars. To fit more of them in, I guess."

The four children trooped across the empty field, following the path beaten into the dirt. The grass on either side at first was clipped and neatly mown, but soon turned tall and untrimmed, waving feathery grass heads in the light breeze which blew from the ocean, as the path wound up the hill, increasingly steeper as the path climbed higher and higher. They passed by wind-tortured pine trees, bent into shapes like gnarled rope, with cloud-shaped bunches of green needles at their ends. The trees on the hill of tombs were shaped like larger versions of those miniature trees in shallow pots, which were everywhere in the little shops outside the base gates.

Carolina was tired from walking and climbing the hill. Her shoes were covered in dust, and she had a scrape on her knee from where she had slipped, going up a particularly steep stretch, a hill so steep that even halfway up they could look back and see the bright white sand beach and blue ocean far below and beyond the long runways and flight line which dominated the base. Despite her skinned knee, she still hoped to see a see an Okinawan ghost – a ghost as friendly as Kimi and Suki.

"Here," Junior whispered, as the path reached a level place, where the hillside had been terraced, and a wall set into the steep hillside opposite. "They come and bring food for the dead kinfolks, and burn black incense, so the ghosts can taste the food. That's what my father says." Carolina looked at it, vaguely disappointed. It looked as if it was a small house, but built into the hill, with only the front wall showing. The roof edge was curved, like the shell of a turtle, seen from the front. There was a solid wooden door reinforced with iron set in the wall, but it was closed and locked with a heavy iron lock. There was a small, paved courtyard in front of the closed door, a space about the size of the bedroom that she and Frankie shared, with a low stone wall along two sides, with a wide opening in the third. There were no ghosts, on a bright and breezy summer day. No flowers either, save the last of a scattering of last years' dead leaves and pine needles blown into the corners.

"Maybe we should have brought food for the ghosts," Carolina suggested.

"I dunno if they would like American food," Danny replied, but he turned out his pockets and put a piece of wrapped candy on the wall. The wrapper had Okinawan lettering on it. "There's a hole in the fence back of my house," he said, by way of explanation. "The Okinawan kids sneak through sometimes, and we trade candy with them – Hershey bars for Okinawan candy."

They waited patiently for a ghost to appear, but none did. With a sigh, Danny retrieved his candy, and they continued following the beaten bath farther up the hillside. The woods and stands of tall bamboo closed in around the path. There were more tombs, embedded in the hillside, some partially ruined and overgrown by bushes and weeds. All the tombs were sealed with closed doors, some chained closed with weathered locks hanging from the chains – all but one, which was the most ruined of all. There was no walled terrace in front of this last one, at the very top of the hill, and the eaves of the curved roof were broken in places.

A rusted grill of iron rods welded together covered the dark opening. There was no means of opening the grill, and the spaces between the rods were too small for anyone to climb through. Surely there was a ghost here, one who might be able to waft through the grill. They took turns, peering into the cave, but it was too dark inside to see anything but what lay in a small square of light close to the opening; a square of dirt and some broken pieces of stone or pottery was all that could be seen. None of the boys had thought to bring a flashlight. Carolina regretfully gave up on the notion of seeing a Okinawan ghost, and so did the boys. It was already late afternoon tending to early evening, and long shadows reached out across the grass. Lightening bugs sparked briefly, as they flitted among the gnarled trees. As much as they hurried down the twisting pathway, it was late by the time they reached Junior's house, even later when Carolina and Frankie reached their house. The sun had already gone down below the horizon. Daddy was already home, and dusk had fallen. Lights shone from the windows, and Daddy was standing on the porch, waiting for them.

"Supper's almost ready," Daddy said. "Your mother was getting worried. Where were you?"

"At Junior's house, playing baseball," Frankie replied, and Daddy looked rather stern.

"Your mother called Mrs. Babcock – and Junior's mom said you were out on the hill behind their house. What were you doing out there – really? And tell the truth, kids."

Frankie gulped; he was not a practiced liar. "We were up on the hill, where all the old Okinawan tombs are, looking for ghosts."

"And you took your little sister with you?"

"She wanted to see ghosts, too," Frankie admitted, and Daddy shook his head.

"Frankie, you shouldn't have done that. Some of those old tombs are derelict – dangerous, even. You might have gotten badly hurt. And besides ... poking around those old tombs is rude. You're trespassing on a family graveyard; that is a place that you ought to treat respectfully. Going around the tombs looking for ghosts is not respectful."

"Sorry, Daddy," Frankie said, and Carolina echoed it. "You won't tell Mama, will you?" Frankie pleaded.

Daddy grinned; both Frankie and Carolina were relieved. Daddy wouldn't tell Mama on them. He was a good sport. "You didn't have to go all the way up the hill, looking for ghosts. They tell me that the northeast gate out to Chibana is haunted by the ghost of one of our own soldiers, with his fatigues all splattered in blood. He asks the gate guards for a light and vanishes as soon as he gets it. Some of the guys swear that a Japanese Samurai warrior in full armor rides his horse up and down Stillwell Drive, or around the golf course." Daddy's face sobered. "The fighting in the war around here was fierce, kids. Men and women died, either in battle, or by killing themselves when it looked like we were winning. It's no wonder at all that some places around here are haunted. Leave the ghosts alone – they deserve some respect. Supper's almost ready, and your mother made chocolate pudding for dessert. You best go inside and wash up."

"Yes, sir!" Frankie ran into the house, Carolina on his heels, both feeling like they had been reprieved. Mama's displeasure was sharp, and pointed, her anger was something to be dreaded, but Daddy was always mild, indulgent, and never angry.

Later that evening Frankie told Carolina that once he and Junior had snuck away to go to the tombs and they were some that were wide open, and they could just walk right into them. Frankie told her that one time he even knocked over a vase and ashes spilled to the ground. Carolina said "Oh, no Frankie! I hope the ghost don't come get you!" That night when Carolina went to bed, covered with the mosquito net, she slept and had bad dreams of scary ghosts.

. . .

An example of Daddy's indulgence was the evening at supper when Carolina asked, "Daddy, can I have a cigarette?"

Mama drew in a sharp breath and began to cough, while Frankie stared in astonishment. Before Mama recovered her voice, Daddy said, calmly, "Sure, Caro – when you finish your milk, come into the living room and I'll let you have a smoke."

"Adam!" Mama hissed, having stopped coughing. Daddy gave her a look and a tiny nod of reassurance.

That evening, Carolina drank her glass of chalk-tasting milk eagerly, and without complaint. Smoking a cigarette after supper was a Mama and Daddy thing, a grown-up thing in which they took pleasure, and now she was going to share in it. How exciting! She could hardly wait. When she had drained the last of the revolting reconstituted powdered milk from the tall glass, she slid down from her chair and ran to the living room, where Daddy sat in the big armchair under the standing lamp where he liked to read. Mama remained in the kitchen, overseeing Frankie and his own glass of milk, while Kimi washed the supper dishes.

"Ready?" He shook out a single cigarette from a crumpled packet. "Let me light it ... and when it gets going, put this end between your lips ... lightly, not biting it! And then inhale, all the way down to your lungs."

Carolina obeyed, and her eyes watered. "Again!" Daddy ordered, and for four or five more puffs, she obeyed, until she began crying and coughing, coughing so hard she was afraid that she might throw up her supper and that nasty milk. At that, Daddy took away the cigarette, stubbed it out in the ashtray, and drew Carolina into his lap, holding and cuddling her until she stopped crying.

"Now you know what it's like," he said, gravely. "Smoking is like drinking and cursing – it's a thing for grownups, not little girls to do. Never ask to smoke a cigarette again, Caro. Promise?"

"I promise," Carolina agreed, thoroughly wretched and never, ever wanting to have anything to do with cigarettes again.

Shortly after the ghost-hunting incident, Frankie came home from school in a bad temper. Mama was out, Kimi was minding Carolina. Her brother stomped into the bedroom which he shared with Carolina, threw his lunchbox across the room, where it banged against the concrete wall and fell to the floor. "I hate him!" he shouted. "I hate him! He ruined everything"

"Hate who?" Carolina demanded. Frankie was so angry that his face was red, and he was nearly crying. "What happened?"

"Daddy!" Frankie shouted, and Carolina was horrified. What had happened – something at school. "He changed my name! Teacher said that since that my last name was Visser now, and not Amato, I had to move to another desk, away from Junior and Danny! Now I must sit in the back row, next to Tony Zampareli, who picks his nose! I hate him, and I hate Daddy, for wrecking everything!"

Carolina was horrified – hate Daddy? What difference did it make at all? It apparently meant an awful lot to Frankie.

"It's because you two are officially my dependents," Daddy explained later, over the supper table, the paperwork finally got expedited through the personnel office, and the school." He looked at Frankie, staring sullenly at his plate, and the inevitable glass of horrible, powdered milk. "It matters to your teacher, son – that the class be in alphabetical order, and since you're my dependents, then you are listed with my last name. It's just the way of doing things."

"I'm not your son!" Frankie muttered. "And I don't care!"

Daddy looked resigned. "As far as the Army goes, you are my dependent, you and your sister and mother. And another thing, whether you care or not. My orders came through today. We're going back to the States in another month, anyway. You'll be farther away from your pals than just across the classroom."

CHAPTER 2
HOME AGAIN

Just before leaving Okinawa, Mama bought a souvenir from one of the little off-base shops by the seashore; a ceramic fisherman, sitting cross-legged, mending his net. It sat on a shelf of curiosities in those homes where they lived in after leaving Okinawa, and then in Carolina's own home. For many years, Carolina would stare into the eyes of the fisherman, wondering if he could see her, and imagining him following her with his eyes as she walked away. Okinawa, with all those green hills, haunted tombs, the white sand beaches and the clear water, Suki and Kimi and the little white house with the tile roof and the hibiscus bush in front of the big window – all that became the memory of a beautiful dream, overlaid by more recent memories. Okinawa sank beyond the horizon, veiled by blue haze as the troopship *SS Sultan* headed east into the Pacific, returning the Visser family to the United States.

"I'm glad we're going home!" Frankie whispered, on that first night, as he and Carolina settled into their bunks. He was still sore about how the official adoption had moved his place in the classroom away from his friends.

"I'm not," Carolina replied, wistfully. "I wish we could have stayed. Daddy …" she raised her voice a little, calling across the cabin, to where Daddy and Mama were sitting up for a while. "Daddy, why couldn't we stay in Okinawa forever?"

"Because I have orders to transfer back to the States," Daddy explained in a patient voice. "I have a slot for flight training at Camp Gary. "– orders are orders, Caro"

"Where's Camp Gary?" Carolina asked. It seemed like everything had been done in a rush, the last few weeks at Kadena, what with their things being packed, the house being stripped of their possessions, the rooms now bare and echoing – home no longer, just an empty unit with bare floors and walls in the family housing area.

"Near San Marcos," Mama answered. "Which is close enough to San Antonio that you two can visit Poppa Lew and Granny Margo, and your Aunt Jane and all your cousins as often as we can make the drive. Won't that be good?"

"Oh, yes!" Frankie sounded delighted. Carolina was a little dubious. She didn't remember her grandparents very well, and Marlene's sisters not at all. When she tried to picture them in her mind, all that came up was a series of small black and white pictures with deckle edges, pasted into Mama's photo album and labeled in her handwriting along the bottom border. There was Aunt Bobbie, who was Mama's older sister, and Aunt Jane, the younger sister, and Granny Margo. In the pictures they all had dark hair, and looked alike – Aunt Bobbie, Mama, Aunt Jane. Granny Margo looked hardly older than her three daughters, as she had married very, very young. In her private heart, Carolina went on missing where they had lived in Kadena for a very long time; the green hills, the glitter of the distant ocean, of Daddy coming home every day and playing with her and with Frankie while Mama put the finishing touches on supper.

• • •

Because everything seemed to go horrible and wrong, once the Visser family returned to Texas. They settled into a small, dingy second-floor apartment in New Braunfels, halfway between San Marcos and San Antonio. Daddy could drive to work at Camp Gary in their only car during the week, and then the whole family could go to San Antonio on weekends, to visit Poppa Lew, Granny Margo and Aunt Jane and her family. The apartment building wasn't far from the busy main road between San Antonio and Austin. There was an uninviting yard of brown grass. dirt, and bull thorn stickers, which wasn't any fun at all to play in, not like the mown green grass in the housing area at Kadena. Noise and dust from constant traffic on that road was a constant annoyance, especially on summer nights when the windows had to be open for fresh air; otherwise, the apartment became a hot-box, and the fans barely stirred the air. It was the best that a captain with a wife and two children could possibly afford. Daddy came home late, sometimes well after suppertime, and often much later than that. The only comfort for Carolina was that she made a friend with a little girl her age, who lived in the apartment downstairs; her name was Laura. Laura's family owned a small television set, and her mother let Laura and Carolina watch *The Mickey Mouse Club* in the late afternoons. Carolina liked this. It was great fun, sitting on the floor of the living room with Laura, and arguing over which one of the boy Mouseketeers they wanted to marry when they grew up.

One particular day, Carolina came trooping up the stairs to the Visser's apartment when *The Mickey Mouse Club* and the cartoons that Laura wanted to watch afterwards were over. Laura's family were ready for supper, and the bright afternoon had already fled from the sky. It sounded as if the evening traffic on the highway had slacked off a bit.

Frankie was sitting on the steps, about halfway up. "Don't go in," he said, gravely. "You might want to wait for a bit. They're fighting again."

"Who?" Carolina was baffled, and alarmed. And she was hungry for supper. From an opened window in their apartment, she could now hear Mama's raised, angry voice, every bitter accusation, and angry words clearly audible to the two children.

"Mama and Daddy," Frankie replied. Soberly. "Again. About money – Daddy's Army pay doesn't go far enough, Mama says. She wants Daddy to resign his commission, and get a better job, one where he earns more. Enough to let us move back to San Antonio. Daddy doesn't want to. He thinks the Army is fine, and Mama just isn't used to putting up with the rough parts."

"I'm hungry!" Carolina wailed and began to sniffle. She hated it when Mama and Daddy raised their voices in anger. Or at least, when Mama raised her voice to shriek, as she usually did. Even if Daddy was angry, he never raised his voice above normal. "How long do we have to wait, Frankie? It scares me when they fight."

"I don't know," Frankie considered the matter soberly, and put his arm around his sister. "Don't cry, Caro-san."

Carolina sniffled again. That was how Kimi and Suki called her, back at Kadena, where they all lived in a nice house with a yard, and Mama and Daddy almost never raised their voices at each other, and Daddy came home every evening and played with them in the yard until it was time for supper. "I wish we could go back to Kadena! I don't like it here, at all!"

"Well, I don't!" Frankie replied, with some indignation. "Now, I wish we could go back to San Antonio, with Poppa Lew. I liked living at Poppa Lew's. It was nicer than here."

It was indeed much nicer at Poppa Lew and Granny Margo's house, which was practically a mansion. Their house was large, tranquil and cool, set in a garden of its own, under shady trees, as different as could be from the miserable, hot-box of the New Braunfels apartment. Poppa Lew and Granny Margo's house had many bedrooms upstairs, with views over the garden, and the green treetops. Long curtains of rich fabric hung over tall floor-to-ceiling French doors, and every room was filled with ornate furniture, adorned with fancy china lamps with fluted silk shades. Poppa Lew and Granny Margo's house smelled of lavender and beeswax furniture polish. When Mama and Daddy, Frankie and Carolina came to supper at the grandparents, they ate off fine china plates and with heavy silverware, in a dining room with leaves set into the table, so that there was room for everyone, even the children. Frankie had explained this to his sister. It was because Poppa Lew was very rich. He had invented things, and owned business properties and several businesses across San Antonio.

Now Carolina and Frankie sat huddled close together on the stairs, as the sky darkened. They heard a door slamming in the upstairs apartment, and no more of Mama's voice; it seemed that the fight was over. Carolina looked up at her brother, who stood up. "I think it's safe now," he ventured, just as the front door to the Visser apartment opened, and Daddy peered down at them, lines of strain in his face, clear in the overhead light.

"Supper's ready," he said. "Come in and wash your hands. Your mama has a headache and went to lie down in the bedroom."

. . .

That was not the worst fight between Mama and Daddy. It was only the first of the really bad fights between them as spring wore on. Sometimes Carolina positively dreaded coming home from watching TV at Laura's. Mama would have been sweating all day in the tiny apartment, Daddy would be late, driving back from Camp Gary, sometimes too late in the evening to have supper with Mama, Frankie, and Carolina. Mama would be short and snappish to the children. At least, Frankie could escape to school for most of the day, but that also gave cause for Mama's anger and frustration, as she and Carolina must walk Frankie to school because Daddy had already gone to work, driving the family's only car, even before the children's breakfast. And then again, in the sweltering afternoon, they had to walk to Frankie's school to see him safely home, to do his homework in the bedroom that the children shared, while Carolina slipped away to the apartment downstairs to watch TV with Laura – her own brief escape from the tension in the apartment.

It came to a head, in the heat of mid-summer, after school ended for the year, and Frankie had to share the misery, all day long. Daddy finally agreed to resign from the Army. Mama had won.

. . . . .

Carolina did miss her friend Laura and watching TV every afternoon, but that was about all that she missed, when they moved to San Antonio. At least Mama and Daddy did not fight, or at least, they didn't fight almost every other day as they had since they returned to Texas from Okinawa. They had to stay for a few months at a crummy motel on the Austin Highway, which would have been almost as bad as the rental apartment in New Braunfels. But the motel did have a pool, in the open courtyard between units, so Carolina did not mind at all, since she was now able to run out of the two-room unit and plunge into the cool water. Mama and Daddy eventually found a house in south-east San Antonio, in Highland Park. It was just five houses down the street from Poppa Lew and Granny Margo's big mansion in the garden, which made Frankie happy beyond all words once they moved into it. Frankie adored his grandfather as much as Carolina adored Daddy; an affection returned, as Frankie was Poppa Lew's only grandson.

Poppa Lew was an important businessman and inventor in San Antonio, as Frankie had explained to her. He was a small wiry man with a bristly mustache and a lively interest in practically everything. The house that the Vissers moved into had a big yard, with a lawn, green trees, and pretty flowerbeds – a pleasant and shady place for Carolina to play in, running barefoot on the grass, just as she had been able to play at their house in Kadena. Best of all, she had ready playmates among her cousins; Aunt Jane's children who were close to her age. The only disappointment was that Daddy now had to work very hard, and for even longer hours than when he had been in the Army. That disappointed Carolina very much; she loved to go places with Daddy, or for their neighbors to see them together.

She loved it when people said things like, 'You're the spitting image of your father!' or 'Where did you get that pretty blond hair and blue eyes!' 'I get them from my Daddy!" Carolina would exclaim.

Carolina started school when summer was over, at Highland Park Elementary, just across the street from their new home on Hammond Avenue. Frankie also went to a new school. He started at the Peacock Military Academy; a very strict and prestigious private school, for which Poppa Lew paid tuition. Frankie seemed to spend more and more time with Poppa Lew, working during the summer for Poppa Lew's construction firm – first in the office with Poppa, and then out with Poppa Lew's foreman on the job site. Carolina didn't mind not having Frankie and his pals to play with as she had when they were younger, since she had her cousins, and sometimes friends from school.

• • •

But being close to Mama's sisters and Granny Margo meant that Mama went to the weekly hen gathering every Friday afternoon, Granny Margo, Aunt Jane, and all the female cousins, with a gaggle of their younger children in tow. They met at one or another of their houses after school got out; ostensibly to get together and fix an enormous family supper for everyone – the husbands and the kids and all. The first one of those gatherings that Mama went to with Carolina and Frankie was at Granny Margo and Poppa Lew's comfortable mansion, just a short walk down the street from the new house. Carolina was late that first Friday; her teacher held her back to finish her arithmetic worksheet. It was well past three o'clock when she left her classroom, and then she dawdled all the way to the grandparents' house. When she got there, it was almost four o'clock, and she could already see her cousins playing outside in the yard. She only has girl cousins and by the time she reached them they were beginning to gather on front porch steps leading to the house. Carolina joined them; she was already quite hungry and wondered if she could beg a cookie or something from Granny Margo without risking a lecture on spoiling her appetite for supper. She became faintly worried at the raised voices already drifting out from the open windows. Irate female voices …

"What's going on?" Carolina sat down on the step next to Aunt Jane's oldest daughter, Carole, who was nearly the same age as Carolina. Carole had curly dark hair done in long pigtails; she looked a little bit like Judy Garland in *The Wizard of Oz*, save that her front teeth were coming in slightly crooked. Carole would need braces to straighten them when she was a little older. Carolina had already heard Aunt Jane lament the potential expense and was very glad that her own teeth seemed to be coming in straight. Daddy couldn't afford another bill, and straight teeth were something that Mama would absolutely insist on – she wanted the best for Frankie and Carolina.

Carole sighed and scratched at a mosquito bite on her shin. "They're already drinking. A lot. Granny Margo and her cousin, Martha aren't much better. Then they start to fight about something stupid that someone else said or did, ages ago, they take sides, and then they begin to scream at each other. … honestly, why can't we have a normal family, that doesn't get drunk and get into screaming fights with each other. This doesn't happen with Dad's family!"

"My Daddy's family doesn't do that, either" Carolina agreed. "And it doesn't happen on *Leave it to Beaver*, although I guess they pretty things up for TV." As far as she knew, Daddy's family were a bunch of staid and mild-mannered mid-western Dutch Americans, who hardly ever raised their voices to each other, over anything. It seemed a rather restful contrast, when she thought about it, especially considering the increasingly irate female voices coming from the direction of Granny Margo's kitchen. There was what sounded like a bottle slamming down on the table inside the kitchen, and a fresh outburst of screaming, with her cousin Martha shrieking even louder. Carole flinched.

"Oh, that's done it," she said, in resignation. "Mom will call Daddy at work, tell him to just go straight home. She'll stomp off in a rage, drag us all home with her and if we're lucky, she'll remember to take the meat loaf out of the oven tonight before it burns to a crisp before she finishes telling off whoever she had the fight with over the telephone. Just you wait and see, Caro. You wouldn't believe how many Friday family suppers turn out like that."

Inside the house, there was another undistinguishable noise from the kitchen – The front door was flung open with a crash, and Aunt Jane appeared in the doorway, clutching her purse to her chest. She was breathing hard, and her face was flushed red with anger.

"Carole, get you sister, Martina we're going home!" Aunt Jane snapped, and Carole looked sideways at Carolina.

"Told you so," she murmured, as Aunt Jane stalked across the porch, her heels drumming on the floor like a military tattoo. Even her footsteps sounded angry, Carolina thought. Then her cousin Martha came out the door and gathered her kids and off she went in a huff. The ruckus in Granny Margo's kitchen had died down a little with Martha's departure, at least for a time, so she still had some hope for the family dinner. She was hungry!

But no – five minutes later, it was Mama, telling her that they were going home as well. Mama was also angry and muttering under her breath. At least they lived only half a block away. When Daddy arrived home, three hours later, supper was on the table, but Mama was still toweringly angry. She was on the phone, yelling at Martha, when Daddy came through the door, hanging his hat on the rack next to the door.

"What happened, Caro – I thought we were going to have supper at your Granny Margo's house?" Daddy murmured.

Carolina replied in a whisper, "Mama and her cousin Martha started fighting, and Mama decided that we had best come home.

Daddy, sometimes I wish we could all go back to Okinawa. I liked it there,"

"So do I, sugar – so do I," Daddy replied with a sigh. "Your mother does have quite a temper, doesn't she? At least, she never raises her hand to you and Frankie. I'm grateful for that much."

Carolina liked it much better about being settled down in San Antonio, on those occasions when Daddy and Mama took her to a club they liked to go to with their friends. They never got into fights there, with each other or anyone else. Daddy so tall and fair and handsome, Mama dark and glamorous, and Carolina's full pleated skirt of her dress swirling about her knees as Daddy spun her out and back into his arms. So many of the other club members would stop dancing themselves, just to watch. When she was a little older, Carolina wondered how and where Daddy had learned to dance so expertly, since the Visser family were reputedly so staid and old-fashioned about fast music and modern dancing. When they put on a slow foxtrot record, Daddy would teach Carolina to dance, encouraging her to put her feet on top of his, as they moved, one step back, side, forward and side again.

"You're making a square with your feet," Daddy said. Carolina loved dancing with Daddy.

· · · · ·

As far as Carolina was concerned, the screaming fights among Mama's family were only an intermittent blot on an otherwise contented life – and the fights didn't happen at every single Friday family gathering. Most of those suppers were jolly and uneventful affairs, even if Granny Margo and Mama, and cousins had emptied too many beer cans or bottles of wine before dishing up supper. The worst and most frightening of those fights didn't even happen at Granny Margo's house, or one of the relatives' houses, however. It came about because Poppa Lew had a meeting with an important business client in Victoria. It meant a long drive and a two-night stay in a motel. And Granny Margo was going with him.

"Where's that?" Carolina asked, with intense interest. Mama had been on the telephone with Granny Margo all afternoon, talking about the trip. School was already out for the summer, and she had been home all day, while her brother had been running errands for Poppa.

"It's about a hundred and twenty miles away," Frankie replied. "Maybe three hours in a car, if you take your time." Her brother perked up, wearing a happier expression. "Granny Margo and Poppa Lew want Mama and us to come with them, for the holiday and to keep Granny Margo company while he's at his business meeting. The motel they're gonna stay in is a nice one. It has a pool – and that will be keen!"

And so it was, although the drive was a long one through the rolling country to the south and east of San Antonio, and since it was summer, very hot. They all went together in Poppa Lew's big station wagon, with their suitcases stacked in the back and all the windows open for fresh air. Poppa Lew drove all the way, with Granny Margo in the front seat and Frankie squeezed between them on the bench seat. Carolina rode in the back seat with Mama; she was envious of Frankie because Poppa Lew let him work the gear shift and put his hands on the steering wheel and showed him how to pump gas when they stopped the car to refuel. The road wandered between pastures and meadows, crossing almost-dry creeks on narrow bridges, winding around by thickets of oaks and scrub cedar, and ramshackle fences hung with tendrils of wild mustang grape vines. Now and again, Poppa Lew slowed, as they came to towns – Lavernia, Sutherland Springs, Stockdale, Nixon, Smiley and Cuero, strung along the ribbon of asphalt like beads on a necklace, with perhaps the towers of a feed mill looming overhead. Old-fashioned brick and stone storefronts lined the road for perhaps a block or two, with advertisements along their sides for Bull Durham tobacco, local drugstore, bar or eatery, and the high school football team. For a good part of the journey, the road ran alongside the railroad tracks, and it thrilled Carolina and Frankie when they passed a slow-moving freight train, and they read off the names of the various rail companies on the sides of every freight car.

Several times, Poppa Lew stopped at a roadside grocery or gas station to buy them all cold soda, the sides of the glass soda bottles sweating from the humid summer heat and the last swallows of the soda in them already gone lukewarm by the time Carolina and her brother drank them. It was late afternoon when they arrived in Victoria, hot and sticky from the long drive in the summer heat and located the motel where Poppa Lew had made reservations. They had a single room reserved for their family; a room with two beds for adults; one for the grandparents, one for Mama, and a pair of cots jammed up against the far wall for Frankie and Carolina. Carolina hardly paid attention to the cramped little room, or anything else but the pool – cool and blue and inviting, after a long hot ride with her skin sticking painfully to the vinyl upholstery. She and Frankie changed into their swimsuits and tore across the baking pavement, yelping a bit as the hot asphalt scorched their feet.

"Last one in's a rotten egg!" Frankie shouted, and they plunged into the cool water at the same moment. After the long, hot, sweaty drive, it felt like pure heaven. They swam and frolicked in the shallow and the deep end with energy and enthusiasm, and only reluctantly emerged when Mama and Granny Margo called them in to change into dry clothes for supper. That summer holiday couldn't possibly get any better, Carolina felt. She loved the water, and she could swim very well: Daddy always compared her to a mermaid. In the morning, she and her brother were back in the pool, as soon as Mama permitted them after breakfast. Mama insisted that they wait for a whole hour after finishing a hearty breakfast in the motel's restaurant, over their indignant protests – but Mama didn't yield, especially when Granny Margo backed her up.

Carolina and Frankie waited impatiently for that hour to crawl past. It seemed to take ages, until they could dive into the aquamarine pool, and commence frolicking and going off the diving board into the deep end, where they had left off the afternoon before. They hardly noticed when Poppa Lew drove off in the station wagon to his client meeting at mid-morning, or when Mama and Granny Margo came out to the pool in bathing suits, shady hats, and dark sunglasses, to lie on the loungers. They also didn't notice that by late afternoon, Mama and Granny Margo had been drinking. Drinking a lot.

When Poppa Lew returned from his client meeting, hours later, it was late afternoon and almost suppertime. Frankie and Carolina had given up eating lunch in the motel restaurant so that they could spend uninterrupted time in the pool, so they were both ravenously hungry by suppertime. So was Poppa Lew, after his business meeting, which had gone on for the entire day. They barely noticed how Mama and Granny Margo were drinking steadily all through supper, on top of what they had already drunk during the late afternoon as they sunned by the pool.

Carolina had Salisbury steak, while Frankie asked for baked chicken and Poppa ordered chicken pot pie. Carolina and Frankie asked for ice cream for dessert, ice cream with chocolate syrup and whipped cream on top; Mama and Poppa Lew approved, since they had cleaned their plates of their meal selections. It was just past sundown when they walked back to their room; the sun setting in a smear of pale cloud on the western horizon, and the first pale stars beginning to wink into life.

Frankie and Carolina settled on the bed in front of the television set, full of supper and dessert, and starting to feel drowsy after a long day in the pool and a full supper. They were sitting on Poppa Lew and Granny Margo's bed, after washing up and putting on their pajamas and bathrobes. It was a very great treat to be allowed to stay up so late and watch a movie on a color television so much larger than the one at their grandparents' house – a very great treat. They were so entranced by the movie they were watching that they hardly noticed the adult's voices getting louder and angrier, at first.

Then Mama shouted an ugly name at Granny Margo – and the next minute, Mama had Granny Margo, holding her head up by the hair with one hand, and slapping Granny Margo across the face with the full force of her other hand. Carolina watched, utterly appalled, shaken down to her very soul. She had never seen anything like this, Mama so furiously angry that she had come to physical violence. As often as the other women in the family got drunk and yelled at each other, she had never seen them come to blows. She and Frankie watched in horror, as Granny Margo put her hands to her face, her cheek already bright red from Mama's hand.

"Marlene, please don't do that!" Granny Margo begged over sobs.

Poppa Lew commanded, "Don't you dare hit your mother!"

"I don't care!" Mama screamed. "She has no right to talk to me that way!" She grabbed the two suitcases that had all their things packed in for the trip home the next morning, the smaller under arm, the other in her hand. She pulled Frankie and Carolina off the bed with her other hand. "Come on, children – we're going home, right now!"

Mama blundered out of the motel room door, ignoring Granny Margo's weeping and Poppa Lew's shouted commands.

"But we don't have a car!" Frankie protested, but Mama ignored him. She was stomping so heavily across the parking lot that she broke the heel off one of her high-heel shoes.

"Mama! Where are we going?" Carolina demanded. Mama's fury was frightening, even more so since it was dark, late at night, and they were miles and miles from home, and Mama was limping on the foot with the broken heel.

"Your father has to come get us!" Mama replied. "We can't stay here; he has to come get us!"

"That'll be hours!" Frankie protested and begged. "Can't we watch the rest of the movie?" He had already stubbed one of his toes on the rough asphalt of the parking lot. Neither he nor Carolina had a chance to put on their slippers; they were both barefoot.

"No!" Mama shrieked. "We're going home!"

Carolina was so distraught by this turn of events that she couldn't even bring herself to protest. Mama and the grandparents furious to the point of open violence? What could an eight-year-old do, when all the stable points in her life splintered into fragments? Mama dragged them across the road – fortunately there was no traffic at that hour – to the gas station on the corner, which had a telephone booth outside, although the station itself was dark and shuttered.

"Wait here!" Mama commanded, and Carolina and Frankie sat upon the suitcases while Mama went into the booth and closed the door behind her.

"What is she saying?" Carolina whispered, for she could barely hear Mama now that the phone booth door was shut. She and Frankie huddled close – not because of the cold, for it was summertime and still fairly warm at night, but because she was frightened, and Frankie was always brave. The stars were out, close overhead in the night sky, a darkness broken by a few lights in windows at the motel, and in the motel office. A few cars passed by on the road, their headlights briefly illuminating the gas station as they turned at the corner.

"She's talking to Daddy, asking him to come and take us home," Frankie put his arm around her, after listening carefully to Mama. Her voice was raised at first, and she was crying, too. At first Mama was audible through the closed booth door, begging Daddy to come and get them now this very minute. After a few minutes, Mama's voice dropped to a more normal tone, and the children couldn't make out the words.

"Will he?" Carolina sniffed, disconsolate and already herself close to tears. "I want Daddy – he never screams or hits!"

"I know, Caro," Frankie replied, hugging her close. They sat for some time, waiting for Mama to finish. If Daddy was going to come and get them, it would be hours yet. Carolina wished that she were at home, curled up in her own bed. This wasn't turning out to be a nice vacation at all. She leaned against her brother, drowsy, in spite of her fears, for it was late at night and she and Frankie were both very tired. She must have fallen into a light doze; the next thing she was aware of was Frankie shaking her shoulders.

"Wake up, Caro. We're going back to the motel."

"Are we?" Carolina yawned, still only half awake. *Was the whole episode merely a bad dream?* She thought it must be, but for Mama carrying the suitcases and taking Frankie by the hand, back across the road and the motel parking lot, limping on the shoe with the broken heel. The room that they were staying in was dark, only one small light still on. Mama tucked them into their cots, and in the morning, it seemed like everything was utterly normal, Granny Margo and Poppa Lew taking them for breakfast before starting the long drive back to San Antonio. Nothing was said about the dreadful, alcohol-fueled fight between Granny Margo and Mama. Carolina sometimes wondered if it had just been a nightmare, but Granny Margo's cheek was still reddened, and her eyes were puffy – so it really had happened. What a memory, for what was supposed to have been a pleasant holiday!

. . . . .

In the summer that she was twelve; Carolina got the shock of her life. The occasion was a late afternoon at their house, with the sun sliding down behind the trees across the road, long shadows stretching out across the lawn, and the road. Carolina and her cousins, Aunt Martha's daughters, Emily and her little sister Kathy sat on the front steps of Mama and Daddy's house, tired out and sweating from playing. Mama had let them have a cold soda each, saying that they could each have one and no more, it would spoil their appetites for supper. It would be suppertime, soon and almost time for Emily and Kathy to go home, and for Daddy to come home from work.

Carolina said, proudly, "Daddy's studying every night after supper. He's wants to go to school to be a doctor, now."

To Carolina's utter horror, Emily set down her soda and remarked, "You know, Caro – Uncle Adam isn't your real father."

Carolina stared at her, speechless with shock; *how could Emily possibly say something like that? Of course, Daddy was her real father! She looked just like him! Everyone said so! Everyone had always said so, for as long as Carolina could remember!*

"That's not true!" Carolina cried, in outrage. "He is too my real Daddy! Mama!" she sprang up and ran into the house, through the living room and into the kitchen, where Mama was just starting to fix supper. Emily and Kathy followed close on her heels. "Mama! Come tell Emily that Daddy is my real father! Tell her!"

Mama, just tying on her kitchen apron around her waist, looked at Carolina in mild surprise. "Carolina," she replied, "I thought you knew that already! He isn't really your father in blood at all. He adopted you and Frankie when we got married. You were a toddler, then. I guess that you don't remember."

"Told you so," Emily muttered, with a smug look, and Carolina began to sob.

"I don't believe you!" She screamed. "Daddy will be home, soon! He'll tell the truth – he is too my real father! I'm going to wait for Daddy!"

She waited by the screen door, tears rolling down her cheeks: *Daddy not her real father? It was a horrible lie, it must, it must be a lie!* Finally, when it was twilight, and the streetlights were just coming on, she saw Daddy's car coming down the street. He parked the car around the side of the house, and as he stepped onto the porch, Carolina couldn't wait another single moment. She flung open the screen door and rushed out, sobbing hysterically.

"Daddy – please come in and tell them all that you are my real father!"

Daddy, absolutely boggled, stared at her. "Caro, sweetie ... stop crying. I ... your mother and I ... well, we will explain. Come inside and calm down. We never thought ..."

Carolina, still sobbing, followed him through the door, as Mama came out of the kitchen.

"Emily – Kathy, go home, now." She sounded stern, almost angry. "We need to have a private family talk with Caro, right this very minute!"

"Yes, Ma'am!" Emily dove for the door, with Kathy on her heels, apparently sobered by Mama's anger, which was no inconsiderable thing. Daddy looked helplessly at Carolina and took her hands in his. She had the feeling that if she had been smaller, Daddy would have picked her up, comforting her as if she were still little. But at twelve, she was just too tall for that.

"Let's go and sit down, Caro," Daddy said, and led her to the sofa. She sat between them, as Mama fiddled with her apron, and Daddy held on to her hands. "Sweetheart, we never kept it a secret from you and Frankie. Your mother and I married when Frankie was six years old and you were just a little girl." Daddy smiled, a little crookedly. "I didn't just believe in my heart that your mother was the most beautiful, fascinating woman in all the world, and the one I fell in love with. I fell in love with you and Frankie as well. I liked the thought of a ready-made family, you see."

"You were too small to remember," Mama put in, sounding a little apologetic. "Frankie was old enough, but honestly, it never seemed important, not something to bring up in conversation. Your blood father was my first husband. Gianni Amato. We married during the war when I was only fifteen. He turned out to be a bad choice," She smiled, with a bitter twist to her lips, as she looked across Carolina towards Adam. "A really bad choice. Your father by blood was this Italian boy I met during the war; a handsome guy with a very high opinion of himself. He had a very hot temper and heavy fists to match. We haven't laid eyes on the b --- the jerk since we took the train from Houston and came home to your grandparents' house. It was after that – I met your daddy, when I went with a friend of mine, to see her boyfriend at Fort Bliss – you were just a baby then. That's when I met your daddy. Gianni Amato has never come to see you and Frankie or sent any money to support the three of us, ever since that day. I think he was as glad to get shed of us as I was to get shed of him. Even his parents – your grandparents on his side of the family treated us like dirt, when I begged them for help! Pig-headed Sicilians! I did so much better when I met your daddy. Ever so much better."

"You should understand, sweetheart," Daddy squeezed Carolina's hands between his, and looked into her eyes. "That guy, Gianni in Houston, who never cared enough to come visit the two of you, or to send money to take care of you, read you bedtime stories, or hold you tight when you were frightened, teach you valuable lessons about life – he might be your father ... but I am your real daddy, for doing all of those things. He doesn't really matter ..."

"He wouldn't even begin to matter, even if he ever coughed up the support dough that he was supposed to send us," Mama added. "And I'm not certain I would care to give him the time of day, even if he did," she added, with indignation. "Please don't cry, Caro – Daddy is your real daddy, for all the reasons he said. I ... we just never talked about your blood father, since it never seemed to matter. It doesn't matter now, sweetheart – does it?"

Carolina sniffled a few times; now that it was explained so sensibly, she wasn't nearly as horrified as she had been when Emily blurted it out, about Daddy not being her real father. The man in Houston, her father by blood, the Italian boy – he who had been married to Mama was a stranger, a legend, a bogeyman who wasn't real and had nothing to do with Carolina, really. Daddy was the one who had been a father – and a much more real father than the man in Houston who Mama said was a real jerk and likely had worse names for, if Carolina was any judge of Mama's own temper.

"'S all right," Carolina finally said. She blew her nose on the handkerchief that Daddy produced from his pants pocket. "It was just a shock, that's all – finding out that everyone knew, but me!"

"It just never seemed important," Mama sighed. "Not important enough to talk about, once we were a real family, all together."

Carolina considered the matter. Of course, Mama and Daddy were right. They were a real family. Although now that she did think about it, there never seemed to be enough money from Daddy's work to buy the things that everyone else had, especially Poppa Lew and Granny Margo. Poppa Lew even paid for Frankie's schooling at the Peacock Military Academy, which was a great expense, and one which Daddy couldn't really afford on his salary. Carolina went to school at St. Margaret Mary when Daddy could afford it, but that was expensive too, and Daddy didn't like to appeal to Poppa Lew more often than absolutely necessary. When Daddy couldn't afford tuition for the Catholic school, Carolina went Highland Park Elementary.

"If he owes us money; owes money for supporting Frankie and I – shouldn't he be made to pay it?" she asked, propping her chin on her hands. Mama dropped her eyes to the hands in her lap. She looked harassed and unhappy.

"I know, Caro-sugar, but it's for the courts to enforce it. Gianni Amato hasn't paid a dime in ten years; I honestly don't know if anything I can do now can change that, especially the adoption was final years ago."

"Still, Mama – if he was supposed to pay for our support, then you ought to make him do it," Carolina argued. "Or give it all up. It's just not fair, when you and Daddy can't make ends meet without Poppa Lew helping ... and I'd really belong to Daddy, then." Carolina did notice that Daddy winced a bit at that but thought little of it until much, much later. "You should get that money, Mama. We need it, and it's just not fair that we should be cheated out of it. You wouldn't let someone who owes you a bunch of money get away with never paying it, would you?"

"Put that way, I don't think I would, Caro. Look, I'll see what I can do." Mama cast an unhappy glance at Daddy and murmured. "She is right, Adam – we ought to at least try."

"I don't ..." Daddy started to say, but Mama kissed Carolina's forehead, saying,

"I'll see what I can do ... oh, help, supper is burning!" She leaped up from the sofa and ran into the kitchen, where something had burned dry in a pan on the stove.

Daddy squeezed Carolina's hands again. He still did not look very happy, but Carolina intuited that he was mostly unhappy about not being able to provide for them as well as Poppa Lew did, with his construction business and his inventions and all his other interests.

"You OK, Caro? You know, you'll always be my little girl, and I'll always be your daddy."

"Yes," Carolina replied, tremulously. "Really." She flung herself into his arms, and he hugged her close to him – and it really was OK. He was her real daddy, no matter what anyone said.

• • • • •

Mama did appeal to the court to pursue the back child support that her first husband still owed for Frankie and Carolina. But for all the trouble it took to hire a lawyer and bring the case to court, all she received out of it was a meagre $50 dollars. This was not nearly enough to pay tuition for a year at St. Margaret Mary for Carolina, or even begin paying Frankie's tuition at Peacock Military Academy.

"Gianni owes thousands!" Mama fumed. "More than ten years' worth, and this is all the children get?"

"Well," Daddy observed philosophically, "It was fifty dollars that you didn't have before. Buy something pretty for our little girl, a good book or two for Frankie ... and something nice for the house. If that money doesn't come anywhere near what he owes, at least you all can get some pleasure out of it!"

Carolina, overhearing this as she labored over her English homework at the kitchen table as Mama and Daddy talked in the living room, thought this was eminently sensible. After all, Daddy was her real daddy now, not that man in Houston – and maybe Mama would buy her a new dress...

She did get that new dress. Mama took her to the big fancy department store downtown, Joske's, to pick it out, which made Carolina feel like a grown-up lady. She tried on a series of dresses that Mama approved of, while an elegantly dressed saleslady hovered over them both. The saleslady was older than Mama, with an olive complexion, dark hair streaked with gray and pulled back into a severe bun on the back of her elegant head. She reminded Carolina of a ballerina, moving gracefully on tiptoes, and peering over her glasses, which were secured by a long chain around her neck.

"I think this one is more flattering to your complexion and coloring, Mrs. Visser," the saleslady said, when Carolina modeled a dark blue dress with a full skirt and a pretty flower-embroidered white collar and cuffs on the short, puffed sleeves. Carolina twirled in front of the three-part mirror by the dressing rooms, admiring how the skirt flared out around her knees. Like Mamas' skirt, when she danced with Daddy. Maybe her own skirt would flare, if she wore it, when she herself danced with Daddy. "Such pretty blond hair – and such a lovely tan, too – like a movie star!"

"It's natural," Carolina said, proudly. "I'm part-Italian."

"And the best part, too," the saleslady agreed, with a smile. "My great-grandfather was from Italy; he did stone-carving for most of the important building in town, then. In my family, they say that he worked on the terrazzo floors at the Capitol building and helped build San Francisco de Paolo here in San Antonio."

"How interesting," Mama replied, although she sounded rather bored. "Do you like this one best, Caro?"

"I do," Carolina answered, and turned on her toes before the three-part mirror once more, just to admire the way that the full skirt fluttered. She loved the dress, and wore it for best, and for picture day at school, quite aware that the other girls examined it with mild envy. She came away from Joske's that day with more than the dress; packed into a pretty box, folded into layers of tissue paper. She also came away with the knowledge of how very proud the elegant saleslady was of her Italian grandfather. For nearly the first time in her life, Carolina thought about how she also was part Italian; in history class at school, she had learned about Michelangelo, Leonardo da Vinci, and Botticelli – and from church, she knew about St. Francis of Assisi, and all the other notable Italian saints. Being part Italian was something to be proud of, sharing that same heritage – even if some of the other kids derisively called her a wop. Carolina didn't care about what the other kids said, she knew for certain that they were only jealous, because she was prettier and smarter than just about all of them.

CHAPTER 3
A RING ON HER FINGER

She started the seventh grade that fall, Saint Gerard's; a good Catholic high school, of which Granny Margo and Poppa Lew approved wholeheartedly, as most of the teachers were nuns. Carolina liked it too, even if she did have to wear a school uniform every day, a plaid box-pleated skirt and a plain white blouse with a gray sweater or pullover on cold days. Having to dress the same as all the other girls every day didn't make a particle of difference for Carolina, as she was prettier than most of the other girls. In fact, it made her stand out even more, with her blond hair and bright blue eyes. Within the first week of starting school, she already had a boyfriend. Although he was not officially a boyfriend at first, just a boy from the eighth grade, who began talking to her every day after school, while she waited out in front for Poppa Lew to collect her on his way back home from his office. His name was Gregory; he was handsome, with dark hair and a clear complexion, not spotted with acne like some of the other boys. He played baseball for the school team. He was also a little taller than Carolina. Like most of the other girls her age, she had her growth spurt before the boys, and Gregory was one of the few that she didn't tower over, so that was good. Carolina liked that.

"Hi," he said, on that first day, as Carolina kicked her heels, sitting on top of the low wall which framed the front staircase of the school, as she waited for Poppa Lew's Cadillac to come around the corner. "You're Carolina Visser, aren't you? I thought so. You're in my mom's homeroom class. I'm Gregory Cooley – but most everyone calls me Greg."

"Your mom is Mrs. Cooley?" Carolina replied, slightly astonished. Although she shouldn't be – come to think of it, Gregory did look a little like Mrs. Cooley. She was one of the few teachers that wasn't a nun; it was his height, the shape of his face and the dark hair, mostly.

"Yeah," Gregory acknowledged. He sat on the low wall next to her – not very close, but close enough so that they could talk comfortably. "Dire, isn't? Your mom being one of the teachers. But I've never been assigned to her classes, so it's all good. You know – we must avoid a suspicion of favoritism? Mom is a good teacher, and she never holds it against me at home, what she hears about me at school."

"That's good," Carolina replied. "I don't know if my mom could be a good teacher ... in a school, that is. She has an awful temper. But she's terribly strict with my brother and I, about good manners and all. Saying yes, ma'am and no, sir, and being polite to grownups. But ... well, there were times that money was tight, with Daddy being in the Army and all. Mama saw that Frankie and I were never short of food. What there was, she served us first, and with the best part."

"She sounds like a good mom," Greg replied warmly. "The best kind. Now I wouldn't mind if mine didn't have to work, but my pop was disabled in the War, and can't work, so Mom has to take up the slack."

"Was he in the Army?" Carolina asked, with interest, and Greg shook his head.

"No, he was in the Marines. He doesn't talk about the War much, except to tell me never to volunteer." Greg laughed, and Carolina decided that she felt comfortable with him; a friend of her own age, to talk to and exchange confidences with, almost as if he were one of her cousins, or even Aunt Bobbie – the dearest of all her relatives, after Daddy and Poppa Lew.

• • •

One day in late April, with only a few weeks to go until the summer break, Greg seemed to be a little nervous, apprehensive, when he met Carolina at their usual meeting place, the wide staircase in front of the school.

"I've got something for you," he said, in a conspiratorial voice, after looking around to make certain that no other students were within hearing. He had one hand in his jacket pocket. "Something special. A present. I want you to keep it, forever and always."

"What is it?" Carolina was eaten up with curiosity. He had nothing in his other hand but his notebook and an algebra textbook, so that something special must be small, if it fit into his pocket.

"A ring," Greg confessed. "It's not a going-steady ring, I wouldn't be allowed to go steady, Mom 'n Dad are awful strict with me, since I'm supposed to be a priest when I grow up. It's because you are my special friend. I just want you to have it."

"All right," Carolina agreed. "I don't think I'd be allowed to go steady, either – my parents think I'm way too young, still …" But she frowned, thinking it over. "But Mama first got married when she was fifteen, and so did Granny Margo, so they might think again, when it comes to me. I still have two years to go until my fifteenth birthday. But we're still special friends. Do you really *have* to be a priest?"

"Yep," Greg nodded, his expression glum, as he drew his hand out of his pocket, holding a tiny velveteen covered ring box in it. "Mom insists, absolutely."

"Dire," Carolina agreed. "Always dressing in black and never being allowed to have any fun at all, because the parishioners might see and disapprove …Ooooh – Greg, it's beautiful!"

The ring was gold, and old-fashioned looking thing, set with a flower made of a diamond center and pearl petals, and delicate curlicue gold leaves. Carolina had never seen anything so beautiful, and her heart warmed with affection for her special friend. "I'd marry you – or go steady in an instant, if you weren't going to be a priest," Carolina exclaimed. She took the ring from Greg, and both his hands closed over hers.

"Don't tell anyone," He smiled at her, but his eyes were shadowed. "We're secret best friends ..."

"Best friends forever," Carolina agreed. "It's so beautiful. I love it! I will keep it safe, and I won't tell anyone about it. I'll wear it on a chain around my neck, OK?"

"Sure thing, Caro," he promised, as Poppa Lew's car pulled around the corner, and Poppa Lew sounded the horn, twice and then once again. Carolina tucked the little velvet-covered ring box into her book bag and bounced down the walkway to the curb, where Poppa Lew waited impatiently for her.

When she got home, she took the ring out of the rubbed velvet box and pondered thoughtfully on just how she could keep the ring safe. She had a little cross on a gold chain in the jewelry box that Daddy had bought for her at the PX in Kadena – a carved wooden box of red-tinted wood with a pale stone carving set into the top. She strung the ring onto the chain and put the gold chain around her neck. Perfect. The chain was long enough that the little cross and the beautiful ring hung below the neckline of her tops, and the collared white broadcloth blouses of her school uniform. No one would ever suspect that she was Greg's special friend, sealed with the ring. And true to her promise to Greg, she didn't tell anyone. So she was shocked and horrified to come home from school a week later, to find Mama waiting for her to come up the walk, after Poppa Lew dropped her off at home.

Mama's expression was thunderous; Carolina's heart sank down to the soles of her sensible black saddle shoes. What had she done now? She couldn't think of anything, and that made it worse, not knowing what had made Mama so angry.

"You have to return that ring," Mama said, straight out. "I just got a call from Sister Frances at St. Gerard's. Mrs. Cooley is coming to our house to get it, this afternoon."

"What ring?" Carolina stammered. Oh, not the pretty ring that Greg had given her, so that they could be secret special friends! How had Mama found out about it? Carolina had not told anyone or shown it off, not even to one of the cousins, or Aunt Jane.

"The one that Greg Cooley gave to you," Mama was implacable and furious; Carolina didn't even consider telling Mama a lie. Mama was often angry – with Daddy, Aunt Jane, Granny Margo and Poppa Lew – but she was hardly ever as angry with Carolina and Frankie. Mama's anger was a horrible thing, and Carolina cringed from having it aimed at her.

"But Greg gave it to me," Carolina still protested. "A present! Because we're special friends. He wanted me to have it, for always. It's beautiful – and why can't I keep it if he gave it to me?"

"That ring wasn't his to give," Mama replied, sternly. "It's a family heirloom and very valuable. It belonged to his grandmother and Mrs. Cooley is furious. You must give it back, Caro. It's not yours to keep and it wasn't his to give to you in the first place."

"But ..." Carolina started to protest, before realizing that it was no use, no matter how much her heart ached at having to give up the ring that Greg had given her in all earnest. She couldn't stand against Mama, Mrs. Cooley, and Sister Frances, the senior counselor, as fond as she was of Greg and as much as she loved the diamond and pearl ring.

When Mrs. Cooley's car drew up in front of the house, Greg was sitting in the passenger seat, looking miserable and ashamed. Carolina could see him from her bedroom window, around at the side of the house, as Mrs. Cooley got from behind the wheel, and walked up the path from sidewalk to the front door. Mrs. Cooley's shoes tap-tap-tapped on the walkway – her shoes sounded angry, and as for her face! Even at that distance, Mrs. Cooley looked as if she were smelling something bad. Carolina's heart ached for her friend. She had already taken the ring from the chain around her neck, put it back in the rubbed velvet box and surrendered both to Mama. She heard but didn't see Mrs. Cooley ring the doorbell and the front door opening, Mama speaking in a low voice to Mrs. Cooley. Carolina tiptoed from her bedroom and down the stairs. She walked stealthily out the back door, and around to the front of the house.

Carolina stole closer, looking nervously over her shoulder at the house. Good – Mrs. Cooley was still inside, with Mama. She went to the car, where Greg sat in the passenger seat, staring ahead; his expression glum – the very opposite of the confident boy hero of the St. Gerard's baseball team. His window was rolled down.

"Hi, Greg," she whispered. "I'm so sorry. They made me give the ring back. Can we still be special friends?"

"We can't," Greg replied. He sounded as if he were about to cry, big handsome boy that he was. "I'm sorry, Caro. I'm not even allowed to speak to you, ever again, even at school. Mom said so."

"I'm ..." Carolina started to say, but Greg rolled up the glass window, looking straight ahead, as if he couldn't even bear to listen to her apology – as if this all was her fault anyway!

Carolina felt so humiliated and betrayed. She ran back into the yard, around the side of the house, even as she heard Mama's voice at the front door.

So much for being a special friend.

There were only two weeks until the end of the semester at St. Gerards', but to Carolina they felt like an endless sentence in Purgatory. On the few occasions that she saw Greg in the hallway between classes, or in the lunchroom, he turned away and pretended to be paying attention to practically anything or anyone else. Mrs. Cooley had nothing to say to her in homeroom that wasn't curt and cold. It was so unfair, and Carolina was miserable. She hoped very much that Daddy wouldn't be able to afford St. Gerard in the fall, and she would have to go back to the public school, and that everyone would forget about Greg and the ring, over the summer.

Carolina would spend the summer having fun with her cousins, swimming in the public pool, and having sleepovers at Aunt Bobbie's house.

· · · · ·

Aunt Bobbie's real name was Bernadette, but no one besides Granny Margo and Poppa Lew ever called her anything but Bobbie. In early spring of that year that Carolina went to St. Gerard's, Aunt Bobbie and her husband Bert moved back to San Antonio, from where they had been living in Amarillo. They found a house in Highland Park, close to the family. Carolina loved to visit them – even better if she could spend the night, because Aunt Bobbie was fun. And she and Mama never fought. This was perplexing to Carolina, as Mama, Aunt Jane and Granny Margo fought like cats in a sack, for any reason or for no reason at all.

Aunt Bobbie looked a little like Mama; slim and elegant, with dark brown hair and dark eyes, but Aunt Bobbie had her hair cut short, like Aubrey Hepburn, the movie star. She dressed every day in tight capri pants, commonly called pedal-pushers, with an oversized man's shirt knotted carelessly at her waist, and with the sleeves rolled up to her elbows – just like Aubrey Hepburn in *Breakfast at Tiffany's*. This was terribly daring for the time. There were women who looked askance at Aunt Bobbie and whispered to each other that she was fast and didn't behave in the way which was the least bit proper for a respectable married woman. Aunt Bobbie also mascaraed her eyelashes and shadowed her eyes in dramatic colors, and she adored popular music. Aunt Bobbie had a wonderful voice, and she sang the latest hits in a dramatic mezzo-soprano. And she didn't care for the whispers, either.

Like Mama, Granny Margo and Aunt Jane, Aunt Bobbie also drank.

Drank a lot. But to Carolina, that was almost normal, and anyway, she loved staying at Aunt Bobbie's house. Like Mama, Aunt

Bobbie loved popular music. When Carolina came over to Aunt Bobbie and Uncle Bert's house to spend the night, Aunt Bobbie would spend hours out on the patio, coaching Carolina on singing the latest popular songs and choreographing elaborate dance routines to go with them. Sometimes they were up until early morning, working out a song and dance performance.

The first weekend of summer vacation after leaving St. Gerard's, Carolina spent it at Aunt Bobbie's. Poppa Lew dropped her off there; she had a pair of PJs and a change of clothes for the weekend in her gym bag. She had resolved not to think any more about Greg, and the ring that she couldn't keep. She ran up the walk to the porch, and Aunt Bobbie met her at the door, a beer can in one hand, and a record in a cardboard shuck in the other.

"Come in, darlin'!" Aunt Bobbie exclaimed. "I just got a new copy of Richie Valens singing *La Bamba*! Bert got drunk and broke my last copy, but I just bought a new copy at Joskes! I've worked out a fantabulous routine for us - how's your Spanish, by the way?! Let's get some supper in us so we can work it out on the patio. Bert's doing hamburgers on the grill - his way to apologize, by doing all the cooking for us tonight!"

"Fantabulous," Carolina replied, and kissed Aunt Bobbie on the cheek. Beer and record in hand, Aunt Bobbie embraced her - somewhat in an elevated and distracted mood. All her attention was focused on the song and dance. Carolina's attention would have been likewise, but she was also hungry. She barely paid attention to the burgers - which were slightly charred on the edges, and still pink on the inside, since Bert had been drinking too, but Aunt Bobbie had sliced up tomatoes and torn up lettuce leaves, and put out bakery buns, a bag of potato chips and all the condiments which went on burgers. They weren't quite as good as the burgers at the Bun & Barrel on the Austin Highway, a popular teenage hangout in a slightly shady part of town. The Bun & Barrel was not shady enough to be dangerous, just shady enough to be interesting; so far, Carolina was forbidden to go there alone by her parents.

When they had finished supper, Carolina and Aunt Bobbie put away the leftovers and Bert retreated to the house – probably to drink more beer, as he had been steadily putting them away all afternoon and evening. The sun had gone down, and the backyard was dim. Aunt Bobbie plugged in the portable record player and turned on the outside porch light.

"Now," she exclaimed happily, as the needle hissed and scratched along the track, and then the first bass chords kicked in, then the male tenor voice, sung with fire and energy.

"*Para bailar la bamba...*"

"Now," Aunt Bobbie said, "To dance the *la bamba...* strike a pose, your left foot out, left hand on your hip. Lift your chin, just so..." and she demonstrated, as the music played at top volume. Aunt Bobbie demonstrated the dance routine to Carolina, all the way through, and when the single record scratched to a halt, Aunt Bobbie reset the needle, commanding, "Now, you follow me – and when you have the moves all down, we'll work on the words, and singing tight harmony..."

Carolina loved dancing and singing with Aunt Bobbie; her choreographed routines were the equal of anything ever seen on the *Ed Sullivan Show*. Perhaps someday, she might be under the spotlights, in front of television cameras, performing for the audience on the *Ed Sullivan Show*! That would make Daddy so proud ... and all her school friends so jealous – they would be green with envy. She would be famous! And on television! Strangers might even ask for her autograph!

She and Aunt Bobbie worked for hours, playing the record while the night stars twinkled in the sky overhead, Aunt Bobbie drinking steadily, while Carolina danced and sang, and the distant sounds of the city floated in, the city which was never entirely quiet. They practiced to the music on the record player, over and over again, until every move, every word was pronounced by Aunt Bobbie to be perfect. Carolina even sang a soprano descant, over Richie Valens ... and they had the most wonderful time, right up until the moment that Aunt Bobbie and Uncle Bert's next-door neighbor appeared, bleary-eyed and in bathrobe and slippers.

"Look, I like *La Bamba* as well as the next man," the neighbor drawled. "But it's two in the freaking morning and I hafta get to work at 7 AM. Suppose you can give the music recital a rest for a bit?"

That brought an end to the music that night – but not an end to the fun for that weekend. At mid-morning breakfast, Aunt Bobbie looked at Carolina, and mused,

"Your hair looks so pretty in the sunlight. I used to wish that I had light blond hair like that."

"I wish it were lighter," Carolina took a bit of her pancakes – Aunt Bobbie served them up with fried sweet apples, just like at a restaurant. "It turns really light from the sun, but only if I spend hours at the pool ..."

"You can get the very same effect with peroxide, sweetie," Aunt Bobbie promised, airily. "Why not take a shortcut! Bert!" she yelled into the living room, where Bert was watching a baseball game on TV. "When you go to the store this afternoon – pick up a bottle of peroxide. 'kay, darlin'?"

"Sure thing," Bert replied from the living room. "Soon as the game is over."

He was as good as his word. When he returned from the grocery store that afternoon with more beer, a loaf of bread and some canned tomatoes, he also had a bottle of peroxide. Aunt Bobbie and Carolina retreated to the bathroom, and Carolina wrapped a towel over her shoulders. Aunt Bobbie dribbled peroxide carefully onto Carolina's hair, until it was quite saturated and the bottle empty.

"Is it supposed to be that color?" Carolina asked, dubiously, for her hair was definitely not getting lighter – in fact, it was developing a decidedly orange tint, which only got brighter and more orange, even after she ducked her head under the faucet and Aunt Bobbie rinsed out all the peroxide.

"I don't know what to do, sugar," Aunt Bobbie confessed, utterly baffled. "My friend Sue uses this all the time on her clients at the beauty parlor – it always works for her clients!"

"What can we do!" Carolina felt like crying, as she looked at herself in the mirror. "Mama will be absolutely furious! She won't blame you; she never gets angry at you; she'll be sure to blame me!"

"I'll think of something!" Aunt Bobbie replied. She looked as if she were thinking, furiously. "Here – try and rinse your hair again ... I'll tell her it was my idea."

Despairing, Carolina rinsed out her hair again, and stared into the bathroom mirror. Nope, still brilliant orange. Aunt Bobbie handed her a towel, just as the phone rang.

"Get that, Bert, will you?" Aunt Bobbie shouted, and Carolina heard Bert reply, heard his footsteps crossing into the kitchen, and his indistinct voice as he spoke into the receiver. Then silence.

"Marlene and Adam are on the way," he called, and Aunt Bobbie groaned.

"What are we gonna do?" Carolina asked again, frantic with apprehension. *How on earth could she explain this disaster to Mama and Daddy?* Aunt Bobbie's expression brightened.

"I just had an idea!" she exclaimed. "Dry your hair ... and I've got just the thing to cover it up, until I can get you to a beauty parlor!"

She vanished from the bathroom, leaving a disconsolate Carolina to rub a towel over her hair. Even towel-rubbing her hair didn't help. Carolina heard the closet door open, and hangers rattling, as Aunt Bobbie rifled through the closet looking for something. Her aunt returned with a bright orange scarf in her hands, a triumphant smile on her face.

"Here, Caro – pin up your hair and wrap this around your head. I'll call Sue at the Kurly-Kut first thing Monday morning and get an appointment for you! I'll come and get you – I know that Sue can fix this in no time."

"You're sure, Aunt Bobbie?" Carolina took the filmy chiffon scarf and regarded her still-damp hair, still dubious about this strategy working at all.

"As long as you keep it on, sugar," Aunt Bobbie promised. Carolina did have to admit that with the orange scarf wrapped around her head, it didn't look too bad. Maybe Aunt Bobbie's brilliant plan would work ...

It did seem like it would, at first. Mama and Daddy's car – a newish VW Beetle came tooling around the corner and stopped in front of Bobbie and Bert's house. Carolina ran down the steps, gym bag in one hand, turning to wave goodbye to Aunt Bobbie with the other. She slithered into the back seat, as Mama scooched forward in the passenger seat, without turning her head to actually look at her daughter, although she did ask,

"Caro, did you have a fun time with your Aunt Bobbie?"

"Sure did," Carolina replied. "We stayed up until two in the morning, working on a dance routine to *La Bamba*..." and she began to sing, softly. Mama, who knew all the popular songs, began to sing with her. When they were done, Daddy said,

"Sounds like you had a great time, Caro ... look, I havta stop for a fill-up; won't be a moment." He turned the Beetle right, driving slowly into the blue-tile trimmed Humble Gas station at the next corner, and pulled up to the gas pump under the awning. When he got out to unhook the gas nozzle, Mama turned in the seat, saying,

"Caro, we were ... oh, my Lord, Caro – what did you do to your hair!" Her voice rose to a screech, and Daddy leaned down, puzzled. "Adam – look at her!"

Carolina began to cry. "Aunt Bobbie said ... that she knew how to make it lighter with per-per-peroxide ... but she didn't at all... she said to wait until Monday when she could take me to her hairdresser friend..."

"Vanity, thy name is woman," Daddy remarked, quite unruffled. He even sounded rather amused. "Did Bobbie expect that your hair would turn the color of Bozo the Clown's?"

"That's not funny, Adam!" Mama snapped.

Carolina wailed – the comment did sting, awfully, since her hair now was exactly the color of Bozo's mane. "It shouldn't have come out looking this way!"

"Well, it did," Mama replied, with a deep sight. To Carolina's relief, she didn't sound all that angry – just a bit over the shock of seeing her daughter with bright orange hair. "What did Bobbie think would happen? I suppose she didn't remember about using toner properly."

"She said she would take me to the hairdresser's tomorrow," Carolina sniffled gently. The one good part about this was that school was out for the summer. Daddy saying that her hair was the color of Bozo's was mild, compared to what the other kids at St. Gerard's would have said – and those girls most jealous of Carolina would have been positively vicious.

"That's all right then," Mama said. "We'll all go – just to make certain that it's done right." But her mouth was set in a grim line. "And I will have something to say to Bobbie about this. Straight peroxide! What did she really think was going to happen!"

Even after the peroxide disaster, Carolina still looked forward to another weekend at Aunt Bobbie's. But before that came about, she woke up on a Friday morning with a very sore throat, after a strenuous Thursday spent at the pool.

"You're running a temperature," Mama said, after a quick squint at the glass thermometer. "You'd best stay in bed until it breaks. I think it's your tonsils again."

"Mom!" Carolina wailed. "How can this be my tonsils! I had them removed ages ago!"

"It was a mystery to the doctor," Mama replied, crisply. "And medical science, since it appears that they grew back within a month or so. I expect that you will simply have to have them removed again. Just as well that this is happening during summer vacation, so you won't miss any school."

Miserable, feverish, and barely able to talk above a croak, she didn't get any better by the next week. Mama took Carolina to the doctor, and it was agreed by all that the tonsils would simply have to come out. Carolina didn't mind, particularly. She was miserable enough with the constant sore throats which occurred just about every time that she had a bad chill or a cold. Besides – after the surgery, she could have all the ice cream and cold custard that she wanted; the only foods that could slide down her poor medically-amended throat, until it healed. She missed the Fourth of July celebrations on account of all this, although from her bed at the hospital she could hear the distant *'poom!'* of fireworks exploding in fountains of light all across the city horizon.

Things didn't work out that way once she came home, although the surgery seemed at first to be a success. Carolina had plenty of ice cream ... but the high temperatures continued to plague her. Everything about her seemed to be in a fog. She fell over, faint and dizzy, wobbling like a baby who had just learned how to walk whenever she had to use the bathroom. After the first time she fell, Daddy carried her, lest she hurt herself in falling again. And her bones ached incessantly, especially at the joints. She huddled in bed under covers piled high, shivering, miserable and without any appetite at all. When she could hear Mama and Daddy's low and worried voices coming from the living room, she knew that they were talking about her, even if she couldn't make out the words. She dozed feverishly and woke to find Mama with a bowl of hot cream of wheat cereal in her hand. It was early morning and just barely light outside.

"You must eat something, Caro," Mama pleaded, and spooned a little of it into Carolina's mouth – bland, smooth stuff. Carolina swallowed obediently, and then her stomach lurched in rebellion.

"I can't," she protested, and knew that her face must have been absolutely green with nausea, as Mama didn't press her to take another bite.

"How is she this morning?" That was Daddy, lurking in the doorway to Carolina's bedroom – Daddy, rumpled in pajamas, unshaven … and worried.

"Not any better," Mama replied, looking over her shoulder at him. "It's been two weeks, Adam. She should have been getting better, not worse. I'm worried; I'm going to make an appointment with the doctor, for today, and as soon as possible."

Mama and Daddy went away, after Mama tucked Carolina's covers over her, and she dozed for a while, still feeling very, very ill. Sometime that morning, Mama came back into the bedroom.

"Caro, sweetie – wake up. Put on your bathrobe and slippers – we're taking you to the doctor, right now. They want you to see a specialist, for some tests…"

Carolina was feeling very woozy, wanting nothing more than to crawl back under the covers and go on feeling miserable. But she put on her bathrobe, and slid her feet into slippers, and when she began to wobble, Daddy gathered her up into his strong arms, and carried her to the car. She leaned her head against his chest as he carried her, thinking foggily that it was like she was a little girl again, the age that she had been in Okinawa. She slept in the back seat of the VW Beetle, hugging the wooly blanket which Mama had tucked around her, only waking when Daddy carried her into the doctor's office.

"Oh, dear," she heard a woman's voice remark, sounding as if she were far, far above her. "This does not look good at all – I'll fetch the doctor at once."

Carolina didn't much care, for the someone thoughtfully tucked another blanket around her, as she lay on a tall bed. Now she was cold again, an icy cold that went straight to her aching joints, in spite of the heat of a summer day. She dozed off again, barely aware of footsteps outside, of whispering voices, a light in her eyes, and then someone wrapping a strap around her upper arm, a sharp pinch and jab of a needle drawing blood from her arm, and someone else turning back the blankets and commanding that she pee into a bedpan.

"It'll take a while for the lab to send me the results," someone said, someone who sounded authoritative. "But I'm almost certain it's Bright's Disease – chronic nephritis. I'd have advised strongly against the tonsillectomy, knowing of her condition. That was a hideously dangerous risk and I would have advised against doing the operation."

"Is it ..." She vaguely heard Mama's voice, sounding as if she were about to cry. "... serious."

"Very serious, Mrs. Visser," the doctor sounded grave, "But treatable now, and not nearly so likely to be fatal as it once was, in the previous century. Take your daughter home and make her stay in bed ... stay in bed for the rest of the summer, is my recommendation. As soon as we have the results of her lab tests, we'll prescribe the proper antibiotic dose. But absolutely, she must rest, even if they seem to be having a good effect within days. That's the most dangerous phase in recovery – when the patient feels well enough to go out and about, resume normal activities ... but true recovery is yet days and weeks away."

"We'll do our best," Carolina heard Daddy say, with both amusement and worry mingling in his voice. "But she's a feisty girl, and sometimes doesn't take well to being bossed around, even for her own good."

"She'll stay in bed, if I have to sit on her," Mama said with a firmer resolve. "Or tie her ankles to the bedpost. She'll get her rest, like it or not."

CHAPTER 4
BLINDSIDED

Carolina slowly recovered from the bout of nephritis over the remainder of summer. By the time the new school year started in the fall, she was able to start school again, without missing a grade. She didn't go back to St. Gerard's after all, which was a bit of a relief. It would have been too awful and humiliating to be faced with Mrs. Cooley and Greg again. Instead, she was to start at a new public high school, for Daddy and Mama had decided to move to another neighborhood. Daddy had taken a job with the company that published the Yellow Pages, the business telephone directory, and was frequently traveling on business for them.

"Because your grandparents are moving," Daddy explained. "And because the job with the Yellow Pages pays so much better, what with the travel bonuses and per diem and all."

"Wait until you see the new house," Mama enthused. "Two stories, and a big back yard. You and Frankie have your own bedrooms upstairs – each with a big, walk-in closet! And I have my own little office downstairs, with a separate phone line, for when I do work for your grandfather."

"Could I have a phone in my bedroom, then?" Carolina begged, and Daddy chuckled, indulgently.

"We'll see, sugar," he promised.

Carolina loved the new house. It was just as Daddy and Mama had promised, bigger than the other house in Highland Park. Like that other house, it was just a block away from Poppa Lew and Granny Margo, and it was even newer and fitted out with every modern convenience and luxury. She barely noticed that Granny Margo looked increasingly thin and frail; because Carolina herself was having too much fun; fun dating boys, mostly. She got her driver's license at sixteen, the year after they moved. She also had fun driving Daddy's flashy red Ford T-bird convertible to school. Slim, blond, attractive, and driving that T-bird, she turned heads, and never lacked for a date, for school hops, the yearly high school prom, and the formal balls at Frankie's school, the Peacock Academy, although Daddy didn't altogether approve one hundred per cent of Carolina's constant social whirl.

"It's all right, Adam," Mama said, soothingly. "It's a double date – and Frankie will see that no one gets fresh with his little sister."

Mama was marking and pinning the hem of an elaborate blue sateen formal, which she had sewn for the next big dance, while Carolina wriggled and complained that a pin was sticking into her side.

"But sixteen is just too young for Caro to wear lipstick and stockings!" Daddy protested, and both Mama and Carolina giggled.

"Daddy – all the other girls wear stockings, and they shave their legs, too!" while Mama pointed out that both she and Granny Margo had married when they were younger than Carolina was by a year.

"Let her have fun," Mama said, and Daddy sighed, in resignation.

"But she has a curfew," he said, firmly. "On the dot of midnight. Otherwise, the car turns into a pumpkin."

"Oh, Daddy, you're such a grump!" Carolina pouted, but Daddy never relented about the midnight curfew, and Mama – while glorying in being able to fit out Carolina in beautiful dresses and accessories for the school social events – was similarly unyielding regarding bad grades on her report cards. Invariably, Carolina would be restricted for a month or six weeks following a bad grade; the telephone in her bedroom unplugged, and Daddy sequestering the keys to the T-bird.

On the whole, Carolina preferred Daddy's punishment; he might be stern, and unyielding to tears and promises to be better – but he didn't scream and storm, with an irrational fury mounting to the highest stratosphere, as Mama did regularly, and for the oddest things. Like Carolina not making up her bed properly in the morning. Mama began screaming, ripping the coverlet, blankets, and sheets off the bed, throwing them around the room – and finally turning the mattress over and dragging it to the head of the stairs.

Carolina guessed that Mama was going to throw the mattress down the stairs, but fortunately, Daddy managed to calm her down. She did make the bed properly after that, so as to keep Mama from going off like a hand grenade with the pin pulled out – but her grades in school were all over the place, usually trending towards 'D' and 'F.' Then Mama would have to get up early, and drive Carolina to school... but this would almost always last for two or three weeks before Mama got tired of getting up and dressed early – especially if it was the morning after one of the family get-togethers at Granny Margo and Poppa Lew's new house, when beer and fury had been flowing freely.

It was the semester that she turned sixteen and was regularly driving the flashy red T-bird, the year after she had been so sick after having her tonsils out that she met Buster, the first serious boyfriend, if Greg Cooley really counted as a serious boyfriend at all. Buster Williams was two years older than Carolina, and devastatingly handsome. He had dark hair that was slightly long and swept back. He had beautiful blue eyes. He looked just like James Dean, lean and wiry in a tight tee-shirt and oil-smudged jeans. He worked at a tire shop a few blocks from the new house. Carolina met him one chilly day just after Christmas when she drove the Thunderbird in to get a patch on the spare tire. She noticed him right away, as she pulled up to the garage bay, and got out of the car, looking around for someone to help her.

He appeared out of the bay, hastily wiping his hands on a shop rag, saying, "Miss, can I help you with something?" but the expression in his eyes was that of a hungry dog, appreciating a big T-bone steak, but not daring to take so much as a nibble out of it.

"Hi," Carolina replied, thinking that he appeared so much more assured and mature than the boys who usually asked her to go with them to Frankie's school dances. "I'm Carolina Visser – my dad said that I should bring in the car. He says there's a hole in one of the tires, and he wants it fixed and put back on the car, so that I'm not left stranded someplace by the side of the road."

"Certainly not," he agreed warmly. "I'd not want to see a girl like you in any kinda danger... or even inconvenienced. Give me the keys, and I'll see to it right away. I'm Buster... but my last name's not Brown. It's Williams. The guy's here joke about that all the time. It's embarrassing if you want to know the truth."

"Sorry – I've had jokes about my name too," Carolina replied, thinking how adorably handsome Buster was, even more handsome than a movie star. He looked good enough to eat and stood looking down at her with those melting blue eyes.

"Where do you go to school, then?"

Buster looked slightly embarrassed. "I don't – I'm finished with school. I dropped out. I work here full-time. I... we had some bad family stuff going on, so I came here from Kansas to stay with my big sister and her husband. They have a house with a casita around in back, where I live. It's little, but I have it all to myself, so I don't bother Sis if I have to work early or stay late."

"That is so cool," Carolina enthused. "A job and your own place! Why, you're practically a grown-up!"

"Yeah," Buster agreed, although he sounded rather lukewarm with enthusiasm. "It's nice, I guess."

"I *so* want to be grown-up," Carolina confided, deeply envious of Busters' apparent independence and freedom from parental and scholastic control. "I'd love to be done with school and have a place of my very own, even if it is just a little place. No one to yell at you, or nag you about your grades..."

Just at that moment, an older man in stained overalls – stained especially thickly around his notable paunch – shot out of the garage.

"Hey, Buster Brown, you gonna talk all day to your girlie-friend, or you gonna get back to work?" he demanded, scowling, and both Buster and Carolina started.

"I've got it, Boss," Buster replied, taking the keys from Carolina's hand. She thought she must be blushing all the way to the roots of her hair. "Miss – if you want to wait a few minutes, I'll get right on it."

"Sure, I'll wait," Carolina promised, hoping that she and Buster could continue talking. She sat in the little foyer of the tire shop, the walls covered with advertisements from tire and automobile manufacturers. A stack of tattered magazines sat on a low coffee table; the chairs were old metal kitchen chairs with vinyl-covered seats, now mended here and there with duct-tape. She didn't open any of the magazines, old, crumpled and dog-eared as they were. She had her school notebook, and notes from history class; as pathetic as it was, her schoolwork was better to kill time with than the old magazines. Ordinarily she would have chosen to walk the few blocks home and come back for the T-bird later. But if she could talk a little more with Buster... that would be worth twenty minutes or half an hour of waiting.

While she waited, she had an idea. She wrote her name and her telephone number on a slip of paper torn off from her notebook and folded it very small. When Buster brought in the car keys, she pressed the folded paper into his hand.

"Call me," she whispered. "Maybe we can go to a movie, sometime."

"I'd like that," Buster replied, and Carolina – as young as she was and still a virgin – felt the heat of their mutual attraction like a kind of invisible fire. Still, considering Daddy, his curfew, and his absolute insistence that he personally meet and approve of any male escort taking her anywhere, even if the boy was one of Frankie's school friends from the Peacock Military Academy – she thought she had better let him know to be careful. "If you call, and my Daddy or Mama answer, tell them that you're a friend of mine from school."

"I'll do that," Buster hesitated. "It 'ud be a lie, though."

"You're right... but I'll think of something," Carolina replied. She thought that Buster might have kissed her – on the lips, too! – but for an irritated bellow from the garage drew his attention away.

"I'll call when I can!" he whispered and fled. Carolina walked to the T-bird in a daze. No, Daddy would definitely not approve of Buster, the high school dropout who worked a menial job in a tire shop. If Carolina knew anything at all, it was that Daddy wanted better for her. That was why he was so strict with her and vetted all her dates. He wanted, more than anything, for her to marry a nice man, educated and officer-class, who would be a good father to their children. Buster probably wasn't anything that Daddy would approve of but Carolina thought of him and felt as if she would melt into his arms like warm butter. Buster could do anything that he wanted with Carolina, and she wouldn't protest for a moment.

So, when he called that evening and she answered the phone, luckily well before Mama or Daddy could pick up on the other extension – she made plans to meet Buster on Friday.

"I'll tell Mama that I'm going to hang out with one of my friends!" she said, in a burst of insight. "They won't think a thing. Mama's going to go over to Aunt Janes for the regular family do. They all drink too much and start screaming at each other. I can do without that. So, let's go to the movies..."

"The drive-in" Buster agreed.

And that was how they managed it for months, all through winter and into spring. Carolina perfected her stories. always innocent-sounding ones, about where she was going, and who she was going to see, once Buster was off his work shift at the tire shop. They would meet around the corner from the house, sometimes at his shop. Sometimes she had the keys to the T-bird, although Daddy didn't often approve of her driving such a flashy car after sundown. Mostly, they went out in Buster's own car. Carolina was sunk in helpless envy of Buster's standing in life. He had everything she wanted for herself; a car, his own place, a job, even if it wasn't the most high-class job around – but best of all, he was free from the tiresome surveillance and authority of parents. On Sundays, they might go to Breckenridge Park, or to the zoo, to wander along the semi-deserted paths among the great oak trees, and hug and kiss where there was no one to see. In the evenings, Carolina and Buster went to the drive-in movies, after burgers and a milkshake at a drive-up hamburger place where no one that Carolina might know from school would see and recognize her. Even if Carolina wasn't hungry, after already having had supper at home, Buster usually was. And then they would watch the movie, with Buster's arm around her shoulder, touching her as if she were something rare and precious, and she would run her hand over the bare skin of his chest and his back, feeling the sparse hair on it springing under her fingers, the heat of his skin. She loved touching him, but they were never petted so intensely as to go 'all the way'. She was still a virgin, intended to stay that way for a while, and Buster never insisted on taking the heavy petting that far, although later, at night in her own bed, Carolina sometimes wished that they could have dared to do so.

"My mama says that teenage boys have an appetite for anything that won't try and eat them first," Carolina remarked, one evening in the middle of the week, thinking of her brother Frankie, and his appetite for breakfast and supper, when he was home. Buster paused from wolfing down a double cheeseburger, to grin at her.

"A working man does build up an appetite," he agreed, wiping a bit of ketchup from his lip. "So, when are you going to tell your parents about me? Or do you just want to run away and get married?"

"I don't know," Carolina admitted, with a bit of a pang. "Daddy would be awful hurt…"

Buster swallowed the last bite of his hamburger and shoved his plate halfway across the table so that they could share French fries.

"I meant to keep it as a surprise, but I went and put a wedding ring set on layaway, so we can do it all legal and respectable."

"Oh, Buster, you shouldn't have!" Carolina protested, and Buster helped himself to a French fry.

"But I mean to take it all seriously, and do it right," Buster put on a stubbornly mulish expression. "Look, Caro – I have a mind to just come over to your house and talk to your father, right this very minute. I want to marry you; you want to marry me. So why not get it all out in the open, instead of sneaking around seeing each other, and you telling fibs to your folks. I can't stand this holding back any longer. I want to go all the way with you, tonight and every night."

He wouldn't take any protest on that plan from Carolina, not that she really wanted to, anyway. She loved Buster and wanted to make love to him without control or question. She sniffled a bit in the passenger seat of Buster's car, as he drove through the neighborhood, but only because she was nervous; this was a huge step which would change everything. It haunted her consciousness, though: the certain knowledge that Buster wouldn't meet anything like Daddy's high standard for husband material. Daddy wouldn't approve, she was convinced – and she feared that would put an end to everything.

Buster parked in front of their house, came around and held the door for her.

"Ready?" he asked, as he took her hand in his, and slammed the car door shut. "Do or die, Caro. We need to get this settled. For once and all. Just tell me that you love me, and it's all worth it."

"I love you, and it's worth it," Carolina said, firmly, but she felt as if butterflies were doing tight-formation acrobatics in her stomach. "The front door is open. Daddy and Mama never lock it, until they go to bed." The light in the front window to the living room shown through filmy curtains, the moving flickers of blue-white light hinting that the TV was on. So, Daddy and Mama were still awake; she followed Buster through the door, his hand held tight in hers, as if he were keeping her from drowning in a deep pool.

"Caro!" Mama exclaimed, as she rose from the couch, where she and Daddy had been watching *The Big Valley*. "I thought you were going to the movies with... and who is this?!" Mama looked at Buster with sudden suspicion, and Carolina thought that her sudden awkwardness may have given the game away. "You've been out... alone... with this boy? Caro, you have a lot of explaining to do."

"His name is Buster," Carolina explained, miserably aware that she might be making a mess of it. "Buster Williams. We've been seeing each other... for months. He works at the tire shop, and we want to get married."

"Buster..." Daddy mused, only slightly startled. "Curious, for a given name, I have to say."

"Mr. Visser," Buster stammered. "It's short for Bernard. I'm serious about your daughter, sir. I want for us to get married, proper-like. I have a job and I can take care of her."

"She's only sixteen!" Mama hissed between her teeth, "That's too young to get married!"

Carolina was moved to stand for herself at this piece of Mama's illogic, protesting, "You were fifteen when you got married the first time!" Mama looked as if she had been slapped.

"That was different, Caro – completely different!" Mama's voice began to rise, in agitation, and Carolina wilted in dread. Mama was about to go off on one of her screaming furies. But Daddy took Mama's hand.

"I'd like your permission to marry your daughter, sir," Buster insisted, and Daddy sighed.

"I'll take care of it, Marlene," he urged her, his voice calm and steady as ever. "Take Caro upstairs. It's past bedtime for a school night. I'll talk this over, man to man with young Mr. Williams here, and we'll get it all sorted. Caro..." he looked significantly at Carolina. "Caro, go upstairs with your mother."

When Daddy spoke in exactly that calm, methodical way, Carolina was bound to obey – just as he had spoken to her all those years ago about smoking cigarettes. Just as he restrained and calmed

Mama's irrational furies. Carolina had best obey, for now since Daddy had it all in hand.

She assumed that she might talk to Buster, afterwards, when everything was settled once Daddy had spoken his mind. She thought that she might be called downstairs, even after Mama firmly ordered her to wash up and prepare for going to sleep. She lay on top of her bedcovers, in her slippers and robe, listening to the indistinct rumble male voices downstairs – Daddy's deeper voice mostly, now, and again Buster's light tenor. Next, she heard the front door slam shut. She sat up alarmed. *What was going on!*

"Daddy!" she called and ran to the window on the upper stair landing which looked out to the front of the house. A car engine started up, the sound of it floating off into the night – the red taillights of Buster's car vanishing at the end of their street as he turned the corner. It sounded, from the screech of his tires, that he was speeding. Carolina ran down the stairs, just as Daddy turned from latching the front door. "Daddy, what did you tell him! I love Buster and he wants to marry me! He even got a ring and everything!"

"Then he had better go and get his money back," Daddy's voice was low and weary. "It would be the sensible thing. You are simply way too young to get married to Mr. Williams – and he, despite his good intentions and his job at the tire store, is also too young to be married."

"But Daddy, I love him!" Carolina cried. Daddy was unmoved, and Carolina realized with a pang that Daddy now looked tired... and even old. She thrust that realization away – Daddy was *not* old; he was still tall and fair, handsome and his blond hair had not thinned much at all.

"You think that you do," he explained gently. "But you both are simply too young to be married. You both would have needed parental permission to do so. Realize this – take it to heart and be sensible. Young Mr. Williams did, eventually. I think that you both were more in love with the notion of being married and independent than you were with each other. But you wouldn't have been happy for long. Poverty would have put chains on you both. It would not have worked at the wages that he was making. Not for long, and certainly not when you have children to care for. He had no other ambitions in life than working as a garage mechanic. No education or skills to go any higher, Caro, I'm sorry. He seemed like a nice enough boy; if someone could have only run a lift under him and bolted in a bit more professional ambition. It wouldn't have worked for any longer than it would have taken to comb the bridal confetti out of your hair. I don't think you will see him again, Caro. Now, go upstairs and go to bed. It's late and you have school tomorrow,"

"Daddy..." Carolina was heartbroken. Never to see Buster again! But Daddy must be wrong – she would see him again; he worked at the tire shop, just around the corner, didn't he? "What did Buster say, when you told him all this?"

"He did argue at first, of course," Daddy's eyes were shadowed. "But then he admitted that he truly did care for you and wanted the best... go to sleep, Caro. You have school in the morning."

And that was the end of it, with Buster Williams. Carolina was on restriction again, so Mama had to drive her to school and collect her afterwards – but as was usual, Mama got tired of waking up in the early morning after a couple of weeks. The first chance she had and the keys to the T-bird and the freedom to drive herself again, Carolina stopped by the tire shop on her way home from school.

"Buster?" said the fat manager in the cruddy overalls, when she hesitantly asked after him, keys in her hand and her heart in her mouth. "Oh, he gave notice two weeks ago. Went back to Kansas, so I heard tell. Told me to mail his last paycheck to his sister's address." The manager leered at her, in a perfectly revolting manner. "She'll forward it to him. You want me to send a message, sweetie?"

"No, I don't think so," Carolina replied, and her stomach churned at that lascivious expression. "Thank you for offering."

She drove away, heartbroken and revolted in equal measure. So much for enduring love and promises of marriage.

. . .

She knew, without a doubt over the next few months, that her parents realized very well how serious she and Buster had been about getting married. It was hard to put a finger on exactly how things had changed, but that they had. Mama and Daddy talked to her respectfully, as if she were an adult, no longer a silly girl, or an innocent child. Or perhaps they had realized how very close she had come to eloping with Buster. They might easily have lied about their ages and gone to a JP to get married. As if Mama and Daddy had been suddenly made aware of how close they had come to losing her; only Buster's upright determination to do things the right way had prevented that from happening. Still, Carolina moped. She missed Buster, missed talking with him about things, going to the movies, sharing his French fries, and petting shyly in the shade of the oak trees in Breckenridge Park. Undistracted by evenings spent with Buster instead of paying attention to her school homework, Carolina finished out her sophomore year of high school with good grades – at least good enough that Mama didn't yell at her or take away the telephone extension.

Daddy was home that weekend, after the last day of school. He had been traveling a lot for his job with the Yellow Pages since he started with them. At the supper table that evening, he broached the matter of the new project.

"It's covering the Austin area," Daddy explained. "And that's beyond the limit of being able to drive back and forth every day. They're going to give all of us on the sales team a hotel allowance and per diem for meals during the three months that it will take to wrap up the project. So Dave, our team manager had an idea – why not rent apartments on a short-term lease for the summer; use the hotel allowance and per diem, and have a bit left over. Dave has an old college fraternity brother who manages rental properties. His company has nothing available at the moment, but he has friends among others in the business, and he says that he can ask around, set us all up on favorable terms in nice respectable places. What do you think about spending the summer in Austin? At least – off and on," he added, hastily. "There's lots of things to do, you know. You'd have the T-bird, of course. Museums and things. The Capitol building. Concerts and lectures during the summer."

"It sounds fantastic," Carolina enthused. Austin was the happening city, a cosmopolitan place. The capitol city of Texas, on the Colorado River; the University of Texas was there, and those of her friends in school who were bound for college all wanted to go the university in Austin, if they didn't want to attend the rival school, Texas A&M, or even the women's university at Denton.

Carolina didn't have any particular interest in or ambition for further education when she was done with mandatory high school, but she knew very well that Daddy wished devoutly that she did. Perhaps Daddy hoped that proximity to the University would instill academic ambition in her. Even Mama approved of the plan, although she did insist on the apartment being fully furnished, saying that she had endured enough moves to bare and bleak houses when Daddy was in the Army.

"I am simply not going to unpack an endless series of cardboard cartons, ever again, Adam," Mama said to Daddy, in a tone of voice which brooked no opposition, and of course, Daddy agreed.

The rental apartment that Daddy signed for turned out to be perfect. It was on the ground floor of a tall, three-story tall complex; a luxury suite with two big bedrooms and two bathrooms, attached to a large living and kitchen area, fitted out with comfortable furniture. The very best part of it was that the apartment was right next to the pool... a lovely, lavish, turquoise-jewel colored pool, surrounded by a wide paved deck arrayed with pool chairs and lounges.

Carolina was in heaven, the first few days – a pool! She had it to herself, most mornings, from the moment she walked out for a pre-breakfast dip, just to wake up! It was like having a private swimming pool in the yard. She had often wished that Daddy earned enough from the Yellow Pages job that he could have a pool built at the new house.

She swam every day, luxuriating in the feel of water against her body – and later, the feel of the sun on her skin, sunning on one of the deck chairs adjacent to the apartment. She was beautiful, confident, and graceful. The covert glances of every male resident in the apartment complex, young or old, confirmed that. She took special pleasure from the admiring glances from a handsome fair-haired young man who lived in one of the upper-floor apartments. He also liked to swim and sun, for his tan was gorgeous. He was tall with blond hair and broad shoulders. Most weekend mornings, he was laying on a towel on the far side of the pool. He had friends who visited sometimes in the evenings, and the sound of music floated out of his apartment, along with the sound of male laughter. Carolina welcomed the admiration of that handsome fair-haired young man, as it helped in no small way, getting over the heartbreak of being abandoned by Buster Williams.

Mama often came out and swam and sunned as well, often with a pitcher of margaritas, or Bloody Mary cocktails at her elbow as she lay out on the chaise lounge. Mama also preferred to smoke outside, for the smell of cigarette smoke would spoil the air inside the apartment. Mama also attracted male attention, for she was still slender and smoldering, with only a little silver in her dark hair. Carolina came up out of the water one morning from a vigorous series of laps back and forth across the pool. As she was toweling herself dry, she noticed that the fair-haired young man she had noted before was talking intensely to Mama.

Well, Mama has gotten herself a boyfriend, Carolina thought to herself, with considerable amusement. *Better hope that Daddy doesn't see that – but what should he expect, seeing how good she looks in a bathing suit, still.*

When she had finished drying off, it seemed like a good idea to sit and enjoy the sun for a while, improving her tan and warming up again after a chilly bout in the water. She settled onto the chaise next to Mama. The handsome young man was already gone.

"Who was that? Daddy will be jealous," Carolina ventured, and Mama smiled.

"His name is Mason Rollins, and he lives in one of the units upstairs, overlooking the pool," she replied. "And he was very polite; said 'hello, how do you do' and asked if we had just moved in. He noticed us; you see. I explained that we were only here for the summer, because of my husband's job. He's a student at the university. Third year, studying to be a pharmacist, but he has a regular job during the summer months."

"How utterly boring," Carolina was slightly let down. Such a gorgeous-looking young man ought to be something more exciting; a cowboy or a soldier, or a flier, maybe even a movie star. Such a waste of good looks to sit around handing out pills!

"Your Daddy would approve." Mama replied, rather amused. "It's a good profession for a serious young man. He was asking especially about you, Caro. He wanted to know if you were my daughter and how old you are. I think you have an admirer, sweetie. He thought you were very pretty, and he wanted to know you better."

"He *is* awful cute," Carolina admitted with a sigh. "What did you tell him?"

"What do you think? I said you were, and that you were sixteen, but everyone thinks you are much older." A little smile crossed Mama's face. "And one more thing, Caro – I invited him to supper tomorrow tonight with you and Daddy."

CHAPTER 5
MASON

Carolina had the jitters – anticipatory nervous jitters – all the next afternoon. After helping her mother to ready the apartment for a visitor, organizing the kitchen for a rather more-than-usual supper, and putting four placemats on the dining room table, she went for her usual swim-and-sun in the warm afternoon by the pool.

"He has a job during the day, to help pay for school," Mama warned Carolina, and looked around the apartment's dining room which was merely a nook of the living room by the door into the kitchen. "Oh, dear. Now I wish that we had packed the good china and silverware to bring with us. I do want to make a good impression on him, for your sake."

"Never mind," Carolina replied, with a fleeting kiss on her mother's cheek. "I wouldn't want him to think that we were going all overboard by putting on too much of a show – the good china, that we never use except on holidays or when Poppa Lew and Granny Margo are coming over for a birthday or something – too much of a show. Just a plain family supper. What are you fixing, then? Nothing to awfully fancy, I hope."

"Porcupine meatballs," Mama replied. "Thank God, I brought the pressure-cooker. With potato puffs. And mixed green salad. Lemon chiffon cake for dessert. Nothing fancy."

"Thank you, Mama," Carolina kissed her mother's cheek on an impulse. "Perfect." She thought about Mason – how handsome and tall! – and her heart raced. "We're not going to dress up, or anything like that?"

"No," Mama replied. "Just change out of your wet bathing suit, into something you would ordinarily wear after your swim of an afternoon." She flashed a reassuring smile at Carolina. "Remember, Caro, perfectly ordinary family supper. Six o'clock – but tell him we'll have a bit of wine or beer before supper."

Carolina went out to the swimming pool, still in an excitable flutter. Mason was so handsome, and apparently so agreeable. Having Mama and Daddy approve of him and doing everything possible to make it easy for both was a bit of a boost. Was this how courtship really worked: the parents reviewing prospective husbands and marking them acceptable, or not acceptable – and then making the way smooth for an acceptable potential swain. It had not worked out with Buster Williams, working in a no-end and futureless blue-collar job. When Carolina had to break up – or was forced to give up – she really felt at first that her heart was broken. But it seemed that her heart fell back to a more or less intact condition after a while. Maybe it would be best for Carolina to let her older, wiser parents, especially Daddy, guide her when it came to courtship by potential husband materiel. She always said she wanted to marry someone just like her daddy anyway.

And Mason was sooooo good-looking. Carolina swam the length of the pool, over and over again, relishing in the feel of cool water, the strength and speed of her own body, sleek, tanned, young and strong. When she was pleasantly tired from the strenuous exercise, she climbed out of the pool, toweled herself dry and squinted up at the sun to estimate the time.

Almost five o'clock; in a typical Texas summer, the hottest time of the day. If she had accurately observed his presence before, Mason would be home soon from his day job. And today would be special; he was invited to supper! He finally walked through from the parking lot outside. Carolina watched him through eyes veiled by dark sunglasses, as he paused by the nearest flight of exterior stairs which led to the upper levels.

"Hi," he ventured; he sounded uncertain, even hesitant. "Carolina... I guess we'll be seeing each other at supper tonight. Your mom invited me, but she didn't say exactly what time."

"Oh, hi," Carolina raised up her dark glasses so that she could look directly at him, and made her voice seem casual. "Mason. Yeah, Mama said she had invited you. We usually have supper about half an hour after Daddy gets in from his job and has a beer. Make it six thirty or so."

"Ok." Still, he stood hesitating with one hand on the chipped metal banister and a foot on the first step. "Should I wear anything special?"

"Clothes," Carolina replied, dryly humorous and recovering her social confidence. Mason grinned. In that moment, Carolina knew that he was a definite possible. He had wit and the confidence to accept and respond readily to a bit of teasing; that on top of his handsome looks and excellent professional prospects.

"Clothes it will be," he replied, "See you at six thirty, then." He trotted up the stairs, and Carolina settled her dark glasses over her nose.

She managed to make a pretense of relaxation, laying out on the lounge to get the last of the afternoon sun, but when that sun slipped behind the apartment wing opposite, and the pool area fell into shadow, she couldn't contain her excitement for another minute. She gathered her towel, tube of suntan oil and dark glasses and fairly danced into the apartment.

"I told him 'Six thirty, as soon as Daddy comes home'," She reported to Mama, who was busy rolling small meatballs in uncooked rice and putting them into the pressure-cooker with a splash of tomato sauce. "What do you think – is that too early? I said that Daddy would want a beer before supper. Is that all right – what if he is teetotal or a Mormon or something! Oh, my god – did I say the right thing?"

"Of course, you did, Caro," Mama rolled another meatball. "And no, he's not teetotal. I saw him with a couple of friends of his, last weekend. They were drinking beer on the balcony outside his apartment and having a fine old rowdy time. For hours, until past midnight, at least. We can see the front of his place from our windows, you know."

"Oh, right," Carolina replied, rather abashed. She should have thought of that. "Well... I'm going to change... should I wear anything special? A dress, maybe?"

Mama shook her head. "Just what you usually wear in the evening after a day in the pool. Don't overdo it, Caro – it's just a plain old family supper and Mason is a neighbor we invited over, so that we all can get to better know him."

"Right," Carolina acknowledged. Mama was usually right about things like this. She went to the small bedroom in the apartment – the one whose window overlooked the parking lot and the street beyond – and stripped off the barely-dried bathing suit, in favor of shorts and a sleeveless blouse. She rubbed her hair vigorously with a towel, combed it out, fluffy about her shoulders, and tied a ribbon around her head. She looked just like Sandra Dee. Well, that was enough dressing up.

She heard Daddy coming in through the door, saying,

"Gosh, Marlene, that smells good. What a day! I think we hit every single office or business in San Marcos and points south. Do I have time to wash up before our guest gets here?"

"Just enough, if you keep it snappy," Carolina heard Mama say from the kitchen. Daddy said something to her, in a voice too low for her to hear in her bedroom with the door closed. Then she heard water running in the bathroom; knew that Daddy was washing up, putting on a clean T-shirt after his long, sweaty, and hardworking day on the road, visiting businesses to sell space in the next Yellow Pages issue. Carolina fiddled a bit more with her hair, decided against putting a bit of rouge on her cheeks. Mama was right – best to not overdo it. When she could stand it no longer, she emerged from the bedroom.

"Is there anything that I should be doing? It's a quarter after six, and I told him 6:30."

Mama looked over her shoulder – she was tearing up iceberg lettuce leaves for the salad. It was one of her rules in making a green salad; that lettuce leaves ought to be torn by hand, never chopped with a knife.

"Yes – set the table – four places, salad course first. Salad forks and dinner forks. I've already folded the napkins."

That was another one of Mama's rules for supper, properly starched and folded napkins. Carolina knew the rules for laying out silverware and plates – forks to the left, evenly aligned, knife to the right with the blade pointing towards the plate. She hoped that Mason would be impressed, but not scared out of his mind, the way that Buster Williams would have been intimidated to silence at being invited to eat supper with the Visser family. From the living room, she heard Daddy's voice.

"He's on his way now. Just coming down the stairs. Good. I already like a young man who is punctual."

"Finish setting the table, Caro," Mama called from the kitchen. "Let your father be the host."

"Yes, Mama," Carolina replied, her heart fluttering with anticipation and nerves. From around the corner, she could hear footsteps approaching the door outside, a tentative knock upon it, Daddy's armchair creaking as he got up to answer that knock. The front door opened; a light male tenor voice and Daddy's deeper one exchanging brief pleasantries. "He's here."

"Then bring a beer for him, and another for your father," Mama suggested, and Carolina thought that sounded quite sensible, although her heart was still racing. She took two cold ones from the refrigerator and went into the living room, where Mason sat on the edge of the sofa, making casual conversation with Daddy. Mason still looked a trifle nervous, but he sent a grateful look towards Carolina. Daddy reached out for his beer, and said,

"Caro, sweetie – sit down with us. Mason has been telling me all about his summer job. He works in a record store near the university. It's only until classes start again, though. Then he goes back to part-time and on weekends."

"That sounds amazing," Carolina replied – and she was being honest. "I'll bet you're the first to hear all the hot new record releases!"

"One of the perks," Mason replied, with a grin. He looked as if he were relaxing a bit, since Daddy wasn't interrogating him like a Gestapo villain in a war movie, with the instruments of torture at hand. "And a generous employee discount, too. I've got a great collection. All my friends are green with envy."

"Mama said that you were studying to become a pharmacist," Carolina felt a little more at ease. Mason was so... nice, as well as being breathtakingly handsome. He looked as if he had also washed up for supper, after a day spent sweating at the job. His hair was still damp, with the marks of a comb and a bit of Brylcreem showing in it. "That really doesn't sound as interesting as the record shop, though. Is it worth sitting through all those classes for?"

"It certainly is," Mason's expression lightened, and he began to outline why this would be so. Carolina still thought pharmacology didn't sound nearly as interesting as working in a record store. In fact, it sounded deathly dull, but it was what Mason liked and was studying to work in that field, and for that she could at least put on a pretense of interest.

Daddy threw in the occasional question when Mason sounded like he was running low. By the time that Mama emerged from the kitchen with her own beer, the conversation had turned three-way, rather lively, and self-supporting. Carolina rejoiced inwardly at that. Mama and Daddy liked Mason as much as she did and that would be all to the good. Mason being acceptable and liked by them would make it so much better. Easier. More comfortable. Not sneaking around, telling fibs like she had to do when she was dating Buster.

It turned out to be a wonderful evening, that night when Mason first came to supper at the apartment. He confessed to adoring the meatballs and asked Mama for the recipe so that he could pass it on to his mother. This, after forking up every mouthful. Mama did not fly into one of her irrational rages over anything – and Daddy seemed to enjoy talking to Mason about practically everything. This had to count as a success. At the end of the evening, after the last crumbs of lemon chiffon cake were finished Mama made up another slice of it for Mason, on a paper plate and wrapped in a napkin, in case he was hungry later.

"If you're free, come have supper with us tomorrow," Mama said, and Daddy nodded, as they bade Mason goodnight at the door.

"I'd already promised to hit the Armadillo HQ with my friends on Saturday night," Mason confessed reluctantly. "Our best night to paint the town and groove on live bands, you see. But any other night..."

"Sunday, then," Mama replied, without hesitation, while Daddy looked on, his expression inscrutable. "A proper Sunday supper – roast chicken and hot biscuits. Bring your appetite."

"I surely will, ma'am!" Mason agreed with heartfelt enthusiasm. He shifted the plate with the cake in it to his other hand, took Carolina's hand in his, and kissed the back of it, with a sort of old-fashioned gallantry that Carolina had only seen at the movies. "And I will look forward to your company, Miss Carolina!"

"So will I," Carolina confessed, rather touched, and impressed by that archaic gesture. "Good night, Mr. Rollins..."

"Call me Mason," he assured her, and then looked towards Daddy, so that he could shake Daddy's. "Good night, sir – I am honored. And I am looking forward to Sunday supper."

"As are we all," Daddy replied, and then the front door shut on Mason and his plate of cake. A few minutes later, Carolina watched him through the living room window. She saw him climb the steps to his apartment, open the door and vanish inside. The lights came on, veiled by curtains, but she could tell. At her back, she heard Daddy say,

"Has the young Lochinvar safely arrived home?"

"Mason has," Carolina answered. "Who is this Lochinvar guy?"

"A literary allusion, Caro," Daddy replied. He was sitting with his feet up on the reclining armchair. From the lines in his face, he was already tired enough from the day of recruiting potential clients for the Yellow Pages, and the burden of being sociable over supper following on top of that. "Never mind. He's a nice kid. Got my approval stamp on him, for what it's worth. You do like him too, Caro?"

"I do, Daddy," Carolina replied, "He is soooo good-looking!"

Daddy smiled. "That's all to the good, kiddo. You know, your mom and I love you and just want the best for you. Young Mason – he is one of the best that we have seen. Consider him good to go, as a suitable date – but don't feel that you need to rush into anything."

"Thanks, Daddy," Carolina dropped a kiss on his forehead, and sashayed off to her tiny bedroom, leaving Mama to wash up all the dishes from supper, and still wondering, with a part of her mind, why Daddy looked so tired and harassed.

• • •

Mason did indeed come to supper on Sunday, bringing a small sheaf of fresh flowers rolled in a cone of paper. Such a thoughtful gesture, and the flowers looked amazing, set in a small vase in the middle of the dinner table. And he came to other suppers, almost every night in the following weeks that summer. He slipped into being almost a true member of the family, joking and joshing with Mama over evening supper, discussing serious matters with Daddy... and anything and everything with Carolina. If he were any more a member of the family, Daddy might have given him a door key to the apartment. After a few weeks, he didn't even bother knocking.

And more often in the evenings after supper, when the sky was still a pale oyster-color with a smear of red on the western horizon, Carolina would go up to the balcony of Mason's apartment, to sit there and watch the sunset, evening descending on dark wings, as the first stars began twinkling dimly in the sky. On the 4th of July, they watched the fireworks from his balcony. And there – they would talk of anything and everything – because Carolina could talk about absolutely everything with Mason. She could vent to him about how unhappy she was at school, feeling that she was wasting her life, sitting in a classroom, bored to tears.

He chided her about that.

"Look, Caro, it might not seem like much now … but learning stuff is useful! You never know when knowledge of something will come in real handy. You want the world to be your own personal oyster, stuffed full of pearls? You gotta stay in school, study hard, pass all the tests with flying colors, and get good grades."

It was pretty much what Daddy had always said; it just sounded better, coming from Mason. She could also unburden herself regarding her secret worries about Mama's erratic and violent temper, which she had never done with anyone else, or voice her concern about matters between Mama and Daddy.

"I mean, I love Mama," she explained earnestly. "And Daddy does, too … but it makes us both tired sometimes, tiptoeing around, as if we were walking on eggshells, for fear of setting Mama off about something. My brother Frankie is well out of it. He adores Poppa Lew, so and he lives almost more at their house then ours, and he works with Poppa, when he's not at school. But I'm still at home, and I'm afraid …" she ventured, and then wondered if she had gone too far, in unburdening herself. Mason waited for a courteous moment, and then took her hand.

"What are you afraid about, Caro?"

"I love Daddy to bits …"

"I can see that," Mason replied warmly. "He's a real gent. I'd love him to bits if he were my dad."

"He never loses his temper," Carolina continued. "And he does his best for us, he really does, and he loves Mama and adores us as much as I adore him ... but sometimes I wonder how he can carry on, when nothing he ever does is quite good enough for her. Poppa Lew helps us out financially, but I wonder if Daddy doesn't just find that a bit humiliating. That he must think that whatever he does for Mama just isn't good enough for her. What about your parents, Mase? Don't you sometimes just wonder?"

"Mom and Dad – they're cool," Mason replied, although Carolina noted that he did sigh, a little. "I'm a lonely-only, so I'm the designated heir to the family name and honor. Still..." he shifted a bit in his chair. "I wish that they weren't so ... so nice about it. About everything."

"What are you most afraid of?" Carolina couldn't help teasing him gently.

"That they *are* so nice and understanding," Mason chuckled. "Disappointing them is a bit like kicking a puppy or torturing a kitten. One feels like a brute for even suggesting ... never mind. Honestly, I don't think your dad would ever walk out on your mom. They ... well, they seem so ordinary, every evening at supper."

"I wonder if they aren't just putting on a show for you," Carolina admitted, and their conversation meandered onto something else. But that was a conversation that she remembered later. Much later.

"What do you really want from life?" she asked him one evening, out of an impulse. She was sixteen, almost seventeen. Mama had been married for a year when she was the age that Carolina was now. So had Granny Margo. Down below, on the first level of the apartment block, she could see Mama through the window to the tiny kitchen, washing dishes, while Daddy lay out on one the loungers by the pool, smoking his last evening's cigarette, the end of it a tiny red spark in the gathering evening gloom. Carolina knew that they could both see her, see plainly that she and Mason weren't getting up to anything that would count against them in the eyes of neighborhood gossipers, assuming there were any prying eyes or gossiping tongues in the apartment complex, which mostly catered to a relatively young crowd. "I definitely know what I want - to be married and settled, have a life and a home of my own. Especially a place of my own. What do you want, Mase?"

"To be normal," Mason replied, and took her hand in his, and kissed it. "I want to be normal, Caro - all that, just like you do. A pretty and understanding wife... and to have everyone looking at us and thinking, 'my heck, what a nice-looking couple.'! That's what I want. If I could wake up in the morning and have that all - it would be my dream come true."

"Mine, too," Carolina replied, her heart lifting. Maybe Mason was the one, the special one. Down below, Daddy had finished his cigarette; he stood up and waved to Carolina. If she didn't come down the stairs in the next few moments, Daddy would get on the telephone, call Mason's telephone, and demand that Carolina come home, right that very instant. "Gotta go, Mase... see you tomorrow, OK?"

"Sure thing," Mason replied. "What's for supper, then - so I can start looking forward?

"Chicken a la king," Carolina replied. On an impulse, she leaned down and dropped a shy kiss on his cheek. "See you then, Mase."

"Sure thing, Caro," he replied, and he caught her hand. "We can dream together, some day."

"Sure thing," she echoed, and only with reluctance, pulled her hand from his, and trotted down the stairs to the ground floor level. "Daddy," she ventured, as she and Daddy went inside for the night. "How can you tell if someone is your soulmate? I think Mason might be..."

"That's a hard one," Daddy replied. "If you dream about them at night, and they dream about you. If you finish each other's sentences ... and you can't even think about being with someone else - that person just might be your soulmate. But there's never any absolute guarantee. You just do your best, hope for the best, and carry on as best that you can. Why? Are you getting serious about Mason? Better question – is he getting serious about you?"

"He might be," Carolina replied. "I might be."

"Well, then just be careful. Don't rush into things, I don't want you getting serious about anyone right now. You are too young" Daddy advised, as he latched the front door and turned off the lights in the living room. The light in their bedroom was still on, leaking around the edges; Mama had taken the telephone there and closed the door. She was talking to someone – maybe Poppa Lew and Frankie, since there was a distinct lack of screaming, which would have been the case if she were talking to Granny Margo.

"I won't," Carolina promised, and went to her own room, wondering if she would dream about Mason. She did – a dream where they embraced and kissed, and she clung to his tanned shoulders. She relished every dream-moment.

Daddy might be right.

. . .

The only worm at the heart of the apple – that perfect, sun-kissed golden apple of a summer in Austin was the calendar. Summer would end, and she would have to go back to high school in San Antonio. Daddy's short lease on the apartment would lapse, and then they would all pack up and go home. Would she go on seeing Mason Rollins? Carolina didn't say anything of this to Mason, but chance intervened. Towards the end of August, Daddy and his team planned an extended trip farther to the north, almost to Georgetown and Abilene. This would take him several days on the road and away from Austin. It wouldn't have mattered much, but that Mama had a frantic call from Aunt Bobbie.

"I have to go home for a couple of days," she said, her face tense and lined with worry. "Your grandma has had a bad turn and Bobbie absolutely insists I ought to come home, right now. I'll take the T-bird, Adam, since you'll have the company car."

"What about me?" Carolina ventured, unhappily. Of all things, she didn't want to cut the stay in Austin short, not if it would mean missing those brief times with Mason. Such moments and hours were precious, since Mason also had a job during the day. "I'd ... I want to stay here in Austin. You know – to look after the apartment. And if Daddy's work road trip ends sooner than expected... well, I can fix breakfast and supper for him, can't I?"

"That's all right, then," Mama replied. She sounded distracted, as if she were thinking of a hundred other things. Carolina rejoiced at the thought of staying in the apartment, by herself! Daddy depended on her, that was for certain. So did Mama. "You stay here in Austin: make certain the place looks as if it is lived in. You have to keep up a place like this – otherwise, with all those rowdy students..."

"I don't think we'll have anything to worry about, leaving our girl on her own for a couple of days. You're sure you can manage, Caro?" he added, just a touch anxious, but his face cleared when Carolina affirmed that she could.

. . .

And that was what it turned out to be. Mama took the keys to the red T-bird, and drove it back to San Antonio, to help look after Granny Margo, and Daddy headed off to the sales circuit in the small towns far, far to the north of Austin. She fixed a lonely breakfast for herself, and went for her regular morning swim, wondering how she would fill the empty hours, pottering around the apartment and sunning by the pool, until Mason came home from work. The day seemed to stretch out interminably. She settled onto the lounge on the sunny side of the pool, slathered suntan lotion on her face, legs, and shoulders, closed her eyes and prepared for a long, boring morning. Until she was dampened by a huge splash of cold water from the pool. She sat up, soaked and indignant, to see Mason in his swim-trunks, grinning and about to scoop up another double handful of water.

"Hey, you! I thought you were at work all day today!" Her heart leaped with transcendent happiness.

"Hey you, yourself!" Mason replied, still grinning. "I asked for time off, and since I am such a hardworking, reliable, and effective employee – you know, I am the ruling crown prince of salesmen – I asked for and got two days off. And because I am such champion among salesman – I got them! At mid-week, even! Although," he added fairly, "We have our busiest days on Friday and Saturday, anyway."

"A whole three days!" Carolina exulted. It was Tuesday. Daddy wouldn't be back until the weekend at the earliest, Mama … who knew! "What are we going to do, Mase? Let's do something fun, something that we haven't ever done before!"

"I have just such a notion in mind," Mason's grin turned sober and earnest. "Let's drive to Mexico and get married, Caro. There's no need in Mexico for you to have your folks' permission, even if you're under eighteen. They don't ask questions in Mexico. We can drive down there in a day, get married and drive back. I have my own car. You want to be married and I want to have a regular normal life. What do you say to that!"

"Yes!" Carolina felt as if her heart leaped with joy within her chest. "Yes! Let's do it, this very minute!"

"We can be in Laredo by afternoon, find a JP in Nueva Laredo … and be back tonight." Mason promised. "And honeymoon here at my place or somewhere along the road."

"I don't want to be away for too long," Carolina temporized. "Mama or Daddy might come back – and they trusted me to look after the place."

"It won't take very long at all," Mason promised, his blue eyes gleaming in his tanned face, the water from the pool beading on his shoulders and dripping down his muscular torso. "Just a single day. I guess I forgot the important part – will you marry me, Carolina Visser?"

"Yes, of course – silly! Just give me a chance to dress!" Carolina collected up her towel and bottle of lotion, and Mason mock-leered at her.

"You won't need that excuse for long!"

Carolina giggled, feeling absolutely light-headed with joy and relief; the guy she adored had just proposed, and insisted on getting married at once! Both of their dreams were within a breath of being true. She did consider for a moment how she would explain all this to Daddy, the reckless impulse taking them to Mexico but swept that to the back of her mind. A day … and then a night with Mason as a lawfully married couple, and then days and nights without counting after that! She packed a small suitcase with her night things, a set of fresh underwear, a set of shorts and a blouse, and put on a pretty floral summer dress trimmed with white eyelet, thinking of how pretty it might look in pictures taken that day. She could show such pictures to hers and Mason's possible children and say, *"Look, my darlings – this is your father and I on our wedding day!"*

The runaway-marriage to Nueva Laredo went as if powered by clockwork. Mason carefully kept just below the speed limit, all the way south on the highway to Laredo, and then across the Rio Grande to Nueva Laredo, where just about everything on the street signs was in English and Spanish alike. They were married in a dingy office by a JP who seemed not quite altogether sober after lunchtime. He glanced blearily at their papers which Mason presented with a flourish. Carolina and Mason signed the registry, and escaped, as Carolina hissed,

"Where did you get a copy of my birth certificate and my passport?"

"I have my ways," Mason replied, with a definite air of smugness. "Being a man of infinite resource and sagacity, as well as being an ace salesman. So, do you appreciate being married to me now, Mrs. Rollins?"

"I do," Carolina replied, utterly content and content also to wait upon what would happen next, after the long drive back to Austin.

Which turned out to be only a night of awkward sleep in the twin bed in Mason's apartment. They had run into traffic on the return journey, and it was well after ten o'clock when Mason finally parked at the apartment. Carolina was exhausted as well. At the door of the apartment, Mason concealed a yawn and asked in somewhat anxious tones,

"You don't expect me to carry you over the threshold, do you? I'm so tired from driving I might just drop you on the doorstep. And you wouldn't want that – bad omen, supposedly."

"Not at all," Carolina replied, and she couldn't keep back the responding yawn of her own. "We'll just have a good night's sleep. First dibs on the shower, OK? I'm all nasty and sweaty from the drive."

"Not that I would object," Mason let the whole yawn out, as he unlocked the door to his place. "But ... I'll scrub your back if you do mine. I think we can both fit in the shower..."

"It's a bargain, then," Carolina said. As excited as she was about being with Mason and being legally married so what would happen between them in bed was totally OK in the eyes of everyone, she was so exhausted that she actually felt a bit light-headed, standing under the hot water in the shower. It had been hours since they ate, at a roadside barbeque place outside of D'Hanis. She was hardly able to appreciate the view of Mason – naked and beautiful, and tanned almost all over, save the bits covered by his swimming trunks. For he was beautiful, so beautiful and perfect, like the statue of Michelangelo's young David ... and he took the soap and bathing sponge and lathered her all over with such exquisitely tender care, both standing close under the shower nozzle. She could only think that he also adored her, slim, and tanned and beautiful.

This seemed to be an awkward time for both of them. She was so young and naive and wasn't sure about what the right moves were, and he appeared to be perfectly content with just holding her, and that's all it was their first night together as a married couple.

He was too tired to do much more than pull her close to him under the covers and whisper into her hair how grateful that he was to have her to cuddle, and she was too exhausted from the drive to even think about making love anyway. They fell asleep, linked close in each other's arms, Carolina thinking as she drifted away into deep slumber that it was delicious, cuddling close to Mason. They would have tomorrow, and tomorrow.

• • •

It was well-daylight when they woke up. Sunlight shifted through the bedroom window curtains, and Carolina woke up and realized that she was sleeping against the bulwark of another human body; a welcome and warm one. Mason. She rolled over and reached her arm around him, heard him mumble drowsily, a name that she thought must be hers. Since it seemed to start with the same letters – he must be saying her name.

"Hi and good morning," she swept a rivulet of blond hair off her shoulder and smiled into Mason's suddenly opened eyes. "It looks like a nice day for a good swim ... and then ... whatever. D'you want me to go down and fix breakfast? Mama and Daddy left the 'fridge full of eggs and bacon an' things. Guess they didn't want me to starve, all on my own..."

"You'll never starve, Caro. Not as long as I'm here," Mason assured her – although to Carolina's ears, he still sounded uncertain.

It was as if Mason had just woken from a strange dream and was not at all certain where he stood with her, why she was even in bed with him. The bed was warm, they were rested from the long drive; they were both naked ... and really, what better situation could there be for making love for the first time? Still faintly baffled, Carolina snuggled against his bare chest, and mentally braced herself for what would happen as a natural result of all that. To her vague disappointment, nothing did. Eventually, Mason gave her one final embrace, kicked the covers off, and announced, "What about that breakfast, Caro?"

"On the way!" Carolina replied, almost regretfully, and slid out of bed. "Just give me fifteen minutes and come down to Mama and Daddy's place!" She found her little suitcase and put on the shorts and blouse and scampered down the two flights of stairs to the apartment. She let herself in, humming a pop tune to herself, and switched on the lights.

The apartment was cool and faintly musty. It had an abandoned feel about it, even after being empty for only twenty-four hours. She lit the stove burners and set cold strips of bacon in the biggest fry pan, searched out eggs and milk from the refrigerator, half a loaf of bread from the breadbox. There was jam and butter in the refrigerator, and a half-full tin of ground coffee for the Norelco coffee maker ...

Mama and Daddy had left the apartment refrigerator fully stocked. Carolina was already thinking about what she would fix for supper for herself and Mason, and if it would be too much to have candles on the table for supper that night. Would she be fixing it for her husband (*and Carolina relished the savor of that very phrase – my husband!*) in his apartment? She rather feared that it would be one of those sketchily equipped bachelor kitchens, based upon how often he appeared for supper with Mama and Daddy. She had never actually explored Mason's bachelor pad, since Daddy was in the habit of giving them both a disapproving look and calling Mason's number if they went into it for more than a hot second. Maybe Mason had a can opener in his kitchen. That was probably all that she could count on... and Carolina went on fixing breakfast; something she would feel happy doing now, for all the mornings of her life.

The outside door to the apartment opened, and Carolina fixed a bright smile on her face.

"I've got the eggs almost ready," she chirped.

"Oh, good." Mama replied. Mama dropped her handbag onto the nearest chair and walked into the kitchen. "It smells amazing, Caro, and I'm hungry. What on earth are you doing, up so early? I usually have to pry you out of the sack."

The door behind Mama opened again; Mason, with a look on his face... surprise and shock, almost equaling the surprise and shock that Carolina felt herself.

Like an absolute dummy, she said, "I invited Mason for breakfast – he has the day off today."

CHAPTER 6
ILLUSIONS AND DISILLUSIONS

"Well, that was nice of you, Caro," Mama replied. She looked frazzled. "Is the coffee ready? All I could think of all the way since New Braunfels, was a decent cup of coffee – aren't you going to set another place for me!"

"We weren't ... I wasn't expecting you back so soon," Carolina stammered. "I thought Aunt Bobbie told you that Granny Margo was really sick."

Behind Mama's back, Mason had his eyebrows raised but he had the wit not to speak.

"Oh, your Aunt Bobbie was just panicking," Mama reached up and for a coffee mug from the dish cabinet. "I didn't like to think of you being here all by yourself, so as soon as I knew that your Granny was just fine, and Bobbie was having conniption fits over nothing at all. Any word from your father, then? God, Caro – are we out of coffee creamer already?"

"No, Mama – behind the milk," Carolina replied.

"The bacon's starting to burn," Mason cleared his throat and observed gently. Thoroughly rattled by now, Carolina shifted the pan off the burner and looked closely at the bacon. Yes, almost inedible, burnt so crispy it was black at the ends.

"I'll start another batch," she confessed, feeling doubly miserable. So much for a honeymoon, and a cozy breakfast for two. Carolina cringed at that mental movie of Mama's guaranteed reaction. Her very soul shriveled at the thought of telling Mama what was really going on with the two of them this very minute. Mama would for sure loose her mind and begin to scream at Carolina, without Daddy there to calm her down. And in front of Mason, too – which would make it worse.

"I like my bacon extra-crispy," Mason slid into the chair at the dining table which did not have a place setting before it, and Mama smiled as if this were all acceptable, and handed him a plate from the dish cabinet. Carolina hastily got out bread and set four slices in the toaster.

God, this was turning out to be such a disaster. The sole saving element was that Mason didn't seem about to blurt out everything to Mama about the trip to Mexico, and he and Carolina getting married there. Carolina took out the carton of eggs and cracked two more of them into a glass quart cup measure. As she added a splash of milk, Mama settled to a place at the table, wrapping her hands around that first mug of coffee, and casually asked Mason about why he wasn't heading off to work, since it was well after nine.

"I'm off until Friday," Mason replied. "Caro and I were going to the lake, check out some of the art galleries, too." He looked as if he would say more, glancing at Carolina for her reaction.

"That's nice," Mama beamed approvingly. "Honestly, too much work is bad for a couple. I wish that Adam didn't have to work so many hours but being the family breadwinner takes time and dedication." She began telling Mason about Poppa Lew and his many laundromats and enterprises, and how that allowed the family to live a very comfortable life in a big mansion. It vaguely hurt Carolina that Mama said nothing about Daddy's many hours on the road, working for Yellow Pages, or how he had to give up being an officer in the military because that didn't bring in enough income for Mama's standard of living. Carolina busied herself with the rest of breakfast, stirring the scrambled eggs, turning the new batch of bacon, buttering the toast. Anything to avoid Mama's questions or deal with Mason's bafflement.

. . .

"OK, Caro – why didn't you tell your mother that we are married? Come clean about it." Mason demanded, as soon as they were alone together, getting back into Mason's car. They were indeed going down to Austin's lakeside park; the only way that they could be alone as Mama was guaranteed to pitch a screaming fit if they went up to his apartment and closed the door.

"Because she will absolutely come unglued," Carolina confessed, on the verge of tears. "And I can't handle that. You've never seen her when she really, really goes off on a tear. Only Daddy can handle it. I can tell them when Daddy comes back."

"Hey, it's OK," Mason reached across and gently touched her cheek. "I understand. We can wait until your dad gets back, and then we can both go and explain to him. When is he supposed to be back in Austin?"

"Friday," Carolina sniffled, and Mason brought out a clean handkerchief from his pants pocket. She dabbed at her eyes with it, and Mason started the car.

"Ok, then – we wait until he comes back," he said, with an air of resolve. "Look, Caro," he added, in a voice intended to be comforting. "It's all gonna be OK. We'll just go on as if everything is completely normal, like we have all summer. OK?"

"OK," Carolina was reassured almost at once. Daddy would understand, and fix everything. And after all, he had told her that he approved of Mason, anyway.

. . .

Her hopes were dashed at supper that night. Mason was there, of course, sitting quietly next to Carolina, with her hand in his under the table where Mama didn't notice. Because Mama was in one of her bad moods, with her eyebrows pinched together in an almost-frown, and Carolina felt her heart sink down to her toes. This meant trouble, she knew absolutely.

"Your father called while you were out at the lake," Mama said, as she set down the casserole of tuna and noodles, scattered with crunchy bits of crushed potato chips in the middle of the table. "Two of his team members got sick yesterday and had to go home so they're short-handed. He'll be out in the field doing their jobs and his own, for another two weeks."

Unseen, under the table, Mason squeezed Carolina's hand. "Poor Daddy," she said, while Mason made sympathetic noises.

"That's too bad. It's always rough, having to take up the slack when someone gets sick." He commented, and Mama continued if she hadn't heard a word.

"And school starts the week after next, so this will be our last weekend here in Austin. Caro and I simply have to go back to San Antonio next week. We'll certainly miss seeing you at supper, Mason. I know Adam really enjoyed your company, just as we do. You should come down to San Antonio and see us, once we get settled back at home."

Carolina had very little appetite for supper, after that. Neither did Mason, really, although he complimented Mama on the casserole as he always did when he ate supper with the family. After supper, Carolina went to sit with him on the balcony of his apartment, sick to death with disappointment that they couldn't spend the evening as she wanted do, now that they were married.

Mason was sensible; he waited for a whole minute or two after putting his arm around her shoulder. "Well, what do we do now, Caro? Do you want to take your mama by the horns and tell her that we're legally married? We can, you know. Before you have to go back to San Antonio."

"I'm still underage," Carolina pointed out, her soul still shriveling with dread at the prospect of broaching the fact of their marriage to Mama, without Daddy's calm authority to back them up. "I won't be seventeen until next year! You've never seen her in a temper, like I have. She's never actually hit Frankie or me but when she is in one of those white rages, but she honestly scares me half to death."

"'s all right, Caro," Mason pulled her close. It reassured her that Mason was being so calm and reassuring about the situation. "Look, here's what we'll do. You go on with your mom as if nothing happened. Go back to San Antonio with her, start school, all of that. When your dad gets back to Austin, I'll tell him everything. How's that for a plan? You ok with doing this my way?"

"Sure," Carolina agreed with a sigh, and nestled her head into Mason's shoulder. "Your way. Perfect."

Daddy would understand. He would make Mama understand, and then she and Mason could be together, together as they had been the night after driving back from Mexico.

• • •

It seemed to Carolina that the following weeks were surreal. On the surface, everything was absolutely, weirdly normal. She and Mama packed up their things and drove home to San Antonio in the red T-bird. They returned to the house in San Antonio, which Frankie had been taking care of, and went shopping for new clothes and school supplies, registering for classes. Increasingly, the whole summer itself seemed a dream. The first weeks of school were another dream, something happening to someone with her name, her face, floating through her days, shuffling schoolbooks in and out of her locker – wondering if marriage to Mason, that single night in his arms, crammed side by side into a single bed – if that wasn't a dream also.

If it was a dream. It shattered like a fragile glass Christmas ornament hitting a hard tile floor, at fifteen past three on a Tuesday afternoon, the second week of the school year. School was out; sidewalks crowded with students, bursting out of campus, their arms burdened with books and notebooks, the street crowded with cars, cars driven by parents come to collect their kids, the big orange school buses belching exhaust as they lurched away from the pick-up area ... and there was the red T-bird, sliding into a suddenly vacated parking place, just opposite the main school gate.

Daddy was at the wheel, a grim-faced Daddy, with Mama at his side and Mason in the back seat. Carolina stood stock-still, the shell of unreality in tiny shards at her feet. Daddy beckoned, with a crook of his finger. Carolina obeyed. Daddy slid out of the driver's seat, and held the door open for Carolina, to squeeze herself into the back seat, next to Mason

"Hi, Daddy ... Mason," she managed to say. This was strange, unsettling, with Mama seeming so close to a temper, and Daddy so stern. "I ... we thought that you were in Austin. What are you doing here?"

Mama didn't say anything. Her lips were set in a thin line, and she was looking straight forward through the T-bird's windshield. She didn't even turn her head to look at Carolina, as Carolina scrambled into the back seat.

"You know perfectly well," Daddy replied, and Mason took and squeezed her hand in a way meant to be reassuring. "Is it true that you and Mason went to Mexico and got married last month?"

"It is, Daddy," Carolina replied, clutching Mason's hand, hard. Mason murmured.

"I went and told him this morning, before I went to my first class," Mason still held her hand, "And then we drove straight here, to get it all sorted. Mr. Visser insisted that we do it right away."

"Ah," Daddy replied. He got in, slammed the driver door, and set the T-bird in gear. "Then you are married and should be together. When we get home, you should pack. What you can't take with you in Mason's car, we can have shipped." He turned his head towards Mama, in the passenger seat. "Marlene, it's done. Nothing you can do or say will stop reality – or our daughter. It's done." Then, over his shoulder, Daddy said to Mason. "Thank goodness there is not a baby coming so Caro can finish high school. You'll see that she's enrolled in an Austin school? A good high school?"

"Yes, sir!" Mason agreed. "Caro is not pregnant." That is not the reason we got married." Caro didn't care, for the reality of it all had broken on her like a marvelous sunrise; she felt like a bird, suddenly able to take wing upon breaking the eggshell. Once home, she fairly flew into the house, up the stairs to her room, and began pulling clothes out of her dresser and the closet, piling them onto her bed. *Mason! She would be with her husband this very evening! They would be together, no matter what anyone might say or do! A husband, her dear friend – and a home of her own.*

In a moment, Daddy tapped on the door, which stood half-open, so it was merely a courtesy. He set a pair of empty suitcases just inside the doorway, and stood there, as if he were reluctant to walk away.

"I thought you could use these, Caro," he said, a half-smile curving his lips. "unless you just wanted to pack your things in brown grocery bags. You're completely happy about getting married and moving in together? You and Mason?"

"Oh, yes!" Carolina exclaimed. "Daddy, he's my best friend in all the world, so why shouldn't we get married. You said you approved! You and Mama did everything but bundle us in bed together, letting us have all that time together over the summer."

Daddy said "he's a nice boy, but you are just a teenager, so young, Caro" But there was a shadow in his eyes, which Carolina might have noticed, were he not so happy about having gotten over the hurdle of breaking the news to Mama. "I hope you'll be happy, Caro … he went and called his parents to tell them the news, just before we headed out this morning. They seemed pleased enough, too," Daddy added, almost as an afterthought.

"Is Mama happy?" Carolina began stuffing the contents of the bed into the largest of the suitcases and snapped the catches closed, with an effort. Another benefit of Daddy being home again – he would be able to calm Mama down from her initial fury. "She liked Mason well enough – so she should be. Daddy – are you certain you can be careful with my things, all the things I can't fit into this?"

"Don't worry about it, Caro." Daddy took the first suitcase. "We'll send you all your things. It's just that your mama has always had her heart set on seeing you married properly; all the trimmings; in church, in a white dress and veil and all – and after you finished high school. It's just going to take her some time to get used to the notion that you and Mason just went ahead and did it," Daddy sighed again. "And we wanted to see you set up, with your own proper household. Try to understand how your mother feels now, Caro. Don't be so hard on her. She's in the bedroom, crying her eyes out. She thought there would be time enough over the next year or so to get things sorted properly for you and Mason; plan a wedding, help you find a place to live. But you've always been in such a hurry. A hurry to do things, to be … whatever it is that you wanted to be."

"I know, Daddy," Carolina finished stuffing the rest of the clothing on her bed into the second suitcase. She snapped the latches closed and lugged the suitcase from off the bed. Daddy took it from her and bent to kiss her gently on the forehead. "I really do love you; Daddy and I love Mason almost as much. But you'll get her to understand; I know that you will. Mason and I will have a dozen children, and Mama will adore them all."

"Just give her a bit more time to get used to that idea," Daddy replied. "Ready, baby? We'd throw rice and rose petals for the two of you, but we don't have a rose bush handy and why waste the rice, since it only gives the birds indigestion."

"Perfectly ready," Carolina replied. She went on tiptoes to plant a kiss on Daddy's cheek, and fairly danced down the stairs to where Mason waited, taking little notice of the closed bedroom door, or the faint sounds of a woman crying coming from behind it. Mama still seemed to upset to bid them goodbye, rose petals, rice or not.

Daddy put the suitcases into the trunk of Mason's car and waited by the curb, waving a farewell as they drove away. Carolina settled into the passenger seat of Mason's car, relieved and triumphant, as he drove towards the Austin Highway. They exchanged smiles, at first hesitant and slightly disbelieving, then blindingly happy, relieved that it was all done, after nearly three weeks of suspense and tension. The car radio was on, playing The Supremes *Baby Love*. Ever afterwards, Carolina thought of that melody as 'their song.'

At the first corner, Mason parked the car, letting it idle in neutral, while he pulled Carolina towards him for a swift embrace and kiss.

"We did it!" Carolina exulted. "Just as you planned ... wasn't Daddy so understanding? I knew he would be!"

Mason pulled her closer, and Carolina rejoiced in the feel of him, the strength in his arms around her, the strength and confidence. They were married – and everyone knew! Still, she would have to go to high school for another couple of years to satisfy Daddy and Mama and Mason, even, but that was OK. She had hopscotched from school to school, time and time again. One more wouldn't be a challenge ... because she was married! Her husband was gorgeous and her best friend, and they were in love and could now be together and in their own home. In an excess of happiness, she murmured to his collarbone.

"Daddy said that your parents know about us! Are they really, OK with it?"

"They sure are, Caro," Mason replied. "They're thrilled to bits. They're going to come over this weekend to meet you. Mom wants to take you shopping at Scarbrough's; you know – for house things. She has a charge account there. Wedding presents, Mom says ..." Mason chuckled, softly, and Carolina decided that she loved the feeling of him laughing, as they clung together. "Mom is convinced that I am living in bachelor squalor, with only two saucepans and a can opener, with old sheets hung up over the windows instead of proper curtains."

"You are not!" Carolina giggled in reply. "You have three saucepans and a cast-iron frypan ... I know, I counted."

"Don't let Mom charge too much," Mason advised, "Necessities only! Or I'll hear about it from Dad."

Carolina giggled again. "Let your mom have some fun. I absolutely promise that I won't ask for expensive china and silver. Just the bare necessities ..."

"Bare it is, then," Mason kissed her again, a kiss which promised nighttime delights – the married delights to which she was now entitled.

And so, it did ... although the narrow twin-size bed in Mason's apartment was still too small for the two of them, unless they slept jammed up together. It truly was love, honest and heartfelt, at least on Carolina's part, a love reinforced and solidified when his parents appeared that next weekend.

. . .

A tentative and polite ring of the doorbell of Mason's apartment came on the following weekend, unaccustomedly early on a Saturday morning. Carolina had just broken eggs into a bowl, fried up a pan of bacon to the perfect degree of crisp, and started coffee. Mason was still asleep when Carolina went to answer the door, still in her bathrobe and slippers, and an oven mitt and spatula in one hand. When she opened the door, an older couple was pressed to enter – the female of the two standing closer to the door, carried a gift-box in her hand. She was as fair a blond as Mason, beautifully dressed for so early on a Saturday, her makeup with every speck of rouge, lipstick, eyeliner, and mascara expertly applied. The man stood a little back, looking slightly puzzled; both middle-aged, perhaps a little older than Daddy and Mama.

"I know that this is Mason's place!" the woman exclaimed. "And you must be Carolina – you are, dear! Who else would be fixing breakfast in my son's apartment this late of a morning! What a splendid surprise, the pair of you running off to be married in Mexico! Don't you dare begin to think of me as an awful mother-in-law, just call me Judy! This is for you, sweetie! Oh, open it in private, it's just a little bit of something to entice a husband with ..." Her eyes swept over Carolina, still in her ratty old bathrobe. "I see that we have arrived, just in time. For breakfast ... I know – don't lecture me about being an interfering old biddy, Gordon!" she said over her shoulder to her husband. "And Caro, sweetie – my husband always says that I open my mouth and speak before my brain is properly in gear! We simply couldn't wait another minute before coming down to the city to welcome you properly into the family! Mason has never, ever given us a moment's worry!"

"He hasn't," Mr. Rollins added, with a sideways glance at his wife, as he extended his hand towards Carolina. "Ever. Gordon Rollins, my dear. Don't pay any mind to our Judy; any thought popping into her mind is coming out through her teeth a split-second second later. So pleased to meet you. Just call me Dad. It's what I am used to."

"I... Mason is still asleep," Carolina replied, still stunned. She still had the oven mitt and spatula in her hand. She shifted it to the other and shook hands with both, fighting the feeling that she had just been run over by a very large vehicle. "I was just fixing breakfast. Do you want some? Just scrambled eggs, bacon, and toast. I can put some more on ... do come in. I am so very pleased to meet you. I just thought that it might be at the wedding, or something."

"Never you mind, Caro-sweetie," Judy Rollins enthused. "And yes, we would love a bit of breakfast... Do you have any honey-butter? I think toast is best with honey-butter on it..."

"I don't think we do..." Carolina stammered, and Judy Rollins stepped inside, setting down her purse and the wrapped present.

"Well, then, Gordon will just have to pop down to that adorable little bodega on the corner and buy some for us, while we finish fixing breakfast for our menfolk ... and if they have any of that nice fresh chorizo sausage, get some that, too, and I'll whip up some nice sausage patties and biscuits ... now, dear, show me where the plates are... oh, good morning, sleepyhead!" Judy added, as the bedroom door opened.

"Mom?" Mason's hair was rumpled, and he wore only his pajama bottoms. "What are you and Dad doing here?"

"We've come to meet your lovely bride," Judy replied, briskly. "You should have known that wild horses wouldn't have kept us away. Now, I intend to have a ladies' day out with Carolina, getting things set up properly in this apartment, so you and your father can spend the day amusing yourselves without us. Really, Mason – those curtains are simply horrible. I don't know how you put up with them..."

"Honestly Mom – I never noticed," Mason sounded harassed. "They came with the apartment."

"Well, we plan to do something about that," Judy promised. "Get dressed, then – both of you! We have a big day ahead of us, and Scarborough's opens soon, and we want to be there when they open the doors."

. . .

That evening, as they snuggled in the new double bed – a bed which had been delivered from the furniture department that very afternoon at Judy Rollin's adamant insistence – Carolina whispered to Mason,

"I adore your mom, but oh, is she exhausting! I thought this day would never, ever end!"

"Mom loves shopping," Mason kissed her, and his hand wandered down her shoulder, and along her backbone. "And I will admit that she had the very best excuse of all to go to town. The place does look nice, though."

"Almost everything I've always wanted for my own house," Carolina admitted. It had been exhilarating as well as tiring, bobbling along in Judy Rollin's wake, like a small dingy tied to a powerboat going at full speed. Mason's mother went from floor to floor at the big downtown department store, consulting a list as long as her forearm, a list of all the things that Judy Rollins considered the bare necessities for her son and daughter-in-law's tiny apartment; things like towels, pots and pans, tablecloths, bed-linen and small furniture, aside from the bed, but at least she let Carolina pick out what she liked of what was available at Scarborough's – which was the important luxury department store in Austin, at least as up-scale as Neiman-Marcus in Houston. "Her friends are going to throw a wedding shower for us, too. She set up a registry for us, at Scarborough's, while we were there."

"Nice," Mason mumbled, after a yawn. He was exhausted too; he and his father had been busy at the apartment all day, setting up the bed, unpacking the various deliveries and hanging new curtains. "More stuff. We might have to move to a bigger apartment if Mom has her way."

"Wouldn't mind, but I do like the pool," The yawn proved infectious, Carolina curled up close to Mason, and thought once more how unutterably happy she was – how they were. *Life was perfect.*

• • • • •

And perfect was what her married life in Austin seemed to be, for months and months, until just after Christmas, which they had spent with Mason's parents. They were both in school, Carolina had her own car, her own place, a contented marriage to Mason, her best male friend, ever. Mama got over the shock within weeks; Daddy talking sense to her probably had a lot to do with that. Carolina got into the habit of calling Mama once a week on the phone which Poppa Lew had paid for, so that Mama could take betting calls for him. Mama confessed to being pleased about her marrying Mason.

"At least, you won't turn up getting pregnant by some handsome guy you met at the Bun n' Barrel," Mama remarked, acerbically which stung a bit, as Carolina now knew it would have been a horrible mistake to have stayed with Buster. Thank goodness Buster *was* a gentleman.

She and Mason went to lots of parties. They were mostly parties hosted by his friends, since he had been in Austin for three years, grew up in a small town close by, and knew everyone and everybody. But after a few of these parties, it began to grate on Carolina that increasingly she sat by herself, wearing a social smile and being agreeable. Mason's friends were almost all male, most of them from his classes at the university, and they weren't her friends. There weren't even many girls among them, she noticed, but didn't think anything of it at first. She had casual girlfriends from her high school but not many of them close enough to be really friends with. Not on the same degree of familiarity as Mason did with his guy friends over the holidays. By New Years, she had her fill of going to parties and being ignored by Mason's male friends.

"Can't we just stay home on New Year's Eve?" Carolina asked, on the afternoon of the last day of December, after Mason announced that they were going out to his friend Martin's place to ring in the new year. The two of them were relaxing in the late afternoon sunshine – which was warm enough after a day. The pool was too cold to swim in, during the winter, although some of the other residents occasional braved the death of cold on icy days. "Crack open a bottle of champagne at midnight, and watch the fireworks from the balcony together?"

"No," Mason replied, patiently. "I already told Martin and Gary that we'd be there. It's a party, for Pete's sake, Caro!"

"But I don't want to go," Carolina insisted, suddenly mulish. "I really don't have much fun at your friends' parties – especially Martin's! I sit in the corner for hours, trying to look like I'm having fun, while I hope someone will talk to me, while all the time, you're having a blast with your pals. I don't know why I should go!"

"Then, don't come," Mason replied, abruptly. He got up from the chair. "Stay home if you like. I don't care. I'm going to Martin's. You can do what you like."

Carolina was shocked out of all reasoning. Was this their first fight, as a married couple? And was it so unreasonable, that she didn't want to go to a party, even on New Year's Eve, where she would sit in a corner with a social smile plastered to her face, hoping that someone – anyone – would talk to her. Why didn't Mason understand! He had always understood before; been her best friend, the one she could talk to about anything and everything. And now, she couldn't talk about this at all!

It was soon even worse. When she went into the apartment kitchen to start supper, Mason emerged from the bedroom, already dressed for the evening, a blanket and a pillow in his arms. He dropped the blanket on the softa.

"Don't wait up for me, Caro," he said tersely. "If you don't want to go to Martin's party, I won't force you." He took his keys from the stand next to the door, and added over his shoulder, "Don't wait up for me. I'll sleep at Martin's. And if I come back early, I'll just settle on the couch." And then he was gone, leaving Carolina open-mouthed and with a cooking fork in her hand, stirring a pan full of ground beef.

She flew to the telephone, in tears, and called Mama.

"We've just had our first fight!" she sobbed. "Honestly – what do I do now! I thought we were in love, and this would never happen!"

"Silly child!" Mama replied, from seventy miles away, her voice sounding tinny on the receiver. "You're married; you will have fights. It's normal. When he comes back tonight, try to talk to him. Communication is the best thing in a marriage."

"Are you sure?" Carolina sniffled. It didn't sound logical. Well, maybe for Mama and Daddy since Mama fought with Daddy all the time, and they were still together. But she had never fought with Mason until now. They had always gotten along.

"Certain-sure," Mama replied firmly, and Carolina had to be content with that answer. Maybe Mama was right.

She fixed herself a solitary supper, ate it sitting alone at the table. Then she wandered around the apartment, fiddling with and putting away this and straightening out that, wondering what to do with herself for the evening, aside from watching television – which just didn't seem the same. She and Mason had always watched something together, curled up on the sofa, with Carolina nestled in the curve of his arm, her head on his shoulder. Eventually, she settled on going to bed close to midnight, when she could hardly keep her eyes open any longer. She locked the door, but left the security latch, hoping that Mason would come home after seeing the New Year in. The bed felt terribly empty, without him in it. Carolina curled up in the middle of it, hugging his pillow to herself. It smelled faintly of him – his soap that he used in the shower, the stuff that he put on his hair – the ineffable scent of his warm body. But the pillow was cold, and she eventually fell asleep, wondering why he wasn't there.

When she woke the next morning, and opened the bedroom door, she found him asleep on the sofa, wrapped in the blanket that he had left there the night before.

"I didn't want to disturb your beauty sleep," he said, which almost sounded like the old, fond, loving Mason, but there was an edge to his voice that made her blood, unaccountably, run cold. There was something terribly wrong about this, and Carolina didn't have a single clue towards what she should do about it.

CHAPTER 7
ENDINGS AND BEGINNINGS

That was on the first day of the new year and Carolina wondered if this was a bad omen. It wouldn't do for the two of them to go on as they had the night before, with Mason out with his friend sand then coming home to sleep on the sofa. But it got worse, almost immediately, when Mason drank a cup of black coffee and said that he wasn't hungry. It was a holiday so there were no classes at the university.

"We're doing inventory today at the store," Mason said, as he put his coffee cup in the sink. "I'll grab something to eat once I get there. Likely we'll finish late, so don't expect me for supper."

Once again, Carolina flew to the phone and called her mother as soon as the door closed behind him.

"Mama," she sobbed into the phone, "It's all going wrong with Mason and I have no idea of what it is that I did! Or what I ought to do about it! What should I do now?"

"Stop crying, Caro," Mama said. She sounded on the telephone as if her head ached fiercely. Carolina would guess that she and the rest of the family had drunk a lot, seeing in the new year. "He's not going to come home until late at night. Well then, stay up and to talk to him. Better than going to bed angry."

"But it will turn into an argument, and I don't want to fight with Mason!" Carolina wailed. "I just don't know what went wrong, all of a sudden! It was all his notion to get married, his parents adore me

– but suddenly now out of the clear blue, he doesn't even want to sleep in the same bed! Mama, what should I do now?"

"Make him give you a straight answer," Mama replied. "He ought to respect you enough to do that. Stay up tonight and demand an answer as soon as he gets home."

• • •

Carolina did exactly that, although she dozed off, sitting on the sofa in her nightgown and chenille robe, when she heard Mason's key in the door lock. It was slightly before eleven; he looked a bit taken back, at seeing her there, sitting nervously under the light from a single table lamp.

"I didn't expect you to stay up for me, Caro," he protested. Carolina uncurled her legs and stood up.

"Mason," she said, her voice sounding shaky and uncertain in her own ears. "Look, we were always able to talk about anything. All last summer, we talked about everything under the sun. Now suddenly there is something wrong with us; I don't know what to think! What's happened that you are angry with me all the time?"

"It's nothing that you have done," Mason sighed, which turned into a jaw-splitting yawn, and hung up his coat in the little front closet. "Honestly, Caro – believe me, it's not your fault. It's all on me. It's my own stupid mistake, thinking that getting married would sort everything out. It's not you. It's me. My mistake. My huge mistake, and I'm sorry for involving you in it. I've got to take a shower. Now. Go to bed; we'll talk about it in the morning."

Carolina had no other choice. She waited awake in bed for Mason, while the water ran in the bathroom shower. She was already half-asleep when he turned off the bathroom light, and slipped under the covers with her, but to her distress, he slept on his side of the bed with his back turned towards her. He didn't even respond when she scooched over to lay against him, spoon-fashioned, with her arm around his waist. The cold shoulder went on for another week or so and Carolina tried every day to talk to him until classes started up again. Then one morning, he was gone, after gulping a cup of coffee and heading off to his first class.

"We'll talk later, Caro," he said over his shoulder as he went out the door.

"OK," Carolina had her own classes to go to, but when she came home after school that afternoon, the apartment seemed curiously empty, although she couldn't at first put a finger on why it felt like that. The empty hours stretched on into the evening, and Mason never returned. It was almost suppertime. Carolina, suddenly worried, searched the bathroom cabinet and made an unsettling discovery. His shaving things, his toothbrush and hairbrush and personal things were gone. She examined the walk-in closet in the bedroom: his favorite shirts, trousers, and coat - all gone. His pajamas were also gone from under the pillow at his side of the bed. So was his own bathrobe and the silly souvenir tiki mug from Hawaii that he liked to drink coffee from. She was alone in the apartment, without a word from the man who was supposed to be her husband. She was baffled, until she found the note tucked behind the toaster in the kitchen.

Caro, honey - I'm sorry, but I can't make this marriage work anymore. Like I told you; it's not your fault, it's all on me. I'm moving in with Martin and Gary. The rent on this place is paid through the end of next month. Take what's yours, and what you want of what my mother and father gave us.

Yours - Mason.

She could hardly dial her mother's number, her hand shook so much, and hardly speak, she was so convulsed with sobs.

"Mason has moved out!" she wailed into the receiver. "I'm all alone in Austin now! Mama, I want to come home!"

• • •

Daddy arrived later that evening, grim-faced and at the wheel of his work car. Carolina had already packed her own clothes. They carried her suitcases and a couple of boxes down to the car. What couldn't fit in the back seat, or the trunk was strapped to the roof. Carolina left her apartment key on the kitchen table. The streetlights were just coming on, bright against a sky the color of oyster shell.

"Don't you want any of your wedding presents?" he asked, and Carolina sniffled and blew her nose, as they walked down the steps from the apartment for the last time.

"No," she answered. "I want to forget that I was ever married to Mason Rollins. I don't want anything that will remind me, at all! I just wish that I can forget this entire year!" She reached into her purse for the soggy Kleenex into which she had been crying all afternoon. "Daddy, I just can't figure out what went wrong with us! I loved him and I thought he loved me … but he kept saying it was all his fault! Why did he do this? How could he do this to me! Make a big thing about getting married, and then just walk away, ending it all with a stupid note!"

"Ah, the big question," Daddy replied, soberly considering all the angles as he usually did when it came to dealing with family conundrums. "The tragic ones, where we try and do the right thing for the right reason, but everything comes unglued anyway. No, it's not your fault, Caro-sugar."

"Mason said it was his fault," Carlina hiccupped. "That it was his mistake in wanting to get married. But I don't see how that could be, Daddy – I just don't. We were perfect for each other. He was perfect."

"Ah, that," Daddy signaled a turn, as they came up to a stop light. "I'm afraid we did. You can blame me for that. He *did* seem like the perfect young man for you. Handsome, well-educated, nice family, a good future. And you got along well with him. We all did. But I should have paid much more attention to the signs. And that's my fault."

"What signs – what do you mean by that, Daddy?" Carolina mopped her eyes again and blew her nose. Daddy kept his eyes straight ahead, looking through the windshield at the city traffic.

"Well, you see, Caro, there were certain indications to me, even if you and your mother didn't think anything of them. Indications that Mason was gay. I think he finally realizes he didn't have any interest in women. Men like Oscar Wilde, you know. Handsome, successful, charming. Man of the world. On top of the world, come to think about it. Married a woman, had children with her – but was more sexually interested in men. I believe now that Mason is a queer, a homosexual."

Carolina stopped crying and stared at Daddy, utterly astounded. "But he ... we did it. A lot of times – and it was his notion to get married in the first place!"

"Ah, yes," Daddy replied, his voice infinitely gentle. "But all those friends of his, those friends in Austin – they were all other men, weren't they, Caro? And he moved in with those friends of his, didn't you say?"

"Yes, they were," Carolina acknowledged. And the memory of Mason saying once how he wanted to be normal came to her. That memory sat like a stone in her stomach. *Oscar Wilde. Mason. Mason saying how he wanted to be 'normal'. Oscar Wilde marrying a woman but carrying on an affair with a man... it all made a dreadful kind of sense.*

They had all been fooled; Mama and Daddy, and Carolina herself – by Mason, who wanted to be normal, perhaps even convinced himself that he could be normal. But he couldn't, not for very long. There wasn't any way to get around it. Perhaps she could pretend that it had never happened at all. Carolina couldn't bear the thought of going back to high school. It would be just too humiliating, explaining what had happened to the girls she knew. And they would ask questions; the shame of having been married and divorced and only seventeen! How could he have done this to her? Was she just used as a test so he could figure out who *he* was? Why did he have to take my down for his own self-awareness?

"I'll go to night school," She announced firmly to Mama and Daddy, several days later after her return from Austin. "I want a proper diploma, so that I can go to nursing school and be a regular R.N."

"What are you going to do about college tuition?" Daddy asked when she announced this at the supper table. "You know that college will cost, and it's not something your mother and I can afford, even if we ask Poppa Lew to help."

"And your grandfather is tied up with helping Frankie and Valerie get settled," Mama said, with a thread of worry appearing in her forehead.

That was one of the changes which had happened while Carolina was away in Austin: Frankie and his steady girl, Valerie, had eloped, just before Christmas. Her brother and Valerie got married in front of a Justice of the Peace at the Bexar County Courthouse between one weekend and the next. Now they lived together in an apartment of their own, although Carolina was given to understand that it wasn't nearly as nice as the apartment in Austin that she had shared with Mason for a bare six months. But they were blissfully happy in it, and Carolina felt a dull throb of resentment whenever she thought about them, an emotion which she tried her best to stifle. At least, Carolina told herself mordantly, they didn't have to drive all the way to Mexico and back. She tried her best to be happy for them, although it was often an uphill fight.

"We can get the marriage annulled," Mama said, and Carolina sighed.

"On what grounds, Mama?" They had been over and over all that since she returned to San Antonio. "Just divorce. There's too much to explain, otherwise. I just want to forget that Mason and I ever happened. You and Daddy approved and made it all happen anyway," she added, and from the way that the worry-line appeared on Mama's forehead and how she went silent and began eating her supper Carolina knew that shot had hit fairly home.

The abortive marriage had one effect, though; Mama and Daddy seemed to consider her now as a responsible adult, not a wayward and impulsive teenager. Perhaps the recollection of how they had steered her so catastrophically into a miserable marriage with Mason had something to do with the new consideration from her parents. Carolina eased her broken heart that spring by work. She got a day job working in the box office at the North Star Cinema, on the edge of a brand-spanking-new enclosed shopping center on the north edge of town, selling tickets and making reservations for the movie showings. It gave her time to study and do homework assignments when the rush at the box office eased to a mere trickle after the movie started. Mr. Waggoner, the theater manager, was a stickler for correct behavior among the patrons and staff, although he seemed to like Carolina and approved of her ambition in going to night school. He turned a blind eye towards her studying during working hours, too.

In the evenings, she went to classes at night school. Unexpectedly, she found that she was getting a lot from her classes, more than she ever had before. Her fellow students were mostly adults, who worked during the day, and were there to earn a diploma or advance their skills. It was refreshing, being in a class where everyone was focused and intent on the materiel, no cattiness from other women, or clumsy attempts at flirtation from the guys. All the other students were strictly focused on the business at hand. She finished the term with good grades; all that she had then was to wait on the diploma. In the fall, Carolina intended to begin nursing school, but until then, there was a summer to get through. No lazing around the pool this year; she spent most afternoons in the coolness of the movie theater, but on some evenings, she took to going to the Princess drive-in on Broadway, near the little amusement park, with the merry-go-round and miniature Ferris wheel. She went with Frieda Peterson, a girlfriend from night classes, and some other girls that Frida knew, all crammed into the red T-bird with the top down and the radio blaring away. The Princess drew a large crowd on most evenings, being a hop, skip, and a jump from one of the back gates into Fort Sam Houston, the big Army post.

The burgers at the Princess were fabulous and famous across San Antonio. So were the hot pastrami sandwiches, and milkshakes clotted so thick with ice cream that at first you had to use a spoon rather than a straw. The odor of frying hamburger patties and crisp French fries filled the evening air, mingled with whiffs of automobile exhaust. But food wasn't the draw – it was the guys and cars, their big, fancy, tricked-out cars, coming to hang out, to tune into the same radio station, and flirt, dance and brag under the stars and the streetlamps. The bittersweet memory of last summer, sunning by the pool at the apartment in Austin, and of long hours talking with Mason began to fade. This was fun, this was much more fun than those endless parties with Mason's friends, where she didn't know anyone and sat in the corner with a social smile plastered to her face. At least she could think of them without cringing. Because everything was new; her parents were finally treating her like a responsible adult, she had her high school diploma, her soon-to-be professional career and all. Carolina's future was assured, and Daddy approved. In the fall, she would start nursing school...

She and Frieda and Frieda's girlfriends had already ordered, and they were just waiting for the carhop to deliver their order. She and Frieda were at the center of a group of regulars at the Princess, many of them guys with Army crew-cuts. There was an empty parking place next to the T-bird, and just as the carhop skated up with a fully loaded tray, a guy driving a brilliant blue Corvette Stingray two-seat coupe pulled into that empty place.

"Hey, Kenneth!" Frieda called, as the guy at the wheel of the 'Vette slid out from behind the drivers' side door. "Long time, no see! Where you been, we missed you?"

"I'll bet you did, Free, but not by much! You beautiful heartbreaker, what with all of your hopeful boyfriends!" The driver strolled over to the cluster around Frieda and Carolina, and the others. Carolina looked at him and felt the spark of instant attraction begin to rise, as if from a bonfire when a fresh log had just been thrown onto it. He was lean, handsome, and narrow-hipped. Broad shoulders stretched a pristine white T-shirt almost skin-tight on the rest of his torso. A stray lock of dark-blond hair curled down over his forehead, almost matching the curl of his lips. He looked a bit like a fair-haired Elvis Presley, or the even more dangerous *Wild One* version of Marlon Brando, even to the skin-tight T-shirt and even tighter blue jeans. His gaze smoldered. Carolina felt her knees getting a bit weak. *God, he was handsome!* Here she goes again attracting the good-looking movie star kinda guy.

"Who's your gorgeous friend, Free?" he asked, looking boldly at Carolina. "Never seen her here before – you gonna introduce us?"

"This is Carolina," Frieda replied, with an amused expression on her face. She obviously was past being attracted to that dangerous glamour which rose like smoke from the driver of the blue 'Vette. "A friend of mine from night school. She's been around the block a couple of times, so don't try your usual girl-impressing stunts with her, Ken. Caro, this is Ken Miller. He has the most original line in flattering a girl, so watch out that you don't fall for them. Hey, is that our order? God, I'm starving!"

"Hi," Carolina said, uncertainly and Ken Miller grinned.

"Come here often, Gorgeous?"

"Now and again," Carolina replied. "I love your car – is it a new model?"

"I've had it for a while," Ken admitted, carelessly. "I might trade it in, soon – not certain I'm all that wild about the color. K'n I have a bite of your French fries while I wait on my order?"

"Sure," Carolina yielded, noticing that he wore a heavy silver ring, set with a blue bezel-cut stone, on the hand which he was dipping into her bag of fries. "Say, is that an Air Force ring? My Daddy was in the Army. He was going to be a pilot, but then he changed his mind."

"Yeah – Air Force. My dad, too. But I'm on terminal leave from the Army," Ken explained. "I had quite a few months of leave saved up, and my folks live here in San Antonio. So, what about yourself ... hey!"

At that moment, one of the other guys admiring the Corvette jostled Ken's elbow. In an instant, Ken swung around, his fist bunching threateningly. Volcanic anger flashed across his face, but only for a brief second.

"Sorry, Ken," the other guy gulped. "My fault – sorry." He slid away as fast as he could move, as fast as the jam of cars and the cluster of car aficionados allowed. Carolina blinked, not entirely certain if she had seen that momentary fury on Ken's face or not. It never occurred to her to wonder why an Army guy would be wearing an Air Force ring.

"I ... was living in Austin last year," Carolina explained. "Studying ... next fall, I'm starting nursing school."

"Cool," Ken was admiring. "But a gorgeous chick like you, emptying bedpans and sticking needles into people? You should be a model, or in the movies, or something."

"I can't sing or dance," Carolina replied, with a laugh. She liked Ken, felt comfortable with him, warmed, and attracted by the glow of his honest interest. This was a heady feeling, after the crushing disappointment of marriage to Mason, who only romanced and married her to prove to himself that he was normal and not like Oscar Wilde; one of those men who really loved other men. She had come to an insight, after weeks of consideration, that any other woman that Mason halfway liked would have done just as well for that purpose.

It was purely just fun to lean against the side of the Corvette, sharing her French fries and alternating bites of her burger and Ken's hot pastrami, listening to pop music on half a dozen tinny-wounding car radios all tuned to the same rock station, under the star-lit sky at the edge of the canopy over the parking spaces at the Princess. There was Frieda, dancing the frug to the music of Dion and the Belmonts and waving her hands over her head, with one of her current admirers. There was a cluster of others dancing, too – that was why the Princess was so much fun as a hangout. Carried away by the music – *Why Must I be a Teenager in Love*. Yes, Carolina thought – *why must I be a teenager in love?*

"I'll bet you can dance," Ken swallowed the last French fry, and grinned at her. "With the right partner! Let's! I'll bet you can dance fit to be on *Ed Sullivan*!" and that was when Carolina decided that she was so over the disaster of being married to Mason, and that she liked Ken a lot.

And she wanted to see him again. Often. He set her pulse racing.

• • •

He was there, the next time that she and Frieda went to the Princess, driving the Corvette, smiling that wicked smile, and undressing her with his eyes. They danced, ate burgers, shared piping-hot crisp French fries, and laughed and chatted with their friends under the starlight. At the end of the evening, when she and Frieda were done with the evening, Ken kissed her and said,

"Hey, Gorgeous, let's go see a movie tomorrow night. James Bond in *Thunderball* is showing at the Majestic! You ready for a little sex and violence?"

"I've already seen it," Carolina replied, for that movie had shown at the North Star. "I wasn't impressed. I'd rather go see *Dr. Zhivago*," Carolina giggled, and Ken kissed her again.

"Oh, just more of the 's' and 'v', just with a classier plot. Is it a date? I'll pick you up at five o'clock?"

"Sure," Carolina agreed. "You can pick me up at my parent's ... I'd like them to meet you. And you to meet them."

"Sure thing," Ken replied. Carolina gave him directions to their address, and she and Frieda drove away up Broadway. When she glanced into the rearview mirror, Carolina thought she saw Ken kissing another girl, but she told herself that must be her imagination. At a distance, fair-haired guys in jeans and white t-shirts, with Army crew-cuts sort of looked alike.

. . .

Ken appeared promptly at five the next evening. Carolina answered the door, feeling the mild sensation of butterflies in her stomach. Would Mama and Daddy approve? Would Daddy administer the third degree, as he did with all those boys who had escorted her to school dances? Or would he and Mama continue treating her as a responsible adult.

"Hi, Gorgeous," Ken greeted her with a grin and a swift kiss on her cheek. "Ready to go?"

"You've got to meet my parents," Carolina drew him into the living room. "Mama, Daddy – this is Ken."

"Mark Kenneth Sanchez, sir," Ken shook hands with Daddy, who looked him over carefully, although his face kept a mild expression, as Ken added. "I go by my middle name, mostly. I have a first cousin also named Mark, and it cuts down on the confusion."

Daddy looked down at Ken's hand, the one with the Air Force ring on it.

"Academy?" Daddy looked quizzical, and then puzzled when Ken replied,

"My father's class ring. He passed it on to me, for luck."

"Ah," Daddy replied, but still looked puzzled. Mama looked between Daddy, Ken and Carolina and said, "Remember to take your house key, Caro – we'll lock the front door when we go to bed. Have a nice time at the movie ... although, I do wonder if it isn't like going to work, for you, since you're working at the North Star."

"It's not like work," Carolina replied, with a laugh. "I get to sit down – and see the beginning and the end of the feature. And anyway, I've overheard *The Sound of Music* so many times that I can recite the whole script and sing every one of the songs from memory!"

"Well then, have good time," Mama said. "And you, Mr. Sanchez – be careful when you have our daughter in the car, when you're driving downtown at night."

"Yes, ma'am, always," Ken answered, and Carolina looked at him sideways.

Hadn't Frieda said his last name was something else when she introduced him to Carolina the other night at the Princess?

"I thought your last name was Miller," Carolina ventured, as they went down the walkway from the house. "That's what Frieda said, when she introduced us..."

"Oh, she must have had me mixed up with someone else," Ken explained, and it sounded reasonable enough to Carolina, even though the car parked by the curb wasn't the flashy and spectacular blue Corvette – but an aging Chevy sedan.

"What happened to your car?" That really surprised Carolina; Ken without his trendy 'Vette Stingray? It was almost as if he appeared without his pants.

"Eh ... it was borrowed from my cousin," Ken replied, as he ceremoniously opened the passenger door for Carolina. "I was tired of paying for the gas. The darned thing was a pig for gas and only seated two people, so I gave it back. Look, Carolina – let's have fun while we can. When my leave's done, I have to report back to my unit, and they tell me I have orders then to deploy to Viet Nam. Just call me Mark since that is my real name. I want to have every bit of life that's due to me while I can enjoy it. What do you say, Caro – enjoy it with me? Life's a crapshoot and then you die, otherwise."

"Sure, Mark," Carolina replied.

. . .

And so, it continued over the remaining summer in that fashion; Carolina working at the North Star Theater box office, going to the Princess with Frieda, or even by herself in the red Thunderbird ... the only constant in her life now was Mark. Mark with his dangerous smile, the curl of dark-blond hair hanging down over his forehead. She couldn't think of him without going weak in the knees. They took every opportunity they had to be alone. He would brush back her long blond hair and kiss her on her neck. He showered with much affection. He told her how he loved every day. He was on leave from the Army; he had orders for Vietnam in a month, or so he told her. Carolina despaired at that thought. There was a war going on in Vietnam, and soldiers dying. No – that couldn't happen to Mark. It made their love-making a matter of desperate urgency and Carolina correspondingly reckless. The days until Mark had to report into Fort Hood trickled through her fingers like grains of sand, no matter how she tried to keep them tight in her fist.

He left from his parent's house, after a farewell supper for the long drive back to Fort Hood. Mark's father, Mr. Sanchez, grilled steaks, and chicken quarters on the barbeque grill out behind the Sanchez's house in the Highland Park neighborhood for a handful of friends and relatives. They ate from paper plates under the pecan tree that shaded the back of the Sanchez' little white bungalow. Carolina liked Mark's parents, but for some reason, she sensed that they were wary, as if they didn't quite know what to make of her, or how to talk to her, even though she helped Mark's mother with the supper, and even brought a macaroni casserole that Mama had shown her how to make.

At the end of the evening, she had to go: Mark would be leaving at three in the morning for the drive to Waco. She wished that they could have spent more time together, but Mark belonged to other people than her, people who loved him as much as she did, but for longer. He walked her out to the T-bird, parked incongruously among the shabbier cars along the street, for a last discrete hug and kiss

"Caro, gorgeous," he said, with a serious expression on his face. "Stop worrying so much about me. I'll be back, I promise. It takes a lot to kill a Sanchez, and I'm one of the hardest to kill that there is."

"Promise?" Carolina gulped down a sob. Mark hugged her to his chest, and she leaned against it, felt his heart beating against her own, as if those hearts were in a mad rhythm of their own. She felt the rumble of his laughter against her cheek. "I ... lost the last man that I loved with all my heart. I don't want to lose you like I lost him."

"He wasn't like me," Mark replied, with complete assurance. Carolina sniffled a little and kissed him again.

"Promise that you'll write to me. Every day if you can."

"I will," Mark assured her. He unwrapped his arms from around her and gave her a little push. "Now go, and don't cry. I hate women who cry all over you. I promise a letter, every day that I can write."

Carolina obeyed, putting the T-bird in gear, and driving down the block without looking back. When she had pulled around the corner and well out of sight of Mark and the Sanchez house, she parked the car and cried until every Kleenex in her purse was saturated and her eyes ached.

She waited and waited for the promised letters, even hoping against hope for a phone call from Mark. She dreamed of him at night, wondered where he was and if he was safe, pictured him in rumpled green fatigues, dark with sweat, a rifle in his hand as he walked down a narrow jungle trail ... and sometimes she woke up sobbing. For two weeks she delayed going to work, until the mail had been delivered, always hoping for a letter from Mark – until the day when Mr. Waggoner caught her clocking in fifteen minutes after the start of her shift, because the mailman had been late.

"I shouldn't have to mention this again, Miss Visser," her boss said, sternly. "Just consider this your first warning."

"I'm sorry, Mr. W.," Carolina felt like bursting into tears. "I was waiting on the mail, for a letter from my boyfriend. He's in the Army and he shipped out to Vietnam two weeks ago."

"I'm so sorry, Miss Visser," Mr. Waggoner answered, austere and firm. "I do understand, and I sympathize. But sympathy doesn't open the box office or answer the phones in time for customers at the first showing. Please don't let this happen again, or we will have to let you go and hire a girl with a more developed sense of responsibility for that job."

"Yes, Mr. Waggoner," Carolina gulped. She really did need the job, at least until the end of summer, when she would start her nursing school. But now, heading out to the Princess after work held no savor at all for her, even if she met with Frieda and her friends. It just wasn't the same, making the scene with all of the gang under the stars and the streetlights, if Mark wasn't there.

And then the miracle happened. She came home early one evening after her shift at the North Star, just as twilight fell, wondering if Mama had kept a plate warm for her, as it was already after suppertime. There was a car parked underneath the streetlight in front of the house, a familiar car; Mark's battered old Chevy. And that was Mark himself, leaning against the fender, his blond hair gleaming in the pool of light. Carolina screeched the Thunderbird to an untidy stop, the rear wheels sticking out at a careless angle. She set the hand brake and flung herself out of the car and into his arms, without even bothering to turn the engine off.

"Mark, you nut! What are you doing here? Everyone thought you were in Vietnam!"

"Hey, Gorgeous!" Mark hugged her close to his chest. "I know, I know. I got sick, sicker than a dog at the transit camp before they could ship us out. I passed clean out – so they put me in the post hospital for a couple of days, and then sent me back home to get better. It'll be a bit, Caro. I was really sick. They were talking about how I'd have to go before a medical board, now. I think they're going to discharge me anyway."

"Never mind!" Carolina kissed him passionately. "I was so worried, when I didn't hear from you! Why didn't they send a telegram to your parents or something?! That's what they are supposed to do."

"My parents didn't get it," Mark replied. "They ... it must have gone to their old address," and he kissed her again. Carolina thought only for a moment – *That's odd. I thought his parents had lived in that place in Highland Park since forever.* And then she gave herself up to the relief and joy of having Mark safe in her arms. The threat of Mark being sent to Vietnam was still a real possibility but removed from the immediate future. He was safe for now. They were safe.

Then the morning came, barely a week after Mark's return from the abortive deployment to Vietnam that Carolina realized that her period was more than a week over-due. And she had always been depressingly regular. Almost two weeks and a funny ache in her lower abdomen must mean that she was almost certainly pregnant. *Oh, my God.* She would have to tell Mark and tell him soon. How would he react? Carolina's blood went cold at the thought, remembering the brief and incandescent fury on the night they first met, when another guy jostled his elbow. Mark had a volcanic temper, although she had not experienced that temper directed against her.

So far… a little nagging voice in her head whispered. *Not so far.* This would change everything. No nursing school now for her, as the mother of a baby. All that work for a high school diploma, gone for nothing. And she didn't know how Mark would take it. …would he leave her? He certainly had to own up to some responsibility. She was sure he would.

She was the most astonished of all, once she had stammered out the news to Mark, as they sat in his Chevy, at the Alamo Drive-in Theater on the Austin Highway, not far from the Bun and Barrel drive-in, waiting for the main feature to begin. He sat for a moment, his face utterly blank and taking in the news, under the dim light cast by the enormous movie screen. Then, to her utter astonishment, he took her in his arms.

"That's fantastic news, Gorgeous ... so let's get married!"

CHAPTER 8
MARK

Carolina and Mark went to the courthouse to get married; Carolina didn't dare tell Mama and Daddy that she had married again until afterwards, figuring that telling them that they were to become grandparents in a few months would soften the blow.

It did.

She and Mark stood in the living room of Daddy and Mama's house, nervously holding hands.

"We just got married," Carolina announced. "We're going to have a baby – so we thought we ought to."

"Oh, Caro!" Mama exclaimed, embracing Carolina. "Are you all right ... so that's why you've been looking so sickly lately, I thought you were coming down with nephritis again! You simply must take better care of yourself now, since it's not just affecting you, it's the baby as well!"

Daddy just looked levelly at Mark, a long searching look. Finally, he extended his hand, and shook Mark's. "You take good care of our girl, now. She's a prize, and not one like you can find anywhere."

"I will, sir," Mark promised, in all earnest, and for a month or two, it seemed like he was living up to that promise. He told her that his discharge from the Army had come through, which was a relief, since it meant that no one would be sending him to Vietnam. They moved into a small apartment nearby and Mark began looking for work. At first Carolina felt that she was cherished and protected, as

Mark always wanted to know where she was going and what she would be doing, even if it were only doing laundry in the apartment complex's laundry room. He hovered, like a mother hen with a single chick. Carolina found it rather endearing at first. They had only one car, Mark's battered old Chevy, so of course she felt it was normal to keep him informed, but eventually the intense questioning after she returned from going anywhere by herself, even to visit her parents got to rather tiresome.

"You don't have to give me the third degree, every time I go somewhere," Carolina protested, half laughing one afternoon. Mama had driven her to the doctor for a check-up, and then the two of them had gone out for a light lunch. After that, Carolina had done two loads of laundry in the apartment's laundry room and chatted there with a young woman who lived in the next apartment, and another woman who lived across the courtyard; perfectly harmless and innocent, but Mark had scowled and insisted on knowing every single detail. "OK, when we were done at the doctor's office, Mama and I went to have lunch at Scrivener's on Broadway. Mama had a tuna salad, I had chicken pot pie, if you really want to know. Then when Mama dropped me off here, I did two loads of laundry, and I had a long talk with Avril Gonzalez, she lives in the apartment next to us, her husband works for the city, driving a garbage truck. Her daughter is named Letty, their little baby is named Antonio, and he has three teeth, and I found an extra odd sock when I was done with the laundry. Then I talked with Pam Thompson, who lives in the apartment across from us. She's nice; you would know her, she has the most flaming red hair I have ever seen, and it's totally natural. Her husband is Jerry, who works out at Fort Sam. Was there anything more you needed to know?"

"It's because I care that much, Gorgeous," Mark justified himself. "I don't want you to be doing anything or going anywhere, or hanging out with anyone, without I know about it. It's best for you and the baby, can't you see that?"

"Of course," Carolina replied, thinking at that moment that it was rather endearing that Mark cared so very much.

She was already feeling some small prickles of unease, though. One of them had to do with that Air Force ring, the one which she had first noticed all those months ago, when Mark drove up to the crowd at the Princess drive-in, at the wheel of that flashy blue Corvette. She found it, where Mark had left it on the bedroom bureau one afternoon, when he had gone off in their only car leaving Carolina to her own devices in their small apartment. She was putting away a load of laundry; his and hers when she noticed the ring in the little dish where Mark normally left his keys, small change, his glasses when he didn't need them, and things like cuff links when he wore a long-sleeved shirt. She picked it up in a moment of idle curiosity. It was a heavy silver thing made for a male hand, deeply, elaborately engraved, and set with a dark blue stone the size of a lima bean. There was a name engraved on the inside and Carolina squinted at it under the light from the bedroom window. She took the ring closer to the window and looked at it carefully. Edward S. Dorian was the name engraved on the inside. Carolina felt a cold chill, in spite of the warmth in the apartment. *Who was Edward S. Dorian?* Hadn't Mark said that the ring was his father's, and given it to him as a good-luck token when he was drafted into the Army? Yes, that was what Mark had claimed.

Carolina sat down on the bed; the ring clenched in her hand. Mark's father was named Abel Sanchez. She knew that much for certain. She had been to their house, for God's sake. And the date of the graduating class was part of the ring; 1961. How could this ring possibly have belonged to Mark's father? Abel Sanchez couldn't have attended and graduated from the Air Force Academy a mere five or six years ago. Cadets couldn't be married ... that she knew from Daddy. The military academies were strict about that. This was why so many cadets married as soon as they graduated. That was in all the movies about West Point. They couldn't marry their girlfriends until after graduation day. Their weddings were part of the plot.

This wasn't possible for that ring to have belonged to Mark's father. It just couldn't be ... and that meant that Mark lied. Casually lied, and worse than that – the ring was engraved with someone else's' name? And how had Mark gotten it? That ring was the first warning sign for Carolina. She put it carefully back in the dish and wondered seriously if she should ask him about it ... but felt a bit of unease at the back of her neck. Mark had fibbed about his name when they first met. Carolina was certain that Frieda had introduced him as Ken Miller – and then later, Mark had insisted that Frieda had just been mistaken. What *was* true about Mark? He always had a good and reasonable answer, an explanation for any doubts which Carolina had raised. She must be mistaken, Carolina told herself – she must be. They were married. Her baby had to have a father.

. . .

The next incident wasn't so readily put out of mind, though, because it scared her nearly to death. Two or three weeks later, the telephone rang, as Carolina was at the sink, drying and putting away the supper dishes. Mark had been home all day, poking around under the hood of the Chevy, trying to fix a bad timer, without luck. He had consequently been in a bad mood. Carolina had fixed his favorite meal, chicken a la king, in hopes of cheering him up.

"I'll get that," Mark dove for the phone – he always preferred to answer the phone when he was home. At least this time, he didn't push Carolina aside, or snatch the receiver from her hand, this time. "Hi ... Dave ... you spotted one? Great... no time like now, it's near to dark anyway. Come get us... right. Five minutes."

"What was that about?" Carolina asked, as Mark reached for his light jacket. He scowled, dangerously.

"Come on, get your coat, we're going for a ride with Dave."

"But ... I'm tired, Mark – I want to sit down and rest..." Carolina protested, but Mark grabbed her elbow.

"I said that we're going for a ride – you can sit down and rest in the car." He hustled her out of the apartment so fast that she barely had time to grab her purse and shrug her coat over her shoulders and button it over her expanding belly.

Dave was one of Marks' friends; Carolina remembered seeing him at the Princess sometimes; a tall, dark-haired guy who never had much to say for himself. Among Mark's pals, he was the one who stood out for carrying on the old-fashioned country habit of chewing tobacco. His teeth were normally flecked with brown tobacco crumbs, and he often spat into an empty soda can. Carolina felt her stomach clench, at the thought of sharing a ride with him, but Dave waited in his car at the bottom of the stairs for them.

"Get in. No, sit in the front with us,"

Dave's car had a long bench seat in front; just room enough for the three of them to sit abreast. Carolina slid in and sat wedged between Dave and Mark with her handbag in her diminishing lap. For some reason, Mark had a small tool bag at his feet. The two men talked over her; with few words and cryptic ones at that.

"Round in back of a motel on the Highway, near to Vandiver," Dave said. "Out of state plates. No streetlight nearby."

"Good," Mark replied. "I can work blindfolded on that model – know it like the back of my hand."

"Run it out to the empty lot behind the abandoned warehouse on Gibbs Sprawl," Dave nodded, glancing into the rearview mirror.

"All I need is five minutes, a wrench, and a screwdriver," Mark said, looking out of the passenger-side window, and Carolina felt like screaming.

"What are you talking about!" she demanded, and Mark looked at her.

"Nothing to worry your pretty little head over, Gorgeous," he replied.

Dave chuckled, drawling. "Don't know why you had to bring your sweetie-pie along for the ride."

"Insurance, just in case the cops see us. I can use her," Mark patted Carolina's belly. "I always plan ahead."

Baffled, Carolina remained silent as Dave drove down old Austin Highway at the edge of town; a highway lined with motels and scattered eating places like the Bun n' Barrel drive-in, where she and her friends from high school hung out. At a certain cross-street, Dave pulled into a motel parking lot, and drove around to the back, out of a puddle of light cast on the pavement by the streetlight, and the lights in front of the rows of doors.

There another Chevy sat parked, next to a row of garbage cans and a discouraged tree weeping dead leaves over the cracked pavement.

"Be just a moment," Mark slid out of the passenger seat, with the tool bag in his hand.

"What is he doing!" Carolina gasped, as Mark went to the other car, and opened the driver's side door. He had a screwdriver in his hand.

Dave shot her a glance in which pity and exasperation were mixed and answered. "Free-lance shopping," He spat into the soda can, and Carolina felt the bile begin to rise in her throat. She stared, aghast, as her husband briefly fiddled with the screwdriver, whanging it into the ignition. The engine of that other car roared to life. Without a backward glance, Mark drove off in it. Dave put his own car into gear and followed it, wheels squealing on the broken pavement behind the motel.

"He's stealing that car!" Carolina exclaimed in horror, as Dave shot her an exasperated glance and spat into his soda can again.

"Not much gets past you, does it, Sweetie-pie?"

Carolina could hardly believe what she had just seen. Mark had stolen a car, and Dave ...Dave was helping him do it, and she was sitting right where in the front seat of Dave's car, as her husband hot-wired and stole someone's car! What if they were caught! *This was horrible – what would Daddy and Mama think if the police arrested them all; Mark and Dave and Carolina herself!* Of course,

Carolina hadn't done anything, but she was still there, an accessory to theft! What if they put her in jail, in her pregnant condition – would that hurt the baby!

Oblivious to Carolina's shock, Dave followed the stolen car. To her relief, he drove in a sedate and careful manner; not, as Carolina would have expected a pair of car thieves to drive, recklessly and on two wheels. They drove towards the open country, well beyond the eastern city limits, Mark at the wheel of the stolen Chevy, Dave following closely but not too closely, so as not to attract attention. It was almost dark when the Chevy pulled off, into an empty parking lot beyond city limits, on the grounds of an abandoned warehouse, set in an acre of crumbling pavement. Mark parked it behind the building, in a dark and open space, where they couldn't be seen from the road.

Dave spat into his disgusting soda can one more time and turned off the ignition of his car.

"Back in a minute," he said. He took the car keys with him, leaving Carolina to sit alone in the dark, her heart hammering with apprehension. The two figures of Dave and her husband were shadowy figures in the dark, dimly illuminated by a flashlight under the hood of the stolen Chevy as they worked to extract something from the engine block. Outside the car, the silence of the countryside at night was broken by little save the muffled sounds of metal against metal, and occasionally, a car passing on the road. Finally, the flashlight switched off, and Dave's car bounced a little, as the doors opened, on either side. Dave slid behind the wheel, grinning, and set his toolkit bag on the floor.

"Ten minutes flat," he remarked with a grin. "Let's make like a tree and leave."

"You're going to just leave that car..." Carolina exclaimed, only thinking that it sounded perfectly idiotic, and Mark chuckled indulgently.

"Of course, we're going to leave it, Gorgeous! Didn't we just steal the damned thing!"

"For a ... spare part!" Carolina still couldn't quite believe what had happened in these last forty minutes. "Why didn't you just buy a new timer? Why did you have to steal it!"

"Because I didn't want to spend the cash," Mark replied, still grinning. "And besides, it was more fun this way."

"You stole someone's car!" Carolina was indignant. "It belongs to someone else – and maybe they don't have any money, or they need a car to get to work! What about that, Mark! Oh, don't ever do anything like that again! What if you were caught and sent to prison? What would happen to the baby and me?"

"They'll never catch us," her husband chuckled again, with a dangerous edge to his laughter which suggested that he wouldn't handle any more questions from her. "Anyway, I'll bet you anything the owners of that hunk of junk have insurance!"

Carolina silently simmered, all the way back to the city, where Dave dropped them off in front of their apartment. What to think now; that her husband was a thief and a liar? But her baby still needed a father, needed a father to support them both. She did resolve, though – to try and keep Mark out of trouble with the law, no matter what it took. For a while, there, it seemed like he was reforming, or at least intending to reform.

"I have to go to Dallas for a job interview." He announced, several weeks after the car theft. "I've all but got it in the bag according to the corporate recruiter; the interview is just a formality. It's with Braniff Airlines. When I get hired, it'll bring in enough so that we can move out of this dump. The interview is on Saturday. I'm taking the Chevy and driving. Load up on groceries and stuff so that you don't have to go anywhere," he ordered, almost as an afterthought.

"I don't *want* to go anywhere, anyway," Carolina replied, not even wondering how a corporation might be doing job interviews on a weekend, since Daddy often had to do duty over a Saturday or a Sunday. She was now far-gone in pregnancy and didn't want to do more than lie down and rest, for the exhaustion that often struck her came out of the clear blue, as if some invisible force suddenly opened a tailgate and dumped a truckload of weariness upon her. In addition, she was obscurely glad that Mark didn't want to drag her along in case the excursion turned out to be another planned venture into auto theft.

"Good thing, Gorgeous," and Mark sounded sympathetic. "You do look tired – got dark circles under your eyes. Well, rest up good, 'cause if I get the job then good things will be happening around here, for all of us."

"I do hope so," Carolina replied, in all honesty. She really did have hopes that Mark was going to get the job with Braniff. He was a good mechanic; he kept the old Chevy running, even if he wasn't entirely scrupulous when it came to replacement parts. He left early on Friday, whistling as he bopped down the apartment steps. She watched as the Chevy vanished around the corner, and waved to Avril, who had baby Antonio balanced on one hip and her purse and diaper bag over her shoulder and leading the toddler daughter Letty by her other hand. Avril grinned and waved back, coming across the walkway balcony that connected all the second-floor apartments.

"Going to take our children to see my Tia Fernanda on the South Side," she explained to Carolina. "She's almost ninety and hasn't seen 'Tonio since he cut his teeth. Jesse has the weekend off, so we're making a day of it. Where's that handsome husband of yours off to?"

"Dallas, for a job interview tomorrow," Carolina explained, "to work for Braniff – can you imagine?"

Avril grinned. "Well, I wish him luck. Say, Caro, when are you due?"

"Two more months, the doctor says," Carolina replied. "I can't wait to see what my baby looks like. I would so like a boy."

Avril squinted at her, consideringly. "Well, you're carrying low, so my Tia would say it's a boy. I got some boy-things that 'Tonio outgrew – yours if you want them."

"Be glad of them," Carolina was honestly grateful. Avril's baby son was almost a year old; her daughter was three, and Avril herself was just a little older than Carolina. It was vaguely comforting to have someone close by who knew all about babies and little children.

"I'll bring the clothes and things over on Sunday, as soon as we get back from the South Side," Avril promised. Carolina thanked her again, and then went to lie down in the apartment, feeling unaccountably tired, dispirited and even a bit lonely. Mark's absence reminded her all too vividly of being alone in the Austin apartment after Mason moved out. But now she had their baby to look forward to and he, for she had begun to think of the baby as 'he' had begun moving vigorously, and she could feel him mostly when she was laying down. She ran her fingers over her distorted belly and talked to 'him.'

"Soon, Baby, soon," Carolina promised. "You'll have golden hair and big blue eyes, and we will take you places like Avril does with her babies – and you'll look so adorable, that everyone will admire you and want to make friends... and your Daddy will have a good job with Braniff and we will live in a nicer place ..." she went on, spinning out the dream for Baby, weaving a coverlet of imagining. But Sunday afternoon, when Mark returned from Dallas, sweating through his white button-down shirt, with his one good tie loosened, the pleasant dream died stillborn.

"I didn't get the job," Mark confessed, after drinking a couple of glasses of ice water. "Dammit all, I thought I had it in the bag, too! Sorry, Gorgeous. I know it meant a lot to you, with the baby and all."

"You didn't?" Carolina's heart sank. "What happened? You thought it was all but in the bag! You said so."

"Well, I turned out to be wrong." Mark was snappish. "They wanted me to do an eyesight test then and there – and I forgot to bring my glasses, so I flunked it. You should have reminded me to pack them!"

"But you hardly need them for anything else than reading," Carolina protested, but Mark scowled so thunderously that she didn't dare protest or excuse. But she couldn't help but wonder: If it was that important an interview – how did Mark forget his glasses?

• • •

Baby Justin Andrew was born right on schedule, but Carolina had to be heavily anesthetized for the delivery: all during her hard labor, Mama and Daddy were with her, Mama holding her hand, and Daddy giving her slips of ice to suck on. Delivery of the baby passed in a blur. She only recalled that a nurse, gloved, capped, and masked into anonymity by the requirements of the delivery room – showed her the baby afterwards, wrapped in a striped cotton blanket, his fair hair clotted with blood and other fluids, a tiny red face screwed up in baffled anger.

"He's beautiful!" Carolina exclaimed, groggily, and then she closed her eyes. She meant to close them only for a moment, but the gray, pillowy wave of unknowing pulled her down, like a tired swimmer giving up and sinking deeper into the water. When she opened her eyes again, she lay in a high white bed in a private room; Mark sat there, in a chair by the bed, Mama and Daddy standing on the opposite side of the bed, along with a doctor that she didn't recognize, a tall man with graying hair, and a stethoscope looped around his neck. All four faces bore an expression of concern and apprehension, even the doctor.

"Where's my baby?" Carolina asked, suddenly struck with a feeling of dread. "Where is Justin? I thought he was here, what happened to him?"

"Caro, honey..." Daddy took her hand in his strong one. Her eyes went from face to face; Mark wasn't looking at her – he was gazing at the floor.

"The baby is in the intensive care nursery," Mama sobbed incoherently, "But there's something awfully wrong, and they have to operate now... to fix internal birth defects. I'm so sorry, Caro! They're afraid that he won't live!"

"He has a chance, if they go ahead and operate at once," Daddy was calm as ever. "A fifty-fifty chance. I know it sounds bad, Caro, but life means hope, and Justin Andrew will have the best care possible."

The doctor cleared his throat. "I'm Doctor Shaeffer, Mrs. Sanchez. The main problem which your little boy has is called an imperforate anus," he explained calm, slightly detached tones, which Carolina found to be rather comforting. There was a lot to be said for someone who could explain things clearly, without dissolving into unrequired drama. "It's a very rare birth defect, mostly affecting boys, when their lower intestinal tract does not develop normally, allowing normal defecation. He will need to have a colostomy, of course. His other problem is that we have also diagnosed esophageal atresia. His trachea, esophagus and lungs have not developed as they should, and saliva is passing directly into his lungs. This raises the very real danger of pneumonia. We must also install a feeding tube into his stomach, since he will not be able to take milk normally, until his trachea and esophagus have completely healed from surgery." Dr. Shaeffer continued outlining what was wrong with little Justin, but reassuringly, outlining what could be done surgically, to make it right.

"I want to see him," Carolina insisted. "Now!"

"He's already being prepped for surgery," Dr. Shaeffer shook his head. "Your husband already gave his permission. It was felt that we should operate as soon as possible."

"Then I want to see him as soon as he is out of surgery," Carolina's eyes began overflowing – her perfect, beautiful little son! She might never get to cuddle him close to her heart, rock him to sleep in her arms as she sang lullabies to him.

"You will, Mrs. Sanchez," Dr. Shaeffer patted the same hand that Daddy held. "You will be able to visit him in the ICU for as long as you want. It does a baby good to maintain that maternal connection. I promise that we will do our very best for him. All children are precious – it's just that some need a little more help getting a good start, and that's what our children's hospital is here for."

Meanwhile, Mark remained silent, staring at the floor between his knees. After the doctor left, Mark abruptly rose from the chair and left also, without another word, leaving Carolina to be comforted by her parents.

. . .

Mark never did visit Justin in the hospital nursery, although he did come back to drive her home, when she was released from the hospital. Baby Justin Andrew Sanchez remained behind; sick, fretful, or dozy from medications or anesthesia. It would be many weeks or even months before he could be released, after recovering from multiple surgeries. But Carolina loved him fiercely, from the top of his downy little head, with the soft diamond-shaped spot where the bones in his skull hadn't fused and she could see the regular gentle movement of his pulse, down to his perfect little toes. For her, he could be coaxed to smile. His tiny fingers would wrap around her finger and hold with a grip that promised that he would never let go of that finger or her heart. Justin had those bright blue eyes which Carolina had imagined. She was certain his eyes would not change with age, fringed with long lashes which were a darker shade than the wisps of fair blond hair which eventually covered his head.

Mark spent less and less time with Carolina at the apartment: there were days when it seemed like he couldn't wait to leave, and he never wanted to go with Carolina to the children's hospital for the daily visit to Justin.

"I'm busy," he told Carolina at breakfast, as he scowled at the scrambled eggs and bacon on his plate. "Look, I can take you on my lunch hour, but your mom will have to bring you back. Jesus, Caro – how many times do I have to tell you that I hate watery scrambled eggs? Maybe if you spent more time learning to cook a meal that I can eat, instead of mooning over that *sick* kid of yours ..."

"How can you say that! Justin is your son, too!" Carolina flared in anger, and Mark picked up the plate with his half-eaten breakfast on it and launched it into the sink, eggs, and all. The plate shattered.

Mark snarled, "Yeah, wish I could be sure of that – and I sure as hell wish I had paid for an abortion, in case that kid *is* mine!"

He slammed the door, while Carolina stood there, stunned and disbelieving. And here she thought that Mark would be a good father to Justin, that he would clean up his act, behave like a responsible provider. Instead, since Justin had been born, Mark was more often viciously angry and abusive, blaming Carolina for anything and everything.

That was the day that Carolina had to do laundry in the morning, and get it done before Mark returned during his lunch break. She gathered up the basket piled full of her things, Mark's dirty shirts and trousers, towels and sheets, and the little undershirts and nightgowns for Justin that she took home from the hospital and returned a clean set every day. She carried the basket and the box of detergent down to the apartment laundry room, still baffled at Mark's fury and the way he seemed not to care in the least for his son.

She found Avril there, with her children. Avril's daughter Letty was standing on a chair and solemnly folding dry diapers with touching care, making certain that every single fold was precise, while little 'Tonio babbled to himself and played with one of his rattle-toys on a blanket spread out underneath the table where Avril and her daughter worked. It was a lovely picture of what Carolina hoped that their family might be.

Before Carolina could turn around and retreat, Avril looked up and exclaimed, "'Lina, there you are – how is the little one! Is he well enough to come home, yet?"

"Not quite yet," Carolina sighed. Two of the washing machines were free. She plunked her own basket before them, and began sorting the whites for hot water wash, and the rest for cold. "In a couple of weeks, Dr. Shaeffer says."

"*Pobrecito!*" Avril replied. "Poor little darling! I burn a candle for him, every week at church, and pray that he might grow healthy and strong, and come home to you. 'Tonio would love to have a playmate,

"Thank you," Carolina replied, honestly grateful for Avril's support, and her intimate knowledge of the peculiarities of babies and tiny children. "Avril, I don't quite know what to make of all this! Mark, my husband – he is not happy about Justin. It's almost as if ..." Carolina took a deep breath and gave voice to her deepest concern. "... he is jealous of the baby. He is angry whenever I visit Justin and pay so much attention to him. I'm so concerned! Just now, he threw his plate into the sink with his breakfast on it and said such vile things. What is it with men!?"

"Ah, poor 'Lina," Avril paused in her folding of her husband's underwear and balling his socks in neat pairs. "He is jealous. That is a thing that happens, sometimes, I think – with a spoiled and arrogant man. He believes that you should devote all your care and concern to him, and that the baby is a rival. Worse than a rival, for the baby holds your heart and soul, where a handsome man only holds your ...." And Avril used a very crude word for a woman's special parts. "The child is yours, and yours alone. You can never get another one, exactly alike to that child ... but you can always get another man. I think all men know this, at their heart. Our children are of our own flesh. We hold them first and always in our heart, while our man ..." Avril shrugged expressively. "If he is not satisfactory, there is always another man. The good men know this, and never press a woman on this matter. But your husband ..." Avril paused in her folding of the laundry and regarded Carolina as if she were considering a serious matter. "'Lina, do you remember that weekend when you told me your husband was driving to Dallas to interview for a job?"

"I do," Carolina replied. "You and Jesse and the children were ... you were going to visit your family on the South Side." Carolina's heart hammered with apprehension. Avril looked so solemn, as if she were about to share bad news. Avril drew a deep breath.

"'Lina, I do not want to tell you this about your husband and I take no joy from it, but he did not go to Dallas that weekend. This I know for sure; Jesse and I saw him with this woman, who lives in the same block as Tia Fernanda. We saw them together. I made Jesse drive around the street because I did not believe what I saw. It was his car parked in the street in front of her house, all the time that we were visiting. Tia Fernanda knows of her by reputation – a woman of bad character with many boyfriends. All her neighbor's gossip about this woman. She is a whore."

"You must be mistaken," Carolina protested. "He ... was going for a job interview. He told me!"

"On a Saturday?" Avril snorted in derision. "He lied. The truth is not in him, as my husband says. If he told us that the sky was blue, I would look out the window to be certain before believing. Your Mark was with the other woman. Jesse saw him also and recognized his car from seeing it here every day. It was him, 'Lina – he was not in Dallas that weekend."

"No," Carolina shook her head, fighting the cold feeling of despair in the pit of her stomach. *How many lies had Mark told her already?* "I don't ... Mark wouldn't lie to me..."

Avril shrugged, mildly exasperated. "Believe as you wish. Jesse and I ... we did not wish to make you unhappy, put a shadow between you and your husband. But as God will witness, he was not in Dallas when he told you that he was. He was with that woman. There should be no lies between a man and a wife."

But there had already been lie upon lie, upon lie. Carolina knew this in her heart, but admitting it to Avril, or even to Mama and Daddy was unthinkable. Besides, little Justin Andrew needed a father.

CHAPTER 9
CALLING IT QUITS

Carolina said nothing to anyone, not even Mama and Daddy, about what Avril told her. That Mark hadn't gone to Dallas to interview with Braniff; he had spent that weekend with another woman. She didn't tell them that Mark had a viciously hot temper, stole parts from other people's cars, and things like the Academy ring. Carolina could, with a considerable effort, make allowances for that. But that he was a liar and unfaithful to boot? She couldn't force her mind to accept that. She still hoped that when little Justin came home from the hospital for good, that Mark would see how important it would be to be a good father, as good a father as Daddy had been to Carolina herself and her brother.

Mark was so good-looking, so charming when they first met, began seeing each other, and was so eager to get married, when she found out she was pregnant. What had happened to him? What had happened that he was so angry now, about everything? Now he didn't want her to go anywhere, do anything, speak to anyone else, without his express approval. So much for being her own woman and knowing her own mind! Carolina made a special effort to make Mark's favorite supper that day, and that the apartment was perfectly spic and span. It meant so much, this marriage, after the disaster that had been Mason. *(But she couldn't help but think that at least Mason hadn't ever hit her or forbade her from going someplace that he didn't approve of. And she also wondered if Avril was right – about Mark being the kind of man who didn't want his wife paying attention to anyone but himself.)*

Mark didn't come home for lunch that following day. How on earth was Carolina going to visit the hospital, to visit Justin and take him his freshly laundered things? Justin had needed to have two operations before he was a week old; surgery to close the hole between his trachea and his esophagus so that he could drink milk and keep saliva from running down into his lungs and a colostomy so that he could pass feces. Her arms ached to hold her baby boy – no, she couldn't endure not seeing him, not for a whole day! Was it possible for Justin to forget who his mother really was, if he didn't see her every single day? When Mark didn't show by one o'clock, Carolina called her mother.

"I thought you were at Santa Rosa already," Mama said, with a sigh. "Never mind. I'll come over and take you. I suppose Mark is busy at work and couldn't get away. You'd best leave him a message that you have a ride already."

Carolina did just that, leaving a message with one of Mark's fellow workers. Then she rushed down the stairs from the apartment, as Mama pulled into the drive, in the red T-bird with the top up. Mama looked tired and harassed. Daddy was on another trip, working hard to pay the bills, as hard as he ever had when Carolina and Frankie were still at home. And Poppa Lew's health was starting to go. He was a pale shadow of the force that he had always been. Granny Margo had died very suddenly, just after Carolina and Mark had married. Everyone expected him to move in with Mama and Daddy now that Granny Margo was gone. Carolina and Mama didn't talk much until they got to the hospital. Mama parked the T-bird, and they walked together into the spacious lobby of the pale, honey-colored brick hospital block. They were just passing by the big glass window and the swinging door that led into the hospital's flower shop, when Mark came running in after them, raging and cursing a blue streak. He caught Carolina by the shoulder, spun her around and flung her at the glass window, shouting,

"You stupid bitch, you don't dare go anywhere that I don't approve of! Haven't you learned that lesson, you cunt!"

Carolina, caught by surprise by the torrent of vicious obscenity as well as the violence, fell with all her weight full against the glass window. Luckily it did not break as shards of broken glass would have gashed her to ribbons. Mark stood over her, cursing and aiming a blow at her face, which she squirmed to avoid as Mama shrieked, and went for Mark, swinging her heavy handbag, the fingers on her other hand curled into claws.

"You let her alone!"

Mark cursed again, and shoved Mama to one side with brutal force, but at that moment, two of the black-robed Santa Rosa nuns appeared, as if popped out of a magic lamp by a genie. The nuns were accompanied by a hulking man in a quasi-military security guard uniform, who topped Mark by half a head and was twice as big from side to side. The security guard also had a baton in his hand and a pistol holstered at the belt which just went under his sagging belly. With one hand, he lifted Mark by the back of his shirt and jacket, as easily as if he were lifting a disobedient puppy by the scruff of the neck.

"Buddy, you heard the ladies," the security guard rumbled, in a voice that sounded like an earthquake. "Leave the girl alone. This is a hospital. What the heck are you doing?"

While Carolina picked herself off the hard floor, with Mama's and the assistance of the two nuns, Mark cursed some more and tried to fight back, but the security guard shook him like a disobedient pup. "Keep it clean in front of the ladies and the sisters! Now, are you going to walk out of this here hospital like a man on his own two feet, or do you need me to drag you out like a bum?"

"I'll go," Mark snarled sullenly. When the guard let go of him, he pulled his shirt and jacket straight, and glared at Carolina.

"I'll speak to you, bitch, tonight, when you get home from your little visit to that kid," He turned on his heel, and mumbled something to the security guard which caused the security guard to growl under his breath.

"You need to leave this hospital immediately or I will have you arrested, now beat it, buster," The man turned to Carolina, now on her feet, with Mama's arm around her shoulder. "Are you all right, ma'am?"

"I'm fine," Carolina assured him in a shaky voice, and Mama said,

"Caro - you can't possibly go back to the apartment with him in the mood he is in. Why don't you come home with me for a while, until Mark gets over it."

"I can't," Carolina replied, although on the inside she was curdling with dread. She hoped that Mark would have calmed down by the time they both returned to the apartment. "For my baby's sake - Mark is Justin's father, after all. I'm all right - just startled, that's all."

Mama stared at her, the concern plain in her fine dark eyes. "Caro," she said at last. "It doesn't work out very well in the long run, when a man starts hitting his wife. Tell me that Mark doesn't hit you."

"He doesn't hit me," Carolina assured her mother. "No, he doesn't hit me. Not ever."

No, Mark didn't hit her. Not exactly. He sometimes grabbed her by the throat, or by the arm, hard enough to leave bruises on her neck, or on her arms. Or shoved her hard enough to make her lose balance, or threw something at her; a plate, or anything that came to hand when he lost his temper. But no - he didn't hit her. Maybe he would stop being so angry when she brought Justin home from the hospital. Justin Andrew was his son. Mark couldn't possibly be angry towards Justin, not angry enough to hit a baby, a baby who was medically fragile.

• • •

When Mama drove her back to the apartment later that day, after cuddling with Justin in the hospital nursery. Mark was not home yet. When he did arrive, shortly before suppertime, he was sullen and withdrawn. Carolina treated him as if he were a bomb with a hair-trigger, all but holding her breath lest something - a word, a look, something wrong with supper – set him off. But when he had finished supper, he moved his plate away, saying,

"I'm going out to hang with some friends – don't wait up for me."

"Yes, Mark," she replied, overjoyed with relief, and he looked straight at her and snapped,

"Well, you don't need to sound so happy about it,"

"I'm sorry, really sorry," Carolina quavered, as he looked as if he were going to shove her out of the way as he went through the kitchen, but he didn't. She slowly washed up the supper dishes and their plates and wondered if Mama was right; she should have gone home to Mama and Daddy after the first time that Mark left bruises on her. She should have gone home this afternoon with Mama ... but then how would she care for Justin? There was no answer, really. She felt as if she were at the bottom of a deep pit, and the only way out of it was to dig with a spoon.

. . .

Justin was able to leave the hospital, after a stay of months, while the surgeries healed. He had also survived a bout of pneumonia which delayed the homecoming another week, and a second round of surgery on his lower intestine, but at long last, Carolina was able to carry him home, wrapped in a lacy shawl that Avril's mother had crocheted for him as a baby shower gift. Carolina wondered if the shawl were a way of making up for what Avril had told her, about Mark spending the weekend with another woman, when he had claimed to be driving to Dallas to a job interview. She still didn't know if she quite believed Avril or not, but then Avril and Jesse were neighbors; kind and concerned neighbors. Avril sometimes came and knocked on their door, after Mark had one of his tantrums, asking quietly and sympathetically, if she were all right. Carolina always insisted that she was, but lately had begun to wonder if Avril really believed her.

They met in the apartment complex laundry room, on the second day after she brought Justin home. He slept quietly in a Moses basket at her feet, while she did laundry, as she didn't want to let him out of her sight for a moment. Avril carried in an overflowing basket of dirty laundry, trailed by her toddler Antonio, who was immediately entranced by Justin, since Justin now slept tranquilly under the folding table which had previously been little 'Tonio's domain. Avril marveled over Justin's recovered health, after such a perilous delivery and months and months in the hospital.

"He is beautiful, *pobrecito*!" Avril cooed, smiling at Justin who had grabbed onto the fingers that she held out in front of him. "And a blessing to you and your husband!"

"I suppose," Carolina agreed, although she was certain that Mark didn't consider baby Justin any kind of blessing. Avril looked at her keenly.

"Most children, they are like weeds," she mused, after a shrewd sideways glance at Carolina. "They will thrive and grow, no matter what their mama and papa do, or do not do. They will thrive and grow strong. But then, I think that some children, like your little one, are like orchids, who must be tended so carefully. Tia Fernanda says that those orchid children are given by God to those who may best care for them. So I am certain that your little Justin was meant to be yours, knowing that he would need especial care."

"Maybe not me so much," Carolina replied. "I don't think Mark really cares about Justin much at all, not nearly as much as I do, or Mama and Daddy, and Dr. Shaeffer at Santa Rosa. You know, last month, when Justin had pneumonia again ... they asked me to go to the financial office first before I went up to the nursery. They had to tell me ..."

"Bad news?" Avril supplied, when Carolina relieved that heart-stopping moment, when the hospital's financial director broke it to her. She had honestly felt like she wanted to die herself, because Baby Justin could very well die, without surgeries – and he would go on needing surgery, that was for certain.

"They told me that Blue Cross – that our insurance wouldn't pay for any more medical intervention for Justin." Carolina took a deep breath. "Of course, I was devastated. I started crying right then and there. They were perfectly nice about it but I felt like my heart was just being ripped out. I was crying all the way to the nursery. My poor little boy was going to die because the insurance wouldn't pay for any more hospital care and surgeries! But Dr. Shaeffer, the surgeon who has done all these operations on Justin, was in the elevator, and he asked me what was wrong, so of course I told him everything. He's gotten very fond of Justin, you see. And he is such a good surgeon, all the nurses and nuns simply worship him. He cares so much and does so much good work. Anyway, Dr. Shaeffer told me not to worry about Justin, because he would get the March of Dimes to fund Justin's medical care after this. You know; the polio charity, but now they raise funds to cure children with birth defects like Justin's. I was so grateful ... because everything would work out for Justin, and it did."

"You see?" Avril nodded in satisfaction. "God intended you to care for your little Justin orchid-child, knowing that your Dr. Shaeffer is on your side! He will grow big and strong and healthy, for sure now, just as God intended."

"I hope so," Carolina sighed. "I expect that I just have to care for both of us, since Mark doesn't seem to take an interest at all."

Avril looked for a moment as if she were about to reply but just then, little 'Tonio fell and bumped his chin on the floor, and he began to wail. That put an end to conversation until Tonio was soothed and distracted, and by that time, Avril's last load of laundry was out of the tumble-dryer and piled neatly folded in her basket. Carolina wondered briefly what it was that Avril had been about to say. Probably nothing important, she told herself.

Justin did indeed grow, big and strong, if only intermittently healthy. He went through several more operations to correct those problems in his digestive tract which had not developed normally. His picture was in the newspaper, as he was the poster child for the local March of Dimes; that child which March of Dimes in San Antonio had spent the most on, to keep him healthy and growing. He cut three teeth and walked at ten months, and Carolina fitted him out with high-laced Buster Brown shoes, to support his ankles. She adored Justin with all her heart, and so did Mama and Daddy. Mark just seemed indifferent to the boy, even as his impatience and bad temper with Carolina became even more uncertain. She protected herself from Mark when he was in his worst mood by holding Justin in her arms, reasoning that he would not dare strike her while she had Justin in her lap.

For Mark had gotten to the point of hitting her, striking with his fist or open hand, for a small reason, or most usually no reason at all, other than he had a bad day at work, or upset with a co-worker. Carolina hardly dared ask any questions about what was going on with his day, for fear of setting him off; he was a domestic hand grenade with a loose pin. She explained away the bruises, if anyone like Mama or Avril asked, by saying that Justin had kicked her with his hard soled shoes, when she was changing the diaper over his colostomy opening, for the site was tender, and Justin hated it being touched there at all. It was only when Justin's first birthday was coming up that she dared mention to Mark about a birthday party for the child.

"Mama and Daddy said that we could have the party at their house," she told him, hesitantly. "We want to have a nice gathering of all our friends, the cousins, and their families, with a big cake and plenty of ice cream, and games for all the children, like Avril and Jesse's 'Tonio and Letty." She swallowed nervously and ventured into dangerous territory, because Mark had to be at the party, else it would become too much for Carolina to explain that if he didn't come. "Everyone will expect you to be there. It's such a big milestone for Justin – getting to one year, when they only gave him a fifty percent chance of survival at birth."

"OK, I'll be there," Mark glowered like a thunderstorm, and Carolina thought it best not to press him any farther than that.

. . .

Mama and Carolina planned Justin's first birthday party down to the least detail: balloons and ribbon garlands tied to the mailbox out front, and festooning the living and dining room, his highchair decorated as well, and a banner across the front room, spelling out "Happy 1st Birthday, Justin!" Mama ordered a fancy decorated cake from the most prestigious bakery in town, a cake with as many layers as a wedding cake. The cake was ornamented with circus animals, made from sugar and frosting – a whole parade of them, from layer to layer. There were bowls of punch and lemonade, platters of tea sandwiches cut into elaborate shapes, the icebox in the kitchen filled with soft drinks for children and beer for the adults. They invited everyone from their family, Frankie and his wife Valerie, Carolina's friends, and neighbors in the apartment building where she and Mark lived, as well as Dr. Shaeffer and the nurses at Santa Rosa. There was even a newspaper reporter and a photographer for the *San Antonio Light*, who came and snapped a picture of Justin Andrew Sanchez the miracle baby, gleefully smearing a spoonful of icing and chocolate ice cream on his face. Poppa Lew, now bone-thin and very frail, watched the festivities from his armchair, until he fell asleep, mid-afternoon, with his head slumping sideways, even though the party was still going strong. The small children who were invited; the children of cousins, Avril's little 'Tonio and Letty, all ran around underfoot, dressed in their very best, energized by cake, sweets, and the intrigue of opening presents for the birthday boy. The mood was happy, celebrating little Justin's survival against the odds – a year of life, and the promise of a life that would continue. With this celebration, Carolina was assured that everyone loved Justin just as much as she did.

Almost everyone. About the time that everyone was admiring the cake, and Justin, Mama whispered discreetly, "Where has Mark gone? You said that he would be here for the party!"

"He did," Carolina cast a quick look around the living room, and the adjoining dining room, where the birthday cake and the table of food had been set out. "He was here! He promised that he would be!" Her heart sank. The family would definitely suspect all that had gone wrong with her marriage, if Mark had decided not to stay.

"He told your father and I that he was going to move his car around the corner, to make space for other guests to park on the street," Mama said, with a quick frown. "And I haven't seen him since."

The knot of dread in Carolina's stomach tightened. Oh, surely, Mark would not have … She made a quick search of the house; kitchen, upstairs, glanced out into the back yard, where a lively game of horseshoes was going on with the older children, supervised by Daddy and Frankie. No Mark. She even ran out to the sidewalk and down to the corner, and Mark's Chevy was nowhere to be seen. He had gone, without a single word of explanation. She returned to the house, tamping down her rage and disappointment. Another broken promise from Mark. It was as if he didn't care a single bit; not for Justin, not for Carolina, not even for keeping his word over such a simple thing as to be at his son's first birthday party.

"He must have had to go help out a friend," Carolina explained to Mama, trying to hide her misery and disappointment when she returned to the house, a house filled with celebration and happiness. "He's always doing that. Anything for a friend."

"Even if it takes him away from his family, on important days?" Mama sniffed, disdainfully. Mama kept her voice low, as they spoke on the front porch, not wanting to spoil the party inside for everyone. "Caro, that's not a good thing, especially on a day as important as this is, for you and the baby! You've always been saying that Justin needs a father; if this is the father that Justin has, then your dad and I really wonder why you are so set on hanging on with him!"

"He loves us, and it matters to me," Carolina insisted.

Mama sniffed again. As she followed Carolina through the front door, Carolina thought she heard Mama say, "Can't prove it by me, and if Mark isn't that wretch Gianni Amato all over again, I'll eat my best Sunday hat!"

Oh, him – that was why Mama kept on worrying so much over Carolina. What she saw of him reminded her of her first husband, the biological father whom Carolina couldn't remember, and was certain she had never met. Daddy was the only Daddy she could remember, tall and fair, broad in the shoulders, sincere and responsible as a father. Mama must think that it was happening again, only to her. Was it? That was the uncomfortable thought that Carolina kept pushing away. It was just that Mark's temper, his bent towards violence and outright dishonesty were a quality becoming harder and harder to push aside. *How can he really love me, when I have bruises from being shoved, hit, grabbed by the arm, wrist, or throat? And it wasn't like people hadn't tried to warn her ...*

But she couldn't think about all that today, not with the birthday party for Justin, the miracle baby, in full swing. Carolina resolutely shoved all those doubts aside, went back into the party celebrating Justin's birthday and survival, bathing in the approval and affection of their friends and kin. No, it didn't matter if Mark wasn't there. No, it wasn't. He would only have put a blight on universal joy anyway.

In the end, Daddy had to drive her and Justin home, after the party, although Mama urged them all to stay and spend the night.

"No, Justin wants his own crib, and our regular evening routine," Carolina replied. Her baby boy was over-tired and over-excited by all the people at the party, the fuss being made over him. He was getting to be fractious and tearful – and Carolina herself was nursing a ferocious headache. They packed the back seat with some of the birthday presents, and Mama added a box with several slices of the ornate cake and a plate of sandwiches.

"At least, Mark will have a little bit of the party," Mama observed. Carolina winced; most likely Mark wouldn't have cared or not about missing the party. Justin slept in her arms, on the way home. Daddy drove silently, but as he pulled up in front of the apartment building, he looked sideways at Carolina, saying,

"Caro, you know your mother and I are really worried about you."

"I know," Carolina looked over Justin's downy head. He was half-asleep with his thumb in his mouth, exhausted and surfeited with attention and cake. "It's all right, Daddy. Really."

"If you say so," Daddy didn't sound convinced. Carolina was relieved that Mark's Chevy wasn't there. Daddy might have said something to him, and Mark would likely have taken it out on her, later. "You go on, put the baby down for a nap, and I'll bring in his presents, and the diaper bag."

It was quiet in the apartment, positively blissful after the party crowd at Mama and Daddy's house. And Mark didn't return until early in the morning. Carolina didn't care. It meant that she didn't have to talk to him at all. The next morning, she could see, through stealing covert glances at him as he dressed, that he was waiting impatiently for her to ask where he had been, where he had gone the day before, absenting himself from Justin's big party. He wanted her to ask – wanted it so much that the steam was practically coming out of his ears, all so that he would have an excuse to lash out at her.

No, she would not take that easy bait, Carolina decided with a touch of mild malice, as she set about fixing breakfast; a Sunday breakfast, something a little more elaborate than toast and coffee and eggs. Waffles – yes, waffles and bacon and eggs over-easy, and a little bit of oatmeal for Justin. She even began to hum a little tune for Justin, even as Mark scowled at them both. That she did not ask about yesterday annoyed Mark even more, but Carolina reasoned that he would have no excuse to get violent with her.

"Waffles OK with you?" she asked sweetly, and Mark scowled." Aren't you going to ask me why I didn't stay at the kid's party yesterday?" he demanded, finally – when obviously he could bear it no longer.

Carolina affected a mildly surprised expression. "I guessed you had good reason," she replied. "One of your friends needed help or something. That's what I told Mama and Daddy. There were so many people there for the baby yesterday that I s'pose that I was the only one who really noticed you weren't there at all."

For a brief moment, she wondered if she had gone too far in poking at the angry bear that was Mark in a bad mood, but he merely grunted and pored himself another cup of coffee. Carolina let out her breath. She had gotten away with that mild thrust. Once she finished breakfast, she took Justin into the bedroom to dress herself and him for church. Lately she had taken to going to mid-morning Mass with Avril and Jesse, and the children. Avril had offered her a ride every Sunday, months ago, and Carolina figured that she owed God something for the life of her little boy, even if she wasn't honestly that religious at all.

She changed Justin's diaper for a fresh one which covered the colostomy, put him into a little pale blue trouser outfit with a white shirt, and put him back in the crib to wait for her, as she dressed and put on her makeup. She had just finished patting on foundation, and was working on her eyes – liner, mascara, and all – when Mark came into the bedroom.

"Where are you going, all dressed up?" he demanded, scowling.

Carolina stared at him, baffled and blank of any answer.

"To Mass. I've gone to Mass every Sunday with Avril and Jesse and the kids. You know that Mark."

"Not dressed up and made-up like the whore you are!" Mark snarled and backhanded her across the face, so hard that she toppled to the floor as the spindly dressing table stool fell over. Then he grabbed up the opened bottle of foundation and threw it across the room. The glass bottle shattered against the wall, and pale beige Cover Girl foundation splashed everywhere, on the wall, the closet door, the clothes inside, and on the bedroom carpet.

Carolina sprawled on the floor, momentarily stunned and dizzy from the vicious blow. Her hands involuntarily went to her face.

This was not the hardest that Mark had ever struck her – he had often been much more brutal. But this was the first time that he struck her in front of little Justin. Dressed for church, in his best clean little shirt and trousers, Justin stared at her over the rail of his crib. His soft little baby mouth puckered in dismay, and his eyes were brimming with bewildered tears. Carolina stared into Justin's eyes, as she gathered herself up from the floor. The apartment door slammed with such violence that it seemed like the whole apartment building shook.

This was a moment that changed everything, Carolina realized with a moment of piercing clarity. Mark had struck her, in full view of the baby.

What life lesson was Justin going to take from this? What kind of things was little Justin Andrew Sanchez going to learn, with a father like that? Her dear, sweet, affectionate little miracle boy – what was he going to learn from seeing Mark knock her almost silly and on a regular basis? Was Justin going to learn that it was OK and perfectly normal for a man to slap, beat, and brutalize a woman? For no reason at all?

Carolina sat on the bed, struggling to come to terms with a shattering insight; the realization that she had given more than two years of her life to a lie, turning her face away from the knowledge that Mark was an awful, brutal, abusive liar, and a criminal at that. There was no good, and nothing good which would come, now or ever, from her hopeful pretense that he loved her, or Justin; that he was just in a bad mood from trouble at work or worry about money, when he struck her, grabbed her with brutal hands, shouted abuse at her. It didn't matter that he had given every indication of loving her at the start of their relationship. Even with Mark wanting to know where she went, who she was with ... all of that was a lie. It wasn't love; it was an indefinite prison sentence. And the one thing that she couldn't live with was knowing in the depths of her soul that if she kept on in this sham of a marriage, Mark would make her little miracle boy into a man every bit as angry and brutal as he was himself.

No, not Justin, she thought. *Not my miracle baby. I can't let Mark make him into something so vile.*

There was a tentative knock on the door to the apartment. Carolina stood up from the bed, feeling that she was dragging an unbearable burden, just by the act of standing up. Most likely it was Avril, wondering if she and Justin were ready to go to Mass.

It was Avril, with Jesse at her back, the children with them, all dressed in their Sunday best, Avril with the lacy scarf over her hair, 'Tonio and Letty solemn and Jesse vaguely uncomfortable in the too-tight suit and tie which fit badly over his muscled, working-man's figure, with the hands and fingernails from which the grime could never quite be scoured clean.

"Caro, are you alright?" Avril asked, in swift concern. "We heard … Mark hit you again, didn't he?"

"He did," Carolina looked her straight in the eye. "And I need to leave. Now. Mark and I are done. I can't go on like this. Let me pack up a few things. Can you take the baby and me to my parent's house?"

CHAPTER 10
A NEW BEGINNING

Avril and Jessie agreed to drive Carolina and Justin Andrew to Mama and Daddy's house, straight away.

"He hit you again, didn't he! I knew it! *Bastardo!* There is a bruise coming out on your face, and your lip is bleeding!" Avril exclaimed, scowling, and added a couple of disparaging comments in Spanish, when Carolina nodded, mutely. "Quickly, 'Lina – go and pack, so we can be away before Mark returns and makes trouble for us all." Avril nodded towards her husband, who took Letty by the hand and lifted 'Tonio in his other arm and took the children to their waiting car. Meanwhile, Avril came into the apartment and helped Carolina throw a change of clothes and some of her most precious things into a small suitcase, and the container of Justin's expensive powered formula as would fit into the diaper bag.

"Leave us your key," Avril suggested as she lugged the suitcase and diaper bag out to the car, followed by Carolina with Justin in her arms. "Jesse and I can come back and get the rest of your things whenever Mark is not around."

Carolina only nodded, still numbed by the blow and the rapidity with which all this was happening. In her heart she knew that the marriage to Mark was over. She would never go back to the apartment, just as she had never returned to the place in Austin where she had lived with Mason. She would file for a divorce. There was no way on earth she would reconcile with Mark, not now, not after all that he had done, the many times that he had shoved or struck her, all the times that he had lied, cheated on her, and stolen from other people, like that part for his Chevy in company with his disgusting friend Dave. Barely twenty, and already divorced twice: what a record of failure she had with men! With Justin in her lap, she squeezed into the back seat with Letty and 'Tonio, for the drive to her parent's house. Some of the numb, unreal feeling had passed by the time she walked up to the front door, and opened it, still hugging Justin to her chest.

"Mama," she said, proud that her voice was steady, as Mama appeared, still in her bathrobe and slippers on a lazy Sunday morning. "I've left Mark. He hit me once too many times, and Jesse and Avril gave me a ride home."

"Oh, my God," Mama exclaimed. "Caro – are you all right?! He didn't hit the baby, did he? Come in, come in, honey ... thank God, we were getting so worried, but we hated to press you ..."

Only then did Carolina burst into tears, so drained that she was afraid she would collapse onto the floor, even with Justin in her arms. Mama took the baby from her, and Daddy – barefoot, but already in a white shirt and his suit trousers, put his arm around her. She was vaguely aware of Daddy talking over her head to Jesse and Avril as she sobbed against his chest.

"Give us your door keys to the apartment," Daddy said, finally when she hiccupped the last of those tears, "And get some breakfast. I'm going to call up Frankie, and we'll go back to your place with Mr. Gonzalez for the rest of your things – the baby will need his crib, after all."

"I've already had breakfast," Carolina protested.

Daddy replied, "Well, have some coffee – you look as if you need it."

"Come along, honey," Mama urged her. Mama had Justin balanced capably on her hip, and he was already smiling. He adored his granny, who was always ready to indulge him. "There's room enough in your old bedroom for the crib ... oh, good, you remembered his formula... now, who's my big handsome boy?" she cooed to Justin, who had already decided that everything was on the sunny side now and was grinning and laughing up at her.

"Thank you," Carolina whispered to Avril, who squeezed her hands. "I couldn't have managed without you and Jesse..."

"It's what friends are for," Avril swiftly kissed her cheek. "We'll go with your papa and your brother and get the rest of your things! I dare that *marrano* – that pig of a husband of yours – to stop us!" she added, fiercely.

"He won't dare," Carolina replied, with a shaky laugh. "He only beats up on women. He wouldn't dare start a fight with Daddy and Frankie, and your husband, all three of them together, even if he has one of his scummy pals with him! When you have a chance, tell my friends like Pam and Jerry where I have gone. I just know they will worry and think that maybe Mark has killed me in a temper and dumped my body someplace."

"I will let them know, Lina," Avril assured her, and then she was gone, leaving Carolina curiously feeling weightless, adrift like a fairground balloon, in the living room of her parent's house, the same room where she and all their friends had celebrated Justin's birthday, not more than twenty-four hours ago.

. . .

In the end, she decided that she would go back to her original plan – the plan from before she was sidetracked by Mark and motherhood. She would start nursing school, become a licensed vocational nurse, maybe even a registered nurse, after that. After all, she had the responsibility for Justin, who would always be medically fragile. How better to care for him if she were a nurse herself? It helped enormously that Mama and Daddy adored Justin and even though Daddy still had to be on the road for his job with the Yellow Pages almost constantly. Mama arranged her social life so that she could care for Justin when Carolina had classes, and later on, evening duty as part of her clinics. Poppa Lew, increasingly frail and forgetful, also moved in with them, taking up residence in the room which had been Frankie's. Almost incapacitated by age, he also helped with minding Justin, reading him fairy stories, and singing him childhood songs in a whispery, tuneless voice.

Carolina filed for divorce from Mark, on the grounds of abuse. It wasn't contested: he never even asked for visitation rights with little Justin. As far as Carolina was concerned, after she walked away from the apartment, Mark might just as well have fallen off the end of the earth. She never saw him again, not even from a distance, and he never paid a single penny of the alimony or child support that he had been ordered to pay by the court. Not that she minded not getting child support all that much, because then he could have demanded visitation rights to Justin in exchange for that consideration. Carolina couldn't bear even thinking about the possibility of her precious little boy being neglected or even abused by his father. Better that Mark be gone entirely from their lives. Within a month or so, she learned from Avril and Pam that he had moved out of the apartment without notice and in the dead of night. Typically for Mark, he owed several months' back rent, and left the apartment trashed. Nearly two decades afterwards, she read in the *San Antonio Express-News* that a former convict named Mark Sanchez had been killed in a multi-car pile-up accident on the highway to Austin. Carolina didn't care sufficiently to check and see if it was the same Mark Sanchez to whom she had been briefly married. He wasn't someone who mattered to her anymore since her life had changed so much after that brief and unhappy interlude.

• • •

A half a year had gone by and life for Carolina settled into a comfortable groove, after her abrupt departure from marriage to Mark. She had Justin, her parents, her brother Frankie, and his wife Valerie. She had Poppa Lew, her aunts, and the cousins and a busy schedule of nursing classes. She found even the hardest of those classes absorbing. Of course, her motivation to succeed at them was powerful; she needed desperately to qualify, to find work to support herself and to care for Justin. She allowed herself to slack off only occasionally; mostly to socialize with friends like Avril and Jesse, or Pam and Jerry Thompson.

The Thompsons bought their own house and moved out of the apartment building several months after Carolina left. Pam stayed in touch with her, and when the weather permitted, they invited her to come over on Sunday afternoons, when they did steaks, burgers, and BBQ on the grill for a circle of their friends, on the covered back porch and terrace attached to their new house. Carolina thought wistfully that she would like a house and a garden like theirs some day – a brand new house on a large lot set about with big trees, a place with space enough for the Thompson's small sons and their two dogs to run around and play on their swing set with their friends. Sometimes she brought Justin with her, although he was still too small and frail to actively join in such rowdy play with older boys, and Mama was so very good at looking after him when she simply needed a break.

It was on one of those lazy Sunday afternoons – a sunny day early in spring with cicadas buzzing in the trees – that she noted a stranger among the gathering at Pam and Jerry's. Not a stranger entirely; a young man she thought she had seen before, around the apartment complex where she had lived with Mark. She had never spoken to him, though, as Mark was apt to go off in paroxysm of rage and jealousy whenever she talked to any other young, good-looking man. The not-quite-stranger was a tall, lanky six-footer with a head of flaming red hair just like Pam's and a contagious smile.

"You remember my brother Jeff?" Pam said, as she handed Carolina a tall, frosted tumbler full of rum and Coke. "He's on spring break from the university – his last year there. Jeff, Hun, this is Carolina ... Carolina Visser once more since she is divorcing that no-good Mark Sanchez."

"Hi," Jeff grinned at her. "If you don't remember me, I sure enough remember you. I wanted to make your acquaintance last time I visited, but Jerry said you were married, and your husband was the insanely jealous type. I didn't think it was the gentlemanly thing to make trouble for you."

"Your discretion was a considerate thing," Carolina replied, warming with interest, mostly for the way in which Jeff was looking at her, not with lascivious interest, or lust, but with warm human regard. "But he's not my husband, now. I moved out and filed for divorce."

"A lucky escape for Caro," Pam added. "We could hear their fights all over the place, and I'd be willing to swear on a stack of bibles that Mark Sanchez was a liar, a thief, and an all-round cruddy human being. Don't know how Carolina put up with it as long as she did, but she gave him the shove at last, and he skipped out just before we settled on this house."

"Sounds like a real loser," Jeff replied sympathetically.

"He was, but I don't like to dwell on the past," Carolina replied, determined that she wouldn't fall again for facile charm; bound and determined not to dwell on the marital disaster that was Mark, especially now that she had Justin's welfare to consider. That consideration overruled everything. She may as well lay out all her cards on the table, as Poppa Lew used to say when he played poker. "Let's talk about practically anything else than my criminally inclined soon-to-be ex-husband. I'm almost twenty, I have a little boy that I adore, his name is Justin, I moved back in with my parents, who are magnificent about it all – not just me and the baby, but my Poppa Lew as well. He used to run all the laundromats in San Antonio. Poppa invented the most amazing things and invested well, but now he's old and frail, and my grandmother died, so he moved in with us as well. I'm in nursing school, mostly so that I can get a good job, and I can look after my little boy who was born with complicated medical problems. Now, your turn."

"OK," Jeff replied with another unaffected grin. "Quite a story, but mine isn't quite so dramatic. Let's go sit down, first."

Jeff took her hand and led her to a pair of folding chairs, set out on the broad patio behind the house, where Jerry's big metal BBQ grill sent up a thread of smoke into the spring air. Jerry and some of his other friends were attempting to smoke marinated spareribs, as well as the usual barbeque fare on the grill. The men were gathered around it, supervising the methodical administration of charcoal to ribs, beef hamburger patties and frankfurters, while their wives and girlfriends hovered, and brought out the side dishes, bread, and buns. "Let's just get comfortable – it's not like there's an epic involved with me. I'm Jefferson Henry Foster, but most people know me as Jeff, I am 25 years old. I'm a political science major. I'm in ROTC and will graduate in June from Oklahoma University. I'll be commissioned as an Army officer at that point. I like kittens, puppies, small children, beer in restrained quantities, and harmless and wholesome sporting pursuits. I also like the Army, believe it or not. I'm the patriotic sort. Eventually, though, I want to go into politics. What else do you want to know?"

"Will you have to go to Vietnam once you're commissioned?" Carolina asked, with a cold clutching feeling at her heart, recalling in spite of herself, how she had been emotionally wrecked at the thought of Mark serving a tour of duty there.

"Probably," Jeff replied with a jaunty grin. "My solemn duty as the Department of the Army commands. My dad was in the Army in the big war, World War Two, and then in the Army of Occupation in Japan, afterwards. I can't say how much I am looking forward to swapping lies with him over beers at the VFW."

Carolina forced a smile. "My dad was in the Army, too. The first thing I remember was how we lived on the base in Okinawa. I loved it there; the Okinawan maids indulged me to no end."

"That sounds wonderful," Jeff agreed. "OK, so tell me all about Okinawa"

"It was lovely," Carolina replied. "Lovely, safe ... all but the car that Mama had to drive! My brother and I went everywhere, exploring the hills back of the housing area with Frankie's friends. Daddy came home every night at a bit past five and played with us on the grass in front of the house, while Mama put the finishing touches on supper. We had two maids who helped Mama. They kept the house spotless, did all the laundry and chores, and looked after Frankie and I. I loved them to bits, Kimi and Suki. They wore blue and white kimonos and straw sandals on their feet. Daddy used to take us down to the beach in summer, and you wouldn't believe how glorious that was, all white sand, and watching the fishermen launch their boats and go out with their nets. Sometimes the net floats would break loose and come back to shore on the next tide; blue-green glass balls, in so many sizes, from little ones that would fit into your hand, to big ones, the size of a basketball. I loved it there – it was a bit boring, once we came back home after a few years."

"It sounds wonderful," Jeff replied. "I wouldn't mind a post overseas once I get that commission. Germany would be fantastic. You know, all those castles along the Rhine, and the chance to visit those museums and historic sites and festivals, and go to Oktoberfest in Munich ... I did say that I liked beer in moderation?" He went on talking, and Carolina listened, occasionally sipping at her rum and Coke, marveling over how he was so happy; Jeff loved life, was looking so forward to all that he could experience in the Army. His boundless enthusiasm and interest in life and everything was like warming herself by a blazing fire, on an icy-cold winter day. She wouldn't have to constantly walk on a tightrope with him, the way that she had with Mark. So different from how Mark kept changing the unwritten rules, would snap at her one day for cooking his scrambled eggs the wrong way and then laughing the next day over how the toast was burnt to a crisp. Why couldn't she have met a guy like Jeff, before she met Mark, or even Mason? It was so unfair of life in general, Carolina thought. Sad experience had made her so very wary now that she had Justin. She couldn't risk being wrong again about a man, not if it would endanger her son.

Waving a spatula in one hand, Jerry interrupted them, at last.

"Hey, the ribs are almost ready, are you two – hungry, yet?"

"Ravenous!" Jeff replied, with another one of those engaging grins. "But I'm more of a burger guy. Burgers dripping with melted cheese and grilled onions and bacon ... I did say that I liked bacon too, didn't I?"

"Alas, the first round of hamburger patties are a bit too overdone," Jerry confessed. "I lost all track of time, through messing about with the ribs. But if you like your hamburger sort of crunchy and all charcoal around the edges ..."

"It is truly meet, right, and salutary," Jeff intoned, solemnly, "That we should in all times and all places worship the Lord with burnt offering, and whole burnt offering ... but if that's the case, I'll let the dogs have the first round and I'll wait on the second. What about you, Carolina?"

"I'll try the spareribs," Carolina decided. "They smell absolutely amazing. I know Pam said you were really working on your secret-formula marinade and sauce."

"Great!" Jerry was enthused. "And try out Pam's German potato salad – it's different from the regular potato salad, you know, with mayo and hardboiled eggs and celery and all,"

"Like our grandma used to make," Jeff explained. "Gran-gran wrote out the recipe once. How can you object to a potato salad that has bacon in it?"

"Is that really a salad?" Carolina mused, and she and Jeff went on merrily discussing what constituted a salad as they joined the others around the picnic table. Did a salad have to have green vegetables in it to count, and if so, then what was lime Jell-O with cottage cheese and crushed pineapple in it, if not a salad? No very firm conclusion was reached, especially after throwing the question out to the rest of the party for discussion.

Carolina enjoyed herself thoroughly: she felt comfortable with Jeff, as comfortable as if being with him was like putting on a pair of good, broken-in shoes. Which was silly, as she had only just met him. She had the feeling though, that he was a bit like Mason in that they could talk about anything and everything. Well, nearly everything except that one important thing, which had eventually made marriage to a woman unendurable for Mason. When the fire in the grill burned down to a few ash-covered coals, the sun slipped low in the western sky, casting long shadows over the grass, and all of Pam and Jerry's guests had their fill of ice cream, Carolina pulled herself away from the party with some reluctance. It was so much fun, just being with Jeff... just being with friends, having merry and frivolous conversations about potato salad, and Jerry's secret ingredient marinade and barbeque sauce. With reluctance, she bid them all goodbye and drove home in the twilight, as the streetlights were just coming on.

When she parked in front of Mama and Daddy's house, she could hear the television inside, and little Justin giggling with Mama. Daddy was sitting on the front porch glider, smoking, and looking out into the evening shadows. With a pang, Carolina noted that he looked rather drawn and tired. In the morning, he was supposed to be heading out on another long road trip. So many responsibilities that Daddy carried on his shoulders now; for herself and Justin, Mama, and Poppa Lew – no wonder that he looked worn and weary. Carolina sat down on the glider next to him and kicked off her sandals.

"Nice time?" Daddy asked with a smile.

Carolina nodded. "Jerry and Pam fed us all until we were bursting, with his secret-formula ribs and burgers, and Pam did her grandmother's potato salad. Then we had home-made peach ice cream, and little waffle cookies. I don't think I'll be hungry again until Tuesday."

"Does sound like a nice time," Daddy reflected. They sat in comfortable silence for some minutes. Daddy lit another cigarette. "You want to tell me anything more, Caro? You wouldn't be sitting out here so long if you didn't have something else to say."

"I might just be enjoying your company," Carolina replied, mildly indignant, and Daddy smiled.

"Pull the other leg, Caro-sugar. There are bells attached to it and they play a tune."

"All right," Carolina confessed with a sigh. "There was this guy there. Jeff. Pam's brother, and we talked for the longest time. It was fun, Daddy. He was fun, and so nice. A real gentleman, and funny. I liked him, lots."

"And …?" Daddy prodded gently, and Carolina considered for a bit before replying.

"I … he told me he likes small children, kittens, and puppies. He's going to graduate from OSU in a couple of months. He's in ROTC and wants to be an Army officer and he will be once he graduates. I think that he liked me as much as I liked him. I'm … I'm interested. Daddy. I want to see him again and I'm certain that he wants to see me, since he asked if I was going to be free next Friday to go see a movie or something, before he heads back to Oklahoma. But …"

"But?" Daddy drew deeply on his cigarette, and then breathed out the mellow gray tobacco smoke, and waited patiently for Carolina's reply.

"I thought Mason was my best friend!" Carolina burst out, still baffled and resentful after all this time. "And I married him, because I liked him lots, and you and Mama liked him lots, too! You and Mama thought he was perfectly fine for me to go and hang out with, invite him to supper with us all summer long. But in the end, he didn't really like being married to a woman! Oh, he was sorry and all, but he was a mistake, and we only figured that out later. And then there was Mark, and I should have seen that he was a mistake too, he had red warning flags hung all over him! He practically glowed in the dark, he had so many warning flags! I married him because he sent me crazy and then I got pregnant with Justin; that's the only reason, I swear! And now I could possibly fall crazy-in-love with another guy who seems like he could be my best friend, but what if he is just another sweet-talking jerk and liar like Mark? What should I do, Daddy? Should I go out with Jeff, and let myself really begin to like him?"

"Ah. Let me think about this, for a moment." Daddy fell silent, considering everything as carefully as he always did, smoking the cigarette halfway to the filter, while Carolina waited. She had always trusted Daddy, even if he had misjudged Mason, initially. Finally, he continued. "Essentially you have been twice burnt romantically and scared to give your heart away again. Only sensible, especially since you have the baby to consider now, not just your own well-being. Because if you get involved with anyone, they must accept you and Justin as a package deal. Just like I did with your mother, Frankie, and you. And I never hesitated for a moment. But the problem for you, Caro, is that you are in a hurry; you want to know right this very minute if this Jeff is the one. You just can't rush into things now, the way you did with that boy at the tire dealership – what was his name?"

"Buster. Buster Williams," Carolina answered.

"Right. Young Mr. Williams," Daddy nodded and continued. "You're a grown-up now, and not an impatient teenager. Put aside the childish dreams of instant falling-in-love forever-ever-after. Take the time to get to know this Jeff, and for him to get to know you and Justin both. You can't possibly marry him before your divorce from Mark is finalized anyway," Daddy added with an air of practicality and a sideways glance. "So, you have a year. Use that year to better get to know Jeff. You have the time. Be an adult about him, Caro. There is too much at stake, otherwise. Take the time to really know each other and be certain-sure before you make any permanent decisions."

"Yes, Daddy - I will," Carolina replied, both humbled and reassured by Daddy's calm assessment. He was right, as he so often had been. "I suppose that if we do go out to a movie or something next Friday, that I should have him come here, so that you and Mama can meet him, as well?"

"Of course," Daddy replied, with a steely glint in his eye. "We'll want to be certain that he is good enough for our girl, and for the baby."

"That's what I thought," Carolina got up from the glider. Yes, Daddy did know best.

CHAPTER 11
JEFF

Carolina took Daddy's advice – to really get to know Jeff. He was on a long break between terms, before having to return to finish his classes at the university in Oklahoma, so that there was time enough for several supper dates. The first time he came to collect Carolina for a casual dinner and to see the new Kubrick film, he turned up almost an hour early.

Carolina hadn't even dressed yet, not that she was planning to wear anything really special, or do anything impressive with her hair and makeup, just to give Jeff the wrong sort of idea. She was still in jeans and a casual shirt, barefoot, when the doorbell of Mama and Daddy's house rang. Justin was in his highchair in the kitchen, and Carolina was trying to get him to eat mashed peas.

"Look baby, I know it's green and squishy, but it's good for you!" she pleaded, but Justin just puckered up his little face in a moue of disgust. The doorbell jingled just then, and she yelled. "Mama – can you get the door? I'm trying to get Justin to eat supper before I get dressed!"

Mama called from upstairs, "Sorry – I'm helping your grandfather; can you get it?"

Carolina sighed in exasperation and put aside the plate with several dabs of varying dull-colored mounds of indistinguishable mush on them. No wonder Justin wasn't enthused about eating any of them. She wouldn't have been keen on eating any of it either.

"Coming!" she called from the living room, as the doorbell rang again. She opened it, starting to say, "Is this impor – oh, you're early."

"Yeah, I know," Jeff replied, with a broad grin. "And I'm sorry to take you by surprise – but not much. Hope you don't mind. I wanted for sure to meet your parents ... and your son. You talked so much about him; I gather that he's a real charmer."

"He is," Carolina answered, distracted by a mild clattering sound from the kitchen – a spoon hitting the linoleum, it sounded like. "But he's being a very bad boy – he will not eat his peas!"

"Let me try," Jeff suggested. "I was very persuasive in getting Pam's boys to eat their food. I even got Jerry Junior and Robbie to eat fried liver."

"You must be terrifically persuasive!" Carolina marveled. Jeff grinned again.

"I am – I might even go into politics when I'm done with the Army. But I only got Jerry Junior and Robbie to eat the liver once," he added. "No luck the second time around."

"Well, it was fried liver. Blurgh! No wonder. But come and see if you can convince Justin to eat green peas," Carolina invited him with another sigh. "Except they really aren't green. They are sort of a nasty blaah green..."

"O.D. green," Jeff supplied. "You know – olive-drab, the color of Army blankets and much else. Let me see what miracles ol' Unca Jeff can do! Hiya, cowboy!" he added, as he followed Carolina into the kitchen, where Justin sat, with his face and bib liberally smeared, and kicking his feet against the rails of his highchair. Justin favored Jeff and his mother with a broad grin, showing off all four of his new teeth, upper and lower. "Let's say you take a bite of those nummy-nummy peas, partner! You know, they are really, really good, even though they might not look it." Jeff suggested in a wooing voice, as Carolina picked up the fallen spoon, and washed it under running hot water and dish soap several times.

"Sorry," she murmured, in response to Jeff's raised eyebrow. "I'm a nurse in training and Justin has medical issues. Absolute cleanliness is important!"

"Well, the floor doesn't look too bad," Jeff observed, genially, as Mama came into the kitchen, with a frown on her face which magically vanished as soon as she spotted Jeff.

"It's not!" Mama expostulated, indignantly. "We have to be absolutely sanitary, when it comes to Justin, what with his medical history ... hello – I guess I can assume that you are this Jeff who is taking my daughter out for the evening ..."

"Yes, but I'm trying to get her son to eat some of those luscious green peas, first," Jeff replied. "Mrs. Visser? Now if I were a perfect fraud, I might say that you hardly look old enough to be Carolina's mom ... but you look just like I had imagined you, from what Carolina said. Jeff Henry Foster, at your service."

"Just call me Marlene," Mama replied, regarding Jeff with wary interest, as Carolina held out the spoon. Jeff took it and crouched down on his knees, on an eye-level with Justin.

"Hello, Justin. I hear that you don't really want to eat your vegetables, but you know that you must, and they are really good, in spite of looking like squished green caterpillars. Now if I take a bite of squishy green caterpillars and I have, at summer camp, now you can certainly take a bite of your peas. How about that, Justin? Do we have a deal?"

Justin looked intrigued, although it was possibly just interest in a tall stranger with a friendly face: he gurgled some indistinguishable baby-babble, and when his mouth was open, Jeff swooped the spoon with a morsel of mushy green peas into it. Justin's eyes rounded in surprise, but he did swallow obediently. Jeff grinned in triumph, sideways at Carolina and Mama.

"It's all in the tone of voice," he explained. "And being a stranger. Kids being devious little critters, they have figured out exactly how far they can go with moms and dads and grandparents. But a complete stranger? Whoa, Nellie – that stranger might be able to whisper a magic spell and turn you into a frog! So, best not to take any chances. I love kids because they are so adorably gullible." Jeff aimed another spoonful of peas at Justin. "I've told some of my best made-up stories to my nephews. Like the time we all went to the coast, to Jerry's folks' summer home on San Padre ... and I told them that this big ol' set of refinery towers that we could see across the bay was a special factory to scrape the foam off the waves to made laundry detergent with."

Carolina giggled, in spite of herself. "You are so bad – did they believe it?"

"Hook, line and sinker," Jeff replied with satisfaction. And Carolina began to believe that Jeff was going to be someone special to her.

She let him finish feeding Justin his supper, then left him in the kitchen talking to Mama – he had made himself at home and Mama at ease, almost from the first moment. Most importantly, he treated Justin as if Justin were an important and worthy component of her life. But as Daddy had advised – not to hurry when it came to getting to know Jeff.

They never did get to the Stanley Kubrick movie, that evening. They went to the Barn Door on New Braunfels for steaks – Carolina opted for roast chicken – and fell into such deep conversation over anything and everything, that they suddenly looked up, after lingering over dessert, and realized that the dining room was all but empty. Yawning waitresses and busboys were clearing away the empty tables, lifting the chairs to balance upside down on their seats on the edge of the tables while they swept the floor underneath. It was already half-past ten, too late for a movie. Well, maybe the very last late showing, but that wouldn't get Carolina home much before midnight.

"Raincheck on the movie?" Jeff asked simply, and Carolina nodded, dazed with conversation and exhaustion. He drove her back to Mama and Daddy's house; they exchanged a quiet and comradely kiss in the front seat. There was still an amber light glowing in the living room window, and the flickering blue of a television screen.

"You don't have to see me in," Carolina said. "You must be exhausted. I know that I am."

"Next Friday, then?" Jeff asked. "We can double date with Pam and Jerry. How does supper and a dance at the Fort Sam Officer Club suit you? It's their wedding anniversary, so they want to celebrate."

"Of course, They want to see if I am good enough for you?" Carolina suggested, mischievously. "I'll tell Daddy – of course, he wants to meet you, and make certain that you are good enough for me."

"I already know you are good enough for me," Jeff kissed her briefly, again, just a quick peck on her cheek. "But I'll be early. Pam gave me your phone number – call you again, tomorrow?"

"Of course," Carolina suddenly felt that she could hardly tear herself away. But she had to – tomorrow arrived early, with a cranky child demanding attention, and then she must read ahead and study for a class on Monday. And anyway, she would talk to Jeff tomorrow, and next Friday, he could meet Daddy ...

She climbed up the stairs to the porch and let herself in with her own house key; surprised to see that Mama and Daddy both were still awake, watching the end titles for *The Name of the Game*, before switching over to Dick Cavett.

"We weren't expecting you so soon," Mama remarked, switching off the TV. Very obviously, they had just been killing time until Carolina arrived home. "We thought you'd be out until later, at least."

"We started talking over supper at the Barn Door, and lost all track of the time," Carolina flopped into a chair and kicked off her shoes. "Maybe next weekend, sometime. We're going to go out to supper at the Fort Sam O-Club on Friday, though, with Pam and Jerry to celebrate their anniversary. I do like him." She confessed, "And Justin behaved for him, and ate all of his peas and the rest of his supper, too. He has been a good boy, then? I think he liked Jeff, too. Did he go to bed on time and not fuss for another story?"

"He did," Mama beamed fondly. "I read him a chapter of *Wind in the Willows* and he dropped off to sleep just before we reached the end."

"Sheer boredom," Carolina commented, and Daddy snorted back a short laugh.

"An O-Club dance?" Mama reminisced, with a fond look at Daddy. "I first saw your Daddy at an O-Club dinner dance at Fort Bliss. My friend Betty was dating an officer stationed there, and she simply had to go see him before he shipped out to Korea. This was back a while, just during the Korean War. She married him, eventually. That was a lovely evening, but your Daddy didn't work up the nerve to talk to me until the next day by the pool. That's when I first thought that he might make good husband material."

"I suppose that I will have a chance to meet this paladin myself?" Daddy asked with a sideways glance at Carolina.

"Of course. He's going to call me tomorrow, and I'll tell him to be certain to come early so that he can meet you," Carolina replied firmly.

"I like him already, Adam," Mama nodded, a thoughtful expression on her still attractive, fine-boned face. "From what I have seen this afternoon. He was good with Justin; firm and kind ... and he was respectful with Caro. I think you will like him as well."

"Well, it's not our opinion which will matter in the end," Daddy said, as he got up with a grunt. "In the long run, it will be our girl's opinion." He sent a piercing glance towards Carolina. "Be absolutely certain of his fitness as a family man, Caro, and be certain that he will protect and care for you and Justin both. That's all that we ask."

"I will be, Daddy," Carolina replied, thinking that Daddy surely looked especially wearied, older than his years. "I'll be certain of him, if he is the one. I promise. Remember – twice burned, three times wary."

"That's our girl," Daddy replied, with a grin that momentarily made him look twenty years younger, like the handsome blond officer that Mama had fallen for at Fort Bliss, all those years ago.

• • •

As she had admitted, Carolina was twice burned and well-entitled to be wary, but in her heart, she was certain of Jeff. He was kind, funny and patient, never pressing her. When the spring break was over, and Jeff had to return to Oklahoma for his university classes, he often made a long drive back to San Antonio on weekends to spend time with her and Justin. It was a revelation to her, how good he was with her cherished and fragile baby boy, changing diapers, playing with him, reading him storybooks, carrying him around on his shoulders. He loved to take them both to the San Antonio Zoo, to admire the birds, animals, and monkeys in their cages, to walk through the dim-lit aquarium building and admire the fishes in their tanks.

"He is so considerate of you, Caro," Mama marveled. "Always holding your hand, watching you – so interested in everything that you are doing. And the baby, too. I swear, he has taught Justin twenty new words in one weekend alone!"

In between those weekend trips, he called her on the phone almost every evening. By the time that he graduated in June, Carolina was absolutely certain that Jeff was her princely knight in shining armor. As he had told her, he would be commissioned as a second lieutenant; and as he had also predicted, he was given orders for Vietnam. He was assigned to the 2nd Armor Division, headquartered at Fort Hood, a half a day drive north from San Antonio. She had a color picture of him in his Army uniform, looking so solemn and serious, not like the laughing and humorous Jeff that she had come to love over the eventful spring of 1968. He had thirty-five days of leave before reporting, and he planned to spend every day of it with Carolina and Justin, even as it seemed that the world was burning to ashes around them. Carolina even took a month away from nursing, so they could be together.

"Let's not talk about Vietnam," she said, on the first day. "I don't even want to think about it. I just want to be in the here and now and pretend that this month will never end."

"Agreed," Jeff nodded. "We'll go out to supper and the movies now and again, but we spend the days with Justin. We do family things, for practice. Darling Caro, I wish that your divorce was final this very minute, then we could get married today."

"Not until fall," Carolina admitted regretfully, and Jeff grinned.

"OK, then – perfect, I'll have R&R leave halfway through my tour, in January next year. We can meet up in Hawaii and get married and spend the honeymoon there. Wouldn't that be fantastic? A whole week in a tropical paradise; sand and surf and Mai Tai drinks in cocoanut shells, as we watch the hula girls and the fire-jugglers. What do you say, Caro? How would you like to be the wife of a US senator?"

"Only if you are the senator," Carolina replied, demurely. Jeff had such a way of teasing her. "But yes. Let's get married when you are on R&R."

"It's a promise then, Mrs. Senator Foster," Jeff raised her hand to his lips and kissed it reverently. He twisted his class ring off his hand and pressed it into her palm. "There you go. A ring to bind a promise with. Sorry it's not one of those gold and diamond solitaire things, like in the magazine ads, but I'm only a poor second louie, and must make do."

"It's too big for my hand," Caro giggled. "I'll wear it on a chain around my neck, and not take it off, ever. Unless I have to have an X-ray taken of myself. Is that a bargain?"

"It is," Jeff agreed fervently, and that set the tone of the month that followed. It seemed to Carolina long afterward that the song *Age of Aquarius* by the pop group Fifth Dimension was on the radio incessantly during that enchanted, blissful, haunted month. *Then peace will guide the planets, and love will steer the stars.* But all the time, men were dying in Vietnam; a constant trickle of names listed in the newspaper, a trickle which occasionally widened to a gusher, given the press of operations in retaliation for the Tet offensive earlier in the year.

The night before Jeff left to drive back to Fort Hood to report in, Carolina cried. She cried all the next day after he left, imagining him driving through the Hill Country, past the rocky hills and meadows starred with oak trees and wandering cattle, farther and farther away from her, from Justin. He did call her from a payphone in the officer's transient quarters to let her know that he had arrived safely.

"I miss the sound of your voice already," Carolina sobbed into the phone. From the tone of his voice when he answered, she knew that he was doing his best to cheer her up.

"I know what I'll do, Caro. I'll buy one of those little portable tape recorders at the PX tomorrow, and I'll tape letters for you. You do the same – and yes, even see if you can get Justin to talk into it. I want him to get used to calling me 'Daddy.'"

"I will, I will," Carolina managed to say, as she forced herself to conquer her emotions. She must, she must be brave for him, not be a wet sponge, spilling salt tears. But still – how could she endure months of this, being without Jeff, knowing that he would almost certainly be in danger?

. . .

In the end, she managed to be brave, keep her composure – even laugh at silly jokes that the other nursing students made, and not to break down every time someone casually asked after Jeff. She focused on her work, her classes, and Justin – and lived for the letters which arrived from him every few days. The best letters were the ones with a slender cassette tape enclosed.

She could listen to them with her eyes closed, and pretend that he was in the same room, for he talked to her like he was there. Although sometimes she could detect a strain in his voice, he talked about anything and everything else but the war: about curious things that he saw, about how beautiful the mountains appeared rising like cliffs from the tangled jungle at their feet, like an ancient Chinese drawing, of morning mist twining through luxurious stands of rhododendrons in the craggy backcountry, of old French colonial mansions crumbling away at the center of ruined plantations. He told her about funny things that his soldiers had said and silly things they had done, or things they had forgotten to do, about strange meals in the mess tent – never anything about mud and blood and danger. He was promoted during that time to the rank of first lieutenant. Best of all, he talked about their future, the happy future they would have as a family, his ambition to get into politics and eventually serve as a US senator. She sent him letters, and recorded Justin saying a few words – after much encouragement. She and Mama baked cookies to send to Jeff – the cookies that he liked best and would travel well in the mail, sent mailed small treats and gifts. And best of all, just after Christmas, a letter came saying that he had R&R leave scheduled for the month of January, a letter which had the date that his leave there would begin. The letter also contained detailed instructions as to where she should go, once she got to Hawaii – to Fort DeRussy, the Army recreation center on Waikiki Beach, and to check in at the Visiting Officer's Quarters.

"It's settled, then," she confided tremulously to Mama and Daddy. "We're going to get married there and then spend our honeymoon in Hawaii. I'm nervous…"

"About marrying?" Daddy suggested with a quirk to his lips which suggested a half-smile.

"Daddy! No, not getting married – about flying! I've never flown before!"

"Piece of cake, Caro honey, piece of cake. It will be a marvelous experience," Daddy replied, and the smile broke out into an open grin. "Besides, there is no way to get from the West Coast to Hawaii without swimming, or a long ride in a boat. Flying will be shorter and more efficient, especially as you have no time to spare."

"No, I haven't," Carolina took a deep breath. "Time to spare, that is. Can you all look after Justin, while I'm away?"

"You know that we will, Caro," Mama swiftly reassured her, while Carolina looked at the letter and wondered at how fortunate she had been, to meet Jeff, her gallant shining knight, who treated her like a princess and loved little Justin. It would be all right now. It would be perfect.

. . .

It was. She was nervous to the point that her teeth almost chattered, when that first flight took off from San Antonio for Dallas and the first stopover. That was the first leg of the journey, with United Airways a DC-8 in white, red, and blue livery. From Dallas to Los Angeles, then on to Honolulu. It would take more than twenty hours, almost a whole day, to get to Hawaii. The stewardesses, so very mod in their orange and cream dresses, accessorized with kicky white go-go boots and white gloves, were almost sisterly in their consideration of her, when she told them that she was on her way to Hawaii to marry her fiancée, on leave from Vietnam. When they landed in Los Angeles in late afternoon, one of the stewardesses told Carolina to wait for her at the boarding gate until everyone had deplaned, and she would take Carolina to the departure gate for the flight to Hawaii, just to be certain that she was at the right gate. Carolina, dazed by exhaustion through having gotten up so early for that first early morning connection to Dallas, was terribly grateful for that and said so.

The stewardess grinned. "It's our playground, Miss Visser. We know all the turns and twists. If you want, you might have time to get late lunch at the space-age restaurant in the Theme Building at the center of the parking lot. It looks like a gigantic concrete spider on four legs, and the view of the whole airport from the observation deck is fantastic. But there is also a perfectly nice restaurant and a rest lounge in the United Terminal. I wouldn't bother with the

Theme Building, though. You'll have supper on the flight to Hawaii first thing after takeoff, then they'll turn off the cabin lights so everyone can get some sleep. You'll be landing in Honolulu about mid-morning. From there, you should be able to get a taxi to the Army post."

"That's what my fiancée told me," Carolina agreed, pleased to have what Jeff had written confirmed by someone who also knew the ropes. She was too nervous to be really hungry and didn't want to risk missing the call for the flight to Honolulu. To her mild surprise, she did fall asleep after a marvelous supper served on a tray, dispensed by yet another one of the stylishly clad stewardesses, although the wine that came with supper might have had something to do with it. She settled against a pillow, propped against the side of her seat, and took a last glimpse out of the oval window at a sky already gone dark, like purple velvet and sprinkled with silver stars, silver stars like tiny sequins. Far below, the ocean surface was finely wrinkled like black crepe satin. She went to sleep, soothed by the constant drone of the four powerful engines, confident that every minute, every mile, was bringing her closer to Jeff.

• • •

When she woke up, brilliant sunshine poured through the windows. The captain, on the cabin loudspeaker was saying that they were an hour out from Honolulu. She raised the window shade and looked out – a dazzle of sunshine so bright and fierce that it practically blinded her. Down below, the sea was now dark blue, spotted with darker shadows of clouds, and the tiny shadow of the aircraft itself, dancing over the water. Her heart pounded with anticipation – soon, very soon.

She had no appetite for the breakfast dispensed by the stewardesses, but the glass of pineapple juice was sweet and tart, and very welcome. Soon after that, the captain announced that they were beginning the descent over the island of Oahu. Carolina practically glued herself to the window, ecstatic when she spotted the green jewel of the island, fringed in concentric rings of white surf and white sand beaches. At first Oahu appeared as a distant green dot, growing larger and closer, more distinct, as the aircraft dropped. Lower, lower, the precipitous mountain ridge, steep and sharp angles clothed in green, the hollow of Diamond Head clear; a perfect round pockmark on the landscape, as the aircraft seemed to pivot on one wing, dropping even more. Now Carolina could make out buildings, tiny like Monopoly houses, embedded among more greenery, as the aircraft pivoted steeply again. She could look down at a sweep of blue bay, dotted with ships, and a white structure like a shoebox, anchored in the water over the darker outline of a ship sunk just beneath the surface.

"To your left, you will see Pearl Harbor, and the Arizona Memorial," the pilot announced, "We will be landing in approximately ten minutes, so please return to your seats if you have not already done so and fasten your seatbelts."

Lower, lower ... something seemed to bump, and what had been an aerial view suddenly flattened and transformed into landscape. With a screech and a squeal of landing gear tires against concrete, the airplane slowed to a slow roll, hardly faster than a man could walk. There were no available bridges to the terminal from the aircraft, as there had been for the flight to Los Angeles – just two rolling ramps, snugged up to the front and rear doors. She took up her carry-on bag and her purse, and walked out into bright sunshine, and down the steps, following the straggling line of other passengers. Several women in Hawaiian dancer costumes, with armfuls of colorful flower garlands looped over their arms greeted them in turn.

"Alo-ha – welcome to Hawaii!" they chanted, and Carolina lowered her head so that one of the women could drape a flower lei around her neck. It smelled gorgeous.

She followed the other passengers into the terminal. Oh, yes; luggage retrieval. Her big suitcase which had been tagged in San

Antonio, loaded into the baggage hold and followed her faithfully through the two changes. The suitcase held a week's worth of clothing, bright casual clothing suitable for a tropical holiday, including a new bathing suit. There was a taxi stand outside the baggage retrieval counter, a line of yellow cabs lined up in a row at the curb. They seemed very orderly about it. The driver of the first cab in line helpfully took the heavy suitcase and slung it into the trunk as if it hardly weighed anything.

"Fort DeRussy," she ventured tremulously, and the driver grinned, a flash of strong white teeth in his brown face as he opened the door for her. "I'm to meet my fiancée there. He's on leave from Vietnam."

"Yes, ma'am!"

She settled herself on the seat, and the friendly driver got behind the wheel, asking as he pulled away from the taxi rank if she had ever been to Hawaii before.

"I haven't – but it is so beautiful!" Carolina answered – and it was. Blue, blue skies, scattered with creamy white clouds piled up in scattered formations, and an equally blue ocean and sugar-white sand beaches, glimpsed here and there, between buildings. Palm trees and tropical flowers were everywhere. Carolina wished that her parents and Justin could have been with her, to relish the beauty of it all. The genial driver pointed out landmarks as he drove, gesturing with one hand, pointing out the tower at the harbor which used to welcome the cruise ships that regularly brought visitors in the early days, the state capitol building, across from the only royal palace in the United States, the road that led up the eminence called the Punchbowl, where the military memorial and cemetery were, and the Ala Wai Canal, which had been built early in the century to drain the swampy area along the coast where the beach resorts and Fort DeRussy now were situated. The taxi driver carried her suitcase into the lobby of the VOQ, accepted the fare and a generous tip, and wished her a pleasant stay in Hawaii. She barely heard his words, as she was looking everywhere for Jeff. Surely, he would stand out, with his height and red hair, but it was mostly women crowding the lobby. She finally got to the desk, and asked the receptionist where Jeff was. The receptionist was a comfortable-looking middle-aged woman with an air of confidence about her.

"He was supposed to meet me here, he sent me the date in his letter," Carolina's voice wobbled with disappointment and apprehension. "I just got here, all the way from San Antonio, Texas. Jeff Foster. First Lieutenant Foster, on R&R leave from Vietnam. We're supposed to be married here."

"Lieutenant Foster?" The receptionist glanced down at a list in front of her. "No, not here today. Sorry, sweetie. Most likely on one of the buses from Hickam tomorrow morning, and there won't be any more arriving today - there's quite a crowd waiting for their men, so you aren't alone. But I can check you into a room, so you can have a good rest and freshen up. If he said he would be here, he will be here." She added kindly. "But MAC - you know, Military Airlift Command is like that - sometimes things are out of control, especially when it comes to flights in and out. Sometimes they say that MAC really stands for 'Maybe Airplane Come'."

Carolina accepted a key to a room, still confused and only partially relieved by having a place to stay and wait for Jeff. "What time are the buses from Hickam expected?"

"Usually about 10AM every morning," the woman replied, "It all depends on the weather, and the MAC flight arriving on time."

Well, that was reassuring. Carolina had been waiting for a reunion with Jeff for six months. She could wait another day, at least. At least, she had a place to stay while she waited.

In the morning, she joined the crowd of women waiting in the lobby, and spilling out onto the terrace and lawn outside, all wondering when the buses with their men would arrive. Some of the women carried small babies or led their older children by the hand. It was all terribly confusing. Someone was making an announcement on a public address speaker. Carolina couldn't hear the words. Was it about the buses from Hickam AFB arriving? The tension ratcheted up to unbearable levels, and the crowd of women and children began moving ... but to where? Were they being directed to where the buses would arrive? Oh, no – the crowd moved sluggishly, towards another doorway, a large double door, which opened into a big, echoing room, some kind of assembly or conference room, with a wooden podium at the front, in front of rows of folding chairs. There weren't enough chairs for the larger-than-expected crowd.

A large man in Army green with a lot of ribbons on his chest and silver eagles on his collar got up before the podium and began speaking. The microphone kept cutting out, and Carolina was standing at the back of the room, so she missed most of what he was saying. It sounded like some kind of briefing for the wives; telling them to expect that their men might be changed through their experiences, since they had seen them last, urging the women to be patient and understanding... well, of course they would! The scenes of war on the nightly news were horrifying enough to viewers! To men who had experienced them, it must have been unimaginable. Carolina wondered why the colonel was belaboring the obvious, but then, some of the wives looked very young, almost as young as herself. Finally, and to her vast relief, the officer stopped speaking. Obviously, the briefing was concluded. Carolina was one of the first in the surge for the doors, and to join the line of women and their children outside, under the swaying palm trees, with the glittering blue ocean beyond.

"They're here!" someone called, in excitement, as the first in a line of blue military buses drew into the Fort DeRussy grounds and into the half-circle driveway where the crowd of women waited impatiently. The woman standing next to Carolina in line drew in her breath and held it, as the first bus rumbled to a halt, and the folding doors opened. Men burst forth from the bus, first one, then the other, running towards their wives and families, meeting in a fierce embrace, with tears and exclamations. Carolina looked for

Jeff, frantic with worry – what if he were not on this bus, this day? She didn't think she could endure another day of tension and worry.

"There he is! Pete!" gasped the woman next to her as a burly sergeant emerged from the bus and stood, dazedly looking around. The woman crumpled in a dead faint, and Pete caught her in his arms before she hit the ground.

Women locked their husbands in a passionate embrace, cried, and murmured incoherent endearments. Small children clung to their daddy's legs, or even smaller ones howled in protest at being handled by a relative stranger. And where was Jeff? A sense of panic began to rise; Carolina was certain that she would begin to cry hysterically, if he didn't appear … and then, miraculously, there he was. Tall, and red-haired, the silver lieutenant's bars on his shoulders, stepping from the second bus and looking around for her. He had a haunted, wary look in his eyes, lines of tension grooved under them, but all that didn't matter, it didn't matter a bit, because he was there, and she was there, and everything was going to be all right.

CHAPTER 12
LOVE AND THE LOSS THEREOF

Carolina clung to Jeff as if she would never let go, feeling his arms around her. It seemed that he was leaner, harder. She buried her face in the front of his military tunic. When she could speak again, she gasped,

"I was so worried when you didn't show up, yesterday. All that they would tell me was that you might be on the bus this morning, but they couldn't tell me for certain one way or the other."

"Never mind, Caro, I'm here now, and that's all that matters," Jeff replied, and his embrace of her finally loosened, although he kept an arm around her shoulders, as if he couldn't bear not to be in physical contact with her. "We have a whole seven days together, so we'll make the most of them. And I have plans to have the most fun here, in this tropical wonderland. We'll eat steaks, and learn how to surf, and listen to Don Ho and his group sing at his nightclub, and beachcomb, looking for shells and driftwood … didn't you tell me once, about looking for those Japanese glass fishing floats? D'you suppose any of them have drifted across the Pacific from Japan to Waikiki …" he drew her to him and kissed her, with almost frantic urgency. "And don't forget that our first order of business is to get married. Let's get your suitcase. I made a reservation at the Outrigger Hotel; Let's catch a taxi. It's right on the beach…"

"OK," Carolina replied. Everything was going to be all right now. She was tranquil. And they had seven days, seven days of holiday in this lush tropical paradise.

They walked down to the white sand beach, away from the crowds, the voices, the men and their wives and children. The two of them passed over a green lawn shaded and fringed by palm trees, their leaves rustling in the constant sea breeze, and went down to the white sand beach. They walked past an enormous concrete buttress on the very edge of Fort DeRussy – a surprisingly ugly structure for so lovely a place.

"Is that the fort that this place is named after?" Carolina asked, idly, and Jeff laughed.

"No ... well sort, of. It's the Randolph Battery. It's part of the coastal defenses, built at enormous cost to the military establishment, sometime around the turn of the century. It's the support structure for an enormous pair of guns – fourteen-inchers. That means," Jeff explained, in a professorial voice, "That they fired ammunition that measured fourteen inches across."

"Golly," commented Carolina. "That must have made a horrendous bang when they were fired." She kicked off her sandals, to walk barefoot in the sand, and Jeff did the same, tucking his socks and boots into the olive-drab green canvas B-4 bag that he slung over his shoulder.

"It certainly did," Jeff chuckled in deep amusement. "The one time they did fire for effect, just after Pearl Harbor, sometime in 1942 as part of a defense exercise, the concussion broke every single glass window for about half a mile around. The Army had to pay damages, of course, and the expense was so horrendous that they never did that again. Supposedly, they tried to demolish the battery after that war, but the concrete was too thick, and the thing was too well-built. Best they could do was to plant ivy, I guess." The gentle surf washed in and out, and the scent of frangipani and plumeria teased over the fresh smell of salt water and pungent drying seaweed. There was a scattering of early sunbathers, their towels spread out on the beach, and another scattering of swimmers on the low platform anchored a little way offshore. The waves broke and scattered with a gentle hissing sound, spreading a thin layer of foam, and then retreating, until the next wave broke in a froth, which reminded Carolina of how Jeff had pranked his nephews, telling them that the oil refinery towers were a factory scraping foam off the waves and manufacturing it into detergent.

The long white sand beach described a gentle curve ahead of them; the blue and ever-moving ocean on one hand, the green jungle of the shore on the other, interspersed with hotels and spanking-new high-rise buildings. The shapes of the glass-walled high-rise hotels sent shadows lying across the beach, as the sun rose. Ahead of them, the craggy green bulk of Diamond Head crouched like an enormous resting lion, and the sky arched overhead, a faultless blue bowl, dotted with pure and cotton-white clouds. They strolled past the old-fashioned sugar-pink sprawl of the Royal Hawaiian, set in its own grove of palm trees and lush gardens. The Outrigger Hotel, in contrast, was tall, oblong and farther down the beach, a severe modern stack of a building with balconies all across every floor, like a chest of drawers with all the drawers pulled out.

"How is Justin doing, since your last letter?" Jeff asked, after a long and restful moment of silence. "And your family – your mom and dad?"

"Justin was sick again. I think I wrote you about that." Carolina answered with a sad sigh. "He is constantly developing pneumonia since he tends to aspirate stuff into his lungs. But Mama and Daddy are looking after him as carefully as I would."

"Another good reason to get married," Jeff said, firmly, as they walked up the steps to the beach-front side of the Outrigger. "As soon as I get back to my duty station, I'll put in the paperwork to adopt him. That way, his medical care is assured at Brooke Army Medical. How's everyone else?"

"Mama is as gorgeous as ever," Carolina reported. "But Daddy looks tired. I think his job is wearing on him, too much. But whenever I ask, he says that he is all right. Poppa Lew ... well, he is old and failing. Frankie and Valerie are fine. She's just found out that she is pregnant. About two months along. Boy or girl, it will be a summer baby."

"I guess I'll get to meet the little toddler when I get home," Jeff looked ridiculously pleased. "I can hardly wait! It'll be good for Justin to have a little cousin. Someone to get into trouble with. I like to think about all that, Caro – all that normal stuff. Babies and kids. You and I and Justin; thinking about the real world helps keeps me sane, with all the madness going on."

"Is it ..." Carolina hesitated, before plunging ahead. "Is it as bad as it looks in the TV news?"

"Worse," Jeff replied grimly. "So much worse. But I don't want to think or talk about Vietnam now. I just want to get settled into our hotel room, enjoy our love together, get a good stiff drink, and go lay out in the sun for the rest of the day. Although tomorrow morning, we ought to go shopping for wedding rings. One of my guys who came back from R&R last month says there's a big shopping center between Ala Moana and Kapiolani where you can get just about anything in the world. Reckon we'll go there and look for a jeweler or something. But tomorrow," he added, as he held the door open for Carolina. "Today, we rest. Tomorrow, we recreate!"

And so, they did; a leisurely lunch, some drinks on the terrace and an afternoon sunning on the beach and Carolina felt the tension of the last few months and days all magically drain away. They were together, in the morning they would go buy wedding rings and find the justice of the peace and get married. Third time is the charm, she reminded herself.

As it turned out, the best place they could find for plain gold wedding bands was at the Sears store, at the shopping center a brief taxi ride away from the Outrigger.

"I suppose that we could find nicer ones, if we spent more time looking," Carolina confessed, regretfully, as they came out of the shopping center, and looked to flag down a taxi. "But I am fine with anything we can get, just as long as you give it to me."

"I'll buy nicer ones when I get back to the States," Jeff promised, as they spotted a cruising yellow cab at the end of the block. Just as he stepped to the edge of the sidewalk to wave down the cab, another car passing on the opposite side of the street backfired, with a sound like a pistol shot, which reverberated among the tall buildings along the avenue.

Jeff's reaction was instantaneous; he grabbed Carolina and violently pulled her down with him, huddling behind the bulk of a big concrete planter. Carolina felt the hammering of his heart against her cheek, the jerk and gasp of his breath as he held her fast, practically squashing her between his body and the planter.

When she could speak again, she exclaimed, "Jeff! It was just a car – backfiring! What is ..." and she almost said '*what is the matter with you*' but realized exactly what was the matter. In his mind, Jeff was still in a war zone, where instant reactions counted, where such a reaction could save a life. "It's OK - we're OK. Let me up. We're OK. Did that taxi see us ... never mind, we'll get the next one. We're OK," she repeated, as Jeff climbed slowly to his feet, and lifted her with one arm to stand with him. She was mildly embarrassed – what would everyone looking at them think? Had anyone noticed at all? There were half a dozen pedestrians along Ala Moana, and at least that many automobiles.

"Yes, we're OK," Jeff replied, somewhat distantly, as if his mind were somewhere else altogether. But in a few seconds, he seemed to have recovered presence and composure, as he flagged down another taxi. "We're getting married, remember? City Hall, then. I guess that's where we find the justice of the peace in these parts." He added to the taxi driver, who was holding the door for them.

"For certain, boss," the taxi driver grinned at them. When he heard that they planned on getting married, he drove around the next corner and whistled to a flower seller, who brought up two leis of fragrant plumeria blossoms. Both the taxi driver and the flower seller refused payment for them, the taxi driver saying expansively, "He is my second cousin, and owes me a favor, so my gift, OK?"

"OK," Jeff acknowledged, although when they were dropped off on a tree-lined street in front of a vaguely Spanish-looking building, with a red tile roof and lattices and galleries, he did give a generous extra tip to the driver. "Ready to take the plunge, Mrs.-soon-to-be Foster?"

"Always," Carolina replied firmly.

. . .

They called their families from the Outrigger when they returned that afternoon. It was already late in the evening for Mama and Daddy, and for Jeff's sister Pam, since San Antonio was five hours ahead of Honolulu. When they were done talking on the telephone, Jeff flung himself face-up on the bed, and bounced in the middle of it several times. His old merry grin was nearly back to what it was when Carolina first met him at Pam and Jerry's house.

"Mission accomplished!" he exclaimed. "Mrs. Foster, are we ready now for some serious and heart-to-heart rest and recreation?"

"I am – and we are!" Carolina threw herself down on the bed beside him – it was a king-sized one, so there was plenty of room and lots of bounce in the box springs.

. . .

They made the most of that week, in that sun-drenched city of tropical flowers and swaying palm trees. They swam every day – sometimes first thing in the morning, even before breakfast – running barefoot across the beach into the ocean right at the Outrigger's door, glorying in the clean, salt-smelling surf, the breeze that rustled the palm leaves overhead, and the distant view of Diamond Head, like a sleeping lion. Carolina tanned to a fair golden brown, and her hair blond hair glistened with golden from the sun.

Sometimes they went sightseeing in the afternoon; there was a lavishly landscaped international market on the other side of the Outrigger, of garden-planted alleyways around a huge, many-trunked banyan tree with a treehouse in it. Clusters of artful little buildings representing little villages of Japan, Korea, China, and the South Seas had been built and decorated in the quaint style of their country of origin, all scattered among the garden, offering art, keepsakes, and souvenirs of every kind, all among the lively bars, and restaurants. Carolina was especially enchanted to discover the Japanese village, where the bits and bobs for sale reminded her piercingly of her early childhood in Okinawa. Jeff bought the loudest and most colorful Hawaiian shirt that he could find, the fabric printed with garish hibiscus flowers, surfboards, palm trees and maps of the Hawaiian Islands and proudly wore it everywhere, although Carolina told him that he was looking so much a tourist that everyone would take advantage.

"As if we don't know tourists, living in San Antonio!" he jeered, and Carolina held any further comment. She loved him too much, and he was having so much fun, flaunting that ghastly rayon souvenir shirt, as if everything that he had seen and experienced in Vietnam was just a fleeting bad dream.

They went to a traditional Hawaiian luau, a feast of whole barbequed pig and other local Hawaiian delicacies, arranged by the Outrigger Hotel for guests on the beach, in the evening just after the sun set in a spectacular display of red, purple, and gold. The luau featured entertainment put on by costumed girl dancers in traditional skirts made of long ti leaves stitched to a waistband, and their male counterparts juggling lit torches ... it was all very touristic, but Carolina and Jeff enjoyed it all enormously. Nothing could be finer, than to sit on woven rush mats, watching the fire-jugglers, while the fresh sea breeze caressed them, and the lights of the city prickled into life, all the way along the long curve of that sugar-sand beach, until they reached the dark lion-shape of Diamond Head. Carolina and Jeff loved the roast pork that was the main dish, and the sweet coconut pudding that was dessert, but confessed later to be dubious about poi... basically the local taro-root porridge.

"It looks like purple library paste!" Jeff whispered to Carolina after it was offered to them. She ate a bite of it, more to be polite than anything else, and just barely refrained from making a disgusted face.

"Utterly tasteless, and more like cream of wheat," she whispered back. "I think it must be something like oatmeal. You must have been fed it from earliest childhood to have any relish for the stuff at all."

And that was their holiday, their idyll in paradise; a riot of sensations, scents of perfumed gardens, the sight of a glorious sunset from the balcony of their room, a glory of colors painting the clouds and sky, the ever-moving Pacific ocean surf, a susurration of the waves and the wind in the palm trees, a swift tropical storm shedding rain for a few sparkling moments and leaving a rainbow arched along the sky as a promise of hope; a whisper of sound as they fell to sleep every night in each other's arms.

Carolina didn't want it to ever end.

But it did – it had to end, for they only had seven days – seven precious days. On that last morning, as they dressed silently and packed away what they had brought with them, Carolina wished for two contradictory things; that it would either go on forever, or that this day could be done and over. She wished that the heartbreaking farewells could be finished, and she could miraculously be back in San Antonio. A knife to swiftly cut off the pain of parting. The taxi driver who appeared to take them to the airport – for their separate flights were scheduled to depart within forty minutes of each other – turned out to be the same driver who had driven her from the airport to Fort DeRussy.

"Hey, miss – your husband, now?" He beamed as though he had been solely responsible for their meeting and marriage.

"Yes," Carolina replied, as Jeff finished slinging her suitcase and his B-4 bag into the trunk. "We married – and today we promised each other that we could come back as often as we could and spend our wedding anniversaries in Hawaii."

"That's good!" he beamed all over his blunt features. "Aloha and see you then, OK? A good marriage and many happy children!"

"Aloha," Carolina replied, as that seemed to be the expected response. She and Jeff held hands without speaking, during the short ride to the airport, the airport on the edge of the military bases clustered around the margins of Pearl Harbor. He was headed back to the horrors and violence of the war in Vietnam. Now and again, Carolina wondered if it was deliberately cruel of the Army to have offered that brief break from bloody war to their soldiers. As the taxi drew up in front of the terminal, Carolina leaned her head against Jeff's shoulder.

"I'll count the days, until you rotate out of that place and come home."

"No, don't count the days like a short timer," Jeff replied. "It just makes the tour seem longer. Count down the weeks – that goes much faster."

They checked their bags, got the information about their flights, and Carolina walked with Jeff to the gate where his flight would depart, some forty minutes before hers, if everything ran to schedule. There was nothing much left to say, so they didn't say anything. All the words that would have been had already been said. She sat with him, still holding hands, in the waiting area, until his flight was called for final boarding, the hands with their cheap wedding rings from Sears on them clasping each other.

Finally, he took his hand from hers, hugged her tight and said, "Give Justin a hug for me, OK, Caro? See you real soon," and then whispered in her ear *"Don't worry, everything will be OK."*

Then he was gone from her, striding purposefully down the air bridge to his flight, a tall red-headed man in Army green. He turned and smiled at her, just that once, and Carolina kissed the tips of her fingers and blew on them – but then he had turned and gone, out of sight.

The tropical idyll was done. Now it was back to grim and grinding reality. But she did take his advice, to just count the weeks until he returned to her arms.

• • •

She went home to a quiet house – Poppa Lew was failing. He had never quite gotten over losing Granny Margo. It seemed that he just drifted away from life. Several weeks after returning from Hawaii, Poppa Lew was gone. Frankie was heartbroken, of course. He and Valerie had hoped that he would live long enough to see their baby born and baptized.

Barely five months after returning to San Antonio, Carolina graduated from the nursing program, and began working the day shift, from 7 AM to 3 PM at the Baptist Hospital downtown – inordinately proud of having completed the one plan she had started, intending to provide for Justin. Jeff was proud of her too. He said so in his latest letter. She had sent him a small snapshot of her in her white uniform and nurses' cap. In the letter that he wrote thanking her for it, he claimed that he carried it next to his heart. He also wrote that he had been offered a desk job for the last month of his tour of duty – but had turned it down. *It's only right,* he wrote – *I wouldn't feel right about leaving my guys and sitting all safe and comfortable in the rear with the gear. That's not how I want them to think of me.* Carolina begged him to accept the desk job in her next letter: *I want to know that you are safe, my darling husband,* she wrote. *I couldn't bear it if anything awful happened to you.*

Several nights after sending that letter, Carolina woke – or thought she woke in the middle of the night thinking that there was someone in the room with her; a white filmy shape against the dark wall, a shape with the shadowy likeness of Jeff, and his voice saying, "Don't worry, everything will be OK."

Everything would be OK; the same words that Jeff had said as he went to catch his flight, his parting words to her in Hawaii.

Comforted and reassured, Carolina closed her eyes – or thought she closed her eyes, and obediently went back to sleep. In the morning, she wondered if it were a premonition; a promise from Jeff that everything would be OK, that he would safely return, and they could be a real family with Justin, who was two years old now and already talking very well. Two days later, though, Justin was wheezing when he breathed, and his little face was flushed. Carolina's heart sank – this threatened another round of pneumonia for her darling boy.

"I'm going to take his temperature," Carolina said to Mama that afternoon when she came home from work, after listening to her son's labored breathing, and feeling his forehead. "He feels hot … all right, Baby Boy. Listen, put this under your tongue. That's right," she added as Justin obediently held the thermometer in his mouth. Poor little boy, he was quite accustomed to indignities such as having his temperature taken. While she waited, she murmured to Mama, "If he is still running a fever in the morning, I'll take him to the pediatric clinic at Brooke Army Medical. We can't risk him developing pneumonia, not now."

"No, certainly not." Mama agreed. "And your father can drive you, since he'll be home tomorrow."

They put Justin to bed early; he was cranky at supper and didn't have much interest in food. Carolina dosed him with sweet-tasting liquid baby aspirin and went to bed early herself. Mornings came early for a working nurse, and she would have to clock in by 6:45 for her regular shift, if Justin was indeed better.

He wasn't. He was wheezing even more when she woke up to the sound of the alarm at five in the morning. Carolina sighed and gave him a bit more aspirin. She called the hospital to let the ward supervisor know that she needed to take a day off to take her son to the base pediatric clinic. Carolina had a good rapport with her bosses and the other nurses at the hospital. She had been an exemplary nurse in her time there, and they all knew of poor little Justin's medical issues.

Well, at least she would be able to get a little more sleep, if she didn't have to go to work. The clinic at Brooke Army Medical Center saw walk-in patients beginning at nine. She would be there with Justin as soon as they opened the doors. With her marriage to Jeff, and Jeff applying to adopt Justin as his son, little Justin had care at the military hospital as a dependent of an active-duty soldier, a circumstance which relieved Carolina's worries on that score no end. Carolina crawled back into bed and fell asleep, the sleep of exhaustion, having learned to take her rest when she could get it.

It was early summer; the windows of Mama and Daddy's house stood open to invite the relatively cooler air of night to come inside. The mild noise from the street and from the neighbors' households also came inside as well. The gentle music of suburbia: a dog barking in a back yard three houses away, the distant wail of a fire or police vehicle, the boy on a bicycle with a basket full of papers and his bike brakes squealing, the thump of a thrown newspaper hitting porch or walkway ... and the sound of a car engine, humming slowly down the street and halting before Mama and Daddy's house, in sudden silence. Car doors slamming closed, the sound of footsteps on the walkway.

Carolina woke at the sound of the front doorbell ringing, a jangling, discordant sound which send pleasant dreams fleeing. *Who was at their front door, so early in the morning?* Carolina groggily stared at her alarm clock – it was almost seven-thirty. Time to be up, for a bite of breakfast and some coffee before she and Daddy took Justin to the clinic. She heard heavy footsteps, a man's heavier tread going across the living room – Daddy was answering the door. Was it the paper boy, wanting to be paid for delivering the *San Antonio Light?*

No, those were men's voices, more than one of them. Carolina couldn't hear what they said. She looked for her robe, couldn't find it. What had brought men to the house at this early hour? Carolina's heart turned cold and leaden within her. *No.*

She ran down the stairs, in her bare feet, clad only in her light summer nightgown.

Only one thing brought men in the early hours of morning to the house where the wife of a soldier serving in Vietnam lived. Only one thing. And that would be that one thing that she dreaded, above all else. She came down the stairs, saw that it was three men in Army uniforms, the older of them with the insignia of a chaplain on the collar of his tunic, and Daddy with a grave expression on his face.

"Caro, baby" Daddy said. *He knew exactly what the presence of a chaplain meant.* He had been in the Army himself in a time of war and knew these things. "I'm afraid there is bad news for you..."

No. Not Jeff!

She collapsed in a dead faint into Daddy's arms, knowing that her dream of a loving and happy family had just now been destroyed.

. . .

She was numb all that day, numb with grief and disbelief, aching to understand why this had happened – not her Jeff, so vital, so loving, the tall man with the contagious smile and head of flaming red hair. She didn't cry until much later. The chaplain and the two soldiers – a young officer and a sergeant accompanying him were all very kind. Carolina couldn't remember what they said to her that morning, only that their voices were kind, considerate, and they took care of everything; all the funeral arrangements and those various phone calls which had to be made. Mama cried silently, as she brought them coffee and offered to fix breakfast, which they declined, saying they had already eaten. Daddy wrapped Justin in blankets and took him to the clinic, instead of Carolina, so part of her mind was with her baby boy, when Daddy called home at midmorning to tell her what the pediatrician had diagnosed.

"Justin has pneumonia, sure enough," Daddy reported. "They've gone ahead and admitted him to the hospital, since he must be in an oxygen tent. I've authorized it – I told them about Jeff. But Caro,"

Daddy's voice dropped. "The doctor warned me that it might come to another operation, and sooner rather than later. They'll want to talk to you about it."

"Thank you, Daddy," Carolina said into the telephone receiver, feeling as if she were being torn in two. "I'll do that when I can. How is Justin doing, now? Tell him that I'll come and see him and bring his favorite story books."

"He's as happy and breathing good right now," Daddy replied, in a rueful tone of voice. "He's sitting up in bed, playing with his toy soldiers under the oxygen tent, and charming the heck out of the nurses."

Toy soldiers. Carolina's heart contracted. If she had her way, little plastic toy Army men would be all that her son would ever have to do with soldiers.

Meanwhile, Daddy continued, "Were they able to tell you anything – Chaplain Roberts, or Lieutenant Carver – about Jeff?"

"They said something about the jeep he was driving hitting a land mine. It was instant," Carolina swallowed. "There was nothing anyone could do for him. The funeral will be later this week. At Fort Sam, with full military honors. Daddy… I don't know what to do now. I was so looking forward to him coming home, being safe, being happy and having him as a great dad for Justin … and now all that is gone. Wasted in a stupid war that no one wanted."

"I understand, Caro," Daddy replied. "Grieve for him, I guess – in your own time." Carolina thought that he had hung up the phone, and as she was about to say goodbye and hang up, Daddy added, "You're a strong, resilient woman. You'll get through it. With scars. But you'll get through it. Give it time."

"I will, Daddy," Carolina said, her heart was aching and felt hollow inside and numb. Her poor baby was in the hospital very sick again, how strong can she be? She didn't cry for Jeff until days later, when a letter from him was delivered, a letter written and mailed two days before his death: Carolina nearly fainted when she took out the mail delivery from the mailbox and recognized Jeff's handwriting on the envelope. It seemed as if all the air had been kicked out of her lungs. Without a word to Mama, she took the letter up to her room, and began to read – and that was when she finally dissolved into tears that she had not been able to shed since the moment when she came downstairs to see Daddy talking to Chaplain Roberts. Jeff wrote in that last letter about how much he loved her, how he was looking forward to being home, and settling into family life with herself and Justin ... never with the slightest idea that the only way he would come home was in a metal coffin. Instead of having that happy life as the wife of an officer and maybe even someday the wife of a senator – all she had now was a Purple Heart, a folded flag, and a cheap wedding band from Sears. All those bright dreams were gone, gone with her brave soldier, her knight in shining armor, the perfect daddy for little Justin Andrew, the man who had really loved and considered her his soulmate.

CHAPTER 13
DADDY'S GONE

As a military widow, Carolina received a small income from the government, which was enough to allow her to quit the hospital job and stay at home and care for Justin, day to day. In an attempt to rebuild an independent life for herself, she decided to use part of that income to rent a small apartment nearby for herself and Justin. Daddy was traveling a lot for his various jobs, and she slowly became aware that there was tension between him and Mama, a quiet and unspoken tension. They never fought openly – just seemed distant from each other. Poppa Lew had died several weeks after Carolina had returned from Hawaii, leaving the house seeming even emptier and more echoing. In her misery after Jeff's death, Carolina did not notice this tension at first, but it soon became obvious. This was the other reason for getting her own place, thinking that it would be easier on her parents, relieving them of the strain of her presence. She talked it over with Frankie, who generally approved of her plan to get her own place.

"Be good for you both, I think," Frankie said. "But close by, of course."

"Of course," Carolina agreed. "They love Justin so much; I'd not want to deprive them of visiting often. Oh, and I have some little clothes that Justin has grown out of, all clean and pressed... do you want them for little Jeff?" Tears welled up briefly, but Carolina fought them back. It had been so kind of her brother and Valerie to name their baby boy after Jeff. It was a way of keeping a little bit of him alive in their hearts. But it always made her want to cry a little, remembering how Jeff had written to her, about how he looked forward to meeting Frankie and Valerie's baby. He would have had such a fun time spinning incredible stories for Justin and his infant cousin, about factories making soap out of sea foam. Jeff would have been a wonderful father and uncle. It was so unfair that he was killed so shortly before he was supposed to come home from Vietnam.

"Sure," Frankie replied. "He's growing like a weed," he added proudly. "Valerie says that kids grow so fast they hardly have time to put any wear on their clothes and booties."

"It's true," Carolina agreed, with a fond smile. "There are some things – especially the denim overalls that I swear will take about four or five little boys consecutively to wear out."

She found a little apartment first and moved into it with Justin – finally feeling adult and independent, even having moments of happy contentment. Daddy often stopped by in the mornings, or sometimes in the late afternoons before going home for supper. He was always welcome, although sometimes she wondered if it was because he was reluctant to spend much time at home, sharing an all but empty house with Mama. But Daddy was always calm, cool, and organized. He had started another job, he told her one morning, as they shared coffee in the tiny, sun-drenched kitchen of the apartment. The job was with a cosmetic company in Mexico City, a company which had ambitious plans to expand their market internationally. He seemed enthusiastic about the job and the company's prospects in the United States and was even studying Spanish with renewed intensity. Daddy spoke Dutch and German, as well as English, so a new language was not half the challenge for him that it would have been for someone like Carolina.

"It's a promising company," he enthused to Carolina. "I'll bring home some of their products for you and Valerie and your mother to sample. I'm getting in on the ground floor, in marketing their products to retail outlets and customers in the States. Speaking the language makes me valuable to the company. Success in the American market could also put me into higher management."

"With a higher income bracket, Daddy," Carolina added, wryly, "Buckets and buckets of money. A corner office with a window and a view; a car with a chauffeur to drive you everywhere and a secretary to answer your phone calls and bring you fresh coffee every morning."

Daddy grinned. "Of course. It's how you keep score in the game of life, Caro. I flipped a coin, deciding on which country was going to be my land of opportunity; Australia, which is really a coming place, when you consider booming markets in the Far East – or Mexico. The coin-toss came up on Mexico, which has the benefit of being easier and cheaper to travel to…"

"Well, I hope you make a success of it, Daddy," Carolina got up from the table and poured herself another cup of coffee. "More? No. Anyway, I'll stop in and see Mama this afternoon. What does she think of all this?"

"About the usual," Daddy replied, with a discouraged sigh, as if he had suddenly sunk back into depression at the mention of Mama. "Your mother is a good woman, but she wants so much. Always has. She wants ever so more than I have ever been able to give her, and I just can't give any more. I'm really tired, now. Tired down to the bone." Suddenly, Daddy looked … old. Weary. Defeated. But only for a moment. "Caro, are you really satisfied with this place? A rented apartment? You know, the Veteran's Administration offers a program for assisting veterans and dependent spouses in getting home ownership. I'd like to see you settled for good in a little place of your own. A place that a landlord couldn't decide to raise the rent or kick you out. Build up equity in your own property, not be pouring money down a rental rat-hole."

"Would it cost very much?" Carolina asked, somewhat wistfully. Daddy looked cheerful.

"No. The mortgage loan would not be much more than you are paying in rent now. And at the end of it, you'd own the house, free and clear; and you wouldn't have wasted twenty- or thirty-years pouring money into a rental and having nothing to show for it, except maybe a landlord raising the rent every so often. Do you want me to look into it for you?"

"Yes, Daddy – if you would." Carolina sighed. "I'd like that. A place that's a hundred percent my own, free and clear. Nothing like a mansion, like Poppa Lew and Granny Margo's place, but just big enough for Justin and I."

"I'll look around and see what's out there," Daddy picked up his car keys. "Something small, but in a good safe neighborhood, and with a good elementary school. Jussie will be old enough for kindergarten, soon enough and sooner than you think."

"Sounds like a plan, Daddy," Carolina agreed.

Having suggested the project and gotten Carolina's agreement on it, Daddy moved swiftly to sort it out, between day trips to Mexico City for the cosmetic firm. Carolina finally decided on a small new-built home at the end of a cul-de-sac in a new neighborhood north of the airport; a modern one-story ranch-style house with a single-car garage, and three bedrooms; one large, the other two rather small, with a single bathroom. There was a single large burr oak tree in the front yard. Caroline loved it; her own little place to call home. Daddy assisted her in making out the paperwork to apply for the VA loan. In fact, he took so much time off from his regular paying job over this, that he had to ask her for a small loan of $2,000, in order to pay bills for himself and Mama. Carolina thought this was a little odd. Wasn't he making a lot from the cosmetic company in Mexico? But she told herself that he was taking so much time from work, and anyway, this was Daddy, who had done everything for her, for years without asking anything in return. She loaned him the money and never thought another thing about it until much, much later.

Over the space of a single weekend, Daddy and Frankie helped her move in from the apartment into the new little house. Fresh paint, flowered chintz curtains over the windows, a few scattered area rugs on the plain linoleum floors, and pictures on the walls. The few bits of furniture that she had of her own fitted in perfectly. Carolina put fresh flowers in pretty vases, and thought that it looked like a dollhouse, and not all that much larger. But it was hers, and Justin's alone. The evening that she and Justin were all moved into the little house, she settled onto one of the folding patio chairs on the little back porch with a cold soda at her side and watched the sun set in a blaze of orange and gold, while the city lights winked on. It reminded her of sitting out in back of Jerry and Pam's place, when they held barbeques on Sundays, and watched the children playing in the dusk. So many lovely memories, but sad ones, too – because that was where she first connected with Jeff. For the first time in simply months, she didn't start crying, when thinking about Jeff, and remembering those happy times with him. Maybe Daddy was right; she was strong and resilient. She would recover from the loss of her brave soldier and true love and begin to live again – live in a world without tears.

. . .

She had barely been in the new little house of her own for more than a week or two, when Mama called her on the phone one morning. She sounded frantic.

"Caro, do you know where your father is? He didn't come home last night! He was supposed to call from the airport when his flight got in from Mexico and come home in a taxi. I had supper on the table and all! I stayed up all night, wondering where he was! If he had been driving his own car, I would have thought he had been in an accident... but there was never a phone call! He always called before if he was going to be delayed past suppertime! I don't dare leave the house, in case he calls, but no one can tell me anything."

"Calm down, Mama," Carolina said firmly. "Look, I'll be right over. Have you called his work? What about his friends?"

"I don't know!" Mama dissolved into tears. "He kept so much to himself lately and I didn't really know any of his friends at his work all that well! I wouldn't even begin to know their phone numbers!"

"Calm down," Carolina urged her again. "Maybe he's left something written down in his desk, like his own address book. I'll get Justin dressed ... we'll be over in half an hour. Look and see if any of his things are gone. Where was he going when he left for work yesterday morning? Was he going on another trip to the cosmetic place in Mexico?"

"I... I suppose so," Mama sounded as if she were blowing her nose. "Yes, I suppose he must have been. He left very early – practically the middle of the night. He called for a taxi to pick him up at the house. I was still asleep; but I think I remember the taxi honking, out in the street."

"When I get there," Carolina said firmly. "We'll look through his closet and his personal things and see what there is missing, something that he would have taken with him. OK? Stop crying, Mama – we'll be there as soon as we can."

Perhaps there had been delay at the border, or he might have simply missed a flight ... did any of his other jobs involve an airline flight? Carolina wracked her memory, but she couldn't remember. Now and again, Mama said that she and Justin had gone to the airport to meet Daddy coming back from Mexico. But if Daddy's return flight had been delayed, then why hadn't he been able to call and let Mama know. As she had seen on the trip to Hawaii, there were public pay phones all over the airport terminals. Daddy shouldn't have had trouble finding one if his return flight was delayed. This was all very curious and very worrying. She hurried through feeding Justin the rest of his breakfast, washed his face and little hands, and packed him and his diaper bag into her car.

She parked in front of Mama and Daddy's house. Mama was waiting for her in the kitchen, and the playpen that she kept at their house for Justin was already unfolded in the living room, and a scattering of rattle-toys in it. (Justin really liked noisy toys.)

"I don't know what to think!" she exclaimed, after hugging Carolina and giving Justin a hasty kiss. "He has been acting so different the last few months."

"Different?" Carolina set Justin down in the playpen. "How so?"

Mama wrung her hands. "Just different ... distant. Never telling me anything! He works so hard and such long hours, but somehow there is never quite enough money in the household account to pay all the regular bills ... and the people calling the house at all hours, even in the middle of the night, asking for your father. They sound menacing, as if they don't quite believe me when I say that he isn't home or can't come to the phone."

"Not enough money?" Carolina echoed, suddenly remembering the loan of $2,000 that Daddy had asked for, back when he was helping her get the house. It had been a strain on her budget, but it was for Daddy, who had done so much for her, all these years. "That's curious. I loaned Daddy some money a bit ago. He was spending so much time with me, getting me the house that he was missing out on work. He said that he needed the cash for household expenses."

Mama looked at Carolina, horrified. "He did? How could that be? Oh, Caro, I don't know what is going on!"

"Mama," Carolina ventured carefully. "Don't you and Daddy ever talk at all anymore? About ... you know... things?"

Mama shook her head and confessed. "No, not really. Look – it hasn't been good between us for quite a while. I'm not happy and he's not happy. We talked seriously about divorce, last year – but that was just before Jeff..." Mama gulped. "So, we decided that it wasn't a good time for us to split up, since you needed both of us so badly."

"I see," Carolina replied, although she didn't, really. *Mama and Daddy unhappy? On the verge of divorce? This was sudden and horrible. And that it had happened when she was so caught up in her own sorrows and woes after Jeff's death. What kind of daughter was she, now?* "Look ... let's go look through Daddy's things and see what he might have taken with him. If he really meant to leave for good, aren't there things that he really treasured that he might have taken with him? And what about calling Grandma Visser? Daddy would for sure have talked to her." Daddy's mother, up in Holland, Michigan, was still alive and spry, Carolina knew – although Daddy was only one of two sons. *Surely Daddy wouldn't let his very aged and widowed mother think that he had vanished without a word?* Carolina was already getting a bad feeling about this. Now she continued, bravely. "You just call her, while I get Justin settled. And then we'll go upstairs and look at Daddy's things. And then I'll try calling this cosmetics company in Mexico City."

"All right," Mama agreed, already looking less distressed. "I really don't know what I will do, if he is gone for good..." she murmured to herself, as she went into the kitchen, where the house phone was.

"You be good, Jussie," Carolina whispered to her son, who favored her with a gap-toothed baby grin and began playing with one of his rattle-toys. Carolina put another within his reach and waited until her mother emerged from the kitchen.

"Mother Visser was still asleep in bed," Mama said. "But I talked to Adam's brother, who looks after her and she is certain that they have not heard from Adam since he called her on Mother's Day – weeks and weeks ago."

"All right, then," Carolina replied, keeping her voice level and steady with an effort. *Daddy must have met with an accident in Mexico. Or been taken seriously ill. He must be lying unconscious in a hospital someplace. And wherever he was, they didn't know how to contact his family. Yes, that must be it. They didn't speak or understand English where he was.*

They searched through the dresser drawers which held Daddy's clothes, and the half of the closet where his suits hung, the desk in the corner of the room that they called the den, where he did work when he was at home. There was a bookshelf with his books in it, and collections of pictures, and knickknacks from his travels, and his service in the Army. There were no gaps between the books on the shelves, and the only one of his suits not in the closet was the one that he had left the house wearing. The only luggage missing from the closet was the small suitcase that he used for overnight trips – just large enough for a pair of pajamas, his shaving gear and a change of shirt, tie, socks, and underclothes. Every one of his tie tacks and pairs of cufflinks were still in the top dresser drawer, all but the ones that he had worn when he left.

Mama kept saying, "I know things weren't good between us, Caro – but he wouldn't have just left, not without a word."

"It doesn't look like that, Mama," Carolina replied patiently. "All of his other things are still here in the house. He just took with him what he usually does, if it looks like he might have to spend a night on the road."

Mama was not consoled. "But just leaving, and not saying a word! How could he do this to us, Caro? How could he do it to me! What am I going to do if he never comes back?"

"I don't know, Mama." Carolina repeated, patiently. No good to encourage Mama to get hysterical. She and Mama discussed what to do, and if they should call the police. Not the police, they decided, not yet, although Carolina did make an attempt to put through a call to the cosmetic manufacturer in Mexico. She was utterly baffled in this by not speaking Spanish, and not being able to connect to anyone who spoke English. Besides, those international telephone calls to Mexico cost a fortune and turned out to be dead ends. She couldn't uncover any useful information about what might have happened to Daddy, so making more of those calls was a waste of time and money.

"I guess that we just wait," she said, finally. "For him to call or come home, or for someone to call and let us know what has happened. I guess after a week or so, we can report him to the police as a missing person."

"I don't know what to do, if he doesn't come home!" Mama fussed, and Carolina's heart ached.

Where was Daddy? And what had happened to him, that he should leave without a word to any of them? Carolina drove to her own little house slowly, reviewing all the things that Daddy had said in the last few months, things that might hold a clue to what Daddy might have done, if he left deliberately. That evening, after she had put Justin down for bed, she sat on the back porch of her little house and thought, thought deeply about what had happened. More and more, she wondered if Daddy really had purposely meant to leave. There was the matter of the money that she had loaned him. And he and Mama were not happy, and in fact, had seriously considered divorcing. More significantly and the longer she thought about the matter, she became convinced that everything he had done in the last few months in getting her and Justin in their own little house had been on purpose. Deliberate. He had meant to leave but wanted first to see that she was safe and settled. Carolina found this thought unsettling. Daddy had always been a rock. Dependable, conscientious, protective of her, always. If he had left, it must have been for a good reason. And of course, he would come back. She couldn't imagine otherwise.

She went every day to Mama and Daddy's house, hoping beyond hope that she was wrong – that Daddy would call, or come home. On the seventh day after Mama's first frantic phone call, she arrived at mid-morning, to find Mama sitting at the kitchen table with an opened letter in front of her, a lit cigarette in her hand with half an inch of ash hanging from it, and her eyes unseeing, like those of a zombie character in a horror movie.

"A letter from your father," Mama remarked, in a dead flat voice, as Carolina sat down at the kitchen table.

"Where is he?" Carolina demanded in a rush, "Where is he, and is he going to come home, soon?"

"I don't know, and no, I don't believe so," Mama replied, and Carolina took the single sheet of letter paper that Mama handed to her. Yes, it was in Daddy's familiar handwriting.

Dear Marlene, the note read. *I am sorry that this is the way things turned out between us. This is not how I wanted it to happen. I love you. This is something I had to do. I had to do this. This was best for all of us. Please tell Carolina I love her and let Frank know that I love him too, and that this is something I had to do. I can't tell you why, but I did not want to put you through any more misery. I was only hurting you. I love you. Please take care of the babies.*
I will always love you.
Adam.

Carolina read the brief letter several times over. Yes, it was Daddy's handwriting; of that, she was absolutely certain. The envelope lay on the table next to the ash tray. It was postmarked from Houston.

"What business did Daddy have in Houston?" she wondered out loud and Mama finally stubbed out the cigarette, which had burned down nearly to the filter.

"None that I know of," she replied, her voice flat and emotionless. But underneath that flat affect, Carolina sensed that rage burned, like coals under a thick layer of dead gray ash, "But it's a port. A busy, busy international port. A lot of ships come and go. Ships with international calls."

"Mama," she ventured at last, wondering if a simple question might set off Mama's volcanic rage. "You know something else. What else did you find out about Daddy, besides this letter from him?"

"I had a call," Mama replied, in that same flat voice. "Very late last night. Too late to bother you with what I learned. The call was from an old friend of your Poppa Lew, who thought that I ought to know.

Know and accept the worst, on the downlow. You know, Caro, your Poppa had friends all over San Antonio, good dependable friends. This one is high in law enforcement."

"What did this friend tell you about Daddy?" Carolina asked, suffocated by a sense of dread. *Nothing good.* This was like the morning that she had come downstairs in this very house, seeing the Army men at the door, talking with Daddy.

Mama stared at the opposite wall, as if she couldn't bear to look directly at Carolina. "Your daddy was a drug smuggler, deeply involved in smuggling dangerous drugs from Mexico into the United States. That he was a regular drug courier – that's what they call them, you know. He brought back dangerous drugs in his luggage with him on every trip back from Mexico City, and that the cosmetic company that he worked for was just a front. A front for manufacturing illicit drugs. He brought me into it, you know. In a peripheral way. And Justin, too – every time that he asked us to pick him up from the airport, after a trip from Mexico City. Which might make trouble for me, and for you too, if we raise too much of a stink about his disappearing. Adam did all of that, just to look like a normal family man when he went through Customs!" The contempt and rage in Mama's voice tore at Carolina's heart.

She stammered out the question that came to her mind. "No, Mama! Why would he do that! Daddy loved us! That letter says so, over and over again. Why would he do something so criminal and wicked!"

"Because he was in debt," Mama replied, her voice gone flat and emotionless again. "Deeply in dept, drowning so deeply in it, that he could never possibly get out. Hundreds of thousands of dollars. The fool. He gambled, without knowing what he was doing... the fool!"

In a sudden fit of rage, Mama sent the ash tray and her coffee cup off the table with a abrupt slash of her arm. Both shattered on the floor, sending coffee and ashes everywhere, broadcast across the kitchen floor. Carolina's heart sank – Mama was in one of her awful furies, yet again.

"How dare he leave me like this!" Mama raged. "How dare he! No money, without a single word of warning! What am I going to do; go out and get a job, at my age! I haven't held a job in twenty years!"

Carolina, baffled and distraught, went to get a broom, mop, and a dustpan to clean up the mess. When Mama went off like this, it was best not to argue, just tiptoe quietly around, until she calmed down. It was tragic, ironic that Daddy had been the one best able to talk her down from whatever fury Mama had worked herself into, and now Daddy, by disappearing this way, had sent Mama into the highest level of fury that Carolina had seen in years.

Really, the only person left in the family that she could talk to about this horrifying development was Frankie. She called him from her house as soon as she got home that evening. She just said that there was some news about Daddy, but she couldn't say very much on the phone, because it was complicated. Frankie left work early and came over. Carolina and her brother sat out on the little patio, in the twilight, with ice-cold drinks at hand. She was reminded vividly of those evenings when they lived in that dusty comfortless apartment in New Braunfels, after their family had just come home to the States from Okinawa. Daddy and Mama fought so viciously while Frankie and Carolina sat outside on the metal staircase and wished that the fight was over.

"So, what did Mama find out about Dad that was so awful that you couldn't tell me on the phone?" Frankie took a quick swig of his own drink. Carolina sighed; Frankie had to know the worst. Daddy had sent his love to both of them, as well as his wish that the babies, Justin and little Jeff be well looked after.

"He was smuggling drugs from Mexico, or so Poppa Lew's old friend told Mama, and she is furious. He might have involved her as an accessory in the commission of crimes, for all the times that she met him at the airport, which is why Mama really doesn't want to go to the police and file a missing person report. She's afraid that if they investigate too deeply, that she would be considered an accessory to what Daddy was doing."

"I can imagine," Frankie whistled in astonishment. "But why was he involved in such a crooked business in the first place. I'd have said that Dad was one of the most law-abiding straight arrows in the world!"

"He was gambling," Carolina explained. "Gambling big-time. And he had lost simply hundreds of thousands of dollars at it, without ever a chance of winning it back. Not all his fault, though. He wanted to give Mama a good life, provide for us all as well as Poppa Lew did. Only Poppa Lew was good at gambling and good at business, ever so much better than Daddy was, for as hard as Daddy worked at it. Or maybe Poppa was just luckier…"

"He was all that," Frankie agreed, fondly. "Poppa had it down to a science. He sure as hell never mortgaged his life to a loan shark, just to have a flutter at the horse races. Poppa studied the records and the odds like I study chemical compounds. What do they really think has happened to Dad? What did Poppa Lew's old friend say?"

Carolina shrugged. "He didn't really say. Maybe he doesn't really know either, or he just can't tell us. Three possibilities, though." She ticked them off on her fingers. "One – that the Mexican mafia went ahead and killed Daddy once that he was no longer useful to them as a drug courier. They made him write that letter from Houston to throw everyone off the scent. No, I don't like to think that, but it is a possibility. Second – that he is in our government's witness protection program, for his own safety and ours. He turned witness and informed on the drug smuggling network, and our people are giving him another identity in another part of the country. The letter from Houston supports that possibility. He said that it was 'something that he had to do.'"

Frankie nodded in agreement. "That's more in line with Daddy's character. I could buy that he's gone along with this to protect us, keep us all safe."

"The third thing is what Mama believes," Carolina continued, with a shudder. Mama hadn't been that angry in simply ages. "That Daddy has just gone and pulled a vanishing act all on his own. She is furious, as you can imagine, but you wouldn't believe some of the awful things that she said about Daddy. She says that since Houston is a port, and a lot of ships come and go from there. Daddy got himself some fake identity papers, got a ticket or took a job on one of those ships and is going to some other country. He told me once that he thought Australia was the *Land of Opportunity*. I'd like to think that is where he went. And that someday, he will come back. I'd rather think that's the case, and not that he is sick or hurt in a hospital somewhere. I hated to think of Daddy, injured and bleeding."

Frankie grinned, reminiscently. "Yeah, that always did freak you out. Remember when Poppa Lew took a swing at that guy in the beer garden, who got too fresh while dancing with Granny Margo, and Dad went to back up Poppa and got a bloody nose for defending the honor and good name of the family?"

"Ugh ... yes, I was so frightened," Carolina confessed. "Everyone shouting and swearing, Granny crying, and Daddy's nose bleeding all over his white shirt. Then the time when he was on the ladder, setting up the Christmas tree and he and the tree toppled over ... I was so scared. I was afraid he had broken something. I think I was much more upset than Daddy was. I would so much rather think that he just went to Australia or someplace."

"I know, Sis," Frankie mused. "Well, it's better than the first possibility."

Carolina nodded. "It's also why I don't really want to go and file a missing person report, get the FBI or someone else to search for him. It might mess up whatever plan Daddy made, if he deliberately meant to disappear. I'm certain he will come back, someday," she added wistfully.

"Could very well be," Frankie agreed. "And if he is in the witness protection program, then they wouldn't tell us anything anyway."

"I think he also wanted to see us both settled, before he went," Carolina ventured. "You and Valerie and little Jeff; you were all OK, anyway. But Justin and I – he was worried about us. All the time that he was helping me get this house, it was as if he wanted to be certain that Justin and I would be all right. I'm almost certain that Daddy meant to leave. He said in the letter that he loved Mama, but I don't really think that he did, anymore. He was just tired of trying to make her happy and giving her everything that she wanted. They had talked about getting a divorce."

"Well, she has one now," Frankie pointed out. "Desertion is grounds for divorce."

"Yeah," Carolina sighed. "And I think that is one of the reasons that she is so angry with Daddy now. She's really angry at herself, although she wouldn't ever admit it to anyone. A lot of the situation is of her making. She wanted so much from Daddy that he was willing to try all kinds of reckless and criminal things. Just so she could have the things that she wanted."

"Well," Frankie leaned back in the patio chair and contemplated the early evening sky. "What is she going to do now, then? She'll have to get a job, of course."

Carolina nodded. "That. And sell the house and move into a smaller place of her own. There's no way she can keep on with the house, paying the bills and the mortgage and all."

They shared the silence, broken only by the distant sounds of traffic, a radio on in one of the neighboring houses, a dog barking somewhere. Finally, Carolina said,

"I wish that I could have had one more dance with Daddy. You know, like how he taught me to dance when I was little, with my feet on top of his. That was so much fun."

CHAPTER 14
LIVING THE DREAM

They never heard from Daddy again, nor a whisper from any source about where he might have gone. For all intents and purposes, Adam Visser vanished off the face of the earth. Carolina was heartbroken; for all her life as long as she could remember, Daddy had been there always; a calm, strong and utterly reliable constant in her life, and then suddenly he wasn't, leaving a gaping void where he had always been, and questions which were never to be answered.

Mama filed for divorce by posting a notice in the newspaper; if there was no response within thirty days then legally, she would have an uncontested divorce. She sold the big house, and almost all of the furniture in it; everything which Frankie and Carolina didn't want, and Mama had no use or space for. Carolina asked to keep the little statue of the Okinawan fisherman. After a time, Mama got a job as a saleslady in a dress shop; at first part-time, as she did not have the strength to be on her feet tending to customers all day.

"I had rheumatic fever as a child," she explained to Carolina. "It affected my heart, so I have to build up my stamina."

This was news to Carolina; Mama had always seemed strong enough do exactly what she wanted to do when she wanted to do it.

"Don't over-stress yourself unnecessarily then," Carolina replied, diplomatically.

It did hurt a little, to see Mama and Daddy's house emptied out and sold. It had been home for Carolina for almost half her life, a welcome refuge between marital disasters and tragedy. In the back of her mind, Mama and Daddy's house was always there for her, and now it just wasn't. After a time, she avoided driving down the street where the house was; knowing that it wasn't home anymore. Another family lived under that roof, watched television in the living room at night, ate breakfast in the sunny little annex to the kitchen. Another mother and father played catch with the children in the back yard and slept in the bedrooms that had been hers and Frankie's, and Mama and Daddy's. Life had an inconvenient way of going on.

Over the next two years Carolina's life was tied up with the uncertainty of Justin's state of health. He was now almost five years old, and the slightest little thing – the sniffles, a chill, an upset stomach – and back he would go to the hospital. Sometimes she thought that he had slept more nights in a hospital bed than in his own little room. During the time that Justin wasn't in the hospital, Carolina and her son spent evenings and weekends with Aunt Jane, Mama's younger sister.

There wasn't much of a generation gap between Aunt Jane and Carolina, and she sometimes seemed more like an older sister than an aunt, even though Aunt Jane's daughters were around Carolina's age. Like Mama and Granny Margo, she had married very young. Like Mama, she was divorced, although Aunt Jane didn't seem to be as bitter about it like Mama was. She was fun to be with, even more fun than Aunt Bobbie, the oldest sister. On a mild Sunday in autumn after taking Justin to the San Antonio Zoo, Aunt Jane and Carolina sat outside on the patio in back of Carolina's little house. Carolina had decorated the patio with a few more folding chairs and some colorful flowering plants in tubs. The sun was sliding down in the western sky in a blaze of orange. The day had already cooled off. A bird feeder hung from a metal shepherd's crook driven deep into the turf at the fence-line, and of course the late-season birds were fluttering about it, fighting over access to cracked corn and bird seed.

Aunt Jane watched them, with a faint smile, and Carolina, following her gaze, remarked, "I like to watch them, in the mornings, especially. I think some pairs have nested in the tree out front."

"To each, a suitable mate," Aunt Jane agreed, with a sigh. "Simpler for birds than humans. Speaking of humans, Caro; have you considered dating again? It's been two years and a bit since you lost Jeff. You cannot simply lock yourself up like a nun."

"I haven't," Carolina protested. "And as a matter of fact, I have dated! There were two guys, and one of them asked me to marry him."

"Do tell," Aunt Jane raised a skeptical eyebrow. "And what did you say? Don't keep your decrepit old auntie in suspense. Guy behind door number one – spill the beans."

Carolina blew a raspberry. "Decrepit old auntie? My right foot!" before explaining. "They were both doctors. Military doctors – captains, both."

Aunt Jane chuckled. "Oh, poor Caro! With Jussie's medical conditions, I'd bet that the only eligible single guys you meet are doctors!"

Carolina laughed, uncomfortably. "Well, the first guy is Justin's pediatrician. He was there for my little boy, twenty-four seven. He would come and sit with me when Justin was going through another crisis … and it was so reassuring! He was so kind to Justin, so caring! I think he was Justin's next favorite person in all the world. We went out for dinner … and then we would go back to the hospital late at night, after visiting hours, to check on Justin and of course the nurses would have to let me in, because I was with the supervising doctor. It was so comforting for me, being able to go in after regular hours. He took such care of my baby boy – and I am so grateful for that. He even took me to meet his own mother, when she came to town for a visit. I liked him lots, as a friend and as Justin's doctor. But there wasn't any romantic spark. We're still good friends. He's getting out of the military and setting up his own pediatric practice in town."

"And what about the doctor behind door number two?" Aunt Jane prodded.

"A flight surgeon assigned to Lackland," Carolina replied. "Tall, dark, and gorgeous with a dimple in his chin; he looked like that actor in *West Side Story* - George Chakiris. He was from Pennsylvania and going back there when he finished his stint in the Air Force."

"And he was the one who asked you to marry him? A handsome doctor!" Aunt Jane fanned herself exaggeratedly with her hand. "Oh, my! I believe I am getting faint! Why on earth didn't you say yes?"

"Well, because first, I didn't want to move to Pennsylvania," Carolina replied. "And second - he is Jewish and would have expected me to convert, and no, I couldn't possibly have gone through with that. And third - I liked him, but I didn't love him. I couldn't possibly marry someone without loving them. I couldn't marry, unless I knew for certain that I loved a man as much as I loved Jeff."

"A guy that you could love as much as you loved Jeff," Aunt Jane mused thoughtfully. "And you are open to dating again. Well, that's promising ... because I just happened to meet up with a guy who reminded me so much of Jeff. Single and unattached; tall, auburn-red hair, and from Oklahoma, too. Last Friday, a friend of mine was having a pool party at the place where she lives. Lots of people, but this one guy really caught my eye, and we started talking."

"Nah-nah-nah!" Carolina jeered, teasingly reverting to a juvenile taunt. "Jane has a boyfriend! K-i-s-s-i-n-g ..."

"Too young for me, sweetie," Aunt Jane replied, not the least bit ruffled. "I don't do cradle robbing when it comes to dates with guys. As I said, we got to talking, and I happened to mention you. I even went and got my purse and showed him the pictures that I took of you and Justin at the Japanese Tea Garden last month ..."

"Oh, that will put him off, for certain," Carolina remarked with a certain degree of cynicism. "Most single guys will run a mile, if it turns out that a girl that they are interested in has children."

"I didn't detect any attempt to run on his part," Aunt Jane replied. "And as a matter of fact, he asked for your number, and he said that he might call you when he got back into town."

"You didn't give him my phone number, did you?" Carolina demanded, and Aunt Jane giggled like a teenager.

"I did," she confessed. "Look, Caro, he would be perfect for you, so give him a chance. Tall, red-haired, from Oklahoma … his name is Josh. Josh Foster. You have simply got to talk to him when he calls. And he said that he definitely would call."

"What!?" Carolina stared, blankly. "Foster? is he kin to Jeff? My Jeff!?"

"I don't think so," Aunt Jane shook her head. "I did ask because it just seemed much too coincidental. He didn't think so, at any rate; Foster is a pretty common name. No cousins or second cousins who were officers in the Army that he knew of. But it's an amazing coincidence, and sweetie, I am certain that you two would get on perfectly. Promise me you'll give him a chance."

"I'll talk to him, when … if he calls," Carolina promised, although she really wasn't sure about this Josh, who had the same last name as Jeff – the same initials, even!

• • •

It was a week before the mystery Oklahoman with red hair and the same last name as Jeff finally called. Carolina had pretty much written off Aunt Jane's attempt at matchmaking, by the time that the phone rang the next Friday afternoon.

"Hi. Is this Carolina Foster?" A pleasantly resonant male voice, Carolina thought. Very easy on the ear, and when she said that she was, the man continued, "Well, see – I'm a Foster, too. Josh Foster. Your aunt told me about you and your little boy and … well, you sounded really nice. Sorry I couldn't call earlier, but I'm in outside sales for Polaroid and I really can't call until I get home again. My specialty is instant cameras, and I have a huge territory to cover for the company. Keeps me on the road constantly."

"Jane told me about that," Carolina replied. "I can't believe the coincidence, though. You have the same initials as my husband had."

"May as well take a chance," Josh replied, sounding rather relieved, and they continued talking; pleasant, irrelevant chat. They made each other laugh, which was reassuring. He talked about his work, and how he traveled a circuit for his company; the things that he saw, the people that he talked to when he stopped over in a small town on the way to one of his clients, and the curious or amusing things in those towns. She told him a little about herself, about some of her experiences in nursing, about Justin, and how much she was devoted to her little boy. It was a thoroughly engaging conversation, which continued, to Carolina's astonishment, for more than an hour. It was only Justin fussing about supper, which brought them back to earth.

"Look," Josh said, "Let's make it a date next Saturday, when I get back to town. Dinner and clubbing. I'll pick you up and we'll get to know each other. No pressure: we'll just have a fun Saturday night."

"Sure," Carolina agreed. "Six o'clock? I'll ask my mother if Justin can spend the night at her apartment, so I don't have to hurry home because the sitter is waiting up for me."

"Perfect," agreed Josh; he sounded excited and even a little bit relieved. Carolina sensed that perhaps he had been a little in doubt that she would agree to a date. "Looking forward to it."

"See you next Saturday," Carolina said, and hung up the phone. "Aren't you jealous?" she crooned to Justin, who gave her a happy grin, and lifted his arms to her so that she could pick him up. "Your mama has a date for Saturday! Isn't that marvelous – oh, yes, Baby – it is marvelous!" With the experience of hindsight, Carolina wondered how many men got butterflies in their stomachs at the thought of asking a woman out, fearing that she might say no instead of yes, and even worse – laugh at them. Oh, Mark had been afraid of women laughing at him, she thought with a new insight. That's why he had been so angry-violent all the time. Mark must have suspected that women might be laughing at him, with his pathetic pretense of being a military veteran, a tough guy with an expensive car. Very likely Avril had also been correct; that Mark was jealous of the attention that Carolina lavished on Justin; not just because Justin was medically fragile, but because the baby existed at all.

If this Josh had anything else in common with Jeff, Carolina hoped that it would be affection for her little boy. How cruel of fate, to first deprive Justin not just of robust good health, but then of the good daddy that Jeff would have been to him, and after that, his grandfather. After two years of silence regarding Daddy, Carolina was now all but certain that he had been killed by the Mexican drug-dealers that he had been working for when he vanished. Months and years had gone by without a single word, a letter, even a phone call. And Daddy loved her so much. If he were still alive somewhere in the world – Mexico, Australia, wherever he might have gone, on his own or under government protection, Carolina was certain that he would have contrived somehow to get word to her.

. . .

She planned very carefully, that date on Saturday with Josh Foster; wondering all that long week if she was going to experience the same kind of connection that she had with Jeff and yet had not felt with either of the two men she had dated since then. She drove Justin to Mama's apartment in the mid-afternoon, when Mama had gotten home from work, packing with him his special pillow and blanket, pajamas, and a change of clean clothes for the next day. Mama looked tired and drained after a morning in the dress shop. She had kicked off her low heels and answered the door in her stocking feet. None the less, she cheered up when she opened the door to Carolina's knock.

"How is my best little Jussie!" Mama exclaimed and scooped a giggling child into her arms. "Ooof! What have you been feeding my grandchild – bricks?"

"He has gained some weight," Carolina explained, and Mama laughed.

"Oh, don't apologize, Caro; he's a growing boy!"

"Finally," Carolina agreed; it was a matter of concern sometimes. Because of being so often sick, Justin remained very thin, although he was shooting upwards rather like a spindly weed. "Don't let him pig out on ice cream, OK? Or stay up too late watching TV. And definitely no scary movies! Nothing to make him wake up screaming."

"Of course," Mama agreed, although Carolina was certain that Justin would be allowed all the ice cream he wanted and to stay up watching TV with his grandma, in spite of all her admonitions to the contrary. "When is your date picking you up?"

"Six o'clock," Carolina replied. "I wanted to leave enough time to get ready without rushing."

Mama looked at her, very closely, as she let Justin down to the ground. "What do you think of him? Jane couldn't stop talking about him, when she told me that she was going to try and set you up with him."

"We talked on the phone last week, for more than an hour," Carolina replied, honestly. "I liked him a lot, but that was on the phone. It might be different, face to face."

"It might be," Mama agreed. "So don't forget to take enough cash for a taxi home, if the date isn't going well."

"I will," Carolina sighed. An evening date with a man she had only talked to on the telephone, once. Never mind about having met, face to face. This evening would be the first time. She wondered now if she should have just agreed to meet this Josh at a restaurant and driven there in her own car. That way, she could always bail out of the date, if it wasn't working... but too late to consider that now. She kissed Justin, hugged Mama goodbye, and returned home, to consider what to wear. Josh had mentioned going out to a club, so a nice dress. Might as well put on the plain little black dress which Aunt Jane said made her look as elegant as Audrey Hepburn in *Breakfast at Tiffany's*, and dress it up with a pair of dangling pearl earrings. She took care with her makeup, and her hair, washing it and letting it dry natural with her curls flowing past her shoulders. She transferred her wallet and keys to her good, beaded evening bag, and took one last look into the bathroom mirror, just as the doorbell rang.

The bell sounded ... tentative.

"Here goes nothing!" Carolina murmured to herself. She took a single deep breath and opened the door, just as the doorbell rang again.

"Hullo ... Carolina?" said the sharply dressed young man standing on her porch. "I'm Josh. I hope I'm not too late."

"Right on time," Carolina replied, reassured. He wasn't quite as tall as Jeff had been, and his hair wasn't the same red, rather more an auburn. But he had a nice smile, and an open, friendly look to him. "And I'm ready to go. Just let me turn on the porch light."

"Righty-oh," Josh replied. "I hope you like Mexican food. I forgot to ask if you like anything else before I made the reservation."

"I do," Carolina answered, truthfully. Josh took her arm in a chivalrous manner, and at the curb, he opened the car door for her. That reminded her most piercingly of Jeff, but she discovered to her secret relief that he was not otherwise that much like Jeff; he was his own person; a man with an acute sense of humor, sharply observant. He would have to be, since he worked in sales. and possessed of a biting wit, that last quality which he must have kept fairly restrained to continue to work in sales. He kept up a sparkling line of conversation as he negotiated the drive to La Fonda on Main, north of downtown. He had reservations for a table on the patio in the garden, where the margaritas appeared almost instantly. And it was a marvelous evening; they drank, had supper, lingered over crème caramel for dessert, before going dancing at a small club with a rooftop terrace. The evening was too delicious to end, but it did, eventually.

"I have had the most wonderful time," Carolina confessed, as Josh escorted her to the front door, where moths flitted around the porch light overhead.

"So did I," Josh confessed. "You are really something, Carolina. I'm so glad that your aunt fixed us up for tonight. I'm away working my territory first thing Monday morning, but I'll be back next weekend. Shall we do it again?"

"Of course," Carolina replied. "I'd like nothing more than another evening like this."

"So do I," Josh hesitated, and then very respectfully tendered a kiss. Carolina put her arms around him, thinking gratefully how very nice it was to lean against a man's strength, inhale the scent of his aftershave, and to fit her head against his shoulder. "Next week it is, then," he added, as they loosened their embrace of each other. "I'll call you, once I get back to town."

"Ok," Carolina agreed. She fumbled for the house key in her evening bag, knowing that Josh was walking back to his car, but looking over his shoulder; it warmed her, knowing that he wanted to be certain that she made it into the house. She waved to him, before she closed the door. Yes, indeed – it had been a wonderful evening. The last thought that went through her mind before she drifted off into pleasant dreams was gratitude to Aunt Jane for insisting that she and Josh get in touch. Clever, insightful Aunt Jane!

. . .

They dated – mostly on weekends, when Josh was back in town after working his sales territory during the week. He met Mama, and after a careful interlude, got to know Justin, who took to him unreservedly. Josh rough-housed with Justin, but always carefully, keeping in mind the necessary colostomy. They went on day dates, sometimes with Justin, and wholly satisfactory evening dates, with Justin spending the night with Mama, and Josh saying an affectionate, yet respectful farewell at the door. Carolina was resolved not to repeat the same mistake that she had, in sleeping with Mark, and Josh was respectful of that. After a year and a half of weekend dates, and frequent affectionate telephone calls, she was absolutely, deliriously certain – she was in love, and was pretty certain that Josh was just as much in love with her. To be in love was such an energizing feeling, a happy feeling for Carolina. To her secret aggravation, Josh held off saying that he was also in love with her; indeed, saying anything at all about moving on to the next logical step in the progression of affection between a man and a woman.

A year and a half; the weather had turned to a South Texas winter, mild during the day, chilly at night – chilly enough to leave the windows open and turn off the air conditioning. Carolina often felt sorry for people living farther north, burdened with bitter cold and thick snow, while in San Antonio, people put on a heavy windbreaker when the winter winds blew and set about planting their vegetable gardens. She and Josh were having supper at a café out on the west side that featured Cajun food, when Josh put his fork down and looked across the table at her.

"Caro, darling ... they're going to change my territory, next month. Transfer me out of Texas. I'm going to be based out of New Orleans. I'm not going to be able to come back to San Antonio."

"Oh?" Carolina said, around a sudden lump in her throat.

Here was another guy that she really loved, but now was going to leave her. She felt as if her heart was being yanked out of her chest; just when things were going so well for her and Josh, even though the question of marriage had never come up. It was almost Christmas now, a time for joy and happiness, stockings on the fireplace, a Christmas tree and family. For everyone but her and Justin, it seemed. This was so unfair! Something of the devastation she was feeling must have shown on her face, because Josh reached across the table and caught her hand, his expression reflecting urgency and even a little desperation.

"So, I've been giving it serious consideration, Caro. I love you and adore Justin, and I want us to be together as a family. Will you marry me? Can you find it in you, to leave San Antonio and come with me to New Orleans, or wherever they want me to go after that? I know it's a hard thing to ask, but I know that I can make a good life for you and Justin, no matter where we wind up…"

"Oh, yes!" Carolina replied, joyfully. "Oh, so many times yes … I knew that I would be following my husband all over the world, if the Army sent him, so of course I can go with you, wherever your bosses send you."

"Oh, good," Josh's face glowed with happy relief, in the dim corner of the Acadiana Café. "I wasn't certain you would say 'yes' but I hoped that you would. You're a wonderful woman, Caro, and I don't want to let you get away from me. Look, I bought a ring … and if it isn't to your taste, then we can go back to the jewelry store and exchange it for something you like better. I haven't had all that much experience in asking a woman that I adore to marry me!"

"I'm sure I will like it," Carolina assured him, as Josh brought out a little velvet-covered ring box from his sport jacket pocket and opened it on the table between them. He looked at her, expectations mixed with a leavening of doubt. oh, my! It's beautiful, and yes, I do love it,"

"Well then, put it on … it should fit," Josh added, still with a trace of doubt. "Oh, perfect – it does. Well then, Caro – when can we get the deed done? My parents likely want it done in church, and I'd like them to be happy that I am finally settling down to marital responsibilities, instead of being a frivolous bachelor. They're Baptists, but I haven't been to church since I was in high school. But since you're the bride, it's up to your family for the venue."

"I was raised Catholic," Carolina confessed. "But since I was a divorced woman when I married Jeff, and the Church doesn't believe in divorce, even from a criminal wife-beater and abuser, I couldn't take communion, so I stopped going to Mass. Baptist is fine as long as they're OK with me having been divorced."

"Better to marry than to burn," Josh took her hand, raised it to his lips for a brief kiss, and slid the diamond solitaire onto her finger. "Well, Mrs. Foster, soon-to-be Mrs. Foster. Let's get it all done, and as soon as we can."

From despair to joy in the space of a few minutes: for Carolina, a dream was about to come true. All that she had ever wanted was to be happily married, with a family of her own and a pleasant little house in the suburbs, but after so many false starts – Mason and Mark, and the loss of Jeff to war ... maybe that dream was within reach now. She loved Josh, and at long last, it seemed like the stars were finally aligned in her favor.

"It will have to be a small wedding," Mama agreed, when Carolina broke the news to her the next day. "Three weeks! My! You two are certainly in a hurry to be married." She looked very sharply at Carolina. "Caro, sweetie, you're not pregnant, are you?"

"No, I am not!" Carolina returned, indignantly. "The great hurry is all because we *must* be married in three weeks, so that we can go house-hunt together in New Orleans! Josh's company wants him in place for the new year ... and I have so much to do ... see to moving my own things. I suppose I have to sell my little house, but it doesn't matter. Josh and I certainly can afford a bigger and nicer one, after all."

"Let me see what I can do," Mama said, slightly abashed at Carolina's vehement reply. "You'll need a nice dress, of course ... but don't go for white and a veil. Navy blue and cream-colored trim, I think – afternoon-length, but with plenty of flowers. We have just the thing at the shop. A nice small hat to match, and a small bouquet ... no point in making a great pretense of being an innocent virgin going from your father's house to your husband. Your brother can escort you down the aisle, and Jussie can stand with you ... maybe Jane as your matron of honor, and Valerie as bridesmaid? No need to go overboard, just keep your wedding party in the family. Just leave it to me," She looked very sharply at Carolina. "I'm so glad for you. Josh is such a nice man. So dependable. And so nice that you really don't have to change your initials, when it comes to monograms and things."

"Yes, it is," Carolina agreed, because it was ironic and maybe a little bit sad – going from being Mrs. Jeff Foster to Mrs. Josh Foster. Did this mean that a marriage was meant to be? It was so bittersweet.

. . .

It seemed as if it was: Mama conferred with Josh's parents, who put in a good word for them at the church where they were members; Trinity Baptist, on the edge of the Monte Vista neighborhood. They had a small formal wedding in the splendors of that lovely, white-pillared church, with the Reverend Buckner Fanning presiding over the exchange of vows, in front of their families and close friends. There was a lovely small reception in the parish hall afterwards, with a small, white-frosted cake crowned with sugar flowers, and servings of fizzy punch, shared among family, friends and well-wishers like the Reverend Fanning.

"Don't worry about Jussie!" Mama whispered, as Carolina gathered up her purse, at the height of the reception, when everyone had enough cake, and stuck around for the last bit of wedding ritual – the escape of the bridal couple. Josh was waiting for her, having already given over custody of their suitcases to a hugely amused cabbie, who was now leaning against the fender of the Checker cab, waiting on the last element of a traditional wedding; the departure of the bride and groom in a shower of thrown rice. (*The cabbie had absolutely refused to let anyone at the reception tie old shoes and cans to his bumper.*) "We'll have a lovely time together ... my, I am so glad that I rate a paid vacation from the shop, now!"

"Don't spoil him too much," Carolina whispered. "And don't let him catch a chill. If it turns into a cold, he'll have pneumonia again, and that will mean another stay in the hospital. This is the number for the hotel where we'll be staying. Mama, please call if he runs the slightest bit of a temperature or begins to cough. It could be a matter of life and death."

"Caro, I know," Mama returned evenly. "Look; I raised both you and Frankie, so I reckon I know something about children ... don't worry about Jussie. You just have a nice honeymoon with Josh ... find our baby boy a nice house with his own little bedroom, in a good neighborhood, close to a good school. All right, Caro! Go throw your bouquet to the girls, they're getting impatient!"

A last hug and a kiss from Justin, who was more interested in the treats that his grandmother had promised him; a whole week of being spoiled and indulged! Outside the main doors to the parish hall, Carolina threw her small bouquet over her shoulder to a small group of single girls. She and Josh dashed laughing and hand in hand, down the pathway towards the street in a small storm of thrown rice to where the taxi waited – the taxi which would take them to the airport. It was everything traditional that she had ever dreamed of in a wedding; a dream which had finally come true.

CHAPTER 15
CORPORATE WIFE, CORPORATE LIFE

The taxi pulled away from the church in a flurry of rice and shouted good wishes. Carolina sighed happily. This was what she had always wanted; a nice wedding, a solid marriage to a good guy, the prospect of a comfortable life with him. There was a glow to the day, to this special day, after so many false starts and disappointments. Josh had his arm around her; and she rested her head against his shoulder.

"Happy, Caro?" he asked, and she replied, with absolute contentment.

"I never thought it possible to be so happy as I am right now. A week in New Orleans for a honeymoon! I've never been there."

"The food's fantastic," Josh assured her, "And so is the night life. We have reservations at the Place d'Armes. That's a luxury hotel in the French Quarter, right around the corner from Jackson Square. We can have beignets and coffee every morning at the Café du Monde, and sightsee ..."

"But in the afternoons, we house-hunt," Carolina reminded him. "We can't spend all our time being tourists,"

"Of course not," Josh agreed. He bent his head a little and kissed her forehead. "We'll spend some time in bed, too."

"Why Mr. Foster, are you making improper suggestions?" Carolina replied, in mock indignation.

"Of course," Josh agreed, and kissed her again.

. . .

Carolina loved New Orleans from the moment they landed. As Josh had promised, they stayed for the week at the Place d'Armes, just off Jackson Square, in the heart of old New Orleans; a district of narrow streets and 19th century two- and three-story buildings adorned with ironwork balconies and other adornments which looked for all the world like wrought-iron lace. Their room at the Place d'Armes overlooked the quiet inner courtyard, rather than the somewhat noisier St. Anne Street. Josh was right about the food. The food in the French Quarter was magnificent, and there were storied restaurants around every corner. During that week, Carolina and Josh sampled as many of them as they could.

"They say that New Orleans has the finest French food, outside of France," Josh assured her, over supper in the garden patio of Broussard's. Late into the evenings, they listened to live music at Preservation Hall, and in various clubs around Jackson Square. Usually, they ordered room service for an early breakfast, or walked around the corner to the Café du Monde for chicory/coffee and beignets buried in drifts of powdered sugar for an early brunch.

In the afternoons, Josh and Carolina looked for a house.

"I'd love to live in the French Quarter," Carolina said, once, "The music, and the restaurants, and the historic buildings and all, and being able to walk everywhere to anything interesting. But it's one thing to live in a tourist attraction, and another to just visit. And besides, I want a house and a yard, near a decent school for Justin."

By the end of the week, they had found a comfortable three-bedroom ranch house on Elizabeth Street in Metairie, an outlaying suburb, close to a day school where Justin could start kindergarten. The suburb was an older one, the houses constructed on underground pilings as that land had all been marsh, until it had been filled in and built up. By the middle of January 1972, Josh, Carolina, and Justin were settled in New Orleans. Josh was on the road for his company during the week, but he had weekends at home, which Carolina loved. Her Texas Licensed Vocational Nursing license was accepted in Louisiana, and she very soon found a job, working for the head of the ophthalmology department at the Ochsner Clinic in New Orleans an eight-to-five job helping the doctors of the clinic see patients, so that she could be home for Justin.

She and Josh loved everything about New Orleans; the music, the food, the raucous Mardi Gras parades, and the occasional sight of the star football player for the New Orleans Saints, Archie Manning driving his flashy Corvette on Airline Drive. Carolina considered herself to be a weekend hippy, living in rowdy New Orleans; bellbottoms, gauzy peasant blouses, love beads and her long hair parted in the middle like Peggy Lipton on the TV show *The Mod Squad.* She baked pot brownies and only occasionally drank too much Annie Green Springs wine, especially when she and Josh had friends over on weekends and alcohol flowed like water in the nearby canal. Carolina remembered those awful family gatherings when she was a child, and Granny Margo, Mama and the aunts all drank too much and fought like cats in a sack; no, Justin would not have unpleasant memories like that of his childhood, so she managed to keep a lid on her own consumption.

But Josh drank heavily, which worried her, sometimes. One Friday he arrived home late from a long trip out through his territory, pulling into the driveway in front of the house, with the front bumper, and hood all bent and crumpled, the headlights shattered. She couldn't believe that he had been able to drive the car to the end of the block, much less hundreds of miles home.

"Josh!" she exclaimed, as he climbed from behind the wheel, rumpled and sweaty from a long drive in the muggy Louisiana spring weather. "What happened to the car! Are you hurt?"

He looked at her in mild astonishment. "No, I'm all right. Ralph and I had a bit too much to drink last night, and I guess that I hit a tree, or a deer or something. The car's fine. Only body damage, nothing important."

Carolina bit her lip. She didn't want to fight with Josh. Instead, she said, "You'll have to drive a company car next week, until you can get it fixed. Come on in, supper is nearly ready."

She did have words with Josh over the dune buggy that he bought from another salesman; a lightweight thing with fat tires and no roof or windows, built on the chassis of a VW Beetle and made to go charging around off-road, on levees, sand-dunes, and dirt tracks out in the country. Josh loved to take the dune buggy and go bouncing along the grass levee in any weather, and Justin loved to go with him, strapped into the passenger seat. But the dune buggy was open to the weather; no doors or roof, only a rollbar over the two passengers for safety in case the buggy tipped over on a steep slope. That didn't bother Carolina so much as did Josh's penchant for taking Justin out on days when it was cold, wet, or windy, or all three, and it did get cold in New Orleans, chiefly in winter.

"You have to be careful, exposing Justin to the cold!" Carolina stormed on one of those weekends, when rain swept in from the Gulf and Josh was all for an excursion along the levee close to Elizabeth Street. "He could catch cold, his death of cold and pneumonia!"

"You're forever mollycoddling the boy," Josh replied, irritated. "How is he going to learn to be anything but a spoiled little mama's boy, tied to your apron strings! He's got on a warm coat, a muffler, and a hat! There's no harm in going out in the buggy!"

"Fine!" Carolina flared to anger at last, knowing that Justin was ready in his warm clothes, watching her and Josh with wide and apprehensive eyes. "But if Jussie gets sick again and winds up in the hospital with pneumonia, yet again! I'm putting it all on you! You take him to the hospital, you sit with him under an oxygen tent, you talk to the doctors!"

"Fine!" Josh replied, buttoning his own coat, and taking down the keys to the buggy from where they hung on a rack by the back door. "Wrap your boy in cotton wool if you want! We're going out – Jussie?"

"Yes, sir!" Justin quavered with a nervous look at Carolina. "I won't get sick, Mom, I promise."

"Come back home the minute you start to cough!" Carolina ordered, and the two of them left through the door into the carport where the dune buggy waited, leaving Carolina feeling rather resentful.

But then she wanted a good daddy for Justin, and weren't ventures like this supposed to be part of it? Justin was growing up; he couldn't be kept as a baby for much longer. He was already going into the first grade.

• • •

They lived in New Orleans for two and a half years and loved every single minute of it; the music, the party scene, the food and Mardi Gras and all, but during the summer that Justin was between first and second grade, Josh returned from a consultation with his immediate supervisor, who had come down to New Orleans on a flying visit from company headquarters.

"I've got good news and bad news, Caro," Josh said glumly, and Carolina's heart sank. "Which do you want to hear first?"

"The bad news," Carolina replied. Yes, she would rather know the bad news. Nothing good had ever happened to her when she didn't face up to bad news. Josh nodded.

"The company wants me to relocate to Cleveland, Ohio, to take on the territory there."

"I don't want to leave New Orleans!" Carolina wailed. "I love it here! I love everything about this place! We're close to family, to my mother and to your folks! I don't want to move and start setting up a home all over again! And Justin; he'll have a new school, new pediatrician, new-everything! I'll have to quit my job at the Ochsner

Clinic! What's so great about Cleveland, anyway! I don't know anyone who ever went to Ohio of their own free will?"

"Well, darlin', there's us, for a start," Josh replied patiently. "The good news is that the company will pay for the move, and a new house, too. It's a raise for me, and a much more prestigious territory." He took Carolina in his arms, pulled her close, and said into her hair, "Caro, it's kind of like the military. I have to go where the company sends me. I love the job that I do, I want to spend the rest of my working life doing it; I can't imagine doing anything else for a living."

"All right," Carolina sniffed, fighting back tears at the thought of uprooting just about everything in the comfortable life that they had in New Orleans. "It's your job and you love it. I understand. My Daddy loved the Army, but Mama hated everything about it, especially once we came back from Okinawa. She nagged and nagged at him until she made him resign his commission, but absolutely nothing that he ever did afterwards ever really did satisfy her ... or made him as happy as he was when he was in the military."

Josh embraced her even more closely. "OK, that's how we need to play the whole thing for Justin. It's fun, and a new adventure. We're a family, a united front. Positive attitude about the move. Promise, Caro? It will make all the difference to Justin. Promise, that you have a good attitude."

"Promise," Carolina relaxed into his embrace, accepting that Josh was right. It was all about her attitude. Recalling how Mama had raged about Daddy's Army career left a bad feeling in her mouth. She didn't want to be the nagging wife, wrecking her husband's life, turning him away from a job, a career that he loved, was good at, and had a promising future. Their happiness as a family was too important to wreck over her unhappiness at having to move. Likely, they would have to move again, after Cleveland. Might as well face the reality of the corporate life and deal, without complaint.

· · ·

Before the summer was out, the house on Elizabeth Street was sold to a new owner, the furniture packed and loaded into crates and in the back of a van – and Josh, Carolina and Justin were headed to the Midwest. All this was paid for by the company, as well as their new house.

"We'll have to stay in an apartment until it's ready," Josh told her, when they arrived at where they were going to stay. "They're not quite finished with fitting out the inside … but this gives us a chance to pick out some of the optional upgrades."

Carolina was still not much pleased over having to move from New Orleans, but she kept herself from saying so, with a bit of an effort. The stay in the rental apartment was not a long one. They moved into the new house as soon as the work was done, and their furniture arrived. It was a sprawling single-story house; a condo-maximum, the builders called it, with a covered carport that they shared with a similar house, and an absolutely enormous back yard, a stretch of lawn running down to a band of woods that fringed the grounds of the neighborhood clubhouse, a clubhouse which offered tennis courts, picnic grounds, and park. Justin started school again, not without some unhappiness over missing the friends that he had made in New Orleans, and Josh went back to work, out on the road during the week, returning home for weekends. All very humdrum, very ordinary, yet Carolina still missed the energy, and the joie-de-vivre of New Orleans. Until that one chilly Friday evening, when Josh came in from the carport, rubbing his hands together to warm them up, and hanging his overcoat on the rack.

"There's a big storm coming in tonight, straight from Canada, so they say on the radio," he said. after pressing his ice-cold hands against Carolina's neck so that she yelped in surprise, as she was taking the supper casserole out of the oven.

"Josh! Don't startle me like that, I nearly dropped it!"

Josh chuckled. "We'll leave the furnace on low tonight and bundle up good when we go to bed. I'm glad I don't have to drive anywhere tomorrow, it's gonna be a real bear, until they get around to plowing the streets."

Plowing the streets? Carolina thought. *How bizarre.* She didn't think anything more about it, although she did make certain that Justin had another warm quilt on his bed, and that he put on his thickest pair of pajamas, after he had his bath. When she and Josh turned off the television set and went to bed that night, she knew only that it was very chilly outside. The inside of the bedroom window was ice-cold, and their neighbor's lighted front porch light had a sort of halo around it.

The next morning, the first thing that struck Carolina upon drowsily waking was how very quiet it was; no traffic noise, no birdsong, not even wind rattling the tree branches. Just a muffled quiet, as if their house and indeed, the whole world had been wrapped up in a thick layer of cotton batting. The floor was cold, so she hastily shoved her feet into slippers and wrapped her heavy winter robe around her and went to look out the bedroom window. She gasped, in surprise, for the world outside had been transformed. The grass lawn was hidden under a thick layer of white snow, as crisp and pure white as cake icing; the evergreen pines at the bottom of their yard were clumped thick with snow, and every limb and bare twig of the bare trees was outlined in a delicate and lace-like edging of white. The sun had risen just above the eastern horizon, and the sky was a pale, achingly lovely shade of blue, against which the new snow sparkled like sugar, wherever a ray of sunlight lay across it. Josh grinned and hugged her to his side.

"Like you've never seen snow before, Caro!"

"Well, I have – in pictures," Carolina replied, somewhat indignant. "But I didn't know that it would be so … so beautiful! Like a Christmas card, or one of those paintings of a winter scene!"

"Wait until you have to drive in it," Josh promised, "Then you'll be looking forward to the spring. When the snow is half-melted, and dirty at the end of winter, and everything is dead or covered in layers of dirt and crud – then you won't think it so beautiful."

"Oh, Mama!" Justin came running in from his bedroom, insane with excitement. "See the snow! Can we go build a snowman?"

"Of course, you can, darling!" Carolina caught her little boy in a hug, swinging him up and off his feet, and in the next moment, chided him for being in his pajamas, with bare little feet on the cold floor. "But quick like a bunny, go put on your clothes ... with the long underwear and good woolen socks and don't even think about going out in the snow without your winter coat, and mittens!? You don't want to get chilled and develop pneumonia ..."

Justin's face fell, but only for a moment. He scampered off to get dressed, and at her side, Josh sighed. "You're mollycoddling him again, Caro. Do you need to constantly remind him of the risk of getting sick?"

"I'm his mother," Carolina replied. This was an old and constant private argument between Josh and herself. "I must keep on him about catching cold because he is medically fragile. I hate that he is, but I also hate having to rush him to the hospital for the least little thing, with my heart in my mouth, and then to have him spend days and weeks in the pediatric ward because he has pneumonia again. And I worry every time because this time, Justin might die. If I lost him, I'd about want to die myself!"

Josh looked out at the newly fallen, pure white snow, blanketing the yard, the trees, and the park beyond. "I know, Caro. I know ... but he is growing up and it's a boy-thing. Trust me on this; boys delight in taking risks and dares, pushing the boundaries. I'm afraid that he will come to push and push and push against you, driven to more and more reckless chances, the more that you fuss over him."

"He's my son," Carolina replied, indignant at how her husband presumed to lecture her about taking care of Justin. "I trained as a nurse, and I know what's best for him!"

"Our son, remember?" Josh replied. "Aren't we a family, then. Look, Caro; just let him go without the constant reminders. In any case, I'm sure he doesn't want to spend any more time in hospitals than you do." He pulled her closer for a brief embrace. "Just go easy on the reminders. Now, let's get dressed and go play in the snow with our boy."

Carolina put on her warmest winter clothes and the heavy coat that she was glad Josh had made her buy when they first moved to Ohio; glad because it was more than cold outside. It was so cold that it almost hurt her nose to draw a deep breath of that ice-cold air. The snow was dry and powdery, crunching softly under her boots, so thick that some of the drifts were over her knees. Justin waded into it, giggling, and threw himself down to make a snow angel. They built a snowman, adorning it with stick arms, a carrot nose, a smile of odd bits of pine bark, and an old rag from the carport as neckerchief. They rolled snowballs and tossed them at each other, and once they were tired and chilled, faces glowing and ruddy from the cold, they retreated to the house for a hearty breakfast of sausage, bacon, scrambled eggs and pancakes.

"Imagine," Carolina said, delightedly to her son. "A real white Christmas!"

"But will Santa Claus know where to find us?" Justin asked, his little face all squinched with the seriousness of it all.

"Of course, he will," Josh replied, quick with the answer, as a good salesman had to be. "I sent a change of address card to the North Pole, last thing before we left Metairie."

"Oh, good," Justin was relieved, and applied himself with renewed appetite to the scrambled eggs and bacon. Carolina sent Josh a grateful look, and her husband grinned. Outside the kitchen window, the snowman grinned as well. Perhaps Cleveland wouldn't be such an awful place to live, after all.

And it wasn't the stay in Cleveland turned out to be even more personally rewarding than New Orleans. Josh's employer became even more generous with the pay and benefits as Josh moved up in management. Just as winter in Ohio began to pall over the long gray months after Christmas, the company held their annual convention in Puerto Rico, and wives were included in the all-expenses-paid stay in San Juan. Marlene flew to Cleveland to stay with Justin while Josh and his three closest friends at the company made plans to take their two weeks of vacation in conjunction with the convention. They flew out to the tropical Caribbean and spent two weeks staying in a rented condominium, exploring the islands, and all the wonderful sights, the lush jungle vegetation, the exotic fruits, vegetables, and drinks at every meal. The four couples shared expenses and then rounded out the two weeks with another week at a five-star hotel in San Juan for the company convention. What a wonderful thing, to glory in the sun, the beautiful tropical beaches in the Virgin Islands, when Cleveland was still sunk in cold, bitter winter!

Life in Cleveland continued to sparkle for Carolina, in a way that she wouldn't have thought possible when Josh first told her about having to move for the company. She had thoroughly expected to be miserable in the upper Midwest. She was not able to get a nursing job, since her LVN license from Texas didn't carry over to Ohio, but since Josh was doing so well, it was not necessary. With Justin in school, she might have found time heavy on her hands, but for the neighborhood community center a short walk from their house. This was basically a public clubhouse with a pool, golf course and tennis courts, which hosted theme evenings, parties and cook-outs, wine-tastings, and weekend get-to-gathers. Carolina took tennis lessons, working up to playing every day that the weather allowed, and also became active in the Women's Club. She took the lead in organizing parties and after school activities for the neighborhood children, which benefited Justin when it came to making friends of his own age. When their second winter in Ohio began, and it was too cold for outdoor sports, Carolina was stuck for a bit when it came to amusements, but then she read a small bit in the woman's section of the *Plain Dealer*. The department store, Halle's was planning a high couture fashion show in the Geranium Room and were recruiting models locally. The models were to show off garments made from Vogue designer patterns, of elegant and very expensive couture dresses, coats and outfits which were also available ready-made at Halle's in the designer shops on the third floor. But any woman who could sew would be able to duplicate one of those expensive designer outfits at home. And cannily, Halle's had a sewing department, selling patterns, fashion fabric and notions on the sixth floor – everything for the home seamstress with a bit of skill.

"That sounds like fun," she said to her Women's Club circle, when they had met at the clubhouse for coffee, after seeing the children off to school. "Everyone used to say that I ought to try modeling. They want applicants to show up tomorrow at the downtown Halle's store. I don't know if I should risk driving all the way, since they've predicted another storm for tomorrow."

"They usually want some near-to-six-foot-tall beanpole," one of her friends said, and then squinted at Carolina. "How tall are you?"

"Five-five," Carolina replied, and the friend said, reassuringly, "But you look taller. I'd say go for it. All they can do is tell you 'No'. And if they say 'yes'? Well, if you dazzle them at Halle's, maybe you'll get an agent and sign with Eileen Ford and be the next Jean Shrimpton! Your face in the fashion magazines everywhere!"

"You're so crazy!" Carolina told her, and the ladies fell apart laughing. But the more Carolina thought about it, the more she wanted to give it a try. As her friend had observed, all they could do was say 'no'. And if they said 'yes', what fun it might be, to sashay down the runway in the Geranium Room, wearing some gorgeous outfit, to hear the murmur of pleased approval from the audience! Yes, she would definitely risk the drive over twenty-five miles on slippery slick roads, with the snow falling like fat white feathers. Halle's was a monumental old-money department store in downtown Cleveland, a square block, ten stories tall, with enormous display windows all along the ground floor, showing off the merchandise. Yes, she would do it. She put on her most slimming, elegant dress, under her heavy winter coat, wrapped a heavy muffler over her head and around her neck, put on her winter driving gloves and ventured out. Nothing ventured, nothing gained... She was a little on the short side, agreed the half-dozen organizers for the fashion show, but they liked her anyway.

"We can always use masking tape to turn up the hems!" one of the managers said cheerily, and Carolina was in. She drove home in somewhat of a daze. It was fortunate that the snow had let up, and that constant downtown traffic had already beaten the snow down to watery, dirty slush. She could hardly wait to get home, to call and tell Mama.

"I've got a modeling job!" she exclaimed into the telephone, and she heard Mama gasp.

"Oh, darling – what fun!" Mama exclaimed. "Is it a one time job, or a regular thing?"

"Only one time," Carolina replied, with some regret. That was the only downside; the fashion show was just a single event. "In three weeks. We'll have several rehearsals before then, and a run-through the day before. But it's at Halle's – the biggest, most fantastic department store in Cleveland! Everyone shops there, if they can afford it, and if they can't they come to look at the windows!"

"Well, I will come and visit, just for your debut!" Mama promised. "I have some vacation time due, I can afford the airfare, and I want to see Jussie again. I miss that little critter something awful!"

Josh was thrilled for her when he arrived home the next day, from doing the rounds of his territory, and heard her fantastic news. "Of course, I'll be there!" he exclaimed, wrapping her in his arms and giving her an affectionate kiss. "It would be fantastic if they ask you back to model in other shows. Think of the useful business contacts you could be making."

"Business contacts?" Carolina replied. "I'm more into the fun it will be! Wearing gorgeous clothes, hanging around in the Geranium Room, seeing all the other ladies all green with envy! I can hardly wait!"

And the fashion show did turn out to be fun, and notable: Mama flew to Cleveland the week before the show, and Carolina picked her up at the airport. It was nearly the first time since they moved to Ohio that she had seen her mother. Mama looked a little bit thinner, but still elegant, still beautifully dressed, since she was still working in the dress shop, with a generous employee discount and first pick at the merchandise going on sale. She looked somehow, indefinably happier, happier than she had in years.

"Oh, it's so good to see you again, Caro!" Mama exclaimed, and Carolina hugged her, overcome with a wave of affection; Mama smelled evocatively of her favorite perfume, *White Shoulders*.

"You too, Mama," Carolina replied, as they walked to where she had parked the car, lugging Mama's suitcase and carry-on, between them. "I can't wait to show you the house! It's gorgeous, even nicer than the house in New Orleans. It was newly built, and we got to pick out some of the builder's extra options. And we're just around the corner from the community clubhouse, and the tennis courts, and Justin has finally settled down at school, once he made a bunch of new friends. I sent you pictures of the snow, didn't I? I don't mind snow, now. We've gotten quite used to it, and you wouldn't believe how gorgeous it looks, Christmas lights and fresh snow …"

"Caro, you're chattering," Mama said with a smile.

"I know," Carolina admitted. "I'm just so happy that you can finally visit, and I can show you everything!"

"Well, I have some good news myself," Mama's smile broadened. "I'm getting married as soon as I get back to San Antonio. Clarence and I have decided to tie the knot."

"Clarence? Clarence who," Carolina was vaguely shocked, although she immediately reproved herself. Mama had not been happy for a long time. She deserved some ration of happiness and contentment, just as Carolina herself had gained, after miscalculation and tragedy.

"Clarence Carlson," Mama replied. "You should remember him – he used to go to the club that your daddy and I used to go to when you were younger" Now that Carolina cast her memory back, she did remember Clarence Carlson: a very tall, skinny man with a long chin and a slightly bulbous red nose. For some childish reason, he had always made her feel slightly uneasy, and on that account she didn't much care for him, not when Daddy was just as tall, ever so much handsomer, and every bit as good a dancer. But if Mama liked him enough to marry ... well, that was OK, although the thought of Mama and Clarence Carlson in bed together made her feel just slightly icky.

"That's wonderful," Carolina made herself say, and she thought she sounded enthusiastic enough. Associating with the ladies in the club, and with Josh's business friends had made her much more socially adept, even sophisticated. "You deserve to be happy."

"Thank you, honey! I hoped you would be pleased for us," Mama replied. Carolina grinned, as if she had just had a delightful thought.

"After the fashion show," she promised, "Josh and I will take you to the seventh floor and buy you and Clarence a wedding present – something extravagant and special, china or glass or silver, just for you."

"Only it will have to be something small enough to fit in my suitcase," Mama agreed, and they both laughed, and Carolina promised that it would be.

The fashion show was a wild success. The Geranium Room was jammed for the showing, and Carolina enjoyed every minute of it, from the store makeup artist who did all the model's faces and the in-house expert who styled their hair, to modeling the home-sewn versions of fabulous designer clothes, parading down the runway to a rustle of appreciation and admiration. *This*, she said to herself afterwards, is *the life – a glamorous, successful life!* She hoped that it would go on, for as long as it possibly could.

CHAPTER 16
AN ADDITION TO THE FAMILY

Carolina's life was full; she was happy, with what she felt was a secure marriage, and a rewarding life in the corporate world. Cleveland had turned out to be a good place for Josh, Carolina, and Justin, and so very much more rewarding than she had expected when Josh accepted the assignment to a new company territory. She was even accustomed to snow, and the stark cold winters which blew in from the Lakes. There was something to be said for the beautiful quiet on the morning after a heavy snowfall, and the look of the countryside buried thick in pure white, and how the multicolored strings of Christmas lights on their house reflected on the snow at twilight. No, Carolina was very happy with her life, and wanted no more changes to it. Justin's ongoing medical issues made her hesitant about another child. So, she was on the Pill ... but Josh's work schedule, being away during the week, and the fact that Carolina was forgetful sometimes about whether she had taken the right pill in the right sequence ... what did it matter, if her husband wasn't home most nights and they only made love on weekends? so what did it matter if she forgot, now and again.

It turned out to matter, a lot. She began feeling ... weird, and her period didn't come. It didn't come and didn't come and didn't come. With a feeling of doom, Carolina made an appointment with her OB/Gyn, and carried a small tightly lidded jar with her. A preserve jar, carefully sterilized with boiling water and allowed to cool before she voided into it, containing her first morning's pee. The word came back in a telephone call the next day, from a very chipper-sounding nurse in the practice.

"It came back positive," she said. Standing in the kitchen by the wall telephone, Carolina felt like she had been hit, like Mark used to hit her. "Are you still there, Mrs. Foster? We'll need to make an appointment as soon as you can. Knowing that your first child had extensive ... issues, we all will be concerned..."

"Yes, thank you for letting me know so soon," Carolina replied, grateful that the nurse just said 'issues' and not 'birth defects.' But she knew very well what Justin had gone through, what she had gone through, and what they were both still going through. "And ... if there is a way to let me know regarding ... although my son's problems were not my fault ... his doctors all said so, over and over."

"Of course," the nurse replied, so reassuring and confident. "We can schedule an amniocentesis to analyze the amniotic fluid that ..."

"Yes, I know what an amniocentesis involves," Carolina replied, tersely, "I qualified as an LVN. A thin needle, poked through into a pregnant woman's belly, to sample the fluid surrounding the embryo for evidence of abnormalities." The thought of that needle made her cringe, and she wrapped her arms around her belly, protectively. But she would have to know, and sooner rather than later. "I'll call and make an appointment as soon as I can."

As soon as I tell my husband, Carolina added silently, as she hung up the receiver. *And what is Josh going to do? Was this unexpected news going to ruin the comfortable life that she had built for herself and Justin, for Josh?* Well. She had another day to think about it all. Josh would be home, in time for a late supper on Friday. There was time enough to set the scene; put him into a good mood, and then tell him that their lives were about to change...

Carolina fed Justin an early supper that Friday, and read to him until he fell asleep, early in the evening. A quick look at the clock; Josh would be on his way home, arriving at any minute. She added another two logs to the fire burning in the fireplace, which sent a wave of sparks crackling up the chimney. She had a bottle of champagne chilled in the refrigerator. When she heard his car pulling into the carport, she uncorked the bottle, poured herself a glass and took a sip, just for a bit of liquid courage. She just didn't know how Josh would take this news. He had never talked about having children; didn't even seem interested in the possibilities. She was on the Pill and that seemed to be just OK with him.

The back door opened, admitting Josh and a draft of cold air. He took in the bottle of champagne, the two glasses, and remarked,

"Is this some kind of special occasion?"

"Yes," Carolina replied. "Hang up your coat and come sit by the fire – I have something important to tell you."

"All right," Josh said, in a good-humored way. "Can I hope that it doesn't delay supper? I'm starving,"

"No," Carolina sighed. Josh seemed determined not to take this seriously. She didn't have any notion at all of how he might react. When they were settled on the couch, each with a glass of fizzing champagne in hand, and the champagne bottle sitting on the coffee table, Carolina took a deep breath. "We're going to have a baby."

"Oh, wow!" Josh exclaimed, utterly floored. "I wasn't expecting that! Look, I thought you were on the Pill! Are you sure?"

"I must have missed taking it for a couple of days," Carolina confessed. "And I am certain. My Ob-gyn confirmed it for sure."

"It's a lot to take in," Josh confessed, and sank about half the champagne in his glass, before pulling Carolina closer to him, on the couch. "I'm excited, I guess, but it's a big step. You sure you're up to coping with a baby, Caro? What with Justin being in school now, you'll be starting all over again with baby stuff. The diapers, the crib, the stroller, and all."

"I know," Carolina rested her head on his shoulder. It would be all right. Josh was OK about a baby, even excited. "Now that you know, I can start telling everyone else, Mama, my aunts, my brother, and his wife, all my friends. Your family, too. I hope they love it. I hope that Justin won't get jealous of a baby. He's so used to being the center of attention, being the only child and all..."

"My sister said that the best way around that," Josh reached for the champagne and topped up their glasses, "Is to conscript the older kids as 'assistant parent' materiel. Draft them into helping with what they can do for the baby. Make them compete with you to be a responsible parent ... rather than competing with the baby to be another baby. Helps them feel a bit more grown-up."

"Your sister is a wise woman." Carolina sighed and snuggled against Josh, her head on his shoulder. In her condition, a glass and a half of champagne made her feel giddy and a bit sleepy. "Do you want a boy or a girl?"

"Twins, one of each, for choice," Josh replied lightly, and Carolina knew what he was thinking. He was concerned about her, and about the baby. "But either a boy or girl. As long as they're healthy, all their precious little fingers and toes. You're worried, Caro. I know you're worried that the baby might have birth defects, like Justin."

"It wasn't anything genetic," Carolina reminded him, for that was the single fear that ate at her, or it would, until the results from the amniocentesis came through. "And it wasn't my fault, like I didn't take my vitamins or get enough rest. I did everything I was told, all the way along. Justin just didn't develop like he should have. My OB wants to do a special test when I'm a little farther along. Stick a needle into my stomach, draw out a little bit of the fluid for analysis. They can tell from that if the baby is developing properly. There's a little risk to the baby, but at least we would know beforehand. Be prepared."

"As long as it doesn't pose any risk to you," Josh kissed the top of her head. "I don't want to lose you, Caro."

As soon as Carolina was 16 weeks into the pregnancy, they scheduled her for the amniocentesis at the Cleveland Clinic main hospital. Josh took the time from his route to drive her to the Clinic and go with her into the reception area. They explained to her that there would be some very small risk, but that every care would be taken to minimize it; that one doctor would feel for the baby through the abdominal wall, now that it had grown large enough, and hold it out of the way of the slender five-inch-long needle inserted into the womb and the amniotic sac.

"If the baby moves at all, we'll have to stop," they told Carolina. "And once we start, you will have to hold very, very still."

"I understand," Carolina replied, and readied herself against what would undoubtedly be a painful process. She closed her eyes, the better to concentrate.

"Now," announced the first doctor, and Carolina felt her belly being prodded and punched; an uncomfortable feeling. She could imagine the baby protesting at being held so still, ruthlessly crammed into one side of the womb. There was a slight pinch, a brief electric pain, then numbness ... and she held her breath, tried to still her very heartbeat.

"Got it," said the second doctor triumphantly, at the end of what felt like a small lifetime. "All right, Mrs. Foster, you can breathe again. It will take a while for the results to come in, but we'll be able to tell for certain if there are any chromosomal anomalies or genetic disorders. We'll be able to tell if it's a boy or a girl, too. An extra bonus," the doctor added with a grin.

"I'd almost rather not know," Carolina said. "We'd like it to be a surprise."

They allowed her to rest for some time, before the nurse came in, and listened to the baby's heartbeat, and checked Carolina's vitals, saying that she could get dressed and go home.

"But if you have any vaginal bleeding, or bleeding from the needle site, or begin to cramp badly, the nurse sternly admonished her, "Then go straight to the hospital."

"I will," Carolina promised, already wondering if the risk of a miscarriage for the baby was worth it at all ... she couldn't stand the thought of miscarrying now, especially since Josh was so excited about enlarging the family.

The time of waiting for results seemed to stretch out interminably. In the meantime, Carolina made the nursery ready. She painted it yellow, with white trim, and Justin helped her; or at least helped her with picking out yellow and white bedding, a pretty crib with a canopy, a rocking chair, and a changing table on a set of drawers. Everything was in a cheerful yellow and white. Justin was as enthusiastic about the baby as Josh was, and eager to help as an assistant parent, just as Josh's sister had suggested. In her heart of hearts, Carolina wanted this baby to be a little girl. She already had a boy, now she wanted a daughter. One day, she went to Halle's infant's department and bought a gorgeous, embroidered baby dress with a matching bonnet, and a pair of tiny Mary Jane patent leather shoes. She kept the sales receipt and the price tags and hid them all in the linen closet underneath a stack of sheets and towels, just in case. She thought wistfully of how she would have so much fun dressing a little girl; as much fun as Mama had dressing her. Finally, the call came from the clinic: the baby was absolutely normal; no problems detected at all through the amniocentesis. Carolina nearly fainted in sheer relief. Until then, she hadn't realized how worried she had been.

"No problems at all," reported her Ob-gyn, Doctor Sylvester, when he relayed the happy news at her next appointment. She liked Dr. Sylvester, and had an easy rapport with him, especially since she had worked as a nurse herself. "And we can tell you if it is a boy or a girl, if you want to know."

Carolina shook her head. "No, Josh and I agreed – we wanted to be surprised."

"Have you decided on a name, yet?"

"Oh, naturally. Graham for a boy, Maci for a girl."

"You certain you don't want to know?" Dr. Sylvester grinned, teasingly. "We could get it sorted for you at once and for all."

"No," Carolina giggled. She had a feeling that if she did have another little boy, she would be disappointed, and that would be an awful way to welcome a new life into the world. Might as well put off knowing for certain as long as possible.

"Well, when you get close to your due date, we can schedule for an induced birth. I know your husband travels for his job during the week, and I'd like to know that you aren't having to make a mad dash to the maternity ward all on your own."

"I wouldn't be on my own, entirely," Carolina replied. "My mother is standing by to come to Cleveland to help out with the baby, and our little boy."

"We'll set a date that will work in with your husband's availability," Dr. Sylvester promised. "For one, I'm not any keener on the emergency midnight dash to the hospital with hardly a minute's warning."

"You're in the wrong specialty, then," Carolina cracked. "You should have specialized in optometry. No sudden midnight emergencies for eye doctors!"

"Ah, but I like living on the edge," Dr. Sylvester replied. "Keeps me from going stale."

. . .

The day for delivery of the baby was set for a Wednesday in August: everything was coming together. Josh arranging his schedule to be in town on that day, Mama booked a ticket for a flight to arrive in the afternoon. Justin was staying for a few days with a friend after school and spending the night at the friend's house – all planned beforehand and going like clockwork.

Dr. Sylvester said cheerily, "We'll want you and your husband to get you to the hospital and checked in by 7 AM Wednesday morning. It might take a couple of hours for the Pitocin IV to take effect, but when it does – wham, bam, thank you ma'am, here's your baby. You might even deliver in time for lunch. Supper, definitely."

"It doesn't seem quite real," Carolina replied. "In three days ... my baby!"

"You certain you don't want to know if it's a boy or a girl?"

"I'll know for sure in three days," Carolina replied, firmly.

On Wednesday morning, Carolina got in their car, feeling clumsier and more pregnant than ever. She was so ready for this to be done; tired of feeling fat, clumsy on her feet, her ankles swelling like balloons and having to pee every fifteen minutes. Josh stashed her small suitcase in the back seat, and they drove in silence to the hospital.

"No breakfast for you," Josh said, as she was checked in. "No coffee, either."

"Sadist," Carolina replied, "I would do almost anything for a cup of coffee from Le Monde, and a beignet, too."

Josh grinned. "Maybe after the baby is born, we'll visit New Orleans again, and you can have all the beignets you want."

She was ushered to a labor room, and prepped by the nurse, while Josh waited outside. He was allowed back in, when she was ready, and the IV drip adjusted.

"Not long now," the nurse said comfortably. "I'll be in and out, checking on you, but if I'm not in the room, just press the call button. Let me know when you start feeling strong contractions."

"Sure thing," Carolina replied. Now she was keyed up, nervous, waiting for that regular tightening across her belly. It had gone on for hours and hours, with Justin. This delivery wouldn't take nearly so long since it was her second baby and induced.

"I have to go get your mother from the airport," Josh said, at mid-morning. "But I'll come straight back here with her. Promise you won't have the baby until after we get back?"

"Pffft! I'm only four centimeters dilated," Carolina replied and then held her breath as another contraction briefly turned her belly rock-hard. "Just don't take long, ok?" she added on a gasp.

"I'll try not to," Josh promised. "But you know how traffic is, around the airport."

Carolina regretted that he had gone, almost as soon as the door closed behind him. The contractions were coming hard and fast, much stronger than she could remember with Justin. She wished now that they had just told Mama to take a taxi to the hospital.

"Ten centimeters," her nurse said, shortly after noon, and another excruciatingly strong contraction prevented Carolina from replying. "OK, I think we're ready to get you to the delivery room ... Baby is starting to crown! Here we go!"

The ceiling of the corridor passed in a blur; the double doors to the delivery room whooshed apart, and Carolina closed her eyes against the dazzle of the big lights.

"Look," said the masked anesthetist, "Mrs. Foster, can you sit up long enough for me to administer the epidural? If you can't sit up, you'll have to give birth without!"

"I'll try!" Carolina gasped, against another hard contraction. It was a hard slog, but she managed to half-sit on the delivery table.

"Good... there you go," said the anesthetist, and Carolina felt the blissful numbness spread from her lower back, deadening the wracking contractions. No, she didn't want to feel anything more, and she closed her eyes against the dazzle of the lights for many long minutes – or maybe those minutes were not that long at all.

"Open your eyes, Mrs. Foster," said Dr. Sylvester. "And look at your daughter."

A heavy, faintly damp weight was set on Carolina's chest, and she opened her eyes obediently, staring into the tiny face and wide dark eyes of the baby. A wandering little pink hand emerged from the towel the baby was wrapped in. The baby screwed up her little face and cried in complaint.

"Maci," Carolina said. "Oh, Maci – you are beautiful!" Her arms went around her daughter, the daughter that she had secretly hoped for, all these months. "Shush, my darling, shushie-bye. Doctor – is she all right? All her fingers and toes ... and her rectum... her throat ... there's nothing wrong?"

"All her fingers and toes," Dr. Sylvester reassured her. Carolina just knew that he was smiling behind his surgical mask. "I counted. Ten perfect little fingers, ten perfect little toes, and perfect little intake and outflow openings at each end, which the pediatric nurse will confirm. Six pounds and four ounces; full term."

"Thank god, thank god," Carolina began to cry, in relief and gratitude. She hugged little Maci to her chest – she had her little girl.

Maci had big blue eyes, set in a gamine face, a pointed chin, tiny ears, and a tuft of light brown hair that showed reddish highlights in the sun. Josh adored her, as much as Carolina did, and as for Justin, Carolina did what Josh's sister had wisely recommended. That is, roped him in to be the junior assistant parent. He turned eight, within days of Maci coming home from the hospital. When he had his birthday party and blew out the candles on his cake *(eight and one to grow on)* he begged to take a slice of chocolate cake into the yellow nursery so that his 'bitty li'l sister' could have a bite.

"No, Jussie, she's too little to eat cake," Mama told him, and Justin stuck out his lower lip. He didn't believe Mama, not until Carolina repeated that fact.

"She won't be big enough to play with you and your friends for at least a year," Carolina explained. "But by the time you are ten, she will be two years old; walking and talking, and old enough to play with you, as long as you play gently with her!" Carolina added. "But up until then, you can help me feed and burp her. You can hold her and rock her to sleep when she is fussy, and that would be a great help to your grandmother and I."

"I can do that, Mama," Justin agreed, confidently.

He was a help, every bit as much a help as Mama was in the weeks that she stayed with them. Justin ran and fetched, cuddled Maci and rocked her (under careful supervision) helped by folding clean diapers, and mixing formula, solemnly measuring out the ingredients into the sterilized glass bottles, sealing them up and ferrying them from the countertop into the refrigerator. With Maci safely delivered, and Carolina at home with Mama to help, Josh had gone back to work, hitting the road during the week, and returning on Fridays to spend the weekend with his now-enlarged family.

"Your little man is growing up," Mama confided one evening, as they sat out on the patio behind the house, watching the birds settle into the trees around the community center to roost for the night. A cool evening breeze fanned their cheeks. "Having a little one to be the big brother two is good for him. Oh, this is so much cooler than in San Antonio just now... I am almost envious, Caro."

"Don't be," Carolina warned her. "In about three months, all this will be buried in snow, and we'll barely dare to poke our noses outside, without we have on two sets of long johns, a sweater, a heavy winter overcoat, gloves, a hat, and a woolen muffler. Then I will envy you and Clarence, sitting outside on a December day, in your shirtsleeves. I could kick myself when I think of how miserable I was, when Josh first told me he was being sent here. There is so much to do, even in winter and in summer, we have the community pool, and Justin loves his school! He has so many friends here, too."

Mama laughed. "I suppose that we are advantaged, at that. I am so glad to see Jussie again, and the baby... it's a pity that Josh spends so much time on the road for his job, though. Just like your father!"

"It is," Carolina sighed. "But he loves his work, being on the road and essentially being his own boss without a supervisor hanging over his every move. The company pays him very well for the trouble, so we cope."

"Well paid?" Mama tilted her head, over the glass of wine that she was enjoying, before Carolina dished up supper and Maci had to be fed. "Well, that is a comfort, that you have that. Clarence and I want to move to a nicer place than that tiny apartment of mine, now that we are married," she added, almost irrelevantly.

"Why don't you, Mama?" Carolina ventured. "Can't you afford it?"

"We can't," Mama confessed, dolefully. "I have my pay from the shop, Clarence has only Social Security and we'd need about $3,000 to afford to move to a better place. A safer place. There have been some questionable tenants, moving into the other units. I hate coming back after dark because some of those questionable tenants have very scruffy friends hanging about, and sometimes the drinking and carousing goes on to all hours."

"Like you would mind drinking and carousing!" Carolina remarked, recalling some of the family gatherings at Granny Margo's house, and Mama frowned, then laughed.

"Well, when I was the one drinking and carousing! Seriously, Caro, it's gotten past endurance, listening to what goes on, on weekends after dark at that place! We want to move away, but with the expense of first month/last month rent, a security deposit, and just the cost of moving ... I don't suppose that we could ask your husband for a loan? We'd be good for it, I promise."

"I'll talk to Josh, on Friday," Carolina promised, touched that Mama could ask, after all that she had done, coming to Cleveland in the first place, and then spending weeks helping out with Maci and Justin. It was only fair that they should loan Mama and her husband, Clarence Carlson, the money so that they could move to a nicer place.

"Of course, we can afford to loan your mother that much money," Josh agreed readily, when Carolina broached the question. "Not a problem in the least. I will get a money order that she can take back to San Antonio with her."

"Thank you so much," Carolina hugged her husband, impulsively and with deep affection. "I do want Mama to move out of that place, if it's become as nasty as it sounds. It's a pity. It was rather nice, when she first moved in."

· · ·

Winter came again, veiled in white, piling the snow in thick white drifts. Carolina thought she could never be as happy and as contented as she was that Christmas, watching Justin open the first of his presents from under the Christmas tree, as she cradled baby Maci in her lap. Josh smiled at them both and promised that he would assemble Justin's new two-wheel bicycle as soon as they had breakfast.

"But you can't ride it, until the snow melts," Carolina assured him, and Justin grinned. He was so happy with his Christmas present bicycle, looking forward to riding it to school, and hanging out with his friends – all of whom had bicycles.

"Just you wait until he has a car and a driver's license," Josh promised, and Carolina laughed, thinking that it would be so wonderful for Justin to reach that magical age of teenage independence, after so many days and weeks confined to a hospital bed and oxygen tent, after being sick, or enduring the painful aftermath of surgery when he was younger. Justin was just as excited about his other Christmas present; a brown and white spotted spaniel puppy that he insisted on naming Rex. Rex had his own basket, but he had already attached himself to Justin, and eventually preferred to sleep at the foot of Justin's bed. He also wasn't terribly bright for a dog. In fact, Josh insisted that as dogs go, Rex was a moron, but he was sweet-tempered, loyal, and only occasionally piddled in the house.

Spring came, followed by summer, the school semester ended, and the community pool opened. The first warm day of summer brought Justin clamoring to go swimming. He loved the clear cool waters of the pool, hanging out with his friends; a mob of little boys competing to raise the biggest splash when they cannon-balled into the pool, no matter how loudly the lifeguard on duty blew his whistle and yelled at them to stop.

"All right," Carolina agreed indulgently, hitching Maci higher on her hip. "But we haven't had lunch yet. Put on your swimming trunks and a tee-shirt, and we'll go to the Dairy Queen for a bite to eat. Remember, you must wait at least half an hour before going in the water ... but you can have a milkshake for dessert."

"I want a hot-dog," Justin announced. "With everything on it!"

"Don't bolt it down," Carolina reminded him. "Chew and swallow!"

But of course, he didn't. He was so excited about going swimming, on a bright hot sunny day, that he took a huge bite of his hot-dog with everything on it, swallowed, and then looked at Carlina with frightened eyes. He coughed, once and again. "Mom, I can't swallow. It's stuck."

"Have a drink of your soda, that will wash it down," Carolina said, cold fear beginning to claw at her. No, this couldn't be happening. He had been so well in the last few years; no medical emergencies, no bouts of pneumonia, no long stays in hospital. Justin took a swallow of his Coke, but it all came back up, through his mouth and nose.

"Mom, I still can't swallow it!" Justin gasped, as Coke, saliva and snot all mixed together gushed out of his nose and mouth. Panic-stricken, he began to cry and cough.

"Ok, Ok!" Carolina exclaimed, gathering up Maci from the highchair, and slinging her handbag and diaper bag over one shoulder. She balanced Maci on her hip and took Justin by the hand. "Just stay calm, Jussie. Here's a napkin. Wipe your face, now. Doctor Mason's office is right around the corner. We'll be there in no time – and you like Dr. Mason, I know. He gives you a comic book and Maci a balloon when you have been good about your inoculations for school. He will know what to do ... and crying makes it worse. Be brave, Jussie. Panicking over this makes it worse. Just concentrate on breathing, OK? Just breathe, baby – just breathe!" She was fighting panic herself. At least the hot-dog was stuck in his esophagus and not his trachea, which would stop his breathing. He just couldn't swallow, that was all. But he could breathe. For now.

She hustled the two children, still in their swimsuits, into the car, and around the corner to Dr. Mason's office, the pediatrician who had looked after Maci since birth, and Justin for even longer. Upon explaining the emergency to Dr. Mason's nurse-receptionist, the nurse brought Justin (still stifling sobs) into an examination room and pulled Dr. Mason away from the scheduled patient that he was seeing.

Carolina liked and most importantly, trusted Dr. Mason – an older man, fatherly and reassuring, on the verge of retiring, but who stayed on in practice because he knew that his little patients and their parents depended on and trusted him utterly. He only took on Justin and Maci because Carol Gaskell, one of Carolina's best friends from the Women's Club – whom Dr. Mason had cared for since a baby and cared for her children in turn – had vouched for them, and on her good word, Dr. Mason agreed to be their pediatrician.

Now he appeared in the examination room, washing his hands, at the sink in the corner and going straight to Justin, all reassurance as he told Justin to open his mouth, and say 'ahh!' as much as that young man could. It only took a moment.

"You need to take this young man directly to the hospital," Dr. Mason said, calmly. "I'll phone ahead, brief them about the situation and tell them to expect you. This is more than I want to or can handle: I'm not set up for doing endoscopic surgery here. But it's all right," Dr. Mason added, reassuringly. "Justin will be all right. It's just that there is so much scar tissue built up from all those previous surgeries that the esophagus is narrowed, substantially; exactly the right size to lodge a whole hot-dog inside. This situation usually only occurs with infants, and not sturdy young gentlemen of nine or ten years."

"All right," Carolina agreed, still shaking from her own panic. "Can I use your phone? I need to call Carol and ask her to meet me at the hospital so she can take Maci home with her, so I can be with Justin for as long as it takes."

"Certainly," Dr. Mason replied. "I'll call her myself. Not to worry," he added, with a mock-stern glance at Justin. "Chew and swallow, young man," he added. "Chew and swallow carefully. Don't bolt it like a starving refugee or swallow things whole, else you will have problems like this more often."

Justin only sniffled in response. Carolina could only think with deep regret how awful this day had turned out, after such a promising start. It was not fair: Justin had only wanted to go swimming on a hot afternoon. And now he was faced with another round in the hospital, after having been well for years.

It took hours for the surgical team at the hospital to extract the last bits of that section of hot-dog lodged in Justin's throat, while Carolina waited with rising impatience and worry in the waiting room. As Dr. Mason had told her, the scar tissue from all those surgeries as an infant and small child had narrowed his esophagus to about the size of a baby's.

Justin had been so well, for so long. Now Carolina wondered ... was this emergency a harbinger, a threat of medical complications to come, as he grew older?

CHAPTER 17
CALIFORNIA HERE WE COME

Just after Justin's emergency with the hot-dog, Josh arrived home from a business meeting in a state of suppressed excitement.

"Guess what, Caro!" he exclaimed as soon as he came in the door. "My whole team has been headhunted by another company! We're to organize a whole new division for the new company! Consumer electronics, headquartered on the West Coast! A huge raise, too!"

"And we would have to move again?" Carolina ventured, with a sinking heart. The Women's Club had just offered her the office of president of the local chapter for the coming year. She couldn't accept the club presidency if they had to move.

Josh kissed her, and replied, "Yep! To California! Land of palm trees and blue skies! Hollywood, movie stars and surfing every weekend! I can hardly wait! What do you think? How fast can we pack up, and sell this place, do you think?"

"Before school starts," Carolina replied, slowly. "So that Justin doesn't miss any school."

It was almost too much to take in; another move, and all the things that would have to be done, uprooting Justin and Maci from a comfortable routine, overseeing the moving company one more time and saying goodbye to all the friends that she had made in Cleveland. But it would be an adventure; California, the golden state… Carolina entertained a brief vision of a bigger house, even a mansion, a place with a lovely garden, a swimming pool of their own, in a glamorous location.

Josh was saying, "Make it a road trip ... and he sang a few lines. "*If you ever plan to motor west, Travel my way, that's the highway that's the best! Get your kicks on Route 66!* That's what we'll do, Caro. Ship my car, pack up the kids, Rex and the cat and make a traveling vacation out of it. Get our kicks on Route 66! Stop and look at the sights along the way ... hey, we can even stop over on Las Vegas, play the slots, and look at the lights!" That made the move sound a bit more tempting. They would also escape the miseries of another long, cold, snow-clogged winter; the charm of fresh snow and a white Christmas had palled after a couple of such winters.

The company paid for the move, of course, and Justin was over-the-moon excited about the proposed road trip and moving to glamorous California, the golden state, even though he did lament losing his circle of friends. Their household furniture and fittings all vanished into the back of a huge moving van, swathed with layers of padding, or packed into boxes. One last round of visits to their close friends, and a final gathering at the community recreation center, and then the Fosters turned their faces to the west: Justin and Maci in the back seat of the car, with Rex the brown and white Spaniel, and Snowball the white cat in her little basket between them.

Josh was right; it was a wonderful and leisurely way to travel, perhaps three or four hours daily in the car. They stopped for lunch at midday, almost always a picnic lunch by the side of the road, if not an interesting-looking roadside diner. They also paused in their journey to visit anything interesting, especially if Justin clamored to see it, after spotting particularly enticing roadside billboards. They stayed in motor courts and small motels along Route 66, once they reached Chicago. From Chicago to St. Louis, the road wandered across the farmlands and industrial towns of the upper middle west. At St. Louis, they admired the soaring gateway arch, and crossed over the Mississippi/Missouri River. Carolina told Justin how that river, eventually went all the way south to New Orleans, where they had lived before Cleveland.

"We're in the West, now, kids!" Josh said.

They followed the endless ribbon of Route 66 to Rolla and Springfield, where they took a detour to see the caves.

"Do you know, there is a town named Springfield somewhere in every single one of the forty-eight states?" Josh told them. Just outside of Joplin, they crossed over into Oklahoma. They stopped over in Oklahoma City to visit Josh's sister and her family, and the rest of Josh's Foster kinfolk. Then it was a long hot stretch across the arid Texas Panhandle, to Amarillo, and then the high deserts of New Mexico. They stopped for several days in Albuquerque, to visit the old town and look at the Indian art. Josh bought a silver squash-blossom necklace and bracelets for Carolina, and a little silver bangle set with turquoise stones for Maci. More dusty miles of desert and desolation, to Gallup. Late summer in the high deserts of New Mexico was the monsoon season. Almost every afternoon, they could see storm clouds building, piling up higher and higher; a snowy-white pillar with a flat iron gray underside, and the veil of rain falling from it, moving slowly across the desert. They could often smell the fresh rain coming on the errant breeze. Then they came to the tall mountains at Flagstaff, and the clear clean scent of pine needles blowing down from the high country. West of Flagstaff, they nearly lost Snowball, when they pulled over at a rest stop to let Rex out for a potty break. The white cat shot out from the driver's side door as soon as Josh opened it.

"Snowball!" Justin screamed. Poor Rex looked terrified, as if the humans were all shouting at him, because it was his fault. Meanwhile, Snowball streaked away, vanishing around the side of the bathroom block, and into a stretch of sand and scrub sagebrush. Beyond that was a sagging barbed-wire fence and then more of the same sand and scrub sweeping out to where a line of low hills marked the horizon. Josh swore and followed after where the white cat had run.

"It's all right, Daddy will find Snowball," Carolina assured her son. Justin's expression was tragic. "Give me Rex's leash. I'll take him for a potty break, you stay in the car and mind your little sister." She was struck by an inspiration. "Leave the car door open. If Snowball comes back on his own, he'll be able to jump back in."

She walked Rex up and down, allowed him to pee into a couple of bushes which he had personally selected to leave messages in for other dogs, while Josh hunted for Snowball. She was certain that Snowball had not run in the opposite direction – back towards the highway. A white cat would stand out against the dark asphalt. She watched Josh walk all the way along the fence, calling, "Snowball! Here, kitty-kitty-kitty!"

When Rex was finished, she took him back to the car, where he obligingly jumped back in. Maci was still asleep. "Go use the bathroom, Jussie. Daddy is still looking for Snowball."

"What if he can't find Snowball?" Justin's voice quivered. "Are we jus' going to drive off and leave him?"

"Daddy will find him," Carolina swiftly assured him, but she knew in her heart that they couldn't stay parked at the rest stop for very long, not in the heat of a summer afternoon in the arid, uninhabited desert. If Snowball had run out into the desert ... poor, lost little cat! He was a house cat, a pet, and wholly unfit to look after himself for very long in the wild, against coyotes and whatever predators there were out there.

Justin went to use the bathroom, and when he returned, he was beaming. "Daddy's coming back – he found Snowball."

"Thank goodness," Carolina answered, relieved, and heartened, when Josh appeared, carrying Snowball, one hand firmly on the scruff of the cat's neck.

"He came out of that big bush, meowing his fool head off," Josh stuffed Snowball into the cat basket, and latched the door. "OK, from now on, this is the rule. Snowball goes into his basket, whenever we stop the car, and before we open a door, or the window. That was a close call!"

They got to Kingman in time for a late lunch, to gas up the car, and fill up jugs of water. They had been told, repeatedly by gas station attendants, other travelers and by people they encountered at the motor courts where they stayed, to always have plenty of water with them, driving across the desert in summer; plenty of water to drink, and to re-fill the radiator.

"What the heck – let's go to Las Vegas!" Josh looked across at Carolina, and she replied.

"Oh, lets!" Carolina replied. "We have time enough that we can spend a couple of days, maybe even see some shows." She had been studying the maps. If they went the hundred or so miles north from Kingman on Route 93 north to Henderson and Los Vegas, they would only be detouring a little out of the way.

"Play the slots, even," Josh said, and Carolina shook her head. "Best not," she said, remembering how Daddy had fallen into deep debt and bad trouble through gambling and losing badly.

They would probably get there around sundown; well, everyone said that Las Vegas was fantastic; the main purpose of the food and top-flight entertainment acts were there to lure people to the game tables. Justin and Maci fell asleep in the back seat as darkness fell; Snowball curled up in his basket, and Rex snored and waffled softly in his sleep, wedged between Justin and Snowball's basket. The road unrolled like a long asphalt ribbon, stretching to the horizon, where she could see a glow in the sky – not the afterglow of sunset, but a pale white glow. They came over the top of Railroad Pass, past the signs for the turn-off to Henderson, and there was Las Vegas, an oasis of lights like a black velvet tray full of diamonds and other gems blazing against the dark.

"Almost there," Josh said, and reached over to give Carolina's hand an affectionate squeeze. "Welcome to the Strip... Say, we get to our hotel, get the kids settled, get some supper and grab a show... sweetheart, you're staring like a kid in a candy store." Josh had been to Las Vegas before, as part of the company conferences, so he was rather blasé about the dazzling lights, the ornate fountains and cascades of neon and glittering bands of lights and animated billboards along the Strip. There were so many lights that the sidewalks and the street itself were as bright as daylight. The sidewalk was crowded, as crowded as the streets in the French Quarter during Mardi Gras, the excitement in the streets an almost palpable thing.

"I've never seen so many lights," Carolina confessed. Every building pulsed with gaudy and glorious neon lights, the Golden Nugget, the Dunes, the Riviera, the Stardust, the Mint, the Pioneer Club. "Oh, my goodness, Josh, look at that!"

A sleepy voice from the back seat. "Are we there, yet?" Justin asked. "I'm hungry, and I have to pee."

"Almost there, champ," Josh replied. "I phoned ahead when we gassed up in Kingman. We have a reservation at Caesar's Palace. For a little extra, they will obligingly ignore the presence of Rex and Snowball, as long as they don't shred the upholstery or pee on the carpet."

Caesar's Palace was huge, a sprawling edifice adorned with lines of straight juniper trees which mimicked the colonnade along the curving façade, and a series of fountains which also repeated the vertical columns and fell back splashing into pools. It was grand, it was glorious, and so over-the-top. The parking lot was huge, and the massive lighted sign and marquee at the entrance boasted that Tom Jones was the headline act in the Caesar's Palace floor show.

"I'd love to see Tom Jones, live!" Carolina exclaimed, as Josh pulled up to the valet stand.

"You shall, Caro," Josh replied, as they unloaded their suitcases, and Snowball's travel basket. Carolina cuddled Maci to her. The baby melted as if boneless onto her shoulder, she was that sleepy, and Justin yawned. "Look, ask at the desk for a list of approved babysitters who can watch the kids tonight. Like I said, we get them fed and settled, and then we go have some happy adult fun for ourselves. The food here is so fantastic that I'd stay here for life."

And that was what they did; brought the children, Snowball and Rex to the suite for which Josh had finagled a reservation when he called that afternoon from Kingman. The suite had two bedrooms and a sitting room. The bellboy trundled in their luggage on a fancy cart, a courtesy which made Carolina giggle. All the way from Cleveland, they had lugged their own suitcases into wherever they were going to stay for the night. She could only think this was a bit of luxury, for what would be their last few nights on the road. Justin was already yawning, but he perked up enough after a bath, and a look at the room service menu.

"Remember to chew carefully and swallow!" Carolina reminded him sternly. "We don't know any doctors here, and it would wreck our vacation trip if we had to rush you to the hospital again because you bolted your food."

Josh cleared his throat. "I'll see if they have soup on the menu. Caro, here's the list of recommended babysitters. You want to start calling them, see which one of them you like who can get here in forty minutes. We'll have just enough time for supper before we catch the show."

After he called in an order for the children to room service, Carolina began calling the babysitters; all of them sounded agreeable over the phone, and of course they had all been vouched for by the hotel. She saw that Justin was eating his supper. The boy was terribly impressed that his supper order arrived on a rolling cart with a cover over it, and that the room service waiter set the table for him, put his meal on the table, and poured him a glass of soda before whisking away the cart and cover.

"I like this place," Justin confided. "They treat everyone like they were royalty!"

"Well, it is a Palace," Josh agreed. He was doing up his white shirt and putting on a tie for the first time in weeks. "All set, Caro?"

"She'll be here in twenty minutes," Carolina replied, feeling little bubbles of excitement beginning to rise. "Just enough time for me to wash and change and do my face."

"Perfect," Josh answered. Yes, it did turn out to be perfect. They weren't going to leave the hotel complex itself, so she could pop back to their suite to check on Justin and Maci any time. The babysitter was a nice, plump middle-aged woman who brought a book to read, and said that she would answer the room phone if they called, and she would have management page them if anything like an emergency came up. Feeling totally reassured and almost as if they were on that first date again, Carolina and Josh went for their own supper; drinks at the bar, and a leisurely, lavish meal, with dessert. Then the live show, with Tom Jones, performing all those hits which had made him a sex symbol. Although the hour was late, the theater was crowded, and the audience enthusiastic. Night and day were only theoretical concepts in Las Vegas, where gambling, drinking and entertainment went on twenty-four hours a day, seven days a week.

"You are absolutely forbidden to throw Tom Jones a pair of your underpants," Josh warned her, in jest. "Or our room key."

"There wouldn't be space enough for him," Carolina replied in much the same humor. "What with us, the kids, Rex and Snowball."

"True enough," Josh took her hand in his, as they walked back towards their suite for the night. "What a finish to the road trip of a lifetime! I almost don't want it to be done, but we're only a day away from Los Angeles. We'll hit the road tomorrow and be there in time for supper."

"It's been a blast," Carolina agreed, "But I do want to get settled again. Find a house in a good neighborhood, maybe with a swimming pool ... find a good school for Justin and get him settled in it..."

"A ceee-ment pond of our own," Josh suggested, mimicking the characters in *The Beverly Hillbillies*. Carolina giggled.

"Yes, a ceee-ment pond of our very own," she agreed. "I've always loved swimming. Daddy used to say that it was as if I had been born with fins."

"Whatever you decide," Josh was indulgent. "It'll be OK with me."

And it was. Although when their car came down the highway through Victorville, after another long drive through a desolate, rocky landscape, interspersed with stretches of barren sand and straggling, half-dead sagebrush. Justin looked through the windshield from the back seat, and asked,

"Dad, what's all that brown stuff in the air. Is there a dust storm out there?"

"Smog," Josh replied. "Air pollution, over Los Angeles."

"Yuck," Josh said. "I'd rather go home to Cleveland."

"Sorry, champ. Los Angeles is home for us now," Josh explained. "Or at least, until I get promoted to another big territory."

"Yuck," Justin said again. He was tired and cross from the long, hot drive through the desert, even though they had stopped for lunch at a hamburger place in a tiny little town called Baker, where all the truck drivers stopped. *(Josh had insisted all during this trip that truck drivers and local policemen always knew the little diners and restaurants with good food – and he was generally right.)*

"It will be all right, Jussie," Carolina promised. "We'll have as nice a house as we did in Cleveland, and maybe we'll be able to go swimming every day. And to Disneyland. And the beach. And Hollywood, to see where the movie stars live. It's a whole different world."

"It's still yucky," Justin whispered sullenly. Carolina and Josh exchanged a commiserating glance.

"He'll get over it," Josh promised, and raised his voice slightly. "We'll stay in a nice hotel again, while your mom and I look for a nice house. Orange County is a good place; south of Los Angeles, between the mountains and the ocean."

"OK, Dad." Justin sounded only faintly mollified.

• • •

They found the perfect house in a suburb called Fullerton; a good and long-established neighborhood, wedged in between the hills and the coast. The house was for sale by an elderly couple who wanted to move to an apartment to be nearer their own family, although there wasn't a pool – or a ceee-ment pond in the back yard. They were close to a sprawling country club which did have a pool, as well as tennis courts and a golf course, which suited them perfectly. It was in a good school district, too. A few members of Josh's team also bought houses close by, so Carolina and Josh had ready-made friends even before they moved in.

The one downside was that Carolina's nursing license was not valid in California, so she could not take a job in the nearby medical center – which would have been perfect. Even though Maci was still a baby and demanded attention, the time hung heavy on Carolina's hands. What fun it had been, doing that fashion show at Halle's, back in Cleveland! Why couldn't she do more of that here, in California? The more that she thought about it, the more fun it sounded and being in Los Angeles was the perfect place to go to modeling school and make a career out of it. Josh was out working his territory for days, even weeks at a time. She had to do something; otherwise go bonkers with boredom. And Carolina had always worked, even if only something part-time. Best not be like Mama, suddenly having to go to work after decades of being a housewife and staying at home with the children, although Josh wasn't anything like Daddy... Or was he when it came right down to it? He was spending so many days and weeks on the road, doing business, while Carolina was not much interested in what Josh was doing, when he was on the road. Would it eventually become clear that Josh was also uninterested in what she did, during the weeks and hours when he was away? That was an uncomfortable thought, and Carolina thrust it far, far down into a corner of her mind. With modeling school, she would have something interesting to do, and to talk about with Josh, when he was at home.

• • •

Modeling school opened doors for her, doors into the glittering entertainment world in California. She and Josh went to a live taping of the *Tony Orlando and Dawn Show*, which was almost as exciting as being an extra in a TV special featuring Barry Manilow. She modeled clothes for several local dress shops at local restaurants, and for a floor show at Disneyland, and got to be a contestant on *The Price is Right*. The most exciting was being an extra on a movie about the life of Howard Hughes. She could hardly wait to tell Josh about it when he came home from work.

"Guess who I met on the set the other day!" Carolina exclaimed. "And we talked for simply the longest time! Did you ever think that there is so much time spent, just sitting around on a movie set? Honestly, you wouldn't believe how boring it must be for the actors. Five or ten minutes doing a scene ... and then an hour or so of sitting around waiting to do the next ... or having to do it over and over again, because something went wrong. Something nearly always goes wrong." She added, with the knowledge gathered of late. "You figure for every minute on the screen, there's an hour of work involved."

"Who did you meet?" Josh asked, with a sigh. He didn't sound all that interested, as if he were slightly more concerned with the cold beer that he had just opened. *Honestly, didn't a husband and wife have conversations about things?*

"Tommy Lee Jones," Carolina exclaimed. "He's the star of the movie that I got hired on! He was in *Love Story*, and now he's on *One Life to Live* and everyone says that he's terribly prickly and hostile when some stranger tries to talk to him, but he was sweet to me, when we talked. They had sent me to wardrobe, to try on this fabulous 1940s outfit, down to a matching handbag and hat and gloves – I'll bet Mama would have worn something like it when she met Daddy – but I was sitting outside, waiting ... and he came and sat down next to me, and we started talking. He's from Texas, too; San Saba. Did you know? His daddy was an oilfield hand, and Tommy Lee loves horses. He wants to own a ranch of his own and says that he'll have it someday. I think he will, he's that focused. We had so much in common, being from Texas and all..."

"I guess you did," Josh replied, sounding supremely bored by her enthusiasm. and for the first time since settling in California,

Carolina found herself annoyed by this disinterest. What was happening to them? They didn't fight; they just hardly talked at all anymore, about much of anything. They never clashed, like she had done with Mason over going out to party with friends, and he never raised a hand against her like Mark had done so frequently. but the niggling unhappiness was there, and she sensed that they were growing farther and farther apart. She didn't like the way he spoke abruptly to Justin, and sometimes physically punished her son by spanking him with a belt. Carolina hated it when that happened.

"And another thing," Carolina announced. "This is serious. Justin is getting teased at school, about his medical condition. His sphincter doesn't work well, after they closed the colostomy. He ... soils his underpants sometimes, and the other boys complain that he stinks. I think we might have to transfer him to a private school."

"Whatever you decide," Josh replied. He had always left domestic matters up to Carolina, but the indifference in his voice stung. "We can certainly afford a private school."

"I'll look into it, then," Carolina was a little relieved that he was OK with transferring Justin to another school, but from then on, her restless dissatisfaction with the situation increased.

Josh also drank heavily, sometimes all night with his friends from work, arriving home sodden with alcohol in the early hours of morning; she could smell the alcohol sweating out of his pores for hours the following day. Sometimes she wondered what would happen if he crashed the car, like he had that long-ago time in New Orleans. Now and again, she woke up alone in bed wondering if there was a policeman coming to the house to tell her that Josh had suffered a fatal auto accident on the California highways or had been taken to the hospital in an ambulance. What was frightening about this possibility was her almost total indifference to it: she didn't care, not even enough to remonstrate with him over his drinking. She reached a breaking point, though, the morning that they had a scheduled parent-teacher conference with at Justin's school, and Josh had gone drinking the night before. He absolutely *reeked* of booze, in spite of having showered, shaved and changed clothes in the morning before the school visit.

Carolina raged inwardly at the embarrassment, although the teacher never said a word; her faint expression of puzzled disgust said everything. What did Justin's teacher think of Justin's parents, with his father smelling like a brewery. Carolina herself shamed and humiliated. As if Justin didn't have problems enough at school with his leaky bowel; now everyone would think that he had a drunk for a father.

It was shortly after that parent-teacher conference that Carolina decided she had enough. She was tired of the smell of booze on Josh, like the stink coming off a skunk, of making excuses to Maci about when her daddy was coming home, of Josh belting Justin. It wasn't a marriage anymore, it was just two people indifferent to each other, sharing a house and not much else. It was a morning when Josh was home on a weekend, looking ragged and hung over at breakfast. Maci and Justin were still asleep.

"We have to talk," Carolina said, putting her courage up to the sticking point. She was done with this marriage.

"Sure. Talk," Josh replied. He had refused scrambled eggs, anything but a stiff drink of tomato juice.

"We're done," Carolina said. "With marriage. Let's get a divorce, before we start hating each other."

"OK," Josh agreed, without even looking surprised. "You want to talk to a lawyer about it, first? I won't contest." He looked around the kitchen, adding. "You can have the house. For the kids and all."

"I won't ask for alimony," Carolina conceded, oddly grateful that Josh was surprisingly civilized over this. "Honestly, I'm making enough through the modeling and all. And I can get my widow's pension reinstated, in any case, and military medical care for Justin."

"Let's do it and get it over with," Josh agreed. "We haven't been happy together for a while, and life is just too damn short to spend it being unhappy." He looked around for a long moment, before adding, "I suppose I should move out, first thing I can find an apartment or crash with one of the guys on the team."

"You don't have to rush," Carolina allowed, suddenly sympathetic towards him. After all, they had been married for more than seven years and had a child together. They had been happy and fulfilled for most of that time. It was only that the time had come to call it quits, now. She couldn't take his drinking, traveling and when he would come home, he would stay out with his buddies drinking.

"No, I'll call around. Get a place of my own. Don't worry about it, Caro. But" he added with a suddenly stern expression. "I will insist on visitation rights, Maci, and Justin, too. He doesn't remember any other father; he's coming up on that dangerous teen age. Boys do need a strong hand that moms can't deliver, especially when they get rebellious."

"As long as you promise not to hit him with your belt," Carolina insisted, and Josh briefly scowled, but said nothing more.

. . .

It was a surprisingly civil and painless divorce, at least it was for the first couple of years. It helped that Carolina and Josh said nothing bad about each other to the kids and maintained a civil and unified front in all things to do with them. Carolina, Justin, and Maci went on living in the Fullerton house and Justin and Maci stayed alternate weekends with Josh at his new place. Which they loved, because it was a condo unit with a pool, and Josh did take them to fun places on those weekends; the beach, to Disneyland and Knott's Berry Farm, to the mountains to see the snow. Josh went on paying for Justin's private school. All of this was more than generous of him, and Carolina was grateful. She did get her Department of Defense widow's pension reinstated, and Justin's Social Security as Jeff's dependent had never stopped. Between that and her income from modeling and as a movie and TV extra every now and then, they managed quite well, right up until Josh got serious about Judy, a woman that he began dating seriously.

Justin and Maci were dropped off late on Sunday afternoon by Josh, who waved from the driver's seat at Carolina. There was a woman in the passenger seat next to him, and Carolina thought it was only her imagination that the woman looked daggers at her, as the kids got out of the back. Carolina had an impression of dark hair and eyes veiled by sunglasses. Before, Josh had always dropped off the kids by himself; parked the car, came into the house and briefed Carolina on whatever they had done, over the visitation weekend. On that day, he just let the kids out of the car, handed them their little suitcases, and then got back into the driver's seat without coming into the house. This was curious, a break from an expected routine.

"Who was that, with your dad?" Carolina asked, as the kids came romping up to her, waiting at the front door and Josh's car roared away.

"His new girlfriend," Justin replied. "I'm hungry, Mom. Are we gonna eat soon? Judy didn't want us to go to Sunday brunch with her and Dad, so Maci and I just had sandwiches."

"A new girlfriend?" Carolina tried her best to sound neutral, non-judgmental. Well, Josh was a handsome man, in his thirties and making a good living. It was only to be expected that he would hit the dating scene again. Any sensible woman would think him a good catch, even with having an ex-wife and two children.

"Her name is Judy," Justin explained. "Short for Judith. I think she and Dad are serious. He told her about us, had her over so that we could all go out to the zoo together."

"Is she nice?" Carolina asked, with a brief pang at her heart. "Do you like her?"

"No," said Maci, decidedly. And then added. "I hate her. She's awful."

"No," Justin answered, almost at the same time. "I think she wants Dad all to herself. She looked at Maci and I as if we were something that smelled bad."

"Oh, dear," Carolina said.

This was not going to work out well. Not at all.

CHAPTER 18
CALIFORNIA, THERE WE GO

Carolina and Josh's divorce was amiable, but that was only at first. After the first year, they agreed to sell the house in Fullerton and split the money. Carolina bought a smaller house in Yorba Linda, which suited her and the children very well. With her widow's pension, Social Security for Justin, and what she earned as a model and movie and TV extra, she could live very comfortably. Josh took Justin and Maci for alternate weekends, which is what he had generously agreed to do, but all that came to a screeching halt once Josh married Judy. Carolina had only seen Judy in passing, when she brought the kids to Josh's house, or when Josh brought them home at the end of a weekend visit. Judy was slim, dark-haired, and pretty; an athletic woman whom Carolina would have bet played a killer game of tennis. Just the type of woman to Josh's taste, but whenever Judy and Carolina met, however briefly, Judy looked as if there was something bad smelling under her nose.

"I don't want to go to Dad's." Justin began dragging his feet over the scheduled visits, and since he was not Josh's biological father, Carolina didn't press the issue. It had just been nice of Josh to treat the children the same. Now Justin said, "Judy hates us spending any time with Dad. She even has a tizzy every time Dad talks to you on the phone. She tells him that you are controlling and manipulative."

"But he is Maci's father," Carolina was shocked. "It's only right and I don't see how she can stand in the way of a daddy spending time with his little girl."

Justin shrugged. "She doesn't even like to look at Maci. I heard her tell Dad that Maci just looks too much like you, and she hates your guts."

"That's not fair!" Carolina exclaimed. "Especially not to your sister! I don't even know Judy! I wouldn't have him back if he was offered on a silver platter with an apple in his mouth. How can she even think that I even want to get back together with her husband. I can't even imagine why Josh would put up with that!"

Justin shrugged. "I dunno, Mom. She looks at me like I'm something nasty that Rex dragged in. Don't make me go to Dad's next weekend. I just don't want to spend another weekend with Judy treating me like a piece of......"

"I won't, sweetie," Carolina promised, a little heartsore that Josh's new wife would dare make visitation weekends so miserable for her children. Eventually, Josh would only take Maci for a single day, as Judy would go into their bedroom and not come out the whole time that Maci was visiting her father. This was terribly hurtful for Maci, who was barely six years old. But very shortly, it became a moot point.

"We're moving back to Dallas," Josh announced in a terse phone call. Carolina could hear Judy's spiteful voice in the background.

"Tell that witch that she doesn't have to send that brat of hers to us, every other weekend!"

"Honey!" Josh gave an exasperated sigh, and Carolina bit her lip to keep from saying something just as rude. "I'm sorry about that, Caro. Really. Maybe I'll be able to come out to California now and again and see Maci. But once we go back to Texas, there's just too much expense and hassle to carry on with visitation."

"You needn't trouble yourself, then," Carolina replied, after running through some less-than-tactful responses. "It will be a hassle, I am certain. Maybe you can just send her a Christmas card once a year, and something for her birthday, that is, if Judy gives you permission to remember that you have a daughter!"

"Caro!" Josh protested, but Carolina had already slammed down the phone receiver.

. . .

Shortly after Josh and Judy moved to Texas, Carolina met up with Miller Hatch, who was a musician and part-time actor. He was playing with a band, at a venue where she was doing a fashion show; a big, easy-going guy, built like a shaggy teddy bear. Mostly he reminded her of Buster, the high school boyfriend who worked at the tire shop, who had wanted to marry Carolina, but who had been told off by Daddy, so many years before. Miller was ambitious about nothing but music and his band. He and the band got by, playing for bars and honky-tonks, but his very lack of ambition was restful after Josh's ambition and long hours and days away from home. And Miller was good with Justin and Maci, like a dependable big brother, and a very good handy man. After a time, Carolina gave him a key and he moved into the spare bedroom. Miller worked evenings and nights, slept in the late mornings, and was almost always home when Justin and Maci came in from school. It was rather pleasant, having a reliable male in the house, someone who could see to fixing small things, hang pictures, sort out clogs in the plumbing and change the oil in her car.

When summer came, Mama called, long-distance, and asked if Justin and Maci wanted to come and visit when school was out.

"Oh, Mom – please?" Justin and Maci begged. Justin had always been adored and spoiled by Mama, and it had been a long time since she and Clarence had been to California for a visit; that time being before Josh and Carolina divorced.

"I'll see what I can do," Carolina promised. It was just barely doable, round-trip airfare to San Antonio for two children. Justin promised to look after his little sister. As a big boy of fourteen he was certainly responsible enough to travel by himself and Mama promised to meet them at the airport. Carolina sent them off and checked in by telephone every day or so. It seemed like they had fun, visiting Carolina's family again, Mama and Clarence, Frankie and Valerie, their cousin Jeff, and all the other cousins.

It was after the children returned from Texas that the matter of Justin's medical issues came to the point where surgery had to be done. The bowel incontinence steadily worsened – his sphincter just did not work, and the social embarrassment was becoming unendurable for a teenager – he had been teased so viciously at his public school that Carolina had to withdraw him and pay tuition to educate him at that private school they had talked about. Carolina reluctantly agreed with the consulting surgeon, Doctor Gibbons, at the naval hospital in Long Beach. The best solution was to close Justin's rectum and install another colostomy.

The heartbreaking part was that she must make the decision herself; Josh, with his new wife far away in Texas, could not be less concerned. Miller, as nearly as she could see, was only serious about music, his band, and possibly mind-altering substances; hardly a reliable support when it came to this. Mama was also far away in Texas, and Daddy had vanished, never to be heard from again. She approved the surgery and threw an absolute fit when Justin was brought back to his room, and in considerable pain when the anesthesia began to wear off.

"Mom, it hurts!" he moaned, and she could see that he was fighting back tears.

"I'll see if they can give you something," Carolina promised, and rang for the nurse, who appeared promptly.

"No, there's nothing on the chart about pain meds," the nurse replied, when Carolina asked if an order for them had been issued. "Sorry."

Carolina hit the roof; bad enough that Justin was in severe post-op pain, but the doctor hadn't left an order. She went to the nurses' station, down the hall, the heels of her shoes clicking like angry castanets on the linoleum floor.

"This is unacceptable," she snarled between her teeth. "Get ahold of Dr. Gibbons, have him call, and authorize pain medication for my son ... Now, this very minute!"

She was in a towering mother-bear fury when Dr. Gibbons himself appeared, slamming open the door to the stairwell, red with indignation and the effort of climbing the stairs.

"Mrs. Foster, if you will join me in the waiting room," he snarled, through clenched teeth, and taking her elbow, he hustled her into the waiting room opposite the nurses' station. Carolina didn't give him a chance to berate her.

"My son is in pain," Carolina raised her voice over what he was about to say. "I will not stand for that, as a mother. You left no orders for pain meds for him, and I will not stand for that! And you certainly wouldn't if it was your son!"

Dr. Gibbons opened his mouth, as if to say something just as fiery, but reconsidered just in time. "I understand," he replied, but it was plain that he was holding onto his temper. The telephone message from the nurses' station must have practically melted the receiver at his end. "I am sorry, Mrs. Foster. I will authorize such meds are appropriate. I apologize for my forgetfulness. I was..." and he took a deep breath. "Suddenly called to another patient. For emergency surgery. I am terribly sorry about this. I know how deeply you care for your son. I'm a parent, myself."

"Thank you," Carolina's anger was cooled. Dr. Gibbons was being fair, and she really did understand about medical emergencies which would cause essential details such as writing orders to slip the mind of a man having to deal with them. After all, she had worked in a hospital, and been good friends with doctors.

Justin recovered from the surgery as well and as speedily as could be expected. He came home and normal life picked up again when school started in the fall, but Carolina was restless, dissatisfied. Life didn't have the same savor, the same feeling of endless possibilities as it had when they lived in Cleveland, and in those first years in California. Increasingly, she felt isolated, being so far from family, and Miller was not much help at all. It came to a head, the day that she came home early, and walked in on Miller and one of his bandmates smoking in the house – passing a home-rolled cigarette back and forth, sharing it with Justin and getting mellow.

It wasn't tobacco, they were smoking. That was the moment that Carolina knew that she was done with California. This wasn't what she wanted for Justin and Maci. She wanted to get back to Texas, anywhere in Texas would do. She told Justin that she didn't want to ever hear of him smoking marijuana again, was tight-lipped to Miller and forbade him to ever smoke the stuff in her house and went to her own bedroom to think about how she could manage a move back to Texas.

There wasn't enough in her savings account to finance a move. She didn't have the promise of a job at the other end, the way that Josh had, much less an employer who would cover the cost of a move. She could sell the house, but she drew the line at that. Where would she and the kids live then? When it came down to it, she didn't really want to throw Miller out; he wasn't really any better situated than she was, when it came to housing. She really didn't come up with any solution, until that weekend, when she took Justin and Maci to the mall, for a bit of window-shopping and for lunch in the food court. The kids liked the food court for the choices available. Everyone could have what they liked best, with ice cream for dessert.

A friend of hers from modeling school had a full-time job at a clock and watch store in the mall: Alicia Munoz, who was slim and elegant and carried herself as if she were a ballet dancer; like the beautiful model Iman. But she managed the store, and now and again modeled a watch for the print advertisements. Carolina liked her, for she was acerbic and funny, and took no guff from anyone, much like her neighbor Avril, back in San Antonio – Avril who had encouraged her to leave Mark when he began beating her.

"Hey, girlfriend!" Alicia said, as Carolina walked into the shop. "Long time, no see! What have you been up to, these days?"

"About five-five," Carolina replied. "Seriously, I have a lot on my plate these days."

She looked over her shoulder, where Justin and Maci were enthralled by a display in the window of the Nature Company store, opposite. Watches and clocks bored them, as did their mother talking with a friend, so she had given them permission to go into the Nature Company and browse among the many entrancing displays of fossils, maps, books, scientific toys, and semi-precious uncut stones.

"I heard that Josh and you divorced," Alicia remarked. "And everything was cool between you, until he married again. True?"

"True," Carolina admitted. "But they moved back to Texas six months ago. She hated having the kids for visits. Honestly, it wasn't worth it, sending Maci to see her dad every other week, when his witch of a new wife couldn't stand the sight of her."

"You're well out of it, girlfriend," Alicia replied. She was working the counter and nodded to Carolina; she had to pay attention to a possible customer, and Carolina waited patiently while Alicia dealt with the customer. When the customer departed, with a satisfied, slightly stunned expression and a watch in a fancy box, Alicia returned to the discussion at hand.

"So, what do you want to do now, Caro?"

"I want to go back to Texas," Carolina replied baldly. "To be near what's left of my family, Mama and my brother and his family. California is just not good for us anymore, but I just can't pull up my stakes and leave. Not without having a job, or the promise of a job when I get there. I have the children to consider."

"Hmm," Alicia ventured thoughtfully, and regarded Carolina through squinted eyes. "If you had a guaranteed job, that would make all the difference?"

"It would," Carolina replied.

"Tell you what, girlfriend," Alicia said, "This company is gonna open a couple of stores, just like this one, in the Town East Mall in Dallas and another in Fort Worth, and they're looking for manager materiel. Personable, capable, erudite, and upper-class manner. Think you can sell watches and manage a store?"

"If it gets me back to Texas," Carolina replied, her spine straightening. "I'll have a go."

Alicia giggled. "OK, then. I'll see what I can do to wrangle you an interview with *El Grande Queso* – the Big Cheese. If he decides you will do for managing one of his stores, then you are in. And my good word counts for a lot, since this is one of the best-performing outlets in the chain."

"Would you?" Carolina gasped. This was the solution to everything. Never mind that it was in Dallas. But it was a big city, taken together with Fort Worth. It was big enough that she and Josh and Judy could live their lives without ever encountering each other.

"Sure, girlfriend," Alicia replied. "I got your number. I'll let you know. In the meantime," her gaze went beyond Carolina, to where Justin and Maci were waving to her, from inside the Nature Company. "I think the kids want you to spend some money on them."

"Story of my life," Carolina sighed.

But Alicia was as good as her word; on her recommendation, Carolina got the interview, and the job.

"Congrats, girlfriend!" Alicia said, as soon as Carolina picked up the insistently shrilling telephone. "You got the job! Your interview blew away every other candidate! And I get a nice bonus for having recommended you in the first place, so don't let me down. How soon can you pack up and move to Dallas?" Carolina's heart soared. Yes! She had the job, a well-paying job in Texas, as near to home as several hours drive, not two days or more on the interstate!

"Well, not tomorrow, for sure," Carolina replied, feeling like a door to a dark cell had suddenly opened, and bright sunlight was pouring in. "I'll need to sort out what to do with the house. I don't want to sell it. I'd rather rent it, since everyone else seems to want to live in California and it's in a nice neighborhood. And I'll have to hire a moving company. Is there an allowance from the company for this kind of thing? Josh's employer always paid for our moves."

"Not for new hires, I'm afraid," Alicia sounded quite regretful. "You're on your own with that, girlfriend."

"I'll work out something," Carolina's enthusiasm was somewhat dampened by this intelligence, until she remembered that long-ago loan to Mama and Clarence, a loan that had enabled them to move to a nicer place, and which had never been repaid. "I think I know where to find the funds. Otherwise, I'll just sell everything but the clothes on our backs and drive my car to Texas."

"You really do want to get out of this place," Alicia observed. Carolina giggled.

"If it's the last thing I ever do!" she sang, mimicking the Animals, and the hit that Jeff had once said was the number one popular song with his troops in Vietnam more than a decade ago. Alicia laughed with her.

"Well, stop by the store; they left me with a raft of paperwork for you to fill out and sign. And if you can give us a rough date when you'll be in Texas. The store is still under construction, so you have a couple of months leeway."

"Tomorrow," Carolina promised. Now that the job was in the bag, she wanted to move on it, and move fast. That night she called Mama and Clarence, and told them about the job, and that she was coming back to Texas after more than ten years.

Mama was ecstatic. "Caro, that's fantastic. I can't wait to see Jussie and Maci again!"

"There's one small snag," Carolina ventured. "I need money for the move. Is there a chance that you and Clarence can repay the loan that we made to you, back in Ohio, so that you two could move out of that dump?"

"Of course, we can!" Mama replied, after a brief and muffled consultation with Clarence – Mama put her hand over the receiver on her end, so that Carolina couldn't really hear what they said. "We can't repay the whole thing, sugar; things are tight for us both, what with Clarence being on Social Security and all. Would $1,500 be enough?"

"I think so," Carolina replied. She would make it work, one way or another.

· · ·

And she did. She found a property management company who would take her on as a client, and oversee renting and maintaining the house, although it wouldn't leave her much more than a pittance in rent. She didn't care, although Justin and Maci were a bit downcast at leaving their schools and those friends that they had made. Miller would stay as tenant in the house and assured her that he would keep it all up.

"I can fix most things, Caro – if I didn't like music so much, my pop would have taken me on in construction."

"I know you will," Carolina replied when he made that promise, although in her heart, she thought it more likely that he would forget, and that it was marijuana that he liked almost more than music. But she was going to leave all that behind her. That furniture that she treasured, and the books, and knickknacks, kitchen things and the bulk of their clothes and Maci's toys vanished into the back of the moving van, packed in cardboard cartons, or swathed in padded mover's quilts. On a very early morning in early summer, with the last of the night stars still twinkling in a dark sky, Carolina loaded the last of their suitcases into the car with a hatch back and handed Justin a freeway map of the southwest. Maci was already settled in the back seat with her pillow and favorite blanket, along with Rex the dog, now much grayer around the muzzle than he had been when they first set out from Cleveland.

"You're going to be my shotgun navigator," she told her son, as she jingled the car keys around one finger. "I can't drive and read a map at the same time. You're going to have to study the map and tell me where to turn off, or merge."

Justin grinned at being so trusted. "You can count on me, Mom. We'd better get going before the morning rush hour traffic starts. Corona to Victorville, Victorville to Barstow, Barstow to Needle. If we head out now, I guess we can get through the Mojave Desert before it gets too hot."

"You bet," Carolina replied. "Texas, here we come."

• • •

They were in Dallas in a mere three days. Carolina had no interest in sightseeing, although Justin and Maci asked wistfully now and again if they couldn't stop in at some creatively advertised roadside attraction. They did make frequent stops, every couple of hours to let Rex pee, and for everyone to stretch their legs. When they crossed into Texas, Carolina felt inexplicably lighter, as if a great burden had been lifted.

"Now, remember, your grandma is going to drive up to Dallas and meet us at the motel," she said, as the distance in miles to Dallas on the highway signs began to wind down, on the afternoon of the third day. "She was going to head out from San Antonio first thing this morning."

"I can't wait to see Grandma again," Justin carefully refolded the map along the creases. "Which motel are we staying at?"

"The La Quinta in Richardson," Carolina replied, "Look sharp for the exit for the North Central Expressway."

"On it," Justin sounded jaunty. He had been so very helpful, reading the maps and navigating all along this way. He was the one who could answer Maci's fretful questions from the back seat over how much further the next rest stop was, or a place where they could eat lunch. It had been a long drive; Carolina's neck and shoulders ached and her behind was nearly numb from so many hours sitting in one position at the wheel. But they were almost there – almost home. Mama met them at the La Quinta; she embraced Justin, exclaiming over how much he had grown since she had seen him last. She had already gotten a room for them all, with an additional folding bed. The room would be very crowded with all of them and Rex.

"He's as tall as I am!" she said, measuring the top of his head to hers. "And Maci – not a little baby anymore!"

"I'm starting first grade!" Maci replied proudly.

"Our big grown-up girl!" Mama replied. She embraced Carolina, adding, "Oh, Caro, I'm so glad that you're back in Texas! It has been so long!"

"Too long," Carolina returned the embrace, and told Maci and Justin to carry in their bags. "But I'll bet there's one person – no, two people – who won't be glad that we're back. Josh is furious, and so is his new wife, Judy the Witch. They're already claiming that I'm stalking after them, that I followed them to Dallas! I'm not, it's just that the new job is here. Just a coincidence, but they refuse to believe me."

"Well, never mind," Mama consoled her. "He's an ex-husband, and she's nothing to you!"

"He is Maci's father," Carolina sighed, "But she hates Maci, because she hates me for no reason that I can figure out, and Maci looks too much like me, and she made it awful every time Maci came for a visitation. What a witch! I wouldn't have Josh back on a bet, and yet she is convinced that I would!"

"Never mind," Mama repeated. "You'll have too much to do to even think of hounding your ex-husband."

"For sure," Carolina hefted her own suitcase out of the back. Rex had already followed the children into the motel room, where the air conditioning was on; a cool refuge from the heat outside, baking down on the concrete and tarmac of the parking lot like a blast furnace. "I have to find and rent or buy another house, move our stuff into it, oversee the final arrangements for the store, hire workers and an assistant manager, get the kids into school, find a pediatrician for Maci – and a babysitter, too, a doctor for Jussie, figure out where to shop for the best groceries ... Josh would be lucky if I have even a free moment to think about hounding him and Judy the Witch!"

They stayed a week in the motel. It took only that long for Carolina to find a house in a nice neighborhood that suited them all. The highlight of that brief stay was the morning that Carolina and Mama got up very early, while the kids were still asleep, to watch the wedding of Prince Charles and Lady Diana Spencer on TV. Carolina watched in a rather wistful mood, envying the pomp and pageantry, the sheer grand spectacle of what the news reporters were calling the wedding of the century.

"She's very young for him," Mama remarked. "A teenager, not even twenty – I can't think that they have all that much in common. He's a tedious and boring old sober side and not even all that good-looking, and she's barely out of whatever they call high school. I don't think she has any idea of what she's letting herself in for."

"They move in the same social circles, so I read in *People*," Carolina answered. "She lived in the palace next door. And he dated her older sister for a while. Her dress is gorgeous!"

Mama sniffed, disparagingly. "It's too bunchy for a slender girl. There's too, too much of it, and it doesn't flatter her at all. Enormous sleeves, enormous ruffle, enormous skirt, enormous train; she's swaddled in an acre and a half of silk. Her mother should have talked her out of it; I would have. She should have picked a dress much refined, more elegant." Mama sighed. "And fitted to her, since she does have a nice figure. Well, that wedding dress will be famous now, and copied everywhere. Every young bride will want something like it, and I will have to talk them out of a ghastly, unsuitable dress for a wedding."

"I still think it's beautiful," Carolina insisted, and they watched the recessional, as the new Princess curtsied to her new mother-in-law, the Queen. "I hope they'll be happy."

"You never know," Mama replied, and Carolina agreed silently. Three times divorced and once widowed; that probably made her a subject-matter expert on unhappy marriages.

• • •

She and Mama found the perfect house in a nice area – three bedrooms and a pretty yard with well-grown trees in Richardson near Prairie Creek Park, a short distance away from the mall and close to the elementary school. She and Mama both loved the house, on a cul-de-sac which had been built on a large lot in a kind of mock Tudor-style. The kids were enthralled at the prospect of their own rooms, and a big yard. Maci made friends immediately with several girls her age, whose families lived on the same street, and who would be in the same grade at Prairie Creek Elementary. Mama sensibly loaded up the refrigerator with bread, eggs, cheese, and TV dinners the night before they moved in, and bought paper towels, cleaning supplies, shelf paper, and detergents in preparation for a good cleaning before anything was unpacked.

Their furniture was delivered the morning that they all checked out of the La Quinta; delivered by a huge van which came rolling noisily up the street to where the house was and stopped with a thunderous release of air brakes. From then on, it was a matter of Carolina directing the burly, overall-clad moving men with their dollies, telling them which piece of furniture or packed box was to go to which room. There were only three of them in the moving crew, but it seemed like a swarm, as they emptied out the back of the truck.

"Kitchen… oh, that's the couch. Living room. Bed frame…" Carolina consulted her packing list. "Master bedroom that way. That mattress goes with it. You haven't lost the parts to put the bookshelf together? Oh, good. That bookshelf goes in the living room … those four chairs are part of the dining room set. You didn't lose the table leaf? Put the box of books in the garage for now. One of the small bed frames goes in the back bedroom, next to the bathroom, the other to the little bedroom next to the master. That's the rest of the dining room table! Into the dining room. Just put the box of china in the garage, we'll sort it out later. The wall clock; into the living room. We'll figure out where to hang it later."

"There's a box marked curtains and bedding," Mama squinted over Carolina's shoulder at her master list. "What do we do with it?"

"Go ahead and tell them to open it. We'll need to hang curtains." Carolina sighed. "And lunch. Can you find the box with the toaster oven in it? We can make toasted cheese sandwiches for the kids."

"If we can get to the refrigerator," Mama noted. The kitchen was packed tight with unpacked cartons.

"Mama, start on the kitchen cartons," Carolina looked at her list again. "They wrapped all the dishes in paper, but I think we ought to run everything though the dishwasher before we put them away."

"All right," Mama vanished into the kitchen, stacked high with cartons, and set to work, slashing the tape on the first one open, and unwrapping the first of the dishes.

"I'd like us all to have a place to sleep tonight!" Carolina called, over the rustle of paper, and one of the moving men trundling in another dolly laden with cartons. "Ok; that one goes into the master bedroom, the other two into the garage…"

It was the work of the rest of that day to get enough of the household goods unpacked so that they could all sleep in their beds, after a good supper – even if it was just TV dinners on a tray. Justin even figured out how to connect the TV to the installed house antenna, so they could watch *Little House on the Prairie.*

It was a good start to a new life, back in Texas.

CHAPTER 19
KIRK

Carolina adored the mall where the shop was to open, from the moment she walked into the place for the first time. The mall was formed in a two-story-tall triangular space, with a department store at the end of each arm and a tall, futuristic tower at the very center where the arms met. It was upscale, ornate, filled with high-end mercantile goods and services. The mall atrium and many of the other areas were adorned with lush tropical plantings, beds of flowering plants, and small, well-tended trees. She resolved that the shop, when it was finally finished and open – would be fully worthy of the Town East Mall. At present, it was just an empty, unfurnished space, somewhat inconveniently located to attract customers, with the drywall and ceiling fixtures hung, the former smelling of fresh paint, and the latter still swathed in plastic. The display cases and other furnishings were all still crated, piled high in the back. She had not much to do at the very first, save to be around to answer questions from the workmen doing the renovation, and to interview new employees. She met prospective new hires at the shop and walked them down to the food court for an interview over a cup of coffee or a soda.

"It's not like I ever worked retail before," she confided to Mama one evening, as they shared a glass of wine and the chance for Carolina to take off her high heeled shoes and put her feet up, "But on the other hand, I have shopped high-market retail often enough when I was married to Josh, and I know what ought to be done to draw in customers and keep them coming back."

"You have an open mind, and a willingness to try out new things," Mama agreed. "Because no one ever told you 'No, that's a stupid idea; don't do it.' Clarence says that some people can be taught, some people learn by the experience of watching others, and the rest have to piss on the electric fence for themselves."

"Really, Mama," Carolina replied, but she still laughed.

"Oh, by the way. a friend of yours from California called today," Mama said. "Ann Magnussen. She got your new number from your pal Alicia..."

"To whom I owe the job that I have now," Carolina replied. "She wangled me an interview with her bosses at the corporation. Ann Magnussen is a good friend of ours. Her husband used to play golf with Josh, and she sold Avon and Mary Kay on the side."

"Well, I told this Ann person that you would call back once you got home," Mama said. Carolina groaned, and padded in her stocking feet, to the wall phone in the kitchen. It would still be mid-afternoon in California, and Ann picked up right away.

"Hey, you!" Ann sang out as soon as she recognized Carolina's voice on the other end. "How are you finding Texas?"

"It turned out to be right where I left it," Carolina replied, and Ann giggled. She asked about Justin and Maci, and exclaimed over how surprised she was, when she heard from Alicia that Carolina and the children had packed up and left.

"I thought you were getting on fine in California. That you loved everything about it," Ann said, "And you could have knocked me over with a feather, when Alicia said you had all but done a midnight flit!"

Carolina sighed. "Things turned ugly for us, after Josh remarried," she replied, "And I decided that I didn't want the sort of life for the kids, the way they were turning out. I wanted to be closer to my mother, and the rest of the family, after all."

"I know that feeling," Ann sighed in turn. "Look, things aren't the greatest between Herb and I lately, I have moved out and I was wondering if I came to Dallas, could I stay with you for a while, until I get a place of my own?"

"I can't promise you anything more than the living room couch," Carolina replied, her heart leaping at the thought of Ann, funny, caustic, retail sales-experienced Ann. "My house has only three bedrooms, and my mother is staying with me until school starts, to look after Maci and Justin. But" and she took a deep breath. "I can promise you a job. How'd you like to be my assistant manager?"

"You mean it?" Ann gasped in delight, upon being assured that Carolina really did mean it and had the authority to hire. "Caro, I'll pack my bags and be on the first plane to Dallas in the morning! Count on that!"

"Call me when your flight lands," Carolina said. "And I'll come pick you up at the airport and show you the mall. You'll love it!"

"I can't wait to see you!" Ann said

"It's going to be like the stateroom scene in *Night at the Opera*," Mama said, when Carolina told her that Ann was coming to stay with them, yet they didn't know half of it. A week later, progress at the shop had gone so far as to have the manager's office set up in back and a telephone line connected. Carolina was inordinately proud of having her own office and desk, although it was otherwise a windowless cubicle. Still, it was hers, and she brought in some framed pictures, a potted fern, and the little statue of the Okinawan fisherman that Mama had bought before they left Kadena to decorate it. She answered the phone after the first ring. It was Alicia, in California.

"Hey, girlfriend, how's it going?" Alicia started off, cheerily. "Are you going to meet the deadline in time for the grand opening?"

"The foreman has promised me that they will," Carolina replied, crossing her fingers. Not a lie, but with this kind of thing, you never knew.

"Well, the new manager for the outlet in Fort Worth is heading your way," Alicia replied. "And he'll need a place to stay. The company isn't paying any relocation costs, so he is screwed. Can he crash with you for a while, until he gets his place organized?"

"Oh my god, Alicia, am I running a company flophouse, here?" Carolina asked, somewhat indignantly. "My place is crammed! My mother, my kids, and my assistant manager is sleeping on the living room sofa! The only possible place left is on an air mattress next to the dining room table! And … a man? One that I haven't even met. Are you out of your mind? What if he is a sex fiend?"

"Your dining room floor is perfectly fine," Alicia laughed, and then her voice turned serious. "Look. You'd have no trouble that way with Lars. He's gay. And he's absolutely the sweetest, most gentlemanly guy I know. He's a bit like a fuzzy soft, lovable kitten. I'd feel like an awful brute, sending him out to Fort Worth, all on his lonesome, without someone to look after him. Let him stay with you, even if it's in the dining room. Then I won't feel so damn guilty, like I helped the company abandon a poor sweet little kitten out in the rain and the cold."

"All right," Carolina agreed, somewhat ungraciously. "Give him my address, and he can stay until he can find an apartment or something."

"You won't be sorry," Alicia promised. "Lars has worked as senior salesman and assistant manager for the company for a while, but he's never been out of California."

· · ·

A week later, Lars turned up at Carolina's door, suitcase in hand and his car parked on the street in front of her house; a slender, gentlemanly person, impeccably turned out in a formal tweed suit with a small flower in his lapel. He reminded Carolina irresistibly of the actor Roddy McDowell.

"Hi," he said, tentatively. "Mrs. Foster? Lars Andreessen. Alicia said I could crash with you for a bit, until I get settled in Fort Worth, save up enough for an apartment and get to know the place better."

"Come on in," Carolina was charmed and could also see why Alicia had been so protective of Lars. He looked like he had been the meek little boy who would have been mercilessly bullied and tormented by bigger boys at school. "I'm afraid the house is dreadfully crowded for now. I have my mother staying with me until school starts, and my assistant manager has dibs on the sofa. All that I can promise you is the dining room, but I do have an air mattress…"

"That's perfectly fine," Lars beamed. "I brought a sleeping bag."

. . .

It worked out very well for them all, during that summer: she and Ann hit it off beautifully with Lars. He knew much more than they did about the care and repair of watches, and his long time with the company as a sales associate and manager put him way ahead of both Carolina and Ann. They picked his brains for shop specific management knowledge all summer.

"Sales are a big deal," he assured the two women, on a day shortly before the grand opening of Carolina's store. "That and keeping the customers happy. Don't be afraid to market the store within the mall. There isn't another specialty shop like it at Town East Mall – maybe some of the jewelry stores sell watches, and maybe Sears or Dillards. But you'll be the only one with the ability to repair, and of course, we'll stand by our product in that regard."

. . .

The only fly in the ointment regarding the move to Dallas was, predictably, Josh's reaction. Carolina took the bull by the horns and called Josh's office, not wanting to have any conversation at all with his wife, Judy. But Josh was Maci's father, and Maci still asked wistfully about her father, now and again. Carolina just couldn't bring herself to believe that Josh was like her own biological father, the Italian boy who had married Mama and then had refused to ever have anything to do with Frankie and herself after Mama walked away.

"I thought you should know," Carolina said, as soon as Josh picked up the phone, "That we've moved to Dallas. I took a manager job for a watch store in Town East Mall and leased a house for us in Richardson. Maci starts school at Prairie Creek Park elementary in August..."

Josh swore bitter and harsh curses, and Carolina's heart sank. She didn't even begin to think he would be that angry. Judy must have sunk her claws deep into him, so deep that his relationship with his daughter was all but ruined.

"Jesus, Carolina, why the hell did you do that? What are you trying to do, follow us around the country, wreck my marriage? You and I are divorced – can't you leave us alone?"

"I am leaving you alone!" Carolina snapped. "This was just to let you know that if you ever wanted Maci to visit, that you could see her without flying halfway across the country! And for your information, Mr. Corporate Big-Shot, I moved here because of my job and my family. It had nothing to do with you and your jealous little witch. Oh, by the way, how does it feel, being married to a woman who is jealous of a little girl? Shouldn't someone of that degree of maturity go back to kindergarten herself?"

Josh replied with some very hurtful and insulting things, so hurtful that Carolina completely lost her temper. The first weapon which she thought of to hit back at him was to remind him of that long-ago loan to help Mama and Clarence move.

"You should know that they've paid half of it back!" she shouted spitefully into the receiver, and that made Josh even angrier, although she was certain that he had long forgotten the loan to Mama and Clarence. In the end, she hung up on him, in mid-tirade, thinking that as Dallas was such a large city, it was entirely possible that they could go for years without ever running into each other, accidentally. It was a pity, though – Maci had really missed her Daddy.

• • •

Carolina was a bit depressed by the time that Lars had saved up enough for the first month rent and security on an apartment for himself in Fort Worth, and Ann found a place close by Town East for herself. The house felt emptier for their going. When school began, Mama would be heading back to San Antonio. The whole summer had been like an ongoing slumber party. But her days were busy enough with the shop. Sometimes she looked up from the counter at the ornate clock on the wall and realized that hours had passed – that it was past lunch time, or after five o'clock. She made friends among the other merchants and sales staff at the mall, including Tom Scott, the manager of the mall itself. Tom was the one to be called if there was a problem with the lights, or the lock on the door, or any one of a thousand things. He made the leisurely rounds of the mall stores every day, keeping an eye on things which might have been a concern of the various shop managers, but which wouldn't have been thought important enough to make a complaint. She liked Tom, at first for himself; utterly reliable, competent, and professional, and secondly because he was broad-shouldered and fair, and reminded her a little of Daddy. He was a mad fan of the Dallas Cowboy football team, having tried out for the team himself, in his younger and fitter days, when he had been the star quarterback of his high school team.

"Good morning, gorgeous," he greeted her one morning – not with any flirtatious intent, but because he was one of those gallant Texas gentlemen. "I cannot fathom why a beautiful lady like yourself isn't married. Strikes me that you should have every single man in Dallas laying his heart and fortune at your feet and begging for a consideration. You have brains, beauty, and business sense. It's an unbeatable combination."

"No, I'm not interested." I've been single for 5 years and don't intend to get involved again, at least not for a long time". Carolina replied. "I've married, divorced, and widowed and that's enough."

Tom sighed, theatrically. "Well, I'm sorry to hear that. Are you still all-in, collecting for the football pool this week?"

"Of course," Carolina replied. The football pool was a big deal; almost inadvertently, a lot of the other mall workers and sales associates had been coming to her shop to buy in and place their bets on which team would win at their weekend games. This was likely a result of her efforts to market the shop among the other merchants at the mall. Everyone knew her, and because she was not particularly a partisan of any team, they trusted her to hold the pool until Monday morning.

"Then ten bucks on my Cowboys," Tom said, and took out his wallet. "And I've gotta introduce you to another guy who wants in on the pool – Kirk Davis. He owns the nursery service that takes care of the plants. You might like him," and Tom fixed her with a speculative gaze. "He's about your age, and single, too."

"Maybe." Carolina added Tom's ten-spot to the catalog envelope in which she kept the cash and noted Tom's name and preference on the outside. "But it's my painful experience that someone not happily married by the time they are my age ... there is a darned good reason why they aren't married."

She had practically forgotten that conversation, when Tom appeared the next Monday morning, accompanied by a younger man, clad in jeans and a khaki work-shirt, with the name of the nursery company and "Kirk" embroidered over the pocket. He was handsome, tanned and fit in the way of someone who worked outdoors a lot and thoroughly enjoyed it. His dark hair was brush-cut short, in a way that reminded her of the military men she had been around, when married to Jeff.

"Hey, Gorgeous, this is the guy I told you about," Tom said. "Kirk wants to join the football pool. His company maintains all the plants in the mall. Kirk, this is Carolina Foster."

Kirk stuck out his right hand. "Hi – Kirk Davis. I'm divorced, too."

Well, that was an odd way to introduce himself, Carolina thought, considerably surprised. She laughed, "It just happens, doesn't it? One day married, the next; wondering why you feel like you have just been run over by a truck. Tom said you wanted in on the football pool."

"Sure thing," Kirk agreed, enthusiastically, although Carolina was uncertain of exactly what he was enthused about. "Count me in. Ten bucks, is it? Houston over Cleveland, by at least five points." He handed over a slightly crumpled business card. "My office phone number but I'm usually out here all-day Tuesday. Tom will know how to find me on Mondays. This mall is one of our biggest clients."

"Ok," Carolina took his ten and added his bet to the big envelope. "I'll give you a call, if you win or just stop here on Monday afternoon."

. . .

Amazingly or maybe, it was just beginner's luck, but Kirk Davis won the pool that weekend. She called the number on the business card and left a message. The following day, Kirk showed up at the watch shop, exuding blue-collar masculine charm.

"Hey, Mrs. Foster, I got the message that I won the pool! Always a pleasure, taking home extra money! Can I buy into the next weekend's pool. Now that my luck is running in a good direction."

"Sure," Carolina replied. She counted out the bills in the pool and put them into his hand. He briefly took hers, as she handed them over the counter.

"Hey, look; Can I take you out? Tom says you are new to Texas, you came from California. I'd love to show you a good time; dinner, a movie, dancing ... whatever you prefer. Make it a date?"

Carolina giggled. "I'm from Texas, actually. Born in Houston, raised in San Antonio, mostly. My Daddy was in the Army, but my grandparents were Texas all the way. My brother still lives in San Antonio. Look, you seem like a nice enough guy but I'm still trying to find my feet in Dallas. I have two children still in school, and boyfriends just aren't part of my life plan at present. No hard feelings?"

"None," Kirk assured her with a merry grin. "None at all. I have a daughter in school, myself. Brianna's mom, my ex; she does have her irrational moments, so I do understand. But" and he pressed her hand briefly before he let it go. "Count me in for the next pool. And if I win it, then absolutely promise me that you will go out to dinner with me. No commitments. Just dinner and some fun, going to a bar with live music or something after supper."

"I promise," Carolina said, laughing – certain that the odds of Kirk winning the pool again were approximately the same as being struck by lightning twice in a row.

. . .

But that lightning did strike, twice in a row. Kirk Davis won the next weekend's pool, and when he appeared, grinning triumphantly to collect his winnings, Carolina had to make good on the promise. They made a date for Friday evening, and Ann agreed to stay at her house that night to supervise Justin and Maci. Ann approved of Carolina, agreeing to go out to dinner with Kirk.

"He's a nice guy," Ann remarked. "And good-looking, but not in a pretty-boy way. He seems more like one of your natural Texas cowboys. Rough-hewn but a gentleman. I talked to him a couple of times. He is one of those guys who genuinely seems respectful to women. I guess his mama raised him right. I think he has an eye for you, else I'd ask him for a date myself."

"Well, if we really don't hit it off," Carolina replied, "I'll bequeath him to you."

• • •

The evening together started well enough: he came to the house and picked her up. He was driving a nice Mercedes; not a new one, but several years old and well-maintained. She had half-expected him to be driving a pickup truck. They went to Campisi's, for Italian food.

"Interesting place," Kirk explained, as they looked over the menu. Carolina was thinking of ordering calamari but waited for Kirk to make his choice. "The very first place to serve pizza in Dallas, and all kinds of Italian specialties. The legend is that the original founders were sort of connected to the Cosa Nostra. You know, organized crime, like the Godfather movies. I don't think it likely; I think they just played up that as good marketing. But it is true that Jack Ruby ate here a lot, including the night after JFK was shot."

"My biological father was from Sicily," Carolina mused, remembering how very proud she had been as a teenager to be part Italian. "I'd never met him. He and Mama split up when I was a baby, and he never came to visit us, or send much for support."

"Yeah, there are some deadbeat dads out there, for sure," Kirk agreed. Carolina wondered if Josh was one of them and wished that she hadn't brought up the subject. Kirk apparently noted her expression and read her thoughts. He hastily added, "I'm not one of them. I have Brianna over at my place, every chance that I get. That's my daughter. She's three, almost four. Cute as a button, even if I say so myself. The courts say that I have the right to be in her life, and I insist on it, since she's my own flesh and blood. Tell me about your kids. Tom said that you have a teenage son, and a girl in elementary school."

"Maci," Carolina replied, glad to be on slightly safer conversational ground, as the waitress brought around a glass of red wine for each. "She's in first grade this year. She's quite the dainty little girl; she loves dressing up her Barbie dolls and making up games for them. Everyone says that she is the spitting image of me, only with reddish-brown hair. That's why her father's new wife hates having her come to visit, because she looks so much like me," Carolina added, with an increasing sense of bitterness. She hadn't quite expected Kirk to be such a sympathetic listener. "Justin; that's my son, and I love him to bits. He was born with medical issues, but they're mostly resolved now. He's hit his teenage growth spurt, he's almost as tall as I am now. He grows an inch or two a week. I swear, I'm having to buy new shorts and jeans for him every couple of months; he is growing that fast. He was a fantastic help when we drove all the way from where we lived in California ... read the maps, kept track of when we needed to stop and let the dog out to pee, and he was an enormous help, unpacking and getting settled."

"Sounds like he's big enough to be useful," Kirk replied with a grin. "I've always said that if you can't wow the women with movie star looks, you should aim at being useful. You know; fixing things..."

"I had a male friend like that in California," Carolina giggled. "A musician, but he could fix things. He's renting the house that I left there, now. I hope that someday that he will hit it big, and feature on *Casey Kasem's Top 40*, but I'm not holding my breath until he does."

Kirk laughed; Carolina decided that she liked the sound of his male laughter, hearty and amused. "There's a joke about that; what do you call a musician who has broken up with his girlfriend?"

"I don't know, Mr. Bones; what do you call a musician who has broken up with his girlfriend?"

"Unemployed – *and* homeless," Kirk answered drolly, and Carolina laughed, genuinely, although she did feel a little bit guilty for having done so. She hadn't left Miller homeless. Although if he kept on smoking the whacky tobaccy with his bandmates, he might yet achieve that status. Still, she was enjoying Kirk's company, when she really thought that she wouldn't. The dinner was lovely, the restaurant was a homely, comfortable place with attentive service, and Kirk was fun. Really fun. She had nearly forgotten how enjoyable an evening could be, relishing good food and amiable company. At his urging, they decided to share a pizza with everything on it, and the pizza was fantastic, every bit as good as advertised.

The promising date evening went straight downhill afterwards, when they went to a club for the live music, and some of Kirk's good friends were there. While Carolina sat, silently simmering and toying with a single glass of wine, the friends monopolized their table and a lot of alcohol monopolized Kirk. It got to the point where he was very obviously drunk, slurring his words and walking a slightly wavering line by the time Carolina suggested meaningfully that the evening was late and that he should drive her home. She clenched her hands underneath her handbag all the way to her house, hoping that Kirk would neither cause an accident, nor be pulled over by the police. They reached her house safely enough, and he came around and opened the passenger door for her.

"Time for beddy-bye," he suggested, and Carolina flinched. "I'm smashed, Carolina. Can I stay here for the night and sleep it off in your bed?"

"No," Carolina replied, firmly. The porch light to her house was on, and she could hear the faint heterodyne squeal of a television set; Ann must still be awake, waiting for her.

"Aww, Carolina," he begged. "I'm too damned drunk to drive. I'm OK with sleeping on the couch, then."

"That's also a big fat 'no!'. You were sober enough to get us this far," Carolina pointed out, wrathfully. "If you're too drunk to drive home, then sleep in your car. My friend has dibs on the couch anyway. But I'm not letting you set foot in my house, not when I have my kids to think of. I haven't known you all that long, and I'm not at all certain I really want to get to know you any better. Good night, Kirk. Thank you for the supper at Campisi's; the pizza was fantastic."

She walked briskly up the walk, aware that he had made a futile grab for her arm as she went. But she was relatively sober, and he was drunk on his butt, so evading him was easy. She let herself in with her own key and latched the door firmly after her.

Ann uncurled her legs from the sofa, yawning. She was already in her nightie and bathrobe. "How did the big date night go?"

"It went beautifully, right up until the moment we went to a club, and he got drunk as a skunk with his good old buddies," Carolina replied. She peeked through the little square window in the front door. Kirk's car was pulling away from the curb. Oh, good; she wouldn't have to stumble over his hungover ass the next morning, or have him pounding at the door, or windows, begging to be let in. Calling the cops on him on a late Friday night was just not one of her weekend plans. And it would annoy the neighbors, too. She dropped her handbag on the entry table, kicked off her heels and sank onto the sofa next to Ann.

"I swear – men!" she exclaimed. "Can't live without them, can't live with them, and we can't even just shoot them! God, I am glad this night is over!"

"We can only shoot them if we can claim a legitimate plea of self-defense," Ann replied, and Carolina laughed, in spite of herself.

"We were having a great time," she explained, rather sorrowfully. "He was funny, considerate; a gentleman, right up until he got drunk. I can't stand that. I began to hate it, when Josh would drink and drink, until it came out his pores. You know, if boredom with each other hadn't put an end to our marriage, the drinking sure as heck would have."

"Sorry to hear it didn't go well," Ann sounded sorrowful. "I was certain you would hit it off. Oh, well. Maybe he'll call and apologize in the morning."

"I wouldn't bet on that," Caroline replied.

. . .

She had that weekend off from the shop, and wanted to spend it quietly with the kids, going and doing family things, cleaning the kitchen, and running a few loads of laundry through the washer and dryer. But the phone kept ringing.

Kirk.

"Look, I don't want to talk," Carolina insisted the first time she answered the phone. "We said everything that was relevant last light."

"Carolina, I'm sorry," Kirk sounded desperately contrite. "About how it turned out, last night. Can I ask for a do-over?"

"No," Carolina replied, adamantly. "I have things to do around the house, Kirk. Goodbye." She hung up, but twenty minutes later the phone rang again. Carolina was loading the dishwasher, and her hands were covered with soapy water. Justin answered the phone.

"Mom, it's that Kirk guy," he said. Carolina sighed, theatrically.

"I don't want to talk to him, Jussie."

"Yeah, Mom, but he wants to talk to you. He sounds awful sorry for last night, whatever he did. He sounds like a nice guy, Mom. And Miss Ann said that he was really nice, when she talked to him at work. Do you wanna talk to him?"

"All right," Carolina yielded ungraciously, wiping her hands on a kitchen towel. "I'll talk to him. Satisfied?"

When she picked up the receiver, Kirk said, "I meant it, when I asked for a do-over. But let's not make it an evening thing. Let's just go for a Sunday drive in the country. Maybe out to the lake, stop for a burger or barbeque someplace. Or take a picnic lunch. We can just ... talk. Really get to know each other, without any pressure. Last night was a mistake, and one that I won't make again."

"All right," Carolina yielded; last night hadn't been a drunken disaster until they went to the club, and he got smashed with his old friends, while she silently fumed. Dinner at the Italian place had been perfect, fun, and he had been the soul of Texas gentlemanly conduct. She ought to give him another chance, the do-over that he wanted so badly. "Then we'll go for a drive in the country. No drinking."

"Perfect," Kirk sounded as if the sunshine had just poured into his life again. "I'll pick you up. Say, eleven?"

"Fine," Carolina agreed.

CHAPTER 20
COMPLICATIONS

"Do you want to talk, Caro?" Ann asked, one afternoon in the shop, when Carolina emerged from her office after a long talk on the telephone. Carolina pushed back a straggling lock of hair, and replaced her earring, in the ear which had been pressed to the telephone receiver. Carolina had a harassed and unhappy expression on her face. She looked around and sighed. Business was slow at mid-morning; the one salesgirl could handle any customer who might appear.

"Yes," she replied, with a sigh. "Let's go to the food court for a cup of coffee. "I don't know how much longer I can stand the situation."

"We'll be back in twenty minutes," Ann called over her shoulder to the salesgirl behind the counter, as she led Carolina out of the shop, with a hand on Carolina's elbow. "You look like you need to talk, girlfriend. Are you and Kirk going through a rough patch again?"

"I suppose we are," Carolina replied, with another deep sigh. They got a coffee each from the nearest stand in the food court, and found an unoccupied table, some distance away from any other shoppers enjoying an early lunch or late breakfast. It was mid-morning, so most of the court was empty. Ann looked at her, expectantly, so she began to explain. "The lease on the house in Richarson is up in another couple of months. I could renew, but Kirk wants us to get married and have the kids and I move into his place. And I just don't know!"

"That's wonderful!" Ann exclaimed. "Honestly, why the hesitation? You two are perfect for each other, and your kids adore him!"

Carolina nodded glumly. Justin and Maci did adore Kirk. He treated Justin like a young man, almost an apprentice to the business, teaching him skills like changing the oil on the car, and building simple things with power tools. Maci looked forward to Kirk's visits almost more than she did the very occasional contact with Josh. "And his daughter Brianna likes me, too. She and Maci adore each other; it's as if they were born sisters, even better than born sisters 'cause they don't fight. Mama fought like cats and dogs with my aunts, even after they were grownup, but Bri and Maci are as thick as thieves. It's Kirk. I think he is still a little hung up on Stephanie and wracked with guilt over the divorce even though it was something that she had accepted."

"The ex-wife?" Ann ventured, and Carolina nodded.

"Kirk runs hot and cold, relationship-wise," she confessed. "One day he is all about us as a couple, excited about getting married for real, and I think that everything is all right between us and it's going to be happy-ever-after and … and then the next moment, it's as if he has gotten cold feet, and he starts hinting that he really ought to reconcile with Stephanie. He usually does this after talking to his mother."

"What business is it of hers?" Ann asked, with considerable indignation.

"Well, Kirk is her only child," Carolina explained. "She loves him to death and beyond. According to Kirk, his mother also really loved Stephanie from the first day; she wants them to get back together. She's come right out and said so every chance that she gets, and that's laying a horrendous guilt trip on him. She's also rather devout and doesn't approve of divorce. I honestly don't know what to do. I can't stand this constant will-he-won't-he."

"But you do love him?" Ann suggested, and Carolina put her head in her hands.

"I do," she confessed. "And I must make up my mind about us moving in with him soon. That or renew the lease on the house."

Ann stirred her coffee absently, while she considered Carolina's indecision. Finally, she ventured, "Ok, you do love him, and he loves you, for certain? I said from the first, you ought to take a chance on Kirk. Take another chance."

Carolina looked into her own coffee cup. Yes, most definitely, Ann was right. Kirk was a chance worth taking; one last chance at a happy married life, and security for her children. "I'll do that," she replied finally, feeling a certain amount of relief that she had made the decision.

Ann nodded in agreement. "He'll have to fish or cut bait," she said.

That was how it turned out. Carolina didn't renew the lease on the Richardson house; she and the children and Rex *(who was getting older, stiff in his legs and gray around his muzzle)* all moved into Kirk's house. He had gotten the house when he separated from Stephanie; a large old-fashioned Victorian rambler of a place, with a sweep of lawn edged by flower beds. Kirk's daughter Brianna was thrilled to have Maci move in; friendship between the two girls overshadowed any untoward feelings Brianna might have had towards Carolina as a stepmother. Justin was just old enough to enjoy being treated by Kirk as a young apprentice; as a teenage boy, he craved the approval of mature men. It all went smoothly, until the weekend afternoon when Mrs. Davis appeared, unexpectedly and unannounced, with a covered roasting pan in hand. She came to the kitchen door, and the girls let her in.

"Gran-ma's here," Brianna called into the little sunroom attached to the living room, where Kirk and Carolina were reading the Sunday newspaper. "She brought a baked ham for Sunday supper."

Oh, Lord, Carolina's heart sank. Here, they were having a happy family Sunday, almost the first that they had spent as a family and now Kirk's mother was here to cast a blight over it all. She set the newspaper aside and reached her bare feet out for her comfortable slides, as Mrs. Davis appeared in the doorway.

"Kirk, – I brought you …" her mouth rounded in an 'o' of surprise as she caught sight of Carolina. Mrs. Davis was about the same matronly vintage as Mama, comfortably on the far side of 60ish, her hair already salt-and-pepper gray, but mostly on the salt side. She was dressed as if she had just come from church; a summer dress with a cotton cardigan, just to warm the chill from the conditioning at her church. "What is … she… doing here, Kirk? You promised me that you would try to reconcile with Stephanie! You promised me that you would at least talk to her!"

Carolina reckoned that Mrs. Davis had just barely stopped herself from saying something worse than 'she'. Carolina stood up, trying to keep a lid on her own fury and disappointment with Kirk. His mother was at it again, writing out another ticket for a guilt trip, and Kirk was just standing there, looking ashamed, and not saying a word to defend her.

"I live here, Mrs. Davis. We've moved in!" Carolina said, utterly calm.

"You can't do this!" Mrs. Davis exclaimed, horrified. "It's immoral, I won't let my granddaughter be raised in a sink of iniquity and immorality, miss-who-ever-you-are! My son is married! Let those whom God hath joined together, let no man …"

"They are divorced," Carolina said, between her teeth. Kirk, are you just going to sit there like a lump on a log and let your mother slander me?"

"Mom," Kirk made a helpless gesture, and Carolina was swept by a wave of cold anger, pulled under by a rising tide of disappointment. Abruptly, she was done with this abortive relationship, Kirk's endless to-and-fro, his mothers' relentless verbal sabotage.

"I can't deal with this," Carolina said. She turned on her heel and went out to the hallway, where the telephone sat on an old-fashioned stand in a niche by the front door. She pulled out the Yellow Pages and opened the pages to the listings of hotels and motels. She ascertained the location of the nearest and dialed their number. Behind her in the sunroom, she heard Kirk's voice, low and reasonable, his mother's raised, and on the thin edge of hysteria.

The motel had open rooms, no need for a reservation, the manager told her.

"Good," replied Carolina. "We'll be there in half an hour – a party of three, and a dog. I take it that pets are allowed?"

"An additional fee," the motel manager replied with a sigh. "And I assume that the animal is housebroken?"

"Of course," Carolina snapped. She hung up the phone, and climbed the stairs to the second floor, where the bedrooms were. She took a suitcase out from under the bed, opened it, and began throwing clothes into it, oblivious to the hot tears streaming down her cheeks and dripping onto the bedspread.

She went to the window, where Justin was throwing a ragged baseball for old Rex to fetch and bring back to him; the old dog limped as if his rear legs hurt, but he still adored fetching the ball, until he was so tired that he could hardly move. Justin, bless him, loved the old boy enough to spend a Sunday morning keeping the dog amused.

"Jussie," she called down. "Come in and pack a suitcase. We're going to a motel."

"But what about all our stuff, Mom!?" he called up to her, shocked and disbelieving. "Our furniture and all..."

"We'll send for it later," Carolina replied. "Tell your sister."

"Mom..." Carolina heard that faint protest, but she slammed the window closed, and resumed packing. In a few moments, Justin came pounding up the stairs, and hesitated at the door to the master bedroom.

"Mom, I don't know if this is such a good idea," he ventured. "Just packing and leaving. We just barely moved in. And Kirk's a good guy ... I like him lots, Mom. Even more than I liked Miller, back in California."

"I know, Jussie," Carolina replied. "But I just hit my limit. Kirk's mother ... I just cannot take any more of her sabotage. Just when I think we're all settled, that Kirk and I are going to go ahead and get married for certain, then she comes in and niggles and nags at him, and he gets cold feet and begins talking about reconciling with Stephanie. I just can't stand it. I'll find us another house. Go get your sister. I'm nearly finished with my things..."

"Are you sure, Mom?" Justin hesitated in the doorway.

"Yes. Now, go."

She heard his feet thumping down the stairs again, and the indistinct sound of Kirk and his mother from the sunroom; Mrs. Davis's voice raised indignantly, Kirk's level and calm, although she couldn't make out the words. Not that she cared, not anymore. Carolina finished packing her own suitcase, and snapped the catches closed. Another small bag for Maci's things, a larger one for her Barbie dolls and their accessories. She walked into the bedroom that Maci and Brianna shared, and her heart sank. Maci would be heartbroken, leaving her Barbie house, even temporarily. She began packing a change of clothes for Maci, pajamas, and underwear, resolutely shutting out the distraction from the voices coming from downstairs. She was done with this, with Kirk and his constant state of indecision, his mother's relentless interference. The sooner that she and the kids were out of this, the better – all the easier to start fresh. She wondered vaguely where Maci was, what Justin was doing that he was taking so long.

Footsteps coming slowly up the stairs and along the hallway – heavy footsteps, not Justin's

"Caro?" Kirk's voice, tentative, a little worried. "Caro? Where are you?"

"In the girl's room," Carolina forced her voice to be steady, firm.

"What are you doing?" Kirk appeared in the doorway. He looked worried, as Carolina saw his expression reflected in the dresser mirror over her shoulder. She pulled some more of Maci's clothes from the bottom drawer.

"What does it look like I'm doing?" Carolina replied. "Packing. We're going to a motel tonight. I can't stand this for another minute. Go reconcile with Stephanie, like your mother keeps saying, and draw a line under us. We're finished. Done. Over. I'll send for the rest of our stuff as soon as I find another place for us…"

Kirk took those words as if he had been punched in the stomach. He shook his head, pleading, "No, Caro … that's not like it is, that's not how I really feel. You can't leave!"

"Watch me," Carolina snapped. "It's how I feel, and what are you going to do about it?"

"This," Kirk took the suitcase from her hand, and tossed it onto the nearest bed. "Look, Caro, I love you from here to hell and back. You can't leave, not when I need you so much? I don't want you to go. Can't you see that?"

"Then tell your mother that!" Carolina fairly spat and Kirk took her hand in a grip that she couldn't break, however much she twisted and tried to pull free.

"All right. You can witness it, face to face." He pulled her after him down the stairs and into the sunroom, past the girls, who regarded them with puzzled and distressed faces, Rex the dog, guarding his tattered tennis ball in the hallway, waiting for someone else to go throw it for him.

"Mom," Kirk began, as his mother clutched her purse to her chest. "Mom, look. I have to say this, once and for all. First: Stephanie and I are done. Finished. The separation is final. The end. Period. She does not want to get back together with me. As a matter of fact, Steph has a steady boyfriend now that she is serious about, which you would know about if you only climbed down off your high horse and listened to what she was really saying whenever you had one of your little talks with her. Second: Carolina and I are going to get married soon, and she is not leaving. Not today, not any other day. I love her very much, and I would appreciate it if you tried to be civil and respectful to her, as part of the family from now on."

"Oh, Kirk!" Mrs. Davis looked as if she had been slapped, turning red across the face as if she really had been struck. She began to cry, and Kirk sighed. He dug into his pocket for a handkerchief and handed it to her.

"Mom, stop that," he ordered. "There's nothing to cry about. And" he looked sternly at Carolina. "Caro, you're not leaving, not today, or ever. I'm sorry about all this, I should have spoken up sooner."

Carolina sniffled. She felt like crying herself. But it was as if an enormous stone had been lifted. They were for certain going to be married, and Kirk had finally laid down the law to his mother.

Mrs. Davis softened towards Carolina, and even came to love her very much, once Kirk made it plain how much he loved Carolina. Kirk and Carolina got married, quietly, and began to make plans for a future together.

"I think we should have a new house," Kirk suggested one evening. "A new build, outside Dallas. A place in the country. Make it our own."

"A place that we build together," Carolina agreed, and thought about it. "I can sell the place in California and put the money into the new house, and your nursery business. It's a chore, keeping track of landlord issues, half the country away. At this point, it's not worth the headache."

Kirk took her hand, raised it to his lips and kissed her palm, very gently. "You'd do that? If we're going to be a family and raise your kids and mine together – would you consider quitting the watch company ..."

"And working with you? Oh, of course. When the girls are in school, naturally." Carolina agreed. She sighed and snuggled down close to him. It was all settled. His mother was still unhappy about the marriage, but at least she wasn't still trying to get Kirk to reconcile with his ex. That ship had long sailed; it had gone around the globe, moored up at the home dock, caught fire and sank, which Mrs. Davis finally had accepted, however reluctantly.

. . .

They bought thirteen acres, on the edge of a little country town outside Dallas, signed with a contractor, and by late autumn of that year, the foundation had been poured and the house framed out. Carolina and Kirk had hoped to celebrate Christmas, or perhaps even Thanksgiving in the new house, but construction and finishing out the interior went by staggering fits and starts, and when December rolled around, Carolina began waking up and feeling sick in the mornings. With a feeling of growing dread, she made an appointment with her OBN/Gyn. It couldn't possibly be what she thought – she was thirty-six for God's sake! She and Kirk weren't planning on any children! They were dedicated to raising the ones that they had already; her two, Justin and Maci, and his daughter Brianna. A new baby meant starting all over again, with diapers, a crib, and a highchair; all that nursery furniture and baby accessories like a stroller that she had long discarded in California, if not before. Ugh. The price and the hassle of starting all over again! And just when they were completing the move to the new house in the country and Carolina had already begun working in Kirk's business.

She didn't tell Kirk until her doctor confirmed it.

"Because of your age, you'll be advised to have an amniocentesis done," the doctor's nurse cheerfully informed her. "You know; a long thin needle, inserted ..."

"I know what an amniocentesis involves," Carolina snapped, and regretted her flash of temper when the nurse looked hurt. "I had one for my little girl, because my son, my first child, was born with birth defects. Fortunately, they were medically reversible, and my daughter turned out OK."

"There are some slight risks," the nurse continued, with a slight hesitation.

"I know," Carolina acknowledged. "Look, it's OK. I qualified as a nurse, back in the day. My certification may have lapsed but I know all about this stuff. Just schedule me for the amnio and let me figure out a way to tell my husband, OK?"

"Sure, Mrs. Davis," the nurse replied, and Carolina drove home, rehearsing in her mind the best way to tell Kirk.

He was overjoyed, of course. He wouldn't be the one to have his sleep, or his life and health disrupted, Carolina thought, sourly, and then on seeing how happy that made Kirk upon hearing that he was about to be a father again, she relented.

"I've got to have an amnio," she told him. "To see if there are any problems. I had one with Maci, and there weren't. The good thing is that they'll be able to tell us the sex of the baby. With Maci, we didn't want to know until she was born. But what do you think about knowing, beforehand?"

"I'd want to know," Kirk agreed readily. "That way we can settle on a name right away. And paint the nursery the right color."

Carolina sighed. "There won't be room for a separate nursery. The girls have their room, and Justin has his…"

"He's a senior, now," Kirk pointed out. "He'll be graduating in the spring. Look, Caro, I know he's your son, but does he have any plans for getting a job and moving out once he graduates? What about going to college?"

"I just don't think Jussie is really college materiel," Carolina replied. "Not after all those calls from his school, about all those absences."

"His GPA and report cards are nothing much to boast about," Kirk agreed.

It pained Carolina to even contemplate any indication that Justin, her sweet and charming son was wobbling on the rails, maybe even wobbling to the point of going off them entirely. He was playing hooky from too many of his high school classes and coming home late with his clothing smelling of cigarette smoke, or even stronger stuff. He had made friends with a bad crowd. Carolina didn't like the looks of some of them at all. But she held her peace; her poor baby boy had always had a difficult time, what with the colostomy, and all those surgeries as a child, then being bullied at public school. He had never really learned to manage the colostomy once he reached the awkward age of fifteen or sixteen and resisted being counseled on how best to handle it. Carolina surmised that he just wanted it to go away, and anything that made him think it was going away ... well, that was what Justin was going to do. That he was verging on juvenile delinquency was unthinkable, to her. Justin had been so responsible and helpful when they moved from California, but that was several years in the past. Now ... Carolina didn't even want to think about it. Justin would be all right, she told herself. And the baby would be all right, as well.

This time, the OB/Gyn used ultrasound, spotting the position of the baby within her belly and judging where to insert the needle for a sample of amniotic fluid, rather than holding the fetus in place physically by pressing on Carolina's abdomen. This process was much more comfortable for Carolina and safer for the baby. And it took a couple of weeks or so for the results; the call from the doctor's office came in late afternoon, when the thin sunshine of early spring was already painting long shadows across the newly turfed lawn. Kirk was just finishing up in the office when the call came.

"Everything's good," her doctor explained. "Everything looks good, genetically-speaking."

"And?" Carolina held her breath. The doctor said, "Do you want to know the sex of the baby?" Carolina squealed "Yes, my husband is anxious to you know, also."

The doctor replied, "It's girl!"

"Thank you," Carolina replied. A little girl! What fun that Maci and Brianna would have, being big sisters! It turned out that she had saved the expensive little baby dress she bought at Halle's in Cleveland, for Maci, along with the bonnet and little Mary Jane shoes. She went to Kirk's office, and he looked up expectantly from a plant catalog on the desk in front of him.

"Well? Something I should know?" He asked, and Carolina bent down and kissed him.

"It's a girl," she replied. "Our baby is a girl."

"Praise be!" Kirk grinned. "Her name is Jordyn; Jordyn spelled with a 'y'. Mom will like that," he added, thoughtfully. "She always liked that hymn about the river Jordan."

"Perfect," Carolina agreed, and it did all seem perfect. Baby Jordyn was perfect, the new house was perfect, the girls were thrilled about their new sister, and Kirk's landscaping company was thriving. The only dark cloud in the sky, and at first only a tiny cloud – was Justin.

She and Kirk were called to the high school, several weeks later. The school secretary wouldn't tell them why, only that the principal needed to speak to them, and it concerned Justin. When they arrived, Justin was sitting outside the principal's office with the Truancy Officer, Deputy Forsberg. His backpack was on the floor next to his feet packed with books, notebook and his grubby gym clothes spilling out of the top. His head was down, and he looked defeated. Carolina's heart sank. "Jussie, what is the meaning of all this?" Justin didn't look up. "Mom, I guess I'm in trouble." He mumbled.

From behind the reception counter the school secretary said "Mr. Gwinnet will see you now Mr. & Mrs. Davis, and she gestured towards the principal's private office just off the foyer. The door was open and Principal Gwinnet met them in the doorway and directed them to the chairs before his desk with a sigh.

"Sorry to have to take this step, he confessed, after the initial social pleasantries were done, but we must ask that you remove Justin from school for the remainder of the year."

"What has he done?" Carolina demanded. "He's a senior! That means he can't graduate and get his high school diploma!"

Kirk took her hand in his. "He can get a GED. But what has he done? Why can't he finish school here?"

Principal Gwinnet looked down at the folder on his desk and said "Have you not been seeing Justin's grades? He has failed almost every class the first two semester of the school year, he has been seen going and coming from school. He will show up for one class to be counted then leave right after for a few hours, then it is not only that, I also have teachers reporting that they are smelling liquor on Justin's breath in class. All of this is just now coming to my attention. So, in my experience, I think it would be best to get him into a good residential program, and on a rigorous schedule so he can graduate. Justin is a good kid; he just needs to put some distance between him and the other kids he has been hanging out with. I can get some reference for various establishments from the career counselor. But for now, I think it's best for all concerned that you find one of them that will accept Justin.

Kirk stood up, taking Carolina's hand. "Thank you for the consideration," he said evenly. "And yes, we will look at alternatives for Justin." In the foyer, he nodded towards Justin, adding, "We're going home now. Thanks for keeping and eye on him, Deputy."

"My pleasure," Deputy Forsberg rumbled. As Justin stood up and gathered his backpack with his locker contents in it, Deputy Forsberg added. "I don't wanna ever see you again, in my professional capacity, boy. Understand? Keep your nose clean and stay away from scumbags like you been hanging with, an' you'll do OK."

Justin mumbled an assent, and Deputy Forsberg spared a wink and an aside to Kirk. Good luck, Mr. Davis."

"Thank you," Kirk replied, and Deputy Forsberg commented to the ceiling.

"Yeah, you're gonna need it, all right."

Even after getting him home, with his bag of schoolbooks and the contents of his locker, Justin reverted to being sullen and uncooperative, confined in what amounted to home arrest. Telling him that they could have had charges filed against them for not seeing that he was in school under the Truancy Law. Carolina, almost five months into her pregnancy, barely had the strength or energy to cope. But she worked the phones, calling across Texas, looking for a program which would accept Justin.

Within a few weeks, they found a residential school for Justin, a Christian-based program, based at a ranch some sixty miles outside of Dallas, called Paul Anderson's Boot Strap School. They would help him finish high school, and perhaps impart some lessons in self-discipline. Justin was accepted to the program, which was at no cost for those who qualified, a cause for enormous relief to Carolina. At seven month she had a bout of false labor; labor so intense that Kirk drove her to the hospital, fearing that she was about to miscarry. The hospital kept her for a week, and only sent her home with strict instructions for total bedrest for the next month, trying to keep Baby Jordyn in place until eight months. Delivery at eight months would be OK; early, but OK, and the longer that she could hold off labor, the better. The only reason to get out of bed would be to go to the bathroom. She lay there, consumed with worry about Jordyn. She couldn't bear to lose this baby now that Jordyn, Baby Jordyn, their little daughter, was so real to them both. She was also missing Justin and feeling a tremendous amount of guilt. Was there more which she could have done for him? Got him professional help sooner, paid more attention to the scummy and disreputable friends that he had made at the local high school, put her foot down about his association with them?

There was no real answer to those worries.

CHAPTER 21
JORDYN

As soon as Carolina was allowed off complete bedrest, Kirk assured her that he would take her and Maci to the Boot Strap School where Justin had been enrolled. Carolina had been wracked with guilt and regret over how she had not seen clearly that he was floundering in regular high school, and had, as cautionary novels and movies had it, fallen in with bad company. Stuck lying flat on her back in the master bedroom with nothing to do except read a book, or to watch the TV that Kirk had moved into the bedroom, she had plenty of time to worry about the survival of Baby Jordyn, and to miss her son, and wonder how he was doing in the residential program.

"Once your doctor says that you and Jordyn are all OK," Kirk promised, "I'll drive you out to the school, and you can see for yourself. It looked pretty swanky to me," he added, considerately, "Not lah-de-dah prep school, like in the movies, but more like a real high-class dude ranch, but with classrooms. And its miles out into the country and a pretty big damn property, posted all the way around. Probably discourages visits from distracting influences."

Kirk was as good as his promise. The next Saturday after Carolina was seen by her doctor and told that everything looked good for a normal delivery, he drove her and Maci out to the school, a drive of nearly an hour and a half, through gentle countryside, spotted with small towns and narrow ranch roads, green pastures dotted with slow-moving cattle, and hillsides cloaked in dark green live oaks. It was already mid-summer, too late in for wildflowers, save for yellow coreopsis and banks of wild sunflowers, in fields already beginning to turn from green to pale brown. Kirk ran the air conditioning full blast in his car, as Carolina was feeling the heat dreadfully. There was little to distinguish the turn-off for the school; just a simple ranch road gateway with a rural road address, spelled out in letters cut from sheet steel, painted white and welded onto the arch over the open gate. The car rumbled over the cattle grid just inside the gate and kicked up a plume of filmy dust which followed them.

"Not far now," Kirk said jauntily, and looked sideways at Carolina. "You are doing OK, sweetheart?"

"Fine," Carolina replied, although she was feeling dreadfully tired after the long drive, and the unaccustomed exercise. She longed to see her son, to be reassured that he was doing well.

"I have to pee," Maci piped up from the back seat, and they all laughed.

"There's a nice bush, over there," Kirk replied. "I can stop the car right here."

Maci protested, "Dad-dee, I'm a girl, I can't pee standing up behind a bush!"

The unpaved ranch road led in a casual loop around the base of a low hill, and then the scattering of buildings lay before them; a pretty rush-ringed pond cradled in the lowest part of a shallow valley, surrounded by ranges of buildings, obviously meant to be classrooms and dormitories. There was a baseball diamond, next to a tall building which must be a gymnasium. The only structures which still hinted at the school once having been a working ranch was a rambling house and a scattering of smaller cottages and a couple of trailers which orbited it. There was a rutted parking lot, outlined with old railway ties and indifferently scattered with gravel adjacent to the house, with a dozen cars parked haphazardly in it. Most of them were drawn up under patchy shade along the margins.

"Visiting day," Kirk explained, as he angled the car into the last bit of shade and set the brake. "I called ahead and let Justin and his house parents know that we were coming. Here, sweetheart, let me come around. The ground is pretty broken up..."

"I can manage," Carolina protested. Kirk had a horror of her falling over something, tripping on the stairs, lifting something heavy, and causing her to miscarry.

"I still have to pee!" Maci protested from the back seat.

"Yes, honey! We'll get to a bathroom. I have to go, too!" Carolina replied, her heart in her throat, because she could see Justin, sitting on the steps to the main house. He stood up when he saw the car and came rushing across the parking lot to her arms.

"Hey, Mom, you're as big as a house!" he gasped, when he finally let her go, and Carolina laughed.

"Jussie, you have a gift when it comes to paying compliments! She looked closely at his face, noting with a pang that he looked almost adult. He needed to shave regularly now. Where had her sweet little son gone, the sick baby that she had held so close in her arms, in the bad old days when she was still married to Mark? Justin was near to grown, now; a baby no longer, but still her dear son.

"She wanted to come and see for herself how you were doing at the Ranch," Kirk explained.

Justin made a wry face. "Well enough, I guess. Come on, let me show you my room and the school part. They treat us good here, Mom. And the food is great. Well, they're into athletics here, and athletes run on fuel ..." he urged them away, after a short trip to the visitors' lavatory in the old headquarters house.

Carolina was very pleased with what he showed them; his room was neat and comfortable, with school textbooks neatly lined up on a shelf above the desk, the bed made to military standard, blankets drawn so tight that a quarter could be bounced off it. Her son appeared clear-eyed and confident as if he were finding his feet again. She would have no worries about him now, none of the nightmare imaginings she entertained when stuck at home on strict bed rest were valid. This was a good place for Justin, putting him far away from the temptations posed by disreputable friends. She said so to Kirk, when the visit was concluded, and they were driving back along the dusty unpaved ranch road, between pastures star-scattered with red and black cattle. Her husband looked out through the windshield, his eyes on the road unfurling ahead of them.

"Ah, yes," he remarked. "But when he finishes the program here, and gets back to the outside world, will he be strong enough to stand on his own and resist temptations, then?"

Carolina tried not to think about that, on the principle of today's problems being sufficient for the day. In any case, Justin seemed to be doing well at the Boot Strap School, and it would be months before he graduated with his GED. In the meantime, the heavily pregnant Carolina had more urgent family matters to consider. Baby Jordyn, who was born early in August; a breech birth and delivered with much difficulty. Her birthday was one day before Maci's and two days before Brianna's. She was a gorgeous, sweet-tempered baby, born with a full head of dark brown hair and questioning blue eyes, and Kirk's mother instantly adored her. For the first time since they had gotten married, Carolina really began to feel that Mrs. Davis had not only been reconciled to their marriage but had begun to feel affection towards herself.

"You realize that we'll be able to have a single birthday party for all of our girls?" Kirk said, upon admiring his newborn Jordyn for the first time, swaddled like a baby burrito in a stretchy cotton muslin blanket. She blinked up at him, then yawned a tiny pink kitten yawn and went to sleep.

"Well, that would be efficient," Carolina replied, so very glad to have had labor and delivery done with. "But wouldn't the girls feel hurt, not having an individual day to themselves?"

"Not necessarily," Kirk ventured, thoughtfully. "One big bash for all their friends to enjoy: a pony ride, a magician doing tricks, dressing up the girls and their guests like princesses. It would be fun for them. One big party, instead of three small ones."

"Well, Jordyn won't be big enough to appreciate any of that for a while yet," Carolina said. "If she's really asleep, you can put her back in the bassinet."

"She's beautiful," Kirk kissed the sleeping infant on her tiny forehead, and carefully laid her down in the hospital bassinet. Then he kissed Carolina, also on her forehead. "You two both look exhausted. Beautiful, but exhausted. Rest now. I must get back and make sure Mom has got supper on for our other girls."

"You really don't know exhausted, until you have tried to squeeze something the size of a watermelon out of an opening in your body the size of a lemon," Carolina commented, and Kirk laughed, with an edge of mild discomfort at that thought. "I hope ... I really hope that your mother feels better about us being married, now that she has another granddaughter."

Mrs. Davis had been reconciled to their marriage, even more so when Carolina and Kirk announced that they were having a baby together. She had made a pieced quilt for Jordyn's crib, quilted by hand, every stitch, and had knitted half a dozen little sweaters and matching hats and booties. All of Mrs. Davis's resentment over Kirk not properly reconciling with Stephanie *(who in the meantime, had become engaged to the man she had been dating before the divorce)* had magically been melted away.

"She does," Kirk replied. "Babies have a way of smoothing things over, especially for a woman like Mom, who's crazy for grandchildren."

"I hope that she isn't hoping for any more babies," Carolina felt completely drained. The labor had been exhausting, as Jordyn had been a breech birth. "I'll be forty in another couple of years, and everyone says that's the upper limit. I couldn't handle another child with birth defects, and we'd be risking that, in a big way."

"Understood, Caro," Kirk looked fondly one more time at Jordyn, her tuft of dark hair, and her little pink face composed in sleep. "You don't need to convince me. I'm happy enough with our family as it is. Yours, mine, and ours, all together."

"Thank you," Carolina replied, exhaustion and the various post-delivery sedatives beginning to drag her under, into vast, pillowy waves of sleep.

· · ·

It did work out well, after Jordyn was born. She was a good baby, placid and sweet-tempered. Her sisters, Maci and Brianna adored her. They were united in that, even if Brianna spent alternate weekends with her mother, where she had her own room and wasn't expected to do chores like clearing the table and folding laundry. At Kirk and Carolina's house, Brianna had to share a room and chores with Maci. On the other hand, Maci spent some holiday vacations in San Antonio with Marlene and Clarence, which Carolina thought must even things out. Marlene and Clarence spoiled and indulged Maci at least as much as Stephanie spoiled and indulged Brianna.

The following spring, when Jordyn was almost eight months old, Justin graduated from the Boot Strap School program with his GED and returned home. It was a slightly awkward thing, since the house was so small now, for all four children, and Justin's room wasn't nearly as large as his dormitory room at the school. But at least, Justin had got a job, although he didn't talk very much about it. Something to do with working with one of his old high school buddies, in the business which the buddy's father owned. Carolina wondered briefly if the high school buddy was one of the disreputable, faintly criminal gang which had caused Justin to get thrown out of high school, but Justin assured her that it was straight-forward.

"We're going to share an apartment," he announced, which came as a pleasant surprise. But Justin was 18, after all, an adult for most intents and purposes. Not a child any longer, but a young man capable of earning his own living and establishing a home, even if only a rental apartment shared with two other young men.

"Good to stand on your own two feet," Kirk approved, wholly. He helped Justin move his few things into that apartment on the outskirts of Dallas, even added a few bits of cheap furniture, and Carolina scrounged some bedding and things like bath towels, and a few kitchen pots and pans – things that eighteen-year-old boys establishing their first home wouldn't have thought about.

"I hope they'll be all right," Carolina said, anxiously, as Kirk drove them home after ferrying a carload of stuff for the apartment. Little Jordyn was in the back, strapped into her car seat and babbling baby-babble to herself.

"He's a big boy, Caro," Kirk replied, as he negotiated a crowded intersection. "You have to let go, eventually."

• • •

It was rather a relief for Justin to have gone out on his own, because Carolina not only had the baby to tend, but Maci was having trouble in school, especially when it came to reading.

"She's dyslexic," Carolina reported to Kirk, after an intense discussion with the elementary school's special education counselor. "It means that she has a great deal of trouble recognizing the shapes of letters and associating the shapes of the letters with the sound they're supposed to indicate. And no, glasses won't help. It's not her eyes, it's more like a small short-circuit in her brain. That's how they explained it to me."

"What can they do about it?" Kirk was somber. "Everything in education comes from being able to read well."

"Special tutoring, she told me," Carolina said with a sigh. "Whatever we can afford, over and above what the school can do for her."

"Shouldn't her father be doing more for Maci?" Kirk asked, with a touch of mild resentment. "Look, God knows, I love the kid, for herself and because she is your daughter. But it's hardly fair, when I do all that, I can and am allowed to do for Brianna; child support to

Stephanie and she has visitation rights every other weekend for Brianna but Josh can't be bothered to raise a finger when it comes to his own daughter? Frankly, Caro, the double standard when it comes to the girls is beyond galling."

"You're right," Carolina admitted, for she was at least as much annoyed over Josh's refusal to allow Maci to visit, because Judy, his second wife had gone on being crazy-jealous of Carolina, without any good reason that anyone could see. Carolina didn't want Josh back, didn't want him back even if he was offered buck naked on a silver platter with an apple in his mouth and garnished with springs of parsley. And it was breaking Maci's nine-year old heart, for she had good and fond memories of her daddy, from when they first settled in California and all the good times that they had there. Maci sometimes plaintively asked when she would see him again. This broke Carolina's heart all over again when she had to explain to her daughter about Jealous Judy.

"Well, then." Kirk smiled recklessly. "What are we going to do about it, Caro? Can you get your ex nailed to the wall and spit up everything that he ought to be paying in child support for the good of his daughter. He's a big-shot high-flying executive, isn't he?"

"Yes, he was," Carolina sighed, remembering how well and comfortably she and Josh had lived, when he was the Golden Boy of sales, bringing down monetary rain upon the corporation which employed him. It was not fair, as Kirk had pointed out, that she and Kirk worked and scrabbled hard for every dollar that Kirk's landscape and nursery business brought in. Why, if it weren't for the program at the Boot Strap School, they would have had to pay for Justin's schooling and therapy. It wasn't fair at all, Carolina thought, with a rising sense of indignation, that Josh should skate freely away from all his obligations to Maci, just because Judy was so hysterically jealous. "All right, what can we do about it?"

"We can talk to a lawyer," Kirk smiled, without any mirth in it at all.

"Let's see what we can get through the school, before poking that hornet's nest again," Carolina temporized. That turned out to be a workable plan. Maci stayed after school several days a week, and worked with Karen, a specialist tutor. Maci adored Karen, who was young and pretty, barely out of college herself, and loved kids. Maci began to make progress, even started to enjoy reading. All in all, a promising beginning to Maci's scholastic development, but then the very worst thing broke upon them.

It came during the week after Maci returned after an Easter break visit to Mama and Clarence in San Antonio. Mama had taken Maci to Six Flags, to frolic in the waterpark there, to the Zoo, and to walk through the precinct gardens of the Alamo, to the Riverwalk. Mama had bought her some lovely dresses for Easter Sunday and a pretty pair of Mary Jane shoes with bows on the toes at the Riverwalk Center, taken her to luncheons at the Twin Sisters Café in Alamo Heights. They had walked through the Witte Museum, through Breckenridge Park; the park where Carolina had walked with Buster, her first serious boyfriend, where she and he had tenderly kissed in the sheltering shade of the enormous oaks ... Carolina thought on that, with reminiscent affection.

Only it seemed that Maci had no such fond memories at all. Late at night, several days after she returned from San Antonio, Maci came to the master bedroom, barefoot in her pink pajamas. Carolina and Kirk were already in bed. It was late, and there was a full schedule on their calendar for the next day, and Maci and Brianna had school.

"Mama," she said. "Can I tell you something. Something important?"

"For sure, Maci," Carolina replied. "You know that you can always tell me anything."

"I don't want to go visit Nana ever again." Maci replied, with a serious expression. "Or Grandpa Clarence. He's nasty."

"Oh, honey, why is he nasty?" Carolina asked. Maci looked so apprehensive; Carolina reached out, setting her bare feet out of the double bed, taking Maci into her arms. "You can tell me about it, kiddo. Did something bad happen when you were in San Antonio?"

"Yes," Maci snuggled into Carolina's arms. To the front of Carolina's pajamas, Maci confided, "I told Karen at school today, and Brianna, when I got home. Karen said that I absolutely had to tell you, because that wasn't right for Grandpa Clarence to do, and that you and Daddy Kirk would put a stop to what he would do, as soon as you knew about it."

"What did Grandpa Clarence do?" Carolina asked, with growing unease.

"He shows me his wee-wee. And he makes me sit on his lap when his pants are down. He does this all the time when I visit, whenever Nana is out of the house. I don't want to go see them, ever again. Grandpa Clarence does things. He's nasty," Maci said again, and Carolina's heart went cold within her, cold with outrage and disbelief, even as Kirk threw back the bedcovers, his face contorted with rage.

"Don't say anything!" Carolina hissed to Kirk, alarmed at the murderous fury in his face. With a visible effort, Kirk schooled his countenance to calm expressionlessness. "It's OK, honey. No, we won't send you to see them again. D'you want me to tuck you into bed? Brianna is wondering where you are, I think."

"Can I cuddle with you for a bit?" Maci whispered, and Carolina kissed the top of her head.

"Sure, baby girl," she assured her daughter. "You're my good brave little girl. You can stay with us until you are sleepy, then Daddy Kirk will carry you to your own bed, and I will tuck you in – OK?"

"'Kay," Maci mumbled into the front of Carolina's nightgown. They lay together, Maci wrapped in Carolina's arms. They left the light on Kirk's side of the bed turned to the dimmest setting, so the room was not entirely dark. Maci's breathing gradually slowed, and when she was deeply asleep, Kirk carried her back to her bedroom. Brianna was already fast asleep in her bed on the other side of the room. Kirk laid Maci down on her own bed, and Carolina pulled the sheet and blanket over her, tucking her securely in. She and Kirk padded quietly back to their own beds, not daring to speak until they could close the bedroom door.

Carolina felt sickened, revolted beyond belief by what Maci had told them, barely able to keep control of her anger, lest it frighten her daughter. And Maci wasn't a child given to fantasies or telling lies. She was painfully truthful; if she said that Clarence had exposed himself to her, made her sit on his naked lap ... Carolina felt bile rise in her throat. How could Mama allow Clarence to go as far as to molest her granddaughter? And to complete the horror; how long had this been going on? She had trusted Mama and Clarence, let her children visit them all the time! When had the old pervert begun doing those revolting sexual things ... Carolina couldn't even begin to find words to express her disgust. She had never really liked Clarence; he had always made her feel faintly uneasy, but Mama had married him, he had made her happy. What had Mama been thinking, and why didn't she protect Maci?

"I can't believe that Mama let this happen!" Carolina burst into tears, tears of rage and sorrow. "That nasty old pervert! I could strangle him with my bare hands!"

Kirk drew her close to him, and she cried into the front of his pajamas, and all the while, he held her close. After some minutes, when Carolina had calmed down, he said, "She's a strong girl, just like her mom. We'll do everything we can. Look, we'll talk to Karen, and the school counselor, and get some referrals to some experts in this, people who know how to best handle the situation. Do we bring criminal charges against him, knowing that it will drag through the courts, and make it necessary for Maci to relive it all?" "One thing I know she will never visit your mother again."

Carolina hiccupped. She was done crying, for the time being. "I should call my brother Frankie. I don't know if his son Jeff ever spent any time with Mama and Clarence. But Jeff's a boy ... Oh, God, to you think Clarence ever molested Jeff, too?"

"Caro, I don't know," Kirk sounded thoughtful, as if he were reviewing every encounter he had ever had with Mama and Clarence, which to be honest, had not been very often. "Did Justin ever say anything to you, about Clarence making advances? He visited them often enough."

"No," Carolina thought back on all those times that Justin had visited Mama in San Antonio. Her son had practically grown up with Mama, lived in the same house, visited overnight when Mama had moved to a small apartment after Daddy disappeared. "No, and I'm certain that Justin would have … well, if he didn't say anything to me; he just would have said no to visiting Mama and Clarence, ever again."

"It could very well be that the old perv prefers girls," Kirk concluded. "But still; tell your brother, just in case your mom's husband plays on both teams."

"The nasty old perv!" Carolina was almost too upset to sleep, but Kirk talked to her gently, and rubbed her back, and at last she fell asleep. When she did, she had a particularly vivid dream, of Daddy; tall, blond, handsome, and hardworking Daddy, who had never been quite good enough or rich enough for Mama. But Carolina had loved him so, the perfect Daddy, the rock of reliability all her life, until he had vanished without any more word than that final letter. He would never, in a million, million years, have exposed his privates to a small girl.

It just was not fair.

As near as could be established by careful questioning and a gentle medical examination by the family pediatrician, Maci had not been physically molested, but Clarence had crossed the line into sexual violation, in all the visits to them that Maci could recall. Carolina and Kirk were somewhat relieved on that score, but were still angry, and disgusted with what he had done and that he had been able to get away with over the years. The school counselor gave Carolina the number for a hotline, maintained by an organization whose focus was to support victims of sexual abuse – victims of all ages. Carolina called the number as soon as she got home. She was still shaking with outrage, completely unsure of what she ought to do, or say to Mama.

The woman at the abuse hotline had a pleasant voice, with a faint but soothing Southern accent and a sympathetic attitude. She also seemed to be completely and absolutely bomb-proof unshockable. Her name was Naomi.

"Like in the Bible," she said, introducing herself to Carolina. "Just to make it clear, it is your mother's husband, your stepfather, who exposed his genitals to your daughter, during a recent visit? That is correct? Was this the first time this had happened?"

"No, it had been going on for a while. It happened almost every time that my daughter visited," Carolina replied. They had not wanted to press Maci very much on the issue. That it had happened at all was bad enough.

"Your stepfather," Naomi ventured. "Who is actually not a blood relative to your daughter, at all."

"He married Mama, much, much later," Carolina explained. "After I was married myself and moved away from home. Clarence is not whom I think of as my father, in any way. He's just my mother's third husband."

"That is usually the case," Naomi agreed. "A stepfather, or male friend of the family – not related to the child... there are sociologists and researchers who have some very elaborate reasons for why this should occur, not that it makes a particle of difference to the victim. Do you plan to bring criminal charges against this man?"

"My husband and I talked it over," Carolina replied, slowly, afraid that this nice Naomi counselor would disapprove of their reluctance to do so. "And we decided no, at first. We don't want to further traumatize my daughter, but this is just so awful, and I have never really felt comfortable around him, anyway. So, we are going to press charges."

"Good. You realize that if you didn't, that would leave him free to molest any other children he comes into regular contact with?" Naomi asked, and Carolina sighed.

"There aren't any other children close to my mother and Clarence, that I know of. They're both senior citizens. I don't think that they associate much with children, other than mine, and maybe my brother's son. Both my son and my nephew are teenagers and my aunt's children are all older, as well. I am almost certain that we will press charges, but only if my daughter doesn't have to go through the whole rigamarole of testifying in court. That would just make it all even worse."

"You will have to talk to your mother," Naomi said, and she sounded rather sad. "And tell her what happened during your daughter's visits. You should also explain that unless things change, your daughter will not have any more unsupervised visits with your mother and her husband. She will almost certainly be in denial and refuse to believe you."

"I will protect my daughter," Carolina was filled with stainless steel resolve. "Either she will divorce Clarence or tell him to move out and never let him be alone with my daughter again or she will never see Maci and my other children again. And I will tell my brother about this and my Aunt Jane."

"Your mother probably won't believe you," Naomi warned again. "You absolutely must carry through on your decision to restrict visits to their house and to bring criminal charges."

"Mama loves my children," Carolina replied. "I'm sure she will listen to what I tell her."

"Don't be so certain," Naomi said, with a sad sigh. "But do talk to her. Impose on her the horror that her husband is perpetrating on vulnerable children. Maybe she will be the one in a hundred to value her children and grandchildren, rather than the man in her life. I wish you all the best, Carolina. Please don't hesitate to call, if you need to talk. Ask for me and if I'm not available, one of the other volunteers will be there for you."

"Thanks, Naomi," Carolina replied, with gratitude and hung up. She was already formulating what she would say to Mama.

Mama, who had been there for her without fail, since she was a tiny baby. Mama who stayed with Daddy even though that marriage was collapsing, because Carolina had just lost her own husband to the war in Vietnam, and Mama and Daddy knew that she needed that stability, a secure home. Mama, who taught them all good manners, encouraged both she and Frankie to stay in school and get good grades, never stinted Carolina and Frankie at meals; in fact, fed them the best of what they had in the house. Mama, who had babied Justin through all his medical and developmental challenges, planned every detail of that beautiful (but ultimately unsuccessful) wedding with Josh, come to Ohio to help out for months when Maci was born, again to Dallas for months when Carolina and the children came back to Texas ... a thousand memories of Mama, both good and bad. The time that Mama had fought with Granny Margo so ferociously, that she had dragged her two children across the street in Victoria late at night to call Daddy and beg him to come and take them home. How she and Frankie sat on the iron staircase of the apartment in New Braunfels, waiting for the shrieking arguments with Daddy to end. The drunken family get-togethers, where Mama had fought ferociously with her cousins. Mama, who had wanted a rich life, one that Daddy eventually despaired of giving her. Daddy, who had gone away, vanished completely from their lives because he couldn't give Mama all of what she wanted. Carolina picked up the receiver, and dialed Mama and Clarences' number.

"Mama, I have something to tell you," Carolina said. Her voice trembled a bit, as she outlined what Maci had said. Clarence, exposing his nasty wrinkled privates to Maci, making her sit on his naked lap. How Maci had told her school tutor Karen, her little sister Brianna, the whole sordid story.

At the end of it, Mama said, "Caro, I will have to ask Clarence about this. I'm certain it's not true, not any word of it. I'll call you back, after I've talked to him." Mama sounded ... relatively calm. Not nearly as shocked as Carolina had thought she might be.

"Do as you think best, Mama," Carolina replied, already with the sinking feeling of betrayal. Naomi had been right. Mama would deny everything; no matter what Carolina herself, or Karen, or their pediatrician had said. Mama would deny, even if she sounded shaken, more startled at the horror of what Clarence was accused of, than the horror inflicted on Maci. She did. She called back that evening, saying that Clarence had denied every word.

"You'll never see Maci, Jordyn or Justin, after this," Carolina said, after Mama had finished sprouting vehement denials. She was in her old irrational fury again, a fury that Carolina hadn't witnessed in ages, ever since that awful day when the letter from Daddy had been delivered. Carolina wondered distantly, as Mama's spiteful denials flowed over her, how she had now become so disconnected from someone who she once loved.

CHAPTER 22
A COLD DAY IN HELL

Carolina brought charges against Clarence Carlson for molesting Maci over years and years of visits to Mama; charges which were eventually sustained by the district attorney. Clarence was spared prison because of his advanced age but put on probation and mandatory counseling twice monthly for fifteen years, which essentially meant life for an 82-year-old man. Maci continued to have regular after school tutoring because of her dyslexia, and about the time that she turned ten years old, Josh began to call, and asked if she could visit.

"I guess Judy the Witch has got over being jealous," Carolina observed to Kirk. "What do you think?"

"It's about time he remembered his responsibilities as a father," Kirk replied. He had always simmered resentfully over how Josh had shirked his paternal obligations, obligations which Kirk had generously fulfilled when it came to his daughter Brianna. Kirk loved Brianna deeply, wanted the best for her, and to be involved in her life. That Josh didn't seem to feel the same affection for and interest in Maci was a cause for anger in Kirk. "And maybe paid a bit more in child support for her, now that she's older."

"I'll ask him that," Carolina said. This was true enough. Maci was growing up. It wasn't just the special tutoring, but there were things like ballet and music lessons, school trips, even just some new clothes now and again. Carolina remembered how her own father, the hot-tempered Sicilian boy in Houston had finally disgorged some child support for herself and Frankie, but only enough to buy her a new dress. Josh had been paying out $300 a month for Maci since they divorced. Surely, he could afford to increase child support to $350.

"It'll be a cold day in hell before you get any more of my money!" Josh snarled when she asked him. He was still resentful of the loan he had made to Mama and Clarence Carlson all those years ago, which had only been half-paid back, and to Carolina, never in full.

"You are so going to regret saying that!" Carolina returned, and when Josh had slammed down the receiver on his end, Carolina called her attorney, Barry Mason, and explained what she wanted. Carolina liked Barry very much; an older man, one of those lean, drawling Texan gentlemen, whose mild aw-shucks country-boy exterior concealed the tenacity of a bloodhound, and the ferocity of a hungry shark when blood was in the water, as was usually discovered too late by those he opposed in court.

"Hmmm," Barry replied, thoughtfully. "Your ex-husband is supposed to be one of those corporate high-fliers? Seems rather chintzy that you're only getting $300 a month. That's a pittance in comparison to the corporate C-suite clientele that I have reason to know so very well. Tell you what; let's subpoena his tax returns for a couple of years. That'll tell us what he has for income, and what he should be paying to support your daughter in the style to which she would like to become accustomed. You OK with that?"

"Go for it," Carolina told him.

A week passed, and when Barry called her back, he said, "Are you sitting down?"

"Yes – but why would that matter?" Carolina asked, and Barry chuckled.

"For fear that you would faint away, darlin'. Your ex-hub is pulling down over $110,000 dollars, and that's in his worst year of the last five. You want me to go after him for what he really ought to be paying in support for his daughter, your li'l girl? Which according to my shirt-cuff calculation is more along the lines of $1,100 a month. And he was getting downright obstreperous when you asked for a mere fifty dollars more ..." Carolina could imagine Barry sorrowfully shaking his head, in his office in an expensive office in a glass tower in downtown Dallas. "Tisk, tisk, tisk. Foster, my man. Big mistake. I think we're gonna have to have a li'l talk about how that just ain't right. You want me to go after him, Carolina?"

"Oh, yes!" Carolina replied, her blood fully up and completely mother-tiger-in-defense of cub mode. "Go get 'em, Barry. Try not to have too much fun."

"As long as I am on retainer, darlin'," Barry replied, "I have all the fun that the law and this mortal flesh allows."

"Good," said Carolina, grimly hoping that Barry would indeed have fun, and that Josh and Judy the spiteful witch would enjoy twisting in the legal winds that Barry would unleash upon them. Kirk took on the responsibility of ferrying Maci to and from her infrequent visits with Josh, since Carolina was held close to home by baby, and then toddler Jordyn, and the responsibility of the office telephones for Kirk's business; a business which had expanded exponentially. Carolina wanted nothing much to do with Josh. This was only for Maci, who in spite of being ignored by her father for years, still looked up to and loved him.

It took a good long time for the child support for Maci to be increased. Josh did everything possible to duck and dodge the bailiff attempting to serve him with a subpoena. He was out of town, he wasn't home, he was sought here, there, and everywhere, like the Scarlet Pimpernel. Like the Scarlet Pimpernel, he managed to avoid being served a summons to court for month after month, mostly by hiding whenever anyone came to the front door of his house, or his corporate office, where he was guarded by several layers of staff. He accused Carolina over the telephone of purposefully harassing him by moving to Dallas, not that Carolina gave a waffle-fried damn about any of that. Until Barry came up with the notion of a suit for increased child support, Carolina hadn't even known exactly where in Dallas that he and Judy the Witch lived, when she first moved to take charge of the watch shop in the Town East Mall. Dallas-Fort Worth was a big city.

"Carolina, darlin'," Barry finally said after two months of frustration in trying to serve Josh, "We have to work up another means of skinnin' this cat. When is the next parental visit scheduled?"

"In two weeks," Carolina replied. "My husband is going to take Maci to Josh's house, unless Josh makes an excuse to re-schedule."

"So, here's what you will do, darlin'," Barry drawled. "You call Josh, an' make some excuse at the end of the weekend, that Kirk can't drive Maci home on Sunday afternoon. That Josh must bring her back to your house where the deputy will be waiting to serve up the subpoena."

"That's brilliant!" Carolina exclaimed. "And devious! Josh won't be expecting that."

"That's why I get paid the big bucks, darlin' – for my quick wits and sneakily brilliant inspirations." Barry chuckled, and Carolina laughed along with him.

Josh certainly wouldn't be expecting to be served, especially away from his own home, where he had been dodging being served for months, and on a weekend as well. It would have worked out, Barry's brilliant plan, but when Josh spotted the deputy's squad car when he came down the long gravel driveway to deliver Maci home from the visit, his car spun in a circle, spraying gravel and dust everywhere.

"Oh, my god! He's getting away!" Carolina shrieked. She was watching from behind the living room curtains, as the deputy's squad car peeled out after him. "And Maci's in the car! Oh, my god, stop him!"

"Easy, Caro," Kirk gripped her shoulder. "She'll be all right. Josh won't do anything rash, I'm certain!"

"We don't know that!" Carolina wept. "And he has Maci!"

Almost before she could pick up the phone to call Barry, or Josh's home number, or anyone at all, the squad car was rolling back down the driveway. Carolina pelted out the door, and down the front steps, running toward the sheriff's deputy even before he could get out of the car.

"Sorry, ma'am." The deputy apologized. He was a young man, in a tan uniform and mirrored sunglasses that hid his eyes. "I didn't want to risk chasing him, not with the kid in his car. What do you want me to do, now?"

"Park around in back," Kirk replied. "He saw your car and panicked. Just wait for him somewhere out of sight and serve him as soon as he delivers my stepdaughter safely home."

"Got it," replied the deputy. He parked the oh-so-identifiable squad car around behind the house, out of sight behind Kirk's truck.

"If he doesn't bring Maci back…" Carolina murmured, and Kirk squeezed her hands between his.

"He will," he replied. "It's as much as his wife can stand to have the kid over, even for just a day or so. He'll have to bring her back."

"Otherwise, I am calling Barry," Carolina replied. "And I don't care if it's the weekend." They waited, Carolina pacing restlessly between the living room and the kitchen. It was time to start supper, and to give Jordyn her bath, but she was uneasy, her nerves jangled with worry.

Finally, Kirk said, "There's a car coming down the driveway – I can't see whose' it is … damn, it's a taxi."

The taxi drew up before the door, and Maci got out of the back. Carolina and Kirk both rushed out of the house, Carolina swept her daughter into her arms and Kirk exchanged a few terse words with the taxi driver, as the sheriff's squad car appeared from the back.

"Guy told me he was in a hurry," the driver explained, through the open window. "A plane to catch at the airport, but he had to return his kid to this address. She said that, yes, this was her house. He paid in advance, so have a nice evening, folks." He set the cab in gear and drove off, down the way that he had come

"Damn it, he got away again," Kirk swore in frustration. "Sneaky bastard, palming off Maci on a taxicab."

"Must have guessed that I'd be waiting still," the deputy agreed. "Swift thinking, no doubt. But never fear, we'll get him served him yet. He can't hide from us forever!"

"He's doing very well at it so far!" Carolina sniffed. She was beginning to be discouraged by the failure to serve Josh. It just wasn't fair. But as it turned out, Josh wasn't able to hide from the sheriff for very much longer. He was served the next morning, as he left for work, by a deputy who hid around the corner from the house, followed him to the office and served him as he parked the car. Carolina got the increased support which she wanted, and to which Maci was entitled. At about that time, Kirk's ex-wife, Stephanie, remarried, and Brianna spent more time with her mother and new stepfather, Josh was as erratic as ever in being available for Maci. He was furious about the humiliation of being served and having to pay more in child support. More often than not, Maci had the shared bedroom to herself.

In the meantime, Kirk's business had expanded, from maintaining indoor tropical plants in commercial buildings and malls, into full-scale landscaping and installing irrigation systems to maintain such plantings. It meant more employees for Carolina to do payroll and insurance for, and long hours driving into town with Jordyn in her car seat, when Maci was in school. It came to a head one afternoon, when eighteen-month-old Jordyn had a screaming tantrum in the car, when they were still twenty minutes from home. The baby was tired and hungry, she had not had her regular afternoon nap, and it wasn't as if a toddler could be reasoned with anyway. Carolina's nerves, already scraped raw by fighting city traffic, were further frayed by Jordyn's shrieking. When she finally got home, and carried the howling toddler into the house, the answering machine was flashing a red light, indicating a message waiting.

"Hey Mom," It was Justin's voice, tinny and thin sounding on the recording. "It's not working out, me and the guys. The landlord wants to up the rent, and I think I'm gonna have to move back in with you all. Is that, OK? Call me when you have a chance."

"It's the far frozen limit!' She complained to Kirk over supper. "I know you love this place, and I do too; we planned it together with everything that we wanted in a house, and I love the country and watching the deer and wildlife, and the whole small-town ambiance and all, but I cannot stand the commute into town, and now that Justin wants to move back in with us. Where does it end, Kirk? He'll want his old room back – and the girls had just gotten happy and settled with their own rooms, and Jordyn will want her own room when she gets older … and this house is just too small, and far away from your worksites to keep on as we are."

"I hear you," Kirk replied. "And the commute is getting to me, too. It wouldn't be so bad if we were retired and had just this little country place for ourselves, but you're right. I'm burning too many hours in traffic, between job sites, and then dragging myself out here at the end of another long day. How big a house do we want to look for?"

"Five bedrooms, three baths," Carolina sighed. "Someplace in your old neighborhood would do; a close-in suburb."

"Mom would like that," Kirk agreed. "She's getting up there in age, and I'd like to be close in case of emergencies."

They had just barely made that decision to have their realtor begin looking at houses which matched their criteria when their realtor called.

"You may call this the most amazing coincidence," she announced. "But one of my other clients are looking to sell their house in …" She named a neighborhood which Kirk and Carolina had agreed upon, and which was convenient to Kirk's main nursery yard, "And they want to move to a country place, with acreage where they can keep some horses. I was thinking that perhaps you two could swap properties."

Carolina lowered the receiver. "Kirk, is there room enough for horses, out here?"

"Half the neighbors have horses," Kirk replied. "And cows and chickens. The same way that folks in the big city have dogs, cats and birds."

"There's plenty of room out here for horses," Carolina replied into the receiver, and held it out so that she and Kirk could hear the reply. "How big is the house they want to sell?"

"Five bedrooms, three bath and a little powder room," their realtor replied. "Three car garage with guest or maid's quarters over it; a mini apartment with a bathroom and kitchenette. Mature trees."

"How soon can we see it?" Carolina asked, and their realtor laughed.

"A showing? Any time you like. Let me know when I can show them yours,"

"We love it when you talk dirty to us," Kirk replied, and Carolina could hear their realtor snickering, as she promised to call them back with a showing date and time.

It worked out, it worked out very well. The big house in the close-in suburb suited Carolina and Kirk to a tee, and the original owners of the big house adored the country acreage and the smaller new house that Kirk and Carolina had built, with many designer touches. The country acreage, house and outbuildings were approximately the same market value of the suburban house, and so the swap was made. The girls now had their own separate bedrooms, which made Maci and Brianna inexpressibly happy, and Justin moved from the shared apartment into the little one-room studio apartment over the garage. Kirk shook his head over this, but only commented privately to Carolina.

"The boy's old enough to be on his own, Caro. It's not a good sign that he couldn't handle it, not even for a whole year."

"He's always been fragile," Carolina replied, and Kirk shook his head.

"I don't doubt it, but he has to learn to stand on his own two feet. Hold on to a job, his own place to live, with or without roommates. He can't be tied to your apron strings for the rest of his life."

"Having the little apartment over the garage isn't entirely a step back," Carolina argued. "So, his friends that he was sharing with, weren't that reliable. It's not his fault,"

"No," Kirk replied, Carolina thought he might say more, but he didn't. He was wise enough by now to know when to drop it.

It went well, with Justin having the semi-independence of the apartment over the garage, right up until the phone rang, very early on a Saturday morning. Nothing good was never known to happen at 2 AM. It was the police, almost apologetic.

"Ma'am – Mrs. Davis? Sorry to be calling you this early, but it's about your son... Justin. Justin Foster?"

"Oh my god," Carolina nearly fainted. "Is ... is he alright?"

"A little banged up, Mrs. Davis. but he'll be fine; just scratches and bruises. But he completely wrecked the car he was driving. It's a write-off, already been towed to the junkyard. Single-car accident, no one else involved, mercifully. Mrs. Davis, I'm sorry to tell you that he was driving while heavily intoxicated and will be charged with a DUI."

"Where is he?" Carolina demanded, "Where is he now?"

"At the county jail. He'll be released in the morning, after 9 AM."

"We'll be there," Kirk took the phone from Carolina, and spoke into it. "Will we have to post bail?"

"No, if he's released into your custody," the officer replied.

"Thank you," Kirk hung up the receiver, and looked at Carolina, in her nightgown and barefoot, just as she had tumbled out of bed to answer the phone. "Caro, I was afraid this would happen to your son," he added gravely. "I was afraid that he wouldn't be able to stay away from unsavory influences and now he's gone and done it again. He simply must learn to face up to things himself. He has to want to change himself. Justin is an adult for all intents and purposes now. You can't force him to straighten up and fly right, as much as you want him to do that. His life is his own, to live or to waste as he wants."

"You want me to stand back and let him wreck his life!" Carolina cried, indignantly, and Kirk took her in his arms.

"Caro, Justin's life is out of your hands. He's a big boy now, and yes, that's what I am saying. There are times when you just have to stand back and let 'em fall on their sword. Afterwards, you can help them up, pull out the sword and wipe off the blood, explain at length where they went wrong … but yes. If he is bound and determined to fall on that sword, there's damn little that you can do to stop him. And I won't stand around and let you tear yourself to pieces because you can't stop him; I love you, sweetheart and the girls and Jordyn, too. Justin is going to have to figure out the important life-stuff for himself."

Carolina leaned against his chest, feeling his arms around her. All the bad times, all those times when she was feeling that they couldn't really connect, all the times that she was angry at how he seemed to ignore Maci and favor Brianna; the memory of those times were as nothing in this moment of truth and comfort. Girls were girls and Justin was a man, and if anything at all, Kirk knew men, and how best to deal with them, even boys like Justin who only thought they were men; silly, impulsive men, determined to fall on that sword, until they figured out better.

"All right," she sniffled, and wiped away the last of her tears with the back of her hand.

"All right." Kirk echoed. "We get him from jail and figure out what to do about the DUI. But Caro, don't try any more to steer his life in the direction you want him to go. Give him respect, and let him make his own decisions, as horrendous as they might turn out to be. His life is out of your hands." His arms tightened around her, as he added, "Agreed?"

"Agreed," Carolina sniffled a bit. "I don't want to go back to bed, though – I won't sleep a wink for worry!"

"No, Caro," Kirk replied, firmly. "It's only half-past two. A Saturday. They won't let your son out of jail for seven hours from now, and it's too damn early for breakfast and the morning paper. We go back to bed and sleep, OK?"

"I don't know if I can!" Carolina thought of Justin, her boy, her precious little boy, battered and bruised, in a jail cell, for hours and hours. "I just hope that that policeman told Justin that we would be there in the morning."

"I'm certain they did," Kirk replied, rather grim. "But if they just let him mentally suffer for a few hours, maybe it would do him a world of good."

They went downtown, first thing Saturday morning to get Justin released to their custody and he was let out of jail; unshaved, hung over, and bruised, his shirt and trousers stained with splatters of blood, dirt and oil from the car wreck. The booking desk handed over his wallet, belt, shoelaces, and the now-useless ring of keys.

Kirk only said, "Look, Justin. you can't go on, doing his, drinking and wrecking cars. They're gonna want to send you to rehab, at the very least. Think of how it will hurt your mother, if you manage to kill yourself, or someone else."

Justin mumbled something indistinct and slouched down sullenly in the back seat of the car. He was asleep before they got home.

In the end, Justin did have to spend several weeks in rehabilitation therapy, as an alternative to a jail term. He seemed better upon finishing the course of treatment and counseling and he did not wreck any more cars. When they brought him home, he seemed to have become quieter and even thoughtful, considerate. Finally, one evening at supper, he said,

"Mom, Kirk. I think you were right when you told me about standing on my own two feet. I have a lead on a job in Las Vegas. Las Vegas, New Mexico. It's a job on one of the ranches around there – a friend of mine from the Bootstrap School, his family helped run it.

He spoke up for me, the job is mine if I want to go to New Mexico. And I want to do it."

"You're certain?" Kirk shot him a skeptical look over the table.

"Yeah," Justin replied, and Carolina said,

"Whatever it takes, Jussie. You know that we'll always love you, and that you have a home here,"

"I know," Justin favored them all with that shy smile that made Carolina recall him as a small boy, grinning at her from a hospital bed.

But he wasn't a little boy anymore. He was a young man, and young men had to stand on their own two feet. Justin packed a suitcase and took the Trailways bus off to the mountains of New Mexico. The house did seem emptier for a long time afterwards. Curiously, it was easier not to worry about Justin when he was out of the household.

For almost four years, matters in the family were on an even keel. Kirk's extensive nursery business thrived, and Carolina could draw an easy breath, with Justin working at the ranch in New Mexico. Jordyn was in elementary school, happy and soaking up learning as if she were a little girl-shaped sponge, and Maci was in high school, and doing well. All that after school tutoring had finally gotten her over the mountain of academic problems associated with dyslexia. She was thriving socially, with a wide circle of friends and even a succession of boyfriends. Carolina was relieved over that; she had been afraid for several years that Clarence's perverted behavior might have damaged her daughter for good, as far as men and boys were concerned. In her senior year, though, she had a boyfriend, Dennis Carmody, who at first seemed just ... serious.

He was a handsome, dark-haired boy, who went to another school, a private prep school, as his father was in the oil business and apparently did very well at it. Carolina knew the Carmody family by sight, as they lived in the same neighborhood. Dennis had his own late model sports-car, and his manners were as good as his complexion was clear. Carolina at first thought it was cute and very responsible, that Dennis was driving Maci to and from school. That came to a screeching halt, though, the day that she heard Maci and Dennis at the back door of the house; Maci with her voice raised, and tearful. Dennis – she couldn't hear exactly what Dennis was saying. Only that his voice was low, and heavy with menace. Carolina opened the back door, just in time to see that Dennis had one hand gripping Maci's wrist, gripping so hard that his knuckles were white. There was a red mark on Maci's cheek, as if she had been slapped. Carolina looked from one to the other, a pair of startled teenagers. Dennis was breathing hard, as if he were angry, and that triggered Carolina's bad memories, memories of Mark and his hair-trigger, volcanic temper.

"I thought I heard you two," Carolina made her voice sound cheerful and level. "Thank you for giving Maci a ride, Dennis – we'll see you later. Won't we?"

"Maybe," Dennis growled, and it seemed like he shot a menacing look at Maci before he dropped her wrist. "Or maybe not. I drive a fast car. You'd never see me if I don't want to be seen."

The hair on the back of Carolina's neck prickled. That was just the kind of thing that Mark would have said. She was able to bid Dennis a mild and conventional farewell before she pulled Maci into the house. She took the precaution of locking the door and waiting until she heard the powerful engine of Dennis' flashy sports-car diminishing in the distance before she faced her daughter.

"All right, Maci. What happened just now between you and Dennis before I opened the door? Did he hit you? Has he ever hit you before?"

"Yes," Maci confessed miserably and burst into sobs. "I ... don't want to go out with him anymore. But he ... he just makes me get in the car, and I don't want to make a scene, if he hits me again. It's awful, Mom! It's as if he doesn't want me to have any friends, any fun at all. When school is out, he is always there ... waiting for me, and I can't stand it. He asks me questions and questions and more questions about what I did during the day and who I talked to, and who I sat with at lunch, and who they are and what they said, and if he doesn't like the answers ... Mom, he said that if he wanted to, he would take me to Mexico and that no one would ever, ever find me there!"

"That's it," Carolina declared. She could feel the mother-tiger rising in her, just as it had, long ago when she walked out on Mark after one blow too many, or when Maci had explained what Clarence had been doing with her, whenever Mama's back had been turned. She could tear Dennis to pieces with her bare hands and teeth, for daring to think that he could lay violent hands on her daughter. "And no, you don't have to have anything to do with Dennis. Let me and Daddy Kirk see to that. Good thing that he goes to a different school," she added, almost to herself. "Baby, stop crying. Wash your face and go do your homework. I have some phone calls to make."

"Yes, Mom," Maci replied, and obeyed. As soon as she was out of the kitchen, Carolina went to the phone in her little business office, which they had set up in the den for the use of the business. *(They got a break on the income tax, having that room set aside for business.)* She called Kirk first. As expected, he was furious, and had some extremely salty remarks to make on the spoiled character of Dennis Carmody, his crass oil-patch executive father, and his rich-bitch mother.

"We'll have one of us drive her to school and back from now on," he declared, after the furious monologue.

"He threatened to grab her from school and high tail it to Mexico," Carolina was still nervous. "He has a car, and I would presume a credit card with no limits to go with it..."

"He doesn't speak Spanish, as far as I can tell," Kirk replied. He had a rough grasp of that language, since so many of his workers were Mexican, or Mexican American. "Which means that he couldn't vanish there for very long. But he could vanish Maci. There's a lot of empty deserts in ol' Mexico, and lots of people who would turn a blind eye towards the body of a young woman, even a gringo girl. We'll find a way to peel this spoiled little bastard off our little Maci. Let me think about it for bit."

"I'm going to call his parents," Carolina announced; best to strike while the fury was still hot. "And that fancy school that he goes to. If there is ever a day that he doesn't show up ... I'll demand that they call me. And if they don't cooperate, I'll sic' Barry on them."

Kirk chuckled. "That's my girl!" he said fondly. "Cry havoc and loose the lawyers of war!"

CHAPTER 23
THE END OF A ROAD

Kirk and Carolina drove Maci to and from school every day for more than a month. It tied their workdays firmly to her school schedule, and it put a heck of a cramp on Maci's social life, such as it was. They hoped at first that Dennis Carmody would lose interest, but it soon became evident that he was as firmly fixated on her as ever. Even more worrying was he had begun leaving bouquets of dead roses on the hood of their car, in the dead of night. That was a message that they rightfully read as a threat. His car, the flashy sports job, appeared all too often in their rearview mirror, as they ferried Maci back and forth. And he had taken to skipping his school classes, although the school did keep their promise to call Carolina whenever that happened. Maci often spotted him hanging around her school. Calls to his parents didn't seem to have any effect at all.

"It's like they don't believe us at all!" Carolina fumed, one night after she had discovered yet another threatening bouquet of dead roses, just before she and Kirk went upstairs to bed. It creeped her out, knowing that Dennis might have been lurking nearby, watching the house. Watching Maci, watching the family. Duchess the spaniel, successor as family dog to the late and much-mourned Rex was useless as a guard dog; Duchess considered that barking at the mailman was about the limit of her duties in protecting her humans.

Kirk replied, "Or that he's spinning them a nice believable yarn, all about how Maci is a liar and he's a nice innocent boy getting picked on. I don't know how we can carry on like this, on guard almost around the clock. We're bound to slip up at some point, and that little sneak will have a chance ... a chance to hurt her, even take her to Mexico like he threatened." He sounded despairing. "I have only one idea left, and that's to send her away and keep quiet about where she is. Too late in the year to get her into some foreign exchange program."

"We could send her to my brother, in San Antonio," Carolina ventured. "But I don't think that would be far enough."

"Not for a determined little prick like Dennis," Kirk agreed. They lay together in bed, with the reading light turned down low on Carolina's side. It was discouraging that nothing could be done about the threat posed by Dennis Carmody, unless and until he did something violent and criminal, and by that time, it would be all too late. After a long moment, Kirk ventured, "There is one possible out. Jared and Susan Kenedy; you know them, I think – he sells plumbing supplies, and she loves to ski. I've done business with him, and we have friends in common. A trustworthy guy, and an honest businessman."

"I remember them," Carolina replied. "I've talked to her at PTA meetings. They have a daughter in the same grade as Jordyn. Her oldest – I think there are three or four younger kids. I can't say we're the best of best friends, but she seems like a nice person. The children that I have met all have lovely manners."

"That's the couple I'm thinking of," Kirk nodded. "It seems they are going to move back to Colorado Springs soon. It's where her family is from, and she loves skiing. Their house is already sold, and the movers have come and gone. They're staying in a hotel until after Thanksgiving break. What if we ask them to take Maci to live with them for a year? She can go to high school there, even help out Susan with the kids; kind of like being an *au pair* girl. I'm certain that we can work out an agreement with the Kenedys."

"I hate to think of my daughter being so far from us," Carolina was disconsolate. What an unhappy choice this would be, sending

Maci so far from home, to live with strangers, even though Susan Kenedy wasn't all that much a stranger.

"But she'd be safe from that little a-hole Carmody," Kirk argued. "Colorado is far enough away that even if he does find out somehow ... well, I think his parents would frown on interstate stalking."

"Let me talk to Maci about this plan," Carolina asked. "I want to know that she is OK with it, before we even suggest it to the Kenedys."

She was hoping against hope that Maci wouldn't like the notion. After all, she had long-time friends at her school, friends that were even more important now that she was a teenager. But when Carolina broached the subject, Maci was enthusiastic.

"Oh, yeah, that would be perfect! Real mountains? In Colorado! That's the family of Jordyn's friend Tracy? I took Jordyn to her birthday party at their house! They're way cool. I'd be OK with that, Mom. Really."

Carolina was vaguely disappointed. Justin in New Mexico, now Maci in Colorado. Now there would be just Jordyn, rattling around in the family nest, and Brianna on alternate weekends. The house would seem quite awfully empty.

It was done and done within weeks, the various authorizations signed and notarized. Susan and Jared Kennedy agreed to take on Maci as a part of their family, part mother's assistant, and take her to Colorado with them when they packed up the kids, the dog and all their luggage. They were going to travel in two vans, just to get everything in – their own five children, Maci, the dog, their luggage, and all.

"It's perfect," Susan said on that last morning before they headed out from the hotel where they had been staying for the long drive east. Carolina and Kirk had thoroughly briefed them both about how Dennis Carmody had been stalking their daughter, and the necessity of them keeping a careful watch. Indeed, they had taken the precaution that morning of having Maci get into their own car while it was still in the garage and lay down on the floor until they were certain of not being followed – just in case Dennis was watching the house. "She is a sweetie; Caro and I promise that I'll take good care of her."

"We'll call every Friday at six," Carolina said, as she hugged Maci to her. "OK! And we'll come to Colorado, just to see how you are settling in. And we'll be there for your graduation, depend on that, for certain."

"Love you, Mom!" Maci exclaimed, as she returned the hug exuberantly. She was eager to get started, to get out of the house, to explore a new place, and above all to get away from the threat of the obsessed Dennis Carmody. Still, the departure left Carolina feeling as if her heart would truly break. Maci would never really come home again and live as a child in their house. She, like Justin, had grown up.

• • •

It was several months after Maci had gone to Colorado with the Kenedys, that Carolina answered the phone early one evening. She was in the midst of fixing supper; just for herself, Jordyn and Kirk, since Brianna spent the weekdays and every other weekend at her mother's house.

"Carolina ... is that really you?" the cracked voice of an elderly woman on the other end. Carolina nearly dropped the phone out of astonishment. Mama's voice! It had been five years since she had spoken to Mama, after Mama refused to believe that her husband Clarence had all but sexually molested Maci, had denied what her granddaughter said, claimed it was all vicious lies.

"Mama?" Carolina ventured uncertainly. Mama sounded unaccountably aged and frail, like another woman entirely. "It's been a while," she could think of nothing else to say. "Where are you? Are you all right?"

"Clarence is dead," Mama replied, and began to cry. "It was the cancer that killed him, Caro. Throat-cancer. Now he's dead and buried in the cemetery plot that he bought for us. I thought you should know."

"That's..." Carolina swallowed what she really wanted to say, which was a sincere wish that the old pervert ought to be burning in hell, screaming in agony as demons poked him in his tender parts with red-hot pitchforks. "I'm sorry for your loss, Mama."

She crossed her fingers as she said this. Nope, she wasn't sorry at all, save that Mama had tied herself to the nasty old man for almost twenty years. Turned a blind eye to his nastiness, refused to believe that Clarence had done all those disgusting things to Maci, a child and defenseless! And this after marriage to Daddy, who was kind and wise and sensible … just not good enough for Mama.

Mama went on crying and gulping. "I'm all alone, Caro! Clarence is dead. He left me destitute. Broke! I don't have anything, I can barely afford anything to eat, and I couldn't think of anyone I can call except for you! Frankie won't take my calls, Jane hates me! We couldn't pay for the apartment anymore; he was so sick at the end that the hospital took the last of his Social Security! We put all our things in a storage locker and … we were living in this nasty cheap motel on the Austin Highway! I can't pay for the motel now, and if I can't pay the rent for the storage locker, they said they were going to auction it all off! All of our things, all of my things!" Mama dissolved into incoherent weeping.

Carolina held the phone in her hand, listening to Mama breaking down on the other end, so many miles away. Old and sick, broken, grieving and stony-broke. Destitute. Mama, with her hair-trigger hot temper and stubborn iron will, weeping as if her heart would break … no, her heart was broken, in the mental as well as physical sense. Mama's things, all packed into a rented storage locker; all those relics and prized possessions salvaged from the house that she had to sell when Daddy vanished, leaving her without any income except what she could earn by going to work herself. Her things doubtless included those last little shreds of what Poppa Lew and Granny Margo had left their middle daughter, the remnants of that rich and privileged life that Mama had wanted to live, what she had been able to salvage out of her earnings in the dress shop ... it was all too heartbreaking, listening to Mama, all alone, far away, and stony-broke.

Mama had given a last home to Granny Margo, to Poppa Lew when they were old and helpless, in their final miserable years of bad health... Well, OK, Mama had given them a home and looked after Granny Margo and Poppa Lew because she had probably browbeaten Daddy into offering them a room. But then again, Carolina had come home to Mama and Daddy, time after time. After divorcing Mason, and after that disaster, divorcing Mark the semi-criminal ... and then coming home wrecked with grief after Jeff was killed in Vietnam. They had welcomed her home with open arms after every time Carolina's marital ship ran aground on the rocks of disaster. Mama had also been wonderful in organizing the wedding to Josh, in looking after Justin when Carolina went to school and worked as a nurse.

So many memories. Mama might have been over-the-top and viciously temperamental, and often emotionally abusive, especially when it came to Daddy, her parents, or Aunt Jane, but she had never physically mistreated Carolina or Frankie, in any way. Well, other than inadvertently forcing them to witness her spectacular tantrums. She had never abused them physically or deprived them of anything they might have needed. Whatever Mama had in the pantry or refrigerator, the best of it all went to herself and Frankie, as children. The absolute worst that Mama had ever done to Carolina was to take Clarence's side, when it came to the old perve showing his privates to Maci, over and over again, and refusing to believe a single word of what Carolina had told her about him.

"Mama," Carolina said at last. "Where are you staying? What's the address, and the unit number?"

Mama choked out a response. Carolina cringed; that place where Mama was staying was almost the worst of the nasty cheap motels along the Austin Highway; the natural abode of winos and the down-and-out, before having to move into a culvert or a cardboard box under the interstate.

"Mama, listen to me. We're coming to get you. As soon as Kirk and I can free up our schedule and drive down to San Antonio. We'll see about paying the rent on the storage unit ... and don't worry. We'll take care of everything."

Kirk agreed, of course; he had always been especially close to his own mother. He had been every bit as horrified and disbelieving over the matter of Mama, Mama willfully choosing to believe Clarence's denials over Maci as Carolina had been.

"Of course, we'll go get your mother," he said, firmly, as soon as Carolina told him about the phone call. "And bring her home with us. The studio over the garage should suit her just fine, as long as she can manage the stairs. If that's too much for her, then the guest bedroom."

"She didn't sound well, at all," Carolina was secretly relieved that Kirk was so positive over this.

"And we'll see about the storage locker as well," Kirk continued. "Look, honey; this is what families are all about. How soon can we pull free and drive down to San Antonio?"

"Let me look at the schedule," Carolina flipped through the date book on the desk in her office. "Hmmm. Looks like Friday is good. What about Mama's stuff in storage?"

"We'll take my truck and one of the trailers with us," Kirk replied, having already swiftly gamed out the strategy. "With the crew-cab, there's room enough for Jordyn, and if we have to spend the weekend, getting your mom's stuff sorted, we'll get it done. I'll tell Stephanie this is not a good weekend for Brianna."

They boarded Duchess at a kennel for the weekend, and set off before sunrise, stopping in West for a potty break and an early lunch of kolaches and pecan rolls at the Czech Bakery in West, munching happily on the flaky pastry, and watching the big trucks roll past on the interstate highway. They reached San Antonio in early afternoon and drove straight from the highway to the cheap motel where

Mama had said she was staying. Carolina's heart sank as they pulled into the parking lot. This motel was on the old Austin Highway, located among dives, head shops, tattoo parlors and pawn shops that lined that old main boulevard. It was even worse, even more incredibly low rent than she remembered, from when she was a teenager, and used to hang out at the Bun 'n Barrel, and later when Mark went with his disgusting buddy to boost a car for a part that he needed for his own car.

Kirk shook his head, as he parked the truck. "Caro, tell your mom to grab her things, and come with us, this very minute. We'll all go to a nicer hotel before we go to the storage place. I wouldn't let my dog stay in this dump for another night, let alone my mother."

Carolina nodded in agreement, almost to overcome to speak. This would be the first time she had seen her mother in years, this week the first time they had spoken to each other since Maci's shattering accusations about what Mama's husband had been up to. She slid out from the truck, went to the scarred door of the shabby unit, a door from which the original paint color had faded, and knocked on it tentatively.

Mama opened the door. Carolina heard the security device being unengaged, and the door latch turned. Mama stood in the doorway.

"Oh, Caro, it's so good to see you again!" Mama practically threw herself into Carolina's arms. "It's been so long,"

"It's good to see you again too, Mama," Carolina brought herself to say. She almost didn't recognize Mama, she was so thin, and run-down. Holding her was like holding a skeleton wrapped in a thin layer of saggy flesh, gray flesh that hung like crepe paper on her bones. There were dark bruises on her arms, and the back of her hands. Her hair had gone almost entirely white, and thin; so thin that Carolina could look down on her head and see Mama's scalp through it. So sad – her thick dark hair had once been her main claim to beauty. She was badly dressed and smelled of sickness. Clarence's final illness and abject poverty had run Mama down to a pale shadow of the beautiful, strong, stubborn woman she had once been. "I hope you packed a suitcase, Mama. Kirk is gonna take us to stay someplace else."

Mama sniffled and wiped her eyes with the back of her hand. "But what about the storage unit with all our things?"

"That's what we brought the trailer for," Carolina replied. "tell us where your things are all stored, and we'll pay the rent and pack what we can into the trailer. Let's go, Mama. This place gives me the creeps. I hope you're all packed and ready." She took a quick look around the motel room and shuddered. It was a horrible, low rent place. The walls were cruddy: was that black mold on the wall under the window AC unit? What did it say about the normal run of clientele that the cheap bedside lamp was chained to the equally cheap and battered nightstand, and the blanket on the bed looked to be as thick as a cheap paper towel? Carolina could just imagine the bugs that infested the tattered carpet, and as for the bathroom plumbing … "Get your purse, Mama. I'll get your suitcase. Ugh … just leave the room key here. Management can sort it out."

"I can't forget my pills!" Mama protested. "My heart pills … they're in the bathroom." Mama darted into the bathroom at the far end of the motel room, and returned, tucking several prescription vials into her purse. "I had to have a heart-valve replaced, some time ago, Caro, and the last time I saw a doctor, he was saying that I probably ought to have another operation, eventually."

"Yes, Mama," Carolina pulled the motel room door shut, taking Mama's elbow with her free hand and led her towards the truck, where Kirk waited patiently. She hoped that Mama had not forgotten anything else. Not for any kind of riches would she set foot in that wretched, disgusting motel room again. "We brought Jordyn with us. You haven't seen her since she was a toddler. She's in grade school. And Maci; she's a senior in high school now, living with some friends of ours in Colorado."

"And Jussie? What about Jussie? How is he doing?" Mama asked. "I can't wait to see him again."

"You might have to wait for that," Carolina opened the rear door of the crew-cab and boosted Mama up. "He's working on a ranch in New Mexico, now. He had a bit of trouble in school himself. He fell in with bad company and got kicked out before he graduated, but he got his GED and he's doing OK now. Jordyn, do you remember Granny Marlene? My mama?" Solemn-faced Jordyn shook her head, 'no', and Carolina continued. "Well, she's coming home to live with us, like I told you. Buckle your seatbelt, Mama. You're done with this place."

"My things," Mama clutched her purse to her chest. "Don't forget about my things, Caro."

"We won't," Carolina assured her. "We brought the trailer so we could haul them back to Dallas with us. Don't worry about a thing."

They spent that night at the nicer hotel. The next morning, they emptied out the storage unit of the pitiful contents, loaded the trailer and the back of the truck, and headed back to Dallas by early afternoon.

"Not much to show for twenty years," Carolina commented.

Mama slept for much of the drive back to Dallas. They got home by dinnertime. Increasingly worried about how thin and ill Mama appeared, Carolina settled her in the guest bedroom, and went down to the kitchen to warm up some light broth, with crackers and a bit of salad on the side, which was all that Mama said she had appetite for. Kirk had already turned on the oven and was rummaging through the freezer for a pan of lasagna, which was what he and Jordyn fancied for supper, after the long drive.

"How is she?" Kirk asked, as Carolina put the pan with the broth in it onto the burner to warm.

"Tired. Very tired. She says that she has been having nosebleeds a lot. I'm going to make certain she sees a doctor," Carolina replied. "She had rheumatic fever as a child and heart trouble ever since then. I'm afraid it got worse. Oh, why did she have to marry that disgusting old pervert!" Carolina's regret and irritation boiled over. "We would have taken care of her! We would have! But I couldn't let that nasty old man anywhere near my children, and Mama decided that she had to stick with him, instead of us! Why?! She fought with Aunt Jane over nothing at all, and she hasn't spoken to Frankie in years, after she had a horrible argument with him!"

"Easy, Caro," Kirk set the frozen lasagna in the oven, and took Carolina in his arms. "It's a hard thing to understand, I know. She loved the rotten old bastard, I guess. She must have seen something in him. Wanted to hold on to life and love, be part of a couple. It's all that most of us really want out of life. Love. Companionship. A family. The assurance that we don't go into the dark alone."

"I know," Carolina returned the embrace, still feeling that she would start crying herself, from guilt and regret over the lost years with Mama. "I know. I had enough false starts at that myself. But Mama cut off everyone. Frankie. Me. Her sister Jane."

"You have a chance now, to take care of your mother properly. Have her in your life again … let her get to know Jordyn, see that Justin and Maci are doing well. It's all good."

"I suppose so," Carolina sniffled. Mama appeared so fragile, so ill and pale. It seemed that she was reviving a little, just by being out of that awful motel – a fading cut flower, revived in a vase of fresh water.

Mama's revival only lasted a month, after they brought her home to Dallas. All the boxes and furniture from the storage locker got stacked in the garage. She was frail, a pale gray shadow of what she had been, and her heart was failing. Worse yet – she had developed leukemia, which put another heart-valve operation out of the question. Her only hope was for a new drug to counter leukemia, and such a drug never became available. Barely a month after bringing her to Dallas, Carolina had to put Mama in the hospital; her condition had become so dire as to require medical attention around the clock. She called Frankie in San Antonio, to let him know that Mama likely didn't have long to live, and he should come for one last visit.

"Sorry, Caro I'm done with playing her game," Frankie said, curtly. That last blow-up with Mama had burned out every shred of respect or affection that he had once had for his mother. "Let me know what arrangements you'll make for her funeral, though."

"Cold, Frankie, cold," Carolina said, finally, shocked beyond words.

Frankie snorted. "The things she said to Valerie and I, that last time we spoke, were beyond forgiveness. I doubt she wants to see me anyway."

. . .

"Caro, dear, don't spend much money on my funeral," Mama remarked on one of the last days that she was coherent. "Once my soul is out of my body ... then there isn't much use for an empty shell. Just wrap what's left in a shroud and stick me in the ground. Clarence bought us plots ages ago. I'd want to be buried next to him. It's already paid for. You won't have to spend a penny more."

"Mama don't talk nonsense. You're going to be all right," Carolina argued. "And in June, we're going to take a road trip to Colorado to see Maci graduate from high school. You'll like that, I think. Maci has grown into a beautiful young woman. And she has a serious boyfriend in Colorado Springs. We'll meet him when we visit. Susan Kenedy says he is a nice young man, with a good future. He's in the Army and they want to get married."

"I'm glad for her," A spark of indignation flared up in Mama's eyes. "But she told lies about Clarence ... such horrible vile lines. There was no reason for that, Caro, no reason at all."

There was no use in arguing, Carolina realized. Mama would always take Clarence's side. "I won't start that argument, Mama. I really won't. You fought like hell with Aunt Jane, then with Frankie, and finally with me. Anger is poison. Let it go."

Mama closed her eyes. They had shadows under them, and her face was nearly as pale as the white pillowcase behind her head. "Don't spend money on my funeral, Caro. Promise me."

"We won't spend money on your funeral," Carolina repeated. "Because you're not dying. You'll get better, you'll have that heart-valve replacement, and then we'll all go to Colorado, and maybe Justin can come back and visit…"

"No." Mama shook her head feebly. "I'm done, Caro. Don't spend a lot."

. . .

She lapsed into unconsciousness that afternoon and passed away early in the morning several days after that conversation, without ever waking up. The hospital called to let Carolina know. Mama's death had not been unexpected at all.

Carolina put down the phone receiver and said, "Mama's gone. Early this morning."

"Sorry, Caro-sugar," Kirk enveloped her in a warm embrace, and she leaned her head against his chest and wondered why she wasn't crying. "You did your best for her – the best that you could do, in the time that you had."

"I suppose," Carolina replied, and leaned against him, thinking how fortunate it was that they had managed to stay together, through all the storms that had swept over their marriage at first. "She wanted to be buried in San Antonio, next to Clarence. She kept saying that the plots were already paid for, and that I was not to spend any more than absolutely necessary."

"San Antonio it is, then?" Kirk replied. "I guess you ought to call your Aunt Jane and your brother and let them know."

"Yeah," Carolina sniffled a bit.

In the end, it turned out to be a small funeral. Just Kirk and Carolina, with Aunt Jane and Frankie, standing by the open plot in a drizzle of spring rain. Which Carolina thought appropriate; a bit of rain, misting the stones and the grass growing around that yawning hole in the ground.

"I'll get 'em a proper stone," Kirk promised impulsively. At Carolina's other side, Aunt Jane blew her nose into a handkerchief, as they walked away toward the cars, and the empty hearse which had carried Mama's coffin.

"Don't spend too much money on it," Carolina replied, "You know what Mama said!"

Kirk grinned. "I know."

At her other side, Aunt Jane commented, "Well, once you're gone, you're gone. I've always thought that Marlene wanted those good and expensive things when she was alive. The lush life. A grand house like Pop-Pop's when Bobbie and I and Marlene were growing up. A rich husband and vacations on the Riviera … and she never got all of that. Adam was her best shot, being an Army officer's wife and all, but …"

"I remember," Carolina thought back to the tiny base house in Kadena, how she and Frankie sweltered in that miserable apartment in New Braunfels, while Mama and Daddy fought and fought and fought. Because Mama wanted to go on living as she had in Poppa Lew and Granny Margo's mansion when she was a girl, and that just wasn't on, for Daddy's career as a junior officer. Mama, who reached for so much and then got so little out of it, at the end, after poisoning every relationship with her remaining family that she had.

Aunt Jane continued. "Me, I kept my expectations reasonable … and so I never got so disappointed in life as Marlene. Guess it was punishment enough, living in that dump on the Austin Highway at the end."

In an ironic turn, it seemed that the twin plots that Clarence had brought in the cemetery weren't fully paid for anyway. The stone that Kirk generously paid for couldn't be installed over their graves until they were fully paid for, and Kirk sensibly refused to pay the balance on the plots. To the best of their knowledge, the engraved granite grave marker was stuck away in a storage closet at the cemetery.

· · ·

In the end, it was just Carolina, Kirk, and Jordyn, for the extended road trip to Colorado Springs to see Maci graduate from high school, and to meet her new boyfriend. Jordyn bounced with excitement in the back seat, with the happy expectation of seeing her big sister again. It had been a long time since Carolina had done a long road trip; coming back from California when Maci was a small girl and Justin was just a teenager was the last time. It was different with Kirk at the wheel, calm and competent. Oh, what a thrill it was to see tall mountains again and feel the cool air against their faces at high altitudes, and to finally pull up into the driveway of the Kenedy house.

They had bought a large house on the outskirts of Colorado Springs, a house with lashings of log-cabin style about it, decorated with woolen blankets, sheepskin rugs, Adirondack-style furniture, and a few stuffed deer trophy heads on the walls. They could look out the windows and the see where the mountains rose from on all sides, blue in the distance and ruddy pink against the sunset.

"Oh, Mom! So glad you could come! Daddy Kirk!" Maci hugged them all exuberantly and swung Jordyn into her arms, as she met them at the front door, late in the afternoon, as the sun was turning the eastern peaks all a warm rose-gold color. "Oof! Kiddo, you're grown! Come in! Come in! We were looking for you all day."

Jared Kennedy appeared from the kitchen, beaming broadly, with cans of beer in either hand. "Hey, Kirk; we were getting worried. Have a beer … have two. Or three."

"Traffic was murder, at the last," Kirk accepted a can of Coors. "Glad to get here with paint still on the off side of the truck. I wasn't expecting the roads to be so damn narrow. Or twisty."

"Or with a thousand-foot drop off one side," Carolina added, for she had been sweating some of those narrow roads. Susan beamed at her.

"Oh, you get used to it, soon enough!" She kissed Carolina on the cheek. "Thank you for the loan of your girl! She has been a blessing, all the way along, and the kids all adore her. Now, the graduation ceremony at the high school is the day after tomorrow, so you will be rested up after the long drive. We have all sorts of plans for you tomorrow, but only after you have a long sleep-in and a good breakfast. Do you want to go visit the Air Force Academy? They do give tours, you know."

"And I want to introduce you to Dave," Maci appeared to glow from within, from sheer happiness. David – everyone calls him Dave. I think I told you about him. He's in the Army, doing a technical school course here in Colorado Springs. He … wants to ask me to marry him, but he wanted to ask Daddy Kirk for his permission, first."

"Well, that's a nice old-fashioned attention to proprieties," Carolina approved, although she did feel a pang of regret. At least Maci had waited until she finished high school and turned eighteen, before determining that she wanted to be married. Unlike Carolina herself, Mama before her and Granny Margo before that. But at least – their family was briefly reunited.

CHAPTER 24
DALLAS IN THE REAR VIEW MIRROR

Maci's high school graduation was held outside, in the high school's very modern sports stadium. The graduates, in their billowing robes and flat mortarboard caps, would sit in serried ranks in the middle of the field, called by last name, one by one to a low stage set up in one end-zone. Friends and families crowded in the stepped stands; Kirk and Carolina sat with Jordyn and all the Kenedy family. One more person had joined their party; a handsome, dark-haired boy in an Army uniform. He looked absurdly young to be a soldier, and Carolina's heart ached briefly at the reminder of Jeff; dead in Vietnam twenty years and more ago.

"This is Dave Reyes," Jared Kenedy performed the introduction, as Maci had already gone to join her classmates for the grand processional into the arena. "Private David Reyes. He's the young man who has been keeping company with Maci. Dave, this is Carolina and Kirk Davis. Maci's parents."

"Sir, ma'am," Dave nervously shook hands with Kirk. "Pleased to meet you. I ..."

"I understand you and my daughter are serious about each other," Carolina took mercy on the young man's awkwardness.

"Yes, ma'am ... Mrs. Davis. I ..." Dave Reyes gulped and then found his courage. "I would like your permission to marry Maci. If she wants me."

"That's charmingly old-fashioned of you," Carolina remarked, stifling her amusement. "But honestly, the final decision about getting married is up to Maci herself."

"I know," Dave nodded, and looked straightly at both. "But I was brought up to be a gentleman, according to the old style. Family is very important, that way."

"It is, certainly," Kirk agreed, also hiding his own amusement. "Well, you have our permission, Private Reyes. I'm sure that Maci will be glad to know you've come to see us today. You'll sit with us for the ceremony and afterwards, we're all having a small party for Maci's friends. You'll be there, of course?" he added on a slightly tentative note,

Dave Reyes grinned in relief. "Wild horse couldn't keep me away, sir ..."

Kirk sighed. "Look, son, you can stop calling me sir. Makes me feel old."

"Yes ... s ..." Dave reddened.

Kirk chuckled. "Just work up to it gradually, then." Dave laughed, and they joined the crowd filing into the stands, as the school band was already beginning to play. When the ceremony was over, the graduates spun their mortarboards into the air, and their families and loved ones rushed down from the stands to join them for pictures, hugs, and triumphant laughter. It was a grand and happy day, and Carolina rejoiced in her own heart for Maci, who had endured and overcome so much.

There was a nice crowd at the Kenedy's house that afternoon; cars were parked all the way up and down the street. Jared turned the speakers of his hi-fi towards the opened windows, turned up the music nice and loud, and grilled BBQ chicken, pork ribs and hotdogs on the smoking grill, which sent up a powerful scent of mesquite. Kirk had brought a bag of mesquite chunks all the way from Texas, just for this momentous event.

"What's a party without good old Texas BBQ?" he said, over beers with Kirk, Dave, and a handful of friends. It was such a beautiful day.

Almost everyone was sitting outside on the terrace, or somewhere in the beautiful grassy backyard under the pine trees, eating off paper plates. "Dave, son, if you're going to marry into a Texas family, you've got to learn the proper technique. Speaking of which, do you have any plans for tomorrow?" Kirk looked uncharacteristically sly. Dave shook his head.

"No, it's a Saturday, and I don't have watch duty. Why?"

"I want to take Maci shopping for her graduation present," Kirk replied. "And I thought you would like some input, since likely you'll be in her life."

"What kind of present?" Carolina ventured, thinking that it might be something like a nice piece of jewelry, but Kirk grinned.

"A new car. I made a promise to myself that I'd see our girl with a prime set of wheels, as a reward for applying herself. I asked Jared about reputable dealerships, so I thought we'd do the rounds tomorrow, before we have to head back to Texas."

"Yeah, sure," Dave replied, and it seemed to Carolina that the young soldier regarded Kirk with respect and awe, even more so when Maci threw herself at Kirk, squealing with excitement.

"Well, I want you to have a good reliable set of wheels, honey," Kirk said, as if he were a bit embarrassed by the demonstration of affection. "Susan and Jared told me that you want to stay here for a while, get a job and not come back to Dallas with us after all. It's all OK, Mace. You're a grown-up girl now, you should be the one standing on your own two feet. But I can give you a good start at that, OK. You and Dave both," he added, with a sideways glance at Dave. At that moment, Jordyn, reunited with Susan and Jared's daughter Tracy, and her best friend, came out of the house, hand in hand.

"Mom, there's another car parked down the street," Jordyn said, solemnly. "A red sports-car. And the driver is watching the house. I think it's that Dennis guy, who kept leaving dead roses on our cars."

"Oh, my god," Carolina looked across the back yard. Yes, out along the road, there was a familiar red sports coupe. She recognized that car and recognized the young man leaning over the zig-zag rail fence which delineated the Kenedy's semi-suburban property. "Maci, it's Dennis Carmody! How the hell did he know to find you here, after all these months!"

"He didn't follow us from Dallas," Kirk said, with a grim look on his face. "I'd have seen that blasted red coupe, following us. Maci," he turned sternly towards his stepdaughter. "How did he know that you were living here?"

Maci looked at the ground at her feet. "Because ... well, I sent him a letter, Daddy Kirk, I was sort of feeling sorry for him. I wanted to tell him that it was absolutely, over, and he should just go away, and leave me alone, get a life, find some other girl to pester. I was certain that if I told him about Dave and I ... well, that he would let go!"

"Well, obviously, that didn't work, Maci!" Kirk said, as Dave took Maci's hands in his. "Didn't you stop and think?"

"I was certain that he would drop this whole fantasy of me being his girlfriend, after all this time!" Maci's chin quivered, and she looked as if she would begin crying. Dave put his arm around her, looking fiercely protective.

"I think you should call the police, Jared," Carolina murmured to Jared, who nodded, and set down his beer and the BBQ fork that he had been wielding. "We did call Dallas PD about him several times, but there was nothing much they could do. He always skedaddled by the time they showed, and his parents ... his parents never believed a word of what we told them about what he was doing."

"I know," Jared replied, "I remember you telling me all about the little freak."

He vanished inside the house. Carolina called after him, "When you're finished with calling the police, may I use the phone to call the Carmodys? I want to be the one telling them that their spoiled little boy has gone to crossing state lines to harass my daughter!"

"He had better not think he can get away with hanging around our house!" Susan fumed. "It's the far frozen limit. Maci, you were very silly, telling him you were here, in Colorado Springs, after we went through all this trouble, to keep him away from you!"

"I know, Susan!" And Maci began to cry. "I'm sorry! I thought he would just forget it all, forget me! Go away and waste his time liking some other girl!"

Dave pulled her close to him, "Mace, there's nothing he can do to you now, not if I'm here, ok?"

Jared emerged from the house. He told Jordyn and Tracy to go inside, and for Maci to go with them. His face was grim and determined, as was Kirk's. "The police are on their way. I think you and I should have a little talk with the young gentleman, once they get here. Make it crystal-clear that we will not countenance any further harassment."

"Absolutely," Kirk agreed. "Is he still hanging around?"

Carolina went to the edge of the terrace and looked towards the road. "He's still there. And there's a police car now. Two police cars!" she added, quite pleased at the alacrity with which the local police paid attention to things like this. "Very nice. Are you going to talk to him now?"

"Oh, yes, we shall," Kirk's mouth was a thin, grim line, mirrored by Dave's expression. Carolina and Susan watched their husbands and Dave walk out to where a pair of police squad cars had boxed in the sporty red coupe. They were too far distant to hear what was said, but Dennis Carmody's attitude and body language reflected defensiveness; nothing of the spoiled and arrogant rich kid, certain that no one would dare stop him doing what he wanted.

"I don't suppose that his parents can explain this away," Susan shook her head. "Driving eight hundred miles and crossing three states... that might take a bit of fast talking, convincing your parents that oh, you're just casually hanging around the girl you have a crush on. His parents aren't certifiable idiots, are they?"

"Not so much that you'd see them around town, drooling," Carolina replied. Out in the road by the flashy car, Dennis Carmody looked to be drooping, under the fierce regard of four uniformed officers, a couple of outraged fathers and young Dave, who looked as if he could readily break Dennis in half without breaking a sweat and only needed the smallest of reasons to do so. In a few more minutes, Jared and Kirk returned to the house, trailed by Dave, who turned around several times to look back at Dennis. Dennis Carmody got back into his car, and drove away, closely tailed by one of the patrol cars.

"What happened – what did everyone say? What did the police do!" Carolina demanded. Kirk grinned, triumphantly.

"Well, first they cited him, and didn't take any excuse about how his daddy was rich and his mama is good-looking. They pointed out that he was more than eight hundred miles away from the address on his driver's license. Then they took note of our ongoing complaint against him, all this while young Dave here, glared in the background. Say, thanks for the backup, kid; I think the little shit was about crapping his pants when you were giving him the stink-eye. Anyway, they wrote him up a citation for loitering, told him that if they caught him again hanging around outside this address, that they would tow the car to the city lock-up, and arrest him for vagrancy." Kirk chuckled. "And his parents would have to come all this way to Colorado Springs to bail his useless ass out of jail. Oh, what a pity ... oh, the tragedy!"

"And?" Carolina said anxiously, "That never made him back off before. He always went home to his parents and spun them a web of lies about Maci and us."

"Well," Kirk grinned again. "The fact that one of the police cars went to escort him out to beyond city limits perhaps brought the little shit to think twice about harassing Maci, ever again. Jared and Sue have friends here, and he doesn't."

"Good," Carolina said. She dared to hope that this had truly settled Dennis Carmody for good and all. She hoped that Maci and Dave would indeed marry, Dave would take Maci with him to live in a base house, and that Dennis Carmody would never, ever haunt their footsteps again.

. . .

They drove back to Dallas at the end of the week, leaving Maci in Colorado Springs with Jared and Susan. Maci insisted on it, since Dave was there, and she didn't want to be separated from him for a single day. Carolina, remembering her brief time with Jeff, finally acquiesced to this arrangement.

"After all, when Dave graduates his technical course and gets his permanent duty assignment," Maci pointed out with starry eyes, "Then we can get married, and I'll go with him."

"All right; we won't stand in your way," Carolina sighed. "Remember; do tell us when the wedding will be. We'd like to be there for you and for David."

"Yes, Mama!" Maci hugged her exuberantly, one more time through the passenger window. Kirk said,

"Now, take care of yourself, and your new car. Don't do anything reckless, ok?"

"I won't, Daddy Kirk!" Maci laughed and stood by the fence to the Kenedy's place, waving at the truck until they turned the corner and she and the Kenedy place were out of sight.

They traveled for quite some time in silence, each with their own thoughts: Jordyn reading in the back seat. Fortunate child, she could read in a moving vehicle without becoming motion sick. Kirk had all his attention focused on driving, negotiating all the turns and twists of the road which would take them down from the mountain-side suburb where the Kenedys lived, into Colorado Springs proper, and then to the highway which would lead them back to Dallas. Carolina was immersed in her own thoughts of Maci, and how her daughter had already pulled away from the family and constructed a new and rewarding life for herself, a life with David Reyes. She would stay in Colorado with Jared and Susan, get a job; waitressing, working retail; something like that, and wait for David to graduate his course. And they would be off; the Lord only knew where. Maci wasn't a child anymore. She was grown-up.

"She won't come home to Dallas, ever again," Carolina said out loud. "Maybe for holidays, like Christmas. But her home won't be with us."

"Oh? What brought that on?" Kirk asked, with a swift sideways glance.

"Maci," Carolina explained. "She won't be back. I was just thinking that she will marry David. And she will be eighteen soon. She could marry him the day she turns eighteen if she wanted to." Carolina considered it, and added, "I'm certain that she will marry him, once she is of age and doesn't need to get our permission."

Kirk signaled for a left turn and waited until oncoming traffic cleared. "She would. He's a good kid, Caro. They'll do OK."

Carolina was silent for a bit longer. "You know, the child support from Josh will stop, when she turns eighteen. I have a mind to take his last few checks and set up a bank account for Maci. Just give it to her outright. We really haven't needed it for her support, not with the business going so very well. There's more than a year of support owed. I'll have to call Barry when we get back. Consider it a dowry if you want to look at it the old-fashioned way. Something that she and David can use in setting up a household. They don't really pay Army junior enlisted soldiers very much at all. If it can make their life more comfortable …" Carolina sighed. "Mama and Daddy fought horribly, and all over money. They say that fights over money wreck more marriages than actual unfaithfulness. I can believe it. You wouldn't believe the awful dump in New Braunfels that we had to live in, when Frankie and I were kids, and we came back from Okinawa. It wrecked their marriage in the long run and put a stop to Daddy's career in the Army. He loved the military. Honestly, I think he would have made high enough rank that Mama would have been satisfied. But she was impatient, and that ruined everything."

"You don't want to see Maci and Dave's marriage boat to be wrecked on the shoals of poverty," Kirk replied, putting it more elegantly and perceptibly than Carolina thought it possible. But Kirk had unexpected depths.

"Exactly," Carolina nodded. "I just don't want to have Maci suffer that misery. And it is miserable. Being poor."

"Sure is, Caro." Kirk looked out the windshield of the truck with the same grim expression that he had worn when he and Jared went to lay down the law to Dennis Carmody. "I've been rich – well, OK – comfortable! And I've been poor. And I must admit that being rich and comfortable is way better. You can live a life at your own convenience ... instead of at the convenience of others. Let alone figuring out if you pay the rent or want to eat something more than beans and government cheese."

"Right," Carolina agreed. "I'll call Barry as soon as we get home. There must be a considerable quantity of back child support racked up. Josh had a big commission for a client. He went into commercial real estate after he retired from the corporation. Barry was working on getting the proper share of it for Maci. There was a court order, releasing $10,000 in funds to us and all that was months ago." She thought about it for a moment, and then added. "I wonder why Josh's company has never paid up, and Barry hasn't gotten on their case about it. That's what he's supposed to do, isn't he? That's why he gets the fees that he does, and they're all paid up, as far as I know."

"Busy guy, lots of cases to attend to," Kirk replied. They were coming up to the onramp for the highway that would take them home. "And he's a good friend to you, Caro. He wouldn't do you dirt, would he?"

"I'd hope not," Carolina replied, but all the same, a trickle of unease couldn't entirely be squashed. It was true that Josh's income had fallen somewhat, once he went to work on a commission-only basis, rather than a salary. It didn't really help that much of what was legally pried out of Josh's commissions had to be paid to Barry as fees for his legal work. But it was all for Maci, to give her a good start in life. She added. "You know, as soon as we get back, I'll call the company and ask them where Maci's share of that big commission check is. It's been months, after all. We should have gotten it by now."

• • •

She did indeed call, the next business day after returning from Colorado, impatient for a straight answer from the commercial real estate company where Josh worked.

"Look, the money was supposed to be released by court order, months ago," Carolina demanded.

"I'm sorry, ma'am," the general manager replied, sounding much harassed. Carolina had gotten as far as his desk by insisting on speaking to higher and higher levels of supervisor. "I can't give you that information. It's out of our hands. You had best speak to your lawyer."

"I will do that," Carolina replied, utterly frustrated. "I left a message at his office before I called you." She hung up the receiver, annoyed all over again. Fifteen minutes later, the phone rang. It was Barry Mason and the fury in his voice could hardly be concealed; an inexplicable fury which baffled Carolina.

"Don't you *ever* go behind my back again!" he raged. "You had no standing to call the company about those funds. I am handling it, Carolina! It just takes time!"

"More time than several months?" Carolina replied, stung.

"The wheels of justice grind slowly," Barry said, sounding only a little less angry. "But they do grind fine. I'm handling it, Carolina. Don't worry, and please don't call your ex-husbands employer. Leave that to me. It's my job."

"Ok," Carolina said, but she was not happy, or content. Barry's anger was unsettling, so out of character for him. "Let me know when the check is on the way to us."

"I will," Barry sounded a bit mollified. Carolina didn't really want to have that rage unleased against herself again, so she didn't pursue the matter further, even though another month passed without a sign of the check. What was happening? The court had ordered that Carolina was entitled to the whole amount of that enormous commission check ... and yet Josh was lagging. Again. And what was Barry doing about it?

Kirk had the late news on the television in their bedroom one evening, long after Jordyn was fast asleep in her bedroom, and Carolina herself was about to nod off.

She heard the news anchorman say, "In other Dallas news, the district attorney for Dallas County has filed charges of criminal embezzlement against a prominent local attorney. Our legal reporter, Skye Peterman has more... what can you tell us, Skye?"

"Say, what?" Kirk nudged Carolina with his elbow. "You are paying attention to this, Caro?"

"I was almost asleep," Carolina protested, but then she came wide awake. That was Barry Mason's picture, flashed onto the screen, as bubbly blond reporter Skye Peterman, stood in front of the splendid Romanesque pile of the county courthouse, clutching a microphone as if it were a lollipop. "... Barry Mason, a regular fixture in legal circles in Dallas County was arraigned today on charges of defrauding multiple clients..."

"Oh, my god!" Carolina exclaimed – now completely awake. "That ... skunk! He stole Maci's money! I just know it! That's why he was so angry, when he called me, after we got back from Colorado! I'm one of the clients that he stole from!"

She felt like crying; not so much at the loss of the money, but at the professional betrayal by someone which she had considered a friend as well as a trusted legal advisor. She had trusted him to uphold hers' and Maci's interests ... and yet Barry had just treated them as sheep to be sheared. That was the hurtful part.

• • •

When she thought that she could be civil and professional – when her anger and hurt had calmed down to a mild simmer, and she had talked to the district attorney about adding her name to the lawsuit brought by all those clients who had been defrauded, she picked up the phone and called Barry. To her surprise, he answered the phone at once.

"I know what you're calling about," he sounded weary and defeated – not the same old confident legal shark who had done sterling legal work in getting Josh to pay up for so long. "And I promise, darlin' – that I will pay you back; every penny of what your ex-husband meant for your little girl. It's just that the firm was in a hard place financially, and I couldn't see any other way out."

"The district attorney wanted me to join in the suit against you," Carolina replied. "But we've been friends for too long. I couldn't do that to you."

"Thanks, darlin'." Barry already sounded more like his normal confident self. "I won't forget this. I'll mail you a check once things have calmed down."

. . .

As good as his word, he did mail a check ... but it bounced, and by the time that it finished bouncing, Barry had left Dallas – likely for some place from where he couldn't be extradited. Carolina never laid eyes on him again, never heard a whisper of where he might have gone with all the money he had stolen from clients; all clients who, like Carolina, had trusted him. She never got anything of the money that was due for what she thought of as Maci's dowry fund. At about the time that she resigned herself to the situation that there wasn't much she could do about tracking him down, she received a phone call that Aunt Bobbie had died. Aunt Jane told her there was not going to be a funeral just a memorial. It was very upsetting to Carolina that she couldn't go due to work, with Jordyn in school and Justin returning home to Dallas.

"The ranch was sold," Justin explained over a tinny, long-distance line from New Mexico. "They're going to break it up for development, so my friend's family and all the hands are out of a job. You don't mind if I move back to the apartment over the garage, while I look for a job in Dallas?"

"Certainly not!" Carolina replied, although she was in two minds about it all. Justin in faraway Las Vegas, New Mexico, working on a ranch, was out of sight and out of mind. She didn't worry so much about him when he was not there. Back in Dallas, living over the garage ... she couldn't help but see him every day.

It did go well, for a few months. Justin seemed to have grown taller, bronzed by working long hours out of doors. He rather played up the swaggering cowboy aspect, wearing Levis and boots, the sleeves of his shirts rolled up. He didn't pick up associating with any of his disreputable acquaintances, at least, and Carolina drew a deep breath of relief after a few weeks of him moving back. Justin really seemed to have matured by working on the ranch. Within a short time, he had a regular job and a steady girlfriend. He brought her to the house on a Sunday afternoon several months after returning to Dallas, and proudly introduced her.

"This is Savannah," he said, holding her hand while Savannah looked nervously at Carolina and Kirk. "Savannah Vaughn. We work at the same place but different shifts. Savannah, this is my mom and stepdad, Daddy Kirk ... oh, and my bratty little sis, Jordyn."

"Hi," Savannah was tiny and dark-haired; her hair in a pixie cut, which emphasized her elfin attractiveness, and large brown eyes. "Very pleased to meet you. Justin talked so much about you all."

"My son didn't say very much about you at all," Carolina confessed, while she pretended to notice Jordyn briefly sticking out her tongue at her brother. "But I'm certain that it will be a pleasure, getting to know you. Will you stay and join us for supper? My husband is grilling beef ribs – and there will be plenty to share."

"Sure," Savannah replied, and a relieved grin lit up her countenance. "I'd love it. We don't get too much time off together, so every moment counts."

. . .

They liked Savannah, the more that they got to know her. She seemed to be a steadying influence on Justin, working part-time and going to a local junior college. She told them that she was studying management and office administration and brushing up on her computer skills.

"Well, if she can only run a jack under him, and install some professional ambition to match hers," Kirk remarked, when he talked this over late one night, "Then I'll say she's a good match for him. I like her.

"I wonder if they are considering marriage?" Carolina ventured, and Kirk shrugged.

"If they are, it will be her notion. She's got a level head on those shoulders of hers. Young guys tend to be morons, for a couple of years, until they outgrow it. You know; young and dumb and full of..." He left it tactfully unsaid, what those young men were full of, but Carolina could very well guess.

Still, Carolina hoped. Meanwhile, Justin and Savannah spent every moment they could together, which wasn't really all that much. Eventually they met her parents and the rest of her family. They were all as pleasant and grounded as Savannah. It wasn't entirely a shock, though, that day when Justin came in from work, and baldly announced to Carolina and Kirk,

"Savannahs pregnant. It's mine, of course."

"Well, we all know what causes that," Kirk looked sharply at his stepson. "So, what are you going to do about it."

"It's her decision," Justin replied. "And I support her in it. She's going to keep the baby, of course."

"What about getting married?" Carolina was vividly reminded about how she had broken the news of her pregnancy to Mark, Justin's father. How Mark had confounded her expectations and insisted on getting married. "Did you even think to ask her about marriage? I know that it's not as hard as it was once, for single mothers ... but..."

"I did ask, Mom," Justin sounded aggrieved. "But she said, no, not for now. Until we're sure that we're doing it for the right reasons."

"I'd say that being pregnant is right at the top of the list of right reasons," Kirk snorted. "But she might have a point."

"She said she never wanted it to come up that I married her just because she was pregnant" – and she says that she just couldn't bear the chance of hearing that, not from me or anyone."

"We'll sort it out," Carolina promised, her heart aching for Savannah, whom she had really come to hold in affection.

She could only assume that Savannah's parents were just as surprised as she had been, but they pulled together for the sake of Savannah and the baby. Carolina and Savannah's mother and older sisters organized a series of baby showers. One of the sisters provided a nearly-new crib that her own child had outgrown; another sister had a highchair and a baby rocker, and they both had plenty of baby clothes in all the useful sizes – everything was set. The single disappointment was that Savannah and Justin didn't move in together, which Carolina had halfway expected. The little apartment over the garage was certainly large enough for two adults and a baby, but Savannah continued living at her own little place. She didn't want to discuss moving into the apartment over the garage, although Carolina talked to her about the possibility several times.

"It's just easier this way," Savannah told her. "Closer to my mother. You work at the business full-time; my mom is at home all the time. And ... Justin isn't really that reliable," she added, almost hesitantly. He has his problems still."

"Ok," Carolina let the subject drop. She didn't want to upset Savannah now that she was almost nine months along in pregnancy.

CHAPTER 25
PRISON, FRAUD AND THE SHAPE OF THINGS TO COME

Justin and Savannah's son was born without complications – at first. They named him Andrew, Justin's middle name. He had Justin's bright blue eyes and a tuft of dark brown hair like Savannah's on his little round head. Carolina and Kirk adored him from the moment they first laid eyes on him. There was one curious thing which Carolina noticed almost immediately; Andrew didn't have that soft little fontanel spot on the top of his head, which would eventually close when the bones of his skull grew and fused. From her long-ago training as a nurse, Carolina knew that this might present a problem as Andrew grew, but she said nothing about it on that first day, when Savannah proudly showed off her beautiful little boy to her family and Justin's. No point in ruining the pride and pleasure of that first day. If it were indicative of a serious medical situation, Andrew's pediatrician would bring it up soon enough.

"I guess that I am ready to be a grandmother," Carolina admitted that evening to Kirk, as they readied for bed. "I do wish that Savannah would come around to consider marriage, after all. It will mean so much, later on, especially when he starts school; that Andrew be part of a regular family. You know, with a mother and a father. I was a single mother myself for too many years, to think that it is ideal, as much as the movies and television try to make it all seem normal."

"Justin isn't really pressing her on it," Kirk observed. After a few moments, he added, "And he isn't really rushing in there, auditioning to be father of the year, Caro. I'm afraid the kid has gone back to drinking too much."

"Oh, he wouldn't!" Carolina was shocked, disbelieving. "He couldn't! Not after that last time, before he went to Las Vegas, not after going through rehab! Not with Savannah and the baby, all depending on him."

"She's a shrewd girl," Kirk replied, with a sigh. "She has her head screwed on right and I don't think that she's looking to depend on your son very much at all.

"I like Savannah," Carolina couldn't leave off worrying. "She calls me 'Mama-Cee. And little Andrew is Justin's son; and part of us. I can't bear to watch him mess up a perfectly good relationship, just because he doesn't really see himself as a daddy!"

"He's a big boy now," Kirk replied, practical as always. "Whether he brings himself around to act like a grown-up, or not, there's damn little that we can do about it, other than be there for Savannah and the baby."

"I know," Carolina settled onto her side of the bed. "I know. But I worry, regardless."

· · ·

As it turned out, baby Andrew did need an extensive cranio-facial operation, when he was barely two months old. The joints in his skull had fused already, just as Carolina had feared on the day that he was born. Carolina practically lived in the hospital pediatric ward waiting room for weeks, haunted by memories of how Justin needed extensive surgery as soon as he was delivered, and wondering in her darkest moments if it was something malign and genetic, inherited from Justin after all. Poor little Andrew: he needed the operation so that his brain could grow normally within the bones of his skull without distortion or damage. It was horrific, seeing him immediately after surgery, with his poor little head all swollen, almost to the size of a basketball. Carolina came over faint with fear, remembering how Justin had spent much of the first years of his life in hospitals, and dreading that Andrew's state of health would condemn him to the same, but Savannah was quite calm about his medical situation.

"Andy will be OK," She assured Carolina. "It's only this. And they tell me that once the swelling goes down – it will go down within weeks – and he gets his proper growth, there aren't any other medical conditions. Not like the problems that Justin had, when he was little." She sent Carolina a sideways glance, almost as if she knew that Carolina was relieving the stress of those early years, when she feared that Justin wouldn't live to adulthood. "It'll be OK, Mama-Cee. You'll see. Andy will be fine, and he will never remember any of this."

"I hope so," Carolina replied. "I do hope so!"

• • •

Jordyn was going to start high school in the next school year, and Carolina was already restless and fed up with living in Dallas. Much as she loved little Andrew and thought the world of Savannah, his mother – she could see that Justin was not taking well to the responsibilities of parenthood. He was beginning to drink heavily again and that was something that she just could not bear to watch.

"I think we should relocate to San Antonio," she suggested one late evening. She and Kirk had their best talks just before bedtime, that or in the early morning over breakfast, after Jordyn had hurried off to school. "Maci and David are married, and off to Fort Rucker. Alabama's not a long way from Texas but there's Fort Sam Houston. It would be nice if we could relocate there. San Antonio has always been home to me."

"I'd give it some serious thought," Kirk agreed. "I've pretty well locked up business here. Expanding to the San Antonio-San Marcos-

Austin market might be advantageous. Seriously, Caro – do you really want this? You'd be leaving Justin ... this house, all our friends around here."

"Too many bad memories," Carolina replied. She was tired of all the reminders. How Josh had screwed around with paying child support for Maci, the poisonous resentment of Josh's second wife, Judy the Witch, harassment of Maci by Dennis Carmody for the best part of a year, and that final swindle by Barry of the funds that were meant for her daughter. No, Dallas had cumulatively left a bad taste in her mouth. Carolina was more than ready for a fresh start. A circle back to San Antonio, which she had departed upon marrying Josh and that storybook honeymoon in New Orleans' French Quarter ... dear heavens, had that been twenty years ago?

"I wonder if that little house that Daddy helped me buy might be available?" She mused. "I loved that little house; just Jussie and I, and sitting out in back of an evening with Aunt Jane, watching the sun set..."

"If it isn't. I'm certain you'll find something just as good," Kirk assured her. "So, Caro, if we do expand operations to San Antonio; I'll find the business and you'll find the house and a good school for Jordie. Deal?"

"Deal," Carolina replied, honestly relieved that Kirk was on board and even enthusiastic about a move back to San Antonio. She might even have underestimated his interest in such a move, for he located a likely property within weeks of instituting a search for something suitable.

"Pureleaf & Associates," he read from the listing. "Conveniently located in north central San Antonio. For sale by owner, that would be a Mr. Sefton Blaine, who wants to retire while still young enough to enjoy it. The business occupies ten acres fronting Jones-Maltsberger just north of the San Antonio Airport. A small office building with a lavatory, sheds, and garaging, some of which have full electricity and water installed, secure parking for work vehicles, all of which are included in the sale. No retail sales area, though. A long-established landscape and nursery supplier, with a sound reputation and a good stable of reliable vendors and suppliers. The price he asks for the property and goodwill is ... a little on the higher end of the median, but not entirely out of the question. It's doable for us, assuming there are no liens or unrevealed encumbrances. What do you think?"

"Let's make an offer," Carolina replied. She thought she knew the area where Pureleaf was located; just off Nakoma and Jones-Maltsberger, and south of the NEIST athletic center. It was an area of scrubland with Salado Creek running through it, interspersed with small industry and unimproved land. It wasn't very far from where her little house had been, in the north-east quadrant of suburban San Antonio, outside the Loop 410 which went all the way around the city. "If you are certain you want to do this," she added, hastily. Kirk grinned.

"Nothing ventured, nothing gained, sugar!"

After some dickering over the subsequent weeks, and several long road trips from Dallas on weekends to view the property, buildings, and vehicles, their offer was accepted by Mr. Blaine.

"It's a lock, Carolina!" Kirk told her, upon receiving the final write-up. "So how are we going to handle the logistics. I don't want to spend a mint at staying in a motel, while you look for a house, and sell this one. What say we buy an RV, drive down to San Antonio and park it on site? You and I can stay in it, on site while you house-hunt in San Antonio!"

"We could use it for holiday trips," Carolina replied, somewhat wistfully. "That is, if we can even afford to take time off, after all of this."

"We'll need to take a vacation or two," Kirk advised, "Once we've got the Pureleaf location all up and running, this house sold, and everything moved into the new house. Say, if we can't find anything that really suits, we can do a new build, again."

"Not so far out in the country, though," Carolina insisted, and Kirk looked vaguely disappointed.

Within weeks, Carolina and Kirk found a lightly used, secondhand RV, purchased it outright, and drove it south. Although it was maneuvered on the road with all the grace and agility of a tank and was a hog for slurping gas, it still worked out cheaper than a long-term stay in a motel and the inside of the RV was comfortably personal, furnished with their own bedding, kitchen things, and a few knickknacks from the house, and with Carolina's little coupe towed behind it. Late in April, in the little office building at Pureleaf, the final papers were signed, the bank check for final payment turned over to Mr. Blaine for deposit at his bank. He was a cheery older man, sunburnt by regular work out of doors, and hands knotted like grass-stems from arthritis. He had already cleared his personal things from the little office, but he sat at the worktable under the window, writing out the checks for Pureleaf's various vendors and suppliers. It was part of the arrangement for the sale that all the bills for services and goods dated before the sale should be paid by the seller, so that Kirk and Carolina could start operations with a clean slate.

"Glad to be leaving the firm in good hands," he remarked. "My wife and I ... we put a lot into it, back in the day. Well, that's the last of them." He sealed up the last of the stamped envelopes and gathered them like a deck of cards to be shuffled. "I'll drop them off at the central post office – don't like to leave them in the mailbox. Not safe, to leave checks in a mailbox, not with so many thieves around."

"Yes, it's a good idea," Carolina replied, absently. She was already arranging the various files in the work desk, stocking the supply closet with paper, and new stationery with hers and Kirks' names printed on envelopes and letterhead. "Thank you, Mr. Blaine. Don't worry for a moment. We'll take good care of Pureleaf."

"You're quite welcome," Mr. Blaine hesitated in the door for a second, as he looked around, one last time. "Goodbye then."

"Goodbye," Carolina had already turned her attention back to a folder full of contracts for maintenance. Mr. Blaine closed the door after himself; she glanced up, and saw that he was saying something to Kirk, before getting into his car, and driving away up Jones-Maltsberger. A new start, a new day... Carolina wanted to make certain that all was in order in the office, before she had to drive back to Dallas, to see to prepping the house for sale. They had barely six weeks before the school year began for Jordyn at a good college prep private school. Carolina was totally focused on having the house sale finalized by then. She would also have to see that all their furniture and household things were packed and trucked to Pureleaf for storage in the largest of the sheds in the yard. This would be a huge project. Having the purchase of the Pureleaf location done and dusted – that was one more thing checked off from her enormous to-do list.

· · ·

As soon as she returned to Dallas, it appeared that hers and Kirk's apprehensions about Justin had been horribly realized during that week.

"Mom," Jordyn said, as soon as she walked in the door, tired and aching from long hours in the driver seat. "It's about Justin. He's in trouble. Big trouble."

Carolina dropped her handbag and keys on the kitchen table.

"What kind of trouble, Jordie?"

Jordyn moistened her lips. "He's been arrested again. Another DUI – last weekend."

"Oh, my god!" Carolina exclaimed. "Why didn't you call and tell us? Where is he, now!"

"I couldn't," Jordyn explained nervously. "You were on the road. I tried leaving a message at the Pureleaf number, but the machine kept messing up. He's in jail. And it's the third time for a DUI, so I don't think they're going to let him out."

"Does Savannah know?" Carolina was about to dial the number for Savannah's little apartment when Jordyn nodded. "She does. She was the one who went to the jail downtown and tried to have him released, but they told her that he'll be brought up for trial. Sent to prison if he's found guilty by the judge. She's the one who told me that it is likely they weren't going to allow bail for a repeat offender. She seemed kind of relieved," Jordyn added. "Mom, I really don't think that Savannah is into Jussie much anymore – even if he is little Andy's father."

"I've begun to think so, too," Carolina sighed. One more little tragedy to add to all the larger ones. "I like Savannah, and I adore little Andy, but I'd be the first to admit Justin didn't really add much to them being a couple, even though she gave him every chance, and every chance there was to be involved with Andy. In the end, I'm certain that Savannah looked at the situation as demanding that she be a mom to two children, and that's not what a marriage ought to be. God, Jordie, I've got such a headache!" She flopped into the nearest chair. Unbidden, Jordyn brought her a tall cold glass of iced tea, and two aspirins. "I'll make some calls tomorrow morning … go down to the county jail and figure out what to do. Justin can't go to prison! He has medical issues, he's fragile!"

• • •

It turned out that Justin could and would go to prison. His chronic medical issues did about as much to obliviate the possibility of a criminal sentence as his assigned public defender did, which was nothing at all.

"He needs therapy," she insisted over and over to Justin's lawyer, a bored young man with a briefcase who appeared as if he could hardly be less interested in the case at all. "He had birth defects, and chronic health problems all through childhood. Prison is hardly the place for my son."

"Oh, yes?" The bored young lawyer did make a note of that circumstance but did little else with the information at that moment or on the day of Justin's court hearing. She sat next to Justin in the courtroom, hardly hearing what the prosecutor outlined of his case, the testimony of the arresting officer. It didn't seem to Carolina that the public defender for Justin did very much more than just a perfunctory defense. At the very end, the female judge asked,

"Would you have anything to add, Mrs. Davis, before I pronounce a judgment? You may approach the bench with your son."

"Yes, your honor," Carolina felt as if she would choke on the words. Everything depended on her words now. as Justin's public defender had done nothing at all. She took Justin's hand in hers, and stood up, so nervous that she could hardly speak. "Your Honor, my son is a good person ... it's just that prison isn't what he needs for his problem ... he was born with life-threatening birth defects! He doesn't deserve to go to prison ... and we love him so very much."

"I'm sure that you do," the judge replied, sounding faintly acid. "You may sit down, Mrs. Davis."

Carolina returned to her seat, numb with dread. That wasn't what she had meant to say. She had meant to tell the judge that yes, her son drank and drove, but that he had an illness, like diabetes. What if someone who was prone to seizures and wasn't supposed to drive went ahead and drove anyway, and had a seizure and then a wreck, or were stopped by the police ... well, you couldn't cure them by sending them to prison. You treated them for the medical issue ... and in the case of Justin drinking, treated with therapy... that's what she should have said. That he had an illness...

The judge looked down at the court from her seat, and said, "Justin Andrew Davis, you are hereby sentenced to two years in prison for drunk driving."

Carolina sprang up, horrified, and sickened at the unfairness of the sentence and shouted, "you can't do that!" Justin; her sweet, fragile baby boy, in prison! The judge rapped her gavel and replied,

"I certainly can! Bailiff, will you remove Mrs. Davis from this courtroom?"

Carolina couldn't protest; the very large bailiff had her elbow in a firm grip, and there was nothing to be done but be led from the courtroom, in abject humiliation. At least, they let her have a few words of farewell with Justin, before he also was led away, in handcuffs.

"Jussie!" she called after him, "I'll do what I can! Baby, we love you!"

"Yes, Mom, I know," he called over his shoulder and then he was gone. Carolina was distraught. She drove home fighting tears all the way. Jordyn met her at the door of the house, silent once she saw that Carolina was alone.

"Guilty!" Carolina choked on the words. "Two years in prison."

"I'm sorry, Mom," Jordyn said. "Are you gonna call Dad and tell him, or do you want me to break the news?"

"I'll take care of it, baby," Carolina replied. She felt utterly drained, and utterly helpless in the face of this new disaster. She lay on hers and Kirk's bed, with the door shut firmly after her, and cried until she couldn't cry any more. When she finally dragged herself off the bed, and dialed the Pureleaf office number, it was mercifully Kirk who answered.

"They found him guilty," she said, straight off. "Two years in prison. What are we going to do, Kirk! He doesn't belong in prison!"

"Jesus, Carolina!" Kirk replied, with a deep sigh. "I'm sorry as all get out, but honestly, I'm not all that surprised. It was his third offense, and there's no two ways of getting around it. I've always thought that he was one of those kids who had to be knocked on the head with a 2x4 clue bat to even get his attention. And no, Caro," Kirk added, sounding particularly stern. "I absolutely forbid you to keep beating yourself up about your son. Listen to me, Caro. You did everything and more, trying to get him to straighten up and fly right. There wasn't a damned thing more that you could have done. There wasn't a lot that Savannah could have done for Justin, either. He's thrown away every opportunity that you and life in general presented him to be a responsible adult and a good father. Maybe two years in the Big House is the 2x4 wake-up call… he's out of your hands, now, Caro. There's nothing you can do."

"Well, I can write to our state representative," Carolina affirmed, and on the other end of the line, she knew that Kirk's expression was exasperated. She could tell by his voice.

"Do that," her husband replied. "And send the kid what you can, by way of letters and things. But no cakes with a hacksaw blade baked into it. That would give him another couple of months tacked on to the original sentence. In the meantime, we need you here in San Antonio. As soon as you can hit the road."

"What's the matter with Pureleaf?" Carolina demanded, suddenly alert to the fresh concern in Kirk's voice.

"I've been fielding calls from venders, over the last few days," Kirk replied. "Over old invoices for goods and services for Pureleaf that haven't been paid. Quite a lot more and every one of them dated before we bought the business from Blaine."

"I'll head out tomorrow morning," Carolina replied, with a cold sinking feeling at the pit of her stomach. How could there be unpaid invoices? And then Carolina remembered Mr. Blaine on that last day, writing out checks to pay all outstanding invoices dated before the date of the sale. He had gathered them all up, like a Las Vegas dealer with a deck of cards, saying that he was going to mail them from the central post office. *What if he had not mailed all those checks?* Carolina mentally kicked herself, for trusting Mr. Blaine. But he had seemed to be an honest man. Well then, and so had Barry Mason, and look where that trust had gotten her; cheated out of that $10,000 which was supposed to have been Maci's money.

"I'll go through the old accounts payable books," she promised. "And see what's been going on, as soon as I get down to San Antonio." Something in her voice must have alarmed Kirk. Now he said,

"Caro, what are you thinking?"

"That we've been gypped again," Carolina replied. "We don't have any means of proving that Sefton Blaine mailed out all those payment checks. He told me that he was going to take them to the central post office to mail. It was more secure that way, he said."

"That bastard!" Kirk swore at length and inventively, commenting at length on the deficient morals and character of the previous owner of Pureleaf and Associates. Carolina could hardly blame him. Kirk was one of those whose words were as good as a signed contract. Just about everyone that he had dealt with in Dallas was similarly trustworthy. That the person they had bought the business from would cheat so massively, going against what had been put in black and white in the sales contract.

"We'll sort out something, as soon as I can look over the books," Carolina said, once Kirk had run out of invective. "We need a good relationship with the local vendors. And legally, we can go after Sefton Blaine. It's all there in black and white as part of the terms of the sale, that he would be responsible for paying all vendor invoices dated before the sale to us."

"Hurry," Kirk replied. "I need you here to get all the rest of this sorted."

In the end there wasn't much that they could do about Mr. Blaine's treachery, except changing the name of the company from Pureleaf to Garden-Grow, Ltd., and making an accommodation, including partial payments of the outstanding invoices, with those vendors whose services they absolutely needed. They attempted to pursue charges against Mr. Blaine for fraud, but he turned out to be much more elusive than Josh had ever been over being served for child support.

"I swear, the man must be turning into a bat like Dracula!" Kirk swore in frustration, after this situation had been continuing for months. "He must be hiding out in a cave someplace."

"Or sleeping in a crypt, on a bed of graveyard dirt," Carolina agreed. It was a grating annoyance to them both because the company itself had such a promise of being profitable if it weren't for the lingering odor of bad credit and resentful suppliers. They had sold the Dallas house, and with regret, Kirk's landscaping, and nursery business in Dallas, so that they could focus all their energy and attention as well as their financial resources on Garden-Grow. Having to pay a new lawyer to pursue all legal avenues against Mr. Blaine, as well as making payments on the outstanding bills to necessary contractors put a considerable dent in those resources.

To save as much on expenses as possible while Carolina scouted around for residential property, Kirk had borrowed a small travel trailer from friends. They parked it next to the larger RV, so that Jordyn had her own little bedroom, bath, and kitchenette, to share with Duchess the spaniel. Jordyn's other pet, Cisco the African gray parrot, lived in a huge cage; a cage too large for the travel trailer or the RV, and so they put his cage in the office building by the front door, where he could keep Carolina company every day. Cisco had a mean streak and tended to bite, but everyone who came to the office building was fascinated by Cisco; most of the workers tried to make friends with him. Kirk also had a new washer and dryer installed in the largest of the storage buildings which had electrical service and plumbing. The rest of their household furnishings were all deposited in boxes in the warehouse buildings and storage pods stacked about the property.

"I like this!" Jordyn was thrilled to bits at having her own little place, even if it was on wheels. "It's like being on a permanent vacation. Why can't we just live on the business like this, and not bother with a house at all?"

They were all at breakfast in the RV, one morning late in the autumn, after selling the house and moving everything into storage on the grounds of Garden-Grow, formerly Pureleaf. Jordyn had started at her new school the college prep and co-ed Texas Military Institute and was a stand-out on their girls' basketball team. Carolina had made home-made egg-McMuffins for them all, fried eggs and a sausage patty on an English muffin. It was a weekend, and Jordyn didn't have any classes or games.

"Because we'll all get tired of it, eventually," Carolina replied. "Believe me, having to go rooting through wardrobe boxes every time you want to wear something a little different. That gets old, after a while."

"Having a house here still would be great," Jordyn enthused. "It would be like living upstairs from the business."

"Frankly, after a whole day in the office," Carolina sighed. "I'd like to get a little farther away from it than twenty feet. It would have been nice to have the new house finished so that we could spend the holidays in it ... but maybe it will be finished and move-in ready by next year."

"I like that idea you had about selling Christmas trees here," Kirk set down his coffee mug, after pouring himself a refill. "We could really do it up here. Set up shade cloth over that big open space next to the office."

"Use the medium shed for flocking and storage," Carolina nodded. "Since the trees come all netted and packed tightly, there should be space enough. I know, it's a new idea for us but innovation is the key to retail."

"And we can be on the spot, till hours!" Jordyn was enthused, while Carolina and Kirk looked at each other and sighed. Jordyn continued, not a bit abashed. "We can play Christmas carols over a loudspeaker, and have pretty lights ... and ... and can we borrow some reindeer from someone? That would be so cool, just to let the kids see them! And we can have a Santa Claus! Oh, please, Mom, Dad; can we have a Santa for the little kids!"

"Cool the jets, Jordie," Kirk laughed, while Carolina thought to herself that their daughter was taking all of this way too seriously. "We're only going to have a nice Christmas tree sales floor, not a department store."

"Yes, as far as the Christmas carols on the loudspeaker are concerned," Carolina replied. "And the lights. We can already string lots of lights, especially if we go on selling after dark. There's a heck of a lot of traffic on Nakoma and Jones-Maltsberger, and there's plenty of space for parking out in front, which a lot of those temporary Christmas tree lots don't really have. Maybe we could offer Santa Claus, for a couple of days. We can always rent a costume and see if one of the workers wants to earn a bit extra for having kids sit in his lap for hours, instead of slinging trees. They're already keen for selling Christmas trees; something different, and something that will bring in new business but nix on the reindeer. I don't even know how we would go about borrowing one or two. Red nose or not!"

"Heck," Kirk began to laugh. "Down in Goliad, they have Santa arrive at their Christmas parade, riding on a tame longhorn – they call it a 'reindeer.'"

"You're no help at all!" Carolina laughed and considered throwing an English muffin in Kirk's direction. But otherwise, she was pleased to consider the suggestions. She had already planned to attend a Christmas tree convention and arrange to purchase plenty of stock for this new project.

It could be so much fun, even with the work involved. She had always loved the Christmas season when she ran the watch shop in the Dallas mall; the decorations in the stores, and in the mall spaces, the music, and the crowds of shoppers, inspired to spend money for that perfect present. Or in this case, that perfect Christmas tree. She had it all mapped out in her mind; how it would look, how it would be stocked, run and managed. Even the notion of a Santa Claus – that might be a fun extra touch. October was not too soon to consider all this kind of holiday venture. Indeed, some retail ventures began planning for the holiday season as soon as the last years' holidays were over.

She went to work in the office, giving Cisco a bit of sliced apple – a thing which he loved above all else. It would be a good day … and there was rain predicted for the next week. Well, better get things sorted before then.

CHAPTER 26
FLOOD

By the second week in October, the Christmas tree sales floor had been organized; a network of heavy cables supporting shade cloth. It was all perfect, even down to the rental for a Santa costume, and the boom-box and loudspeaker to play Christmas music. Carolina figured that they would make the last big push; flocking the trees, setting up the displays, stringing the lights to illuminate the area after dusk during the week of Thanksgiving. The forecast for the coming weekend was for rain; there was a tropical storm moving through Mexico and a cold front coming down from the north. Carolina didn't pay much attention, except for thinking that the rain would be as welcome as the cooler temperatures of autumn were, after a blistering hot and dry summer. Rain was always a natural blessing. After it fell, the rain lilies in the wild and overgrown places would put up a single stem, topped with a white six-pointed blossom. Carolina was very fond of the rain lilies. Friday afternoon was cooler and cloudy; rain began to fall well after sundown, first as a gentle patter, then a regular drumming on the metal roof of the RV, falling in a watery fringe off the eaves of the office building and the storage sheds, splashing onto the thirsty ground, and kicking up splatters of mud.

"There'll be water in the creek, for once," Kirk noted, when they turned off the television in the RV and went to bed that night.

"That'll be a welcome change, for certain," Carolina yawned, sleepily. Salado Creek, which wound sinuously through the middle of the property was normally a series of small pools of stagnant water barely ankle deep, cradled between stretches of dry gravel and large rocks scoured bare by old floods. Nothing much larger than tadpoles and mosquito larvae lived in them, certainly not fish of any size longer than one inch or so. A scattering of tall trees hunched over the pools, as if thirsty for every drop of moisture, and Carolina frequently saw egrets, bitterns and cranes haunting the margins, where a slender trickle of water connected the pools for a couple of days after every rainstorm. Other than that, Carolina and Kirk barely noted the creek at all, although it was noted in the survey when they bought the property that the presence of the creek put the property in what they called a 100-year flood zone. A fresh gust of rain slathered the window by the bedroom of the RV with water. Carolina could barely see the shape of the travel trailer between the splatters and runnels of water. There was still a light behind the window of the travel trailer.

"Jordie ought to be going to bed soon," Carolina yawned. "She has a basketball game tomorrow afternoon at Palo Alto."

"She's a big girl," Kirk said, as he climbed under the covers. "And don't fret. If she doesn't want to get a full night's rest before a game, that's her problem. Maybe the team coach's problem ... jeeze, listen to it come down!" he added, as Carolina switched off the bedside light. "I tell you what, if it keeps up like this, I'm going to get up early, go round and make certain the roofs of the sheds aren't leaking. We got all our stuff inside, as well as all the landscape maintenance equipment ... don't want it all damaged by getting soaked."

"Sure," Carolina replied and cuddled up close to her husband. "We've got insurance, if the rain has damaged the roofs." She was certain of that aspect, as she had overseen practical matters like that for the business. In a moment, the light in the travel trailer winked out; yes, Jordyn was thinking of the game the next day.

* * *

All night long it rained. Carolina woke to a gray and dreary morning, when Kirk slid out of bed, began dressing and looking around for his waterproof boots. The RV wobbled at every move.

"I'll start the coffee," she promised, and Kirk grunted by way of reply. He hated having to get up so early on a weekend morning. He sat on the edge of the bed to pull on his jeans and boots. In a moment, he was gone, squelching his way through the wet gravel and mud to the nearest shed. Carolina dressed and flipped on the TV for the local news, as she filled the coffee machine with water and fresh coffee grounds, after letting Duchess out for a quick piddle. The rain had slacked off from the fury of the night before, but it was still drizzling. Eggs, bacon, toast ... Jordyn would be hungry, as hungry as a teenager playing a demanding sport always was.

Oh, it looked like a lot of streets were flooded downtown. Lots of closed high-water crossings, which was to be expected, since so many creeks and storm drains threaded the city. The news channel was running a list of the closed and flooded streets over some aerial shots of the city. At the door, Duchess whined to be let back in; the dog abominated getting wet and cold.

When Jordyn came from the travel trailer, yawning hugely after letting Duchess out to go pee, Carolina said, "Look, sweetie, I think you ought to call your coach and bow out from the game. It looks like a real tangle on the roads today, because of all the rain. Downtown is getting flooded."

Jordyn glanced at the TV screen, and the scrolling list of closed streets. "Oh, wow ... that does look bad. They'll probably cancel the game anyway. Yeah, I don't want to drive across town on a day like this. C'n I use your cellphone, Mom?"

She made the call, and yawning, said that she was going to go back to bed. "It's Saturday. I'll fix something for myself later."

"Sure thing," Carolina was relieved that Jordyn agreed so readily. It was her private conviction that local drivers forgot every single bit of good sense and courtesy when the roads got wet ... and as for the roads themselves ... well, proper water shedding and deep gutters to carry away the rain were just a legend; a concept which had never occurred to whoever had built most of the roads in San Antonio. Every second intersection turned into a lake, and the deep pools along the highway access roads made hydroplaning when coming down an off-ramp at speed a very real possibility. By the time coffee was ready, Kirk had returned, damp and deeply unhappy, scraping mud from his boots on the metal step of the RV before he tracked it inside.

"All the roofs of the sheds leak, in one place or another. I pulled some tarps over the wardrobe boxes, but a few are already soaked through – those roofs are leaking faster than I can do something about them."

"We'll have to unpack the wardrobe cartons, as soon as it stops raining," Carolina sighed. Another chore- not looking forward to. "And run what we can through the dryer."

"I'll go back and see what I can do, for the stuff in the shed that leaks the worst," Kirk accepted a cup of coffee, and slumped onto the banquette in the little dining area. "I think the worst of the rain has passed over. So, we got that, at least."

"But there's closed streets and flooded high-water crossings all over town," Carolina forked strips of nicely crisped bacon from the frying pan and laid them on a pad of paper towels to drain. "Jordie called her coach and said she can't make it to the game. She went back to bed."

"Good," Kirk downed about half a cup of coffee in a single gulp. "She can help, in sorting out all the wet stuff in the sheds." He cast a glance at the television screen, where a fresh list of closed streets and low-water crossings was scrolling. "Jesus. Caro, that's the 281 off-ramps by the Quarry Market! What in the heck is going on?"

"It's just above the dam in Olmos Park," Carolina explained. "It was meant to keep downtown from flooding. Poppa Lew told us when we were kids. All about how the river used to flood out and drown downtown after every winter storm, until they build that dam in ... I guess the 1920s."

"And a lot of good that it did!" Kirk was still looking at the TV screen. "Caro. will you look at that? A guy driving his pickup was just swept away from that off-ramp! Look, we'd better keep an eye on the creek, I think."

"It didn't rain all that much here," Carolina replied, and Kirk shook his head.

"But it rained a heck of a lot up in San Marcos, in the Hill Country and everywhere else to the north of us. That water gotta go someplace. Like downhill."

"I guess it does," Carolina agreed. It honestly didn't seem to her that the rain had been any more intense than usual. "But have some breakfast, first."

"OK," Kirk finished off the rest of that coffee and got up to pour himself another. "No rest for the righteous, I guess. I hope this doesn't put a crimp in the Christmas tree thing."

They ate a somewhat hurried breakfast, before Kirk went out to see what else could be done about the leaking roofs in the storage sheds. Carolina began washing up the breakfast dishes in the RV's small sink, setting them to dry in the drainboard, vaguely regretting the lack of a dishwasher. Until the new house was built, she would be back to washing pots and dishes by hand ... suddenly, the door to the RV was flung open with a bang.

"Grab your purse, Caro. We have to get out of here quick, the Salado is cresting! I'll get Jordyn and Duchess!"

Carolina gasped, but Kirk was already pounding on the travel trailer door, shouting for Jordyn. She looked out the window towards the line of trees that outlined the Salado, and nearly fainted in horror. There was no creek, but a rapidly spreading ocean of pale brown water, pouring between the nearest sheds and storage pods, swirling around the standing oak, cedar, and poplar trees, rising higher and higher in a relentless surge. There was trash; broken tree limbs, empty drums and lengths of lumber that looked as if it had come from a downed fence floating in the flood. She grabbed her purse, the cellphone which lay on the dinette table where Jordyn had left it, before tumbling out of the RV into water that was already knee-deep and rising fast and waded toward Kirk's big three-quarter ton pickup truck, the water already up to her thighs before she reached the passenger door. Jordyn was already scrambling in from the other side, still barefoot and half-asleep, clad in sweatpants and tee-shirt that she wore as pajamas with Duchess in her arms. Carolina clambered in as Kirk turned the ignition. Mercifully, the engine roared into life, even with floodwater up to the floorboards.

"Hang on," Kirk commanded, and Jordyn's arms tightened around the dog on her lap. "Hope to hell I don't hit anything big!" he added. "Christ, Caro! It looked like it was the Johnstown flood, as if a dam suddenly broke!" Water swished and gurgled under the truck, as it moved ponderously towards higher ground along Jones-Maltsberger Road, which ran along the front of the property. A tall chain-link fence ran along the road, a fence broken by a double gate, which normally was kept padlocked on weekends. Frighteningly, the rising water kept pace with the truck. Carolina expected at every yard that the engine would flood out, stranding them in deep water in the middle of their property. When they got to the gate, and Kirk got out to work the combination and open the gate, water splashed up over the hood and washed off to the sides; it was that deep. But the engine didn't stall, and Kirk gunned the accelerator for all it was worth. They roared up onto the paved roadway, a road which had rose steeply as it scribed a straight line up the hill past the athletic center.

"Oh, my god!" Carolina exclaimed, looking out at the spreading lake of brown water behind them. Everything they owned was under water, except for the office building, which looked to have water up to the level of the windowsill. All along the lower road behind them were cars, stranded off the side, up to the windows in water... water which was still rising. It was horrible to watch; motor vehicles overwhelmed by the flood, drifting half-submerged, even as she and

Kirk watched in relative safety. A handful of other cars and trucks were parked along the side of Jones-Maltsberger and Arion Parkway, inching along to higher levels even as the water rose. Otherwise, clusters of people stood together, watching the flood – it was horrible; Carolina couldn't bear to watch, but like everyone else, couldn't endure turning away. She stood with her arm around Jordyn, watching the flood sweep through their property, creeping almost imperceptibly up the embankment. At least the water wasn't coming up in that overwhelming rush, as it had at first. Two fire engines were also parked along with the rest, the firemen in safety gear doing their best to rescue stranded motorists. "Kirk!" Carolina screamed. "We forgot Cisco! He's in the office, still! How could we forget him?"

Kirk paled, under his tan. "All right! I'll go back and get your bird, even if I have to swim all the way."

A fire fighter standing nearby overheard this, and said, "Sir, if you go into that water, we're gonna have to fine you, and double, if we have to go in and rescue you if you get in trouble. It's too dangerous to risk your life in it."

Another bystander, an older man in grubby work clothes asked, "Who's Cisco?"

"Our pet parrot," Carolina said, practically crying. How could they have forgotten Cisco when they had remembered Duchess! "He's in a big cage in our office building down there!"

The man in work clothes scratched his chin thoughtfully. "Lemme see. I have a boat in storage; a fifteen-foot Tracker, not three blocks from here. Give me five minutes to bring it around…"

"Sir, you might be liable to be fined, too, if you take your boat out into this," the fire fighter pointed out, and both Kirk and the boat owner glared at him.

"I'm not one to sit around in an emergency, son," the boat owner replied.

"Do as you think best, then," the fire fighter replied. He sounded as if he were grinding his teeth, but he turned away, and seemed to be deliberately not seeing the man who offered to bring his boat around to rescue Cisco.

In a few minutes, not less than ten, the man returned, towing a trailer with a small flat-bottomed aluminum boat on it. He backed the trailer to the edge of the water and he and Kirk made short work of sliding the boat out onto the murky water and firing up the outboard motor.

"There's a closet by the back door, with a pet carrier in it," Carolina said, breathlessly.

"Right," Kirk nodded, and kissed her cheek before wading to the side of the boat and clambering in. Carolina stood with Jordyn; nerves drawn to the breaking point. She hardly noticed the firefighter at her elbow until the man spoke.

"Miss," he said, speaking to Jordyn. "I'd get some shoes on if I were you. That water is filthy, some of it from busted sewers and septic systems, and if you get an open wound on your feet, you're gonna be in a world of hurt when they get infected."

"I don't have any shoes," Jordyn replied in a small, shaken voice. "I was asleep when Dad woke me up and said the creek was flooding. I didn't have time."

The firefighter sighed. "Well, get into the truck, then. Don't be walking around barefoot,"

Carolina nudged her daughter. "He's right, Jordie – get into the truck and keep Duchess company."

The boat was chugging across the spreading brown lake, in which the various sheds and the office building remained as islands, with water swirling in dirty eddies around them. Within a few minutes, the boat vanished around the far side of the office building, where the back door was, and the sound of the outboard lost in the noise of the flood itself, and traffic on the roadways. Carolina held her breath, counting the minutes. How long would it take Kirk to get in through the back door, find the closet with Cisco's travel carrier in it, struggle through the water to the tall cage by the front door. She could only hope that the water hadn't risen over the cage top, otherwise poor Cisco would have been trapped, and drowned against the cage bars at the top as the water came up ... no, she couldn't bear to think of poor cranky, "bitey" Cisco, dead in such a sudden and appalling manner. They should have remembered to get him from the office!

Before fifteen minutes had passed, the small boat came puttering around from the back of the office, crossing the murky pale brown lake. Kirk was standing in the middle of the boat, triumphantly holding up the travel carrier. He was grinning, she saw as the boat puttered through the opened gate, still deep in floodwater. He wouldn't be smiling so broadly if they hadn't been successful.

"Got him!" Kirk called as soon as they were in earshot. "And just in the nick of time, too!"

The boat angled up, just where the trailer for it was perched at the edge of the flood. The owner of it, that public-spirited and compassionate man, angled the engine until it was back-end to the trailer. Carolina rushed down to take the small carrier from her husband, so that he could help load the boat.

"Cisco!" She exclaimed to the slightly damp and chastened parrot within. "I'm so sorry! We shouldn't have forgotten you! Who else would bite the employees and make them feel wanted when they just offer you a piece of apple! Who's the pretty and brave boy, then?"

Cisco refrained from comment, a cranky and ungracious bird, as always. Carolina put the carrier in the truck, considerably relieved. Kirk finished helping the owner of the boat stow it back on the trailer. Just at that moment, the cellphone in her purse rang.

"Carolina, it's Valerie! Are you OK?! Oh, thank God, you answered!" It was Frankie's wife. She continued, "We just now saw on the news; the KSAT helicopter was live, flying over Nakoma and 281 north of the airport, and it was horrible! Did you all get out in time!"

"Oh, Val, we did, but everything is under water and wrecked!" Carolina felt like crying. "The creek flooded everything! But Jordie and Kirk and I are fine. I'm fine. We're all OK. Even the dog and the parrot. Kirk had to go back in a boat to rescue Cisco, but he's fine, too."

Frankie's voice came on the line. "Caro! Jesus, Caro, what a mess. You've got to come and stay with us, then. We have room. Don't bother with a hotel; this is what family is for."

"I know!" Caro began to laugh, torn between tears and laughter. "We don't have anything that isn't under water. Jordie doesn't even have shoes! She's barefoot..."

"Get to our house," Frankie commanded sternly. "We'll find her some shoes, even if we have to make an emergency run to Walmart. We've been watching the news. You wouldn't believe what a mess that this rainstorm has made. It didn't even rain all that much where we were – it was all the water coming down from the Hill Country."

"That's what Kirk has been saying," Carolina replied. "We'll be there in half an hour."

Now that it was done, Carolina began shaking. She could barely handle the cellphone. It had all happened so suddenly, this nightmare of a sudden flood. It had happened within the space of ten or fifteen minutes, although now it seemed to have been hours. They had nothing but the clothes they stood up in, her purse and cellphone, and the pets, and Kirk's truck. Everything else was under water or swept away. Kirk was thanking the helpful boat owner, shrugging, and looking slightly embarrassed. Then he came up to Carolina, his face full of concern.

"Ma'am – are you OK? You look like you're going to pass out."

"I'm fine," Carolina insisted. "Just reaction. That was my brother and Valerie, on the phone just now. They want us to come and stay with them, right now. I said we would be there in half an hour." She managed a short, humorless laugh. "At least where they are, it's high ground."

"Good idea," Kirk looked back at the flooded nursery grounds, "It's a mess, Caro. There's nothing we can do about it until the water goes down." He helped her into the truck; Carolina thought she must really look dreadful.

"Was it hard to find Cisco?" she asked, as Kirk put the truck into gear.

"No, not really," he replied. "We went around to the back. The water had busted open the door, and then the force of it broke out the front door as well. It was up to my chest, by the time I got to the front. Poor Cisco was a very unhappy bird, clinging to the top of his cage, about a foot above the water. He was very glad to be rescued; he came along quietly." Kirk sighed. "But damn near everything that can be moved is swept out of the building. God knows what's happening to the maintenance gear. I don't know how much of it we can get cleaned up and functioning again. We just won't know until the creek goes down."

"We're together and we're safe," Carolina pointed out. "Even Duchess and Cisco. Which is better than some people have had today, if all those stories on the news are true. Tomorrow we'll think about all that. Let's just get to Frankie's house in one piece." She had another thought. "I'll have to call Maci and Dave, let them know that we're all right. If they saw the news reports, I'm sure they're going to be worried sick. And I can send a message to Justin – he'll be worried, too. Especially if he's permitted to watch TV. I'm sure this is all over the news."

"I'm sure it is, Caro," Kirk answered. "But like you said – one day at a time."

• • •

Immediately they reached Frankie and Valerie's house on the north side, far distant from the flooding downtown, and along the creeks that threaded San Antonio, Valerie drove Carolina to the nearest Target store to buy underwear, pajamas, and a change of clothes for them all, as well as a pair of shoes for Jordyn.

"I'll never think of John Lennon's 'Imagine' song again, without wanting to throw something at the man," Carolina commented, as they went through the checkout stand. "'Imagine no possessions' ... well, I don't have to imagine now, do I?"

"It's easy if you try," Valerie grinned, impishly, and Carolina began to laugh. Well, one had to laugh, either that or break down sobbing. The situation was still completely unreal.

. . .

Kirk and Frankie went back to the site the next afternoon, when the water had receded sufficiently that they could get into the buildings. It was a long wait, for Carolina and Jordyn, at home with Valerie, wondering what the men would find, if they would find anything at all. It was nearly suppertime when Frankie and Kirk returned, dirty, damp and muddy to the knees. Carolina brought them each a beer, once they had changed into something cleaner, and they all sat out in the cool evening, on the back porch, where Frankie had his BBQ grill, and an outdoor refrigerator for cold drinks.

"Oh, Jesus, Caro, it's the most godawful mess I ever laid eyes on. The company vehicles are all jumbled together, piled up like Tonka trucks. Just about everything but the filing cabinets was washed out of the office building; all the papers in them are soaked through. Everything small is ... God knows where, probably miles down the Salado and buried in mud, I think. Computers are shot, likely can't be rebooted, so are the mowers and maintenance gear, although we might be able to salvage them with a bit of work. As for the nursery inventory ... all gone. Swept clean. Somewhere farther down the creek, I guess. Everything in the trailer and the RV is trashed. And all those big trees by the creek ..." Kirk grinned. "Are full of your clothes, Sugar. Hanging from the branches, as God is my witness."

"Well, I'm glad you found something to be amused about," Carolina replied. It was grimly amusing to think of all her wardrobe, hanging from tree branches, rather like a kind of trendy department store display.

Now Frankie said, "You do have flood insurance, I would think. That should help with a lot of the expense, wouldn't it?"

"It's the work of cleaning it all up, sorting out the losses," Carolina explained. "And yes ... It was mandatory with our loan that we have the minimum amount of flood insurance, and I thought I had made it plain to our insurer that we did want additional flood insurance, since the place was in a 100-year flood area."

"Well, that's all right, then." Frankie sounded relieved, but Kirk was still depressed.

"We have to keep the business going, honey," he said. "Not just for the clients ... but so that our guys have a paycheck to depend on."

When the water had receded sufficiently that serious clean-up of the Garden-Grow site could begin, there was so much that needed doing, Kirk and Carolina hardly knew where to begin, once that she had arranged tetanus shots for the two of them, and a handful of employees who had volunteered to work, sorting out the shambles left after the flood.

"We have to go on servicing our clients," Kirk said, looking at the tangled, muddy mess that had been the shed with the mowers and power tools. One of their workers was spraying an ordinary garden hose over it all, washing off the mud as they watched. "And I stayed awake last night, writing down a list of all the existing clients and the details of their maintenance contracts that I could recall. Those contracts we have copies of in the files once they are dried out. But with the computers ruined we have no idea of how much they owe, or when they're due to pay."

"I'll go to the bank and ask for a print-out of our business account records," Carolina replied, her shoulders sagging at the thought of one more thing to do, to recover from the wreckage that the flood had made of their business. "Maybe I can reconstruct the payment histories from the deposits."

"Out of fifteen trucks and vans," Kirk continued, as if he had not heard a word. "We have two which still function, besides the one we drove out in, because Samuel and Juan drove them off-site Friday before the flood so that they could get to clients over the weekend. Our credit is good, so that we can afford a couple of rental trucks for at least a couple of months. But what about the rest of the gear? What do you hear from the insurance company?"

"The adjuster is coming on Wednesday," Carolina replied. "But I can't get them to understand that I did specify that we wanted additional flood insurance included when we set up for this place. We're covered for fire, workman's compensation, and certain other kinds of damage. I'm certain that our underwriter insisted on flood insurance since we were in a zone off the Salado where it was a possibility. And I asked for it, but the people I am talking to insist that nothing other more than the usual coverage."

"See what the adjuster says," Kirk said, with a sigh. "I reckon it's like the old joke about how you eat an elephant; one bite at a time."

"Right," Carolina replied, but there was truly so much that needed attention, it was still hard to get started, when salvaging the sodden paper files from the office meant having to do three or four other tasks; setting up a place in the sun for all the paper files spread out to dry, wedging the file drawers open, and carrying armloads of sopping-wet files before even beginning that task.

One task at a time, one bite at a time. When she had finished with shifting soggy files from the wrecked office, Carolina wandered down to the creek, now returned to something more like the usual condition of small pools, connected by trickles through what looked like acres of mud. Mindful of the warnings about having small scratches and wounds contaminated and infected by contact with the mud, she wore heavy dishwashing gloves, and carried a plastic laundry basket; something to collect those garments still hanging from the tree branches, where the floodwater had deposited them. If they could be salvaged at all, Carolina was willing to take them to the nearest coin-op laundry with industrial-sized washing machines. She picked her way along the bank, snagging what she could reach, wondering if she would ever be able to find her driver's license. It had been lying on her work desk in the office, on Friday afternoon. She had it out to fill in the license number on some bit of state paperwork. At least she had the other necessary stuff that had been in her purse, like her credit cards, and Kirk had his wallet and his own driver's license in his wallet, which had been in his pants pocket on that disastrous morning.

She spotted an anomaly in the mud at her feet – something too regular to be the remains of blunt-ended grass, drowned and then covered by a thin layer of silt. She bent down and took hold of it, pulling it free from the mud and water – a leather jacket, trimmed with western-style fringe. Her own leather jacket purchased not three weeks before the flood – the original store tags still on it, Carolina fought back the urge to laugh and laugh. Of all the things to find, in the aftermath of that awful flood!

CHAPTER 27
STARTING OVER

"Well, we'll see what we can do about the equipment and office stuff damaged by the leaking roofs," said the insurance adjuster after surveying the mud-sodden property. "And the break in the septic system. You're covered as far as that damage is concerned."

"But what about flood damage?" Carolina asked, drawn to the breaking point by anxiety over the mess and the destruction of practically every single household item and personal possessions that they owned. "I'm certain it was a condition of our loan when we finance this property. I'm sure I asked for it to be included since the Salado Creek did present a flood hazard."

"I just didn't see that, anywhere in your policy," the adjuster replied. "Look, I'll have to check with my supervisor ... but I'm pretty certain that you have a minimum amount of flood insurance, but nothing more."

"I don't see how that could be!" Carolina was distraught. "We have to be able to replace all the gear that was ruined – and keep on servicing our regular clients. We'll need that payment for flood damages, I don't see how we can possibly carry on."

"You can ask for mediation with our company," the adjuster replied, which came across as reassuring to Carolina and Kirk both. In her own mind, Carolina was certain that she had asked for additional flood insurance, when they bought the business, knowing very well that the Salado Creek ran across the back end of the property.

• • •

They did go for mediation with the insurance company but lost. Carolina cried her eyes out, afterwards. She felt responsible for not having double-checked the insurance policies and made an almighty fuss when she noted the absence of additional flood coverage. She was, after all, the office manager and co-owner; she was the one responsible for the administration and payroll.

"Look, we can manage," Kirk, always the optimist, tried reassuring her, as they drove home from the mediation. "We can make it work. God knows, we've come close to being strapped before. At least this way, we have a cushion, from the sale of the company in Dallas."

"Not as much as you would think," Carolina shook her head and refused to be comforted. "We burned through a lot of that; paying off all those bills from vendors and suppliers that Sefton Blaine left us holding. Getting the new house finished took another big chunk out of what was left. We simply had to have the insurance payout, Kirk, otherwise we'll be strapped for money."

"We can make it work," Kirk insisted.

• • •

And God knows, they tried. They tried for two years. The one good thing that happened during that period had nothing to do with the struggle to keep Garden-Grow afloat was that Justin was given an early release from prison.

"Either they let him off for good behavior, or they were tired of you incessantly bombing your representative with letters about the boy," Kirk remarked when they received the good news.

"At least something went right, out of these last couple of years," Carolina said, dizzy with relief and happiness, after getting the good news.

They took the day off from work when Justin was released. He came up on the bus from where he had been incarcerated, and they collected him from the downtown bus station. Carolina almost didn't recognize him when he got off the bus. He had bulked out a bit, from working out in the prison gymnasium, although he was not as tanned as he was, upon returning from New Mexico from the ranch job there.

"It's not like I didn't have anything else to do," he said, when she remarked on how fit and muscular that he looked now. "I hit the weights a lot." He seemed different in other ways, though. He held his head up, looked people directly in the eye. Carolina was hard put to define exactly what was that change in him. "I had a lot of time to think. About things. Me. How I screwed up, royally. What I'll miss out on with Andy and Savannah. I met a lot of guys in jail, Mom. Some of them were old – they had spent most of their lives behind bars. And it finally came to me that I didn't want to be like them. I didn't want to look back on a wasted life."

"Sounds like the 2x4 finally connected," Kirk commented later. "And not a moment too soon."

Carolina was just relieved that her baby boy was out of prison. "He should never have been sent there!" she said, and Kirk shrugged.

"Did him some good, in the long run. What is he going to do, now?"

Carolina sighed. "He's going to take the bus back to Dallas. There's a halfway house there, where he can stay for six months, while he looks for a job. And he's going to look for an Alcoholics Anonymous group, I don't know if he can even patch things up with Savannah – but he says that he is bound and determined to be involved in little Andy's life."

"Well, that's good," Kirk allowed. "Especially if he can stick to it."

• • •

But that was the only good thing, in the aftermath of the flood. The day came a little more than a year after Justin's release, when Carolina looked at their business bank accounts, looked at the bills that they still owed, the ruined vehicles and maintenance gear, still sitting rusty and near-derelict, having defied every effort to get them operational again, the tools and equipment that they needed but couldn't afford, the employees that they needed also, but couldn't afford to hire because funds were so tight. At that moment, Kirk came into the office, sweaty and smelling of gasoline and cut grass. He had been all day in the heat, operating the mower and cutting the grass for one of their regular clients. They had to let several employees go, and now Kirk was working alongside the ones that were left. Carolina had a sudden feeling of crystal clarity. It was clear. They were done. It was finished. Beyond recovery. Sefton Blaine cheating them from the outset was bad enough, but the flood was the final blow.

"We can't go on," she said, simply. "It will kill us both, trying to keep on making bricks without straw. I'm going to call our lawyer and see what we need to do to declare business bankruptcy."

Kirk slumped in the nearest chair, a battered metal government surplus item; all that they could afford when it came to replacing those desks, cabinets, and chairs, fitting out the office after the flood. Carolina had gone to a surplus auction at Fort Sam Houston and bid on what she could get.

"Can we keep Jordyn in school?" he asked simply. His eyes were red rimmed from all the dust kicked up by the mower. "She loves TMI – it would kill her to leave in her senior year."

"We'll do everything to keep her there," Carolina agreed. "And one more thing; not a word to her about the money situation. Agreed?"

"She's a clever girl," Kirk nodded. "She'll figure it out, eventually. But agreed."

"It wouldn't be a personal bankruptcy," Carolina pressed her fingers on her eyes. She could feel a headache coming on. "A business bankruptcy. There is a fine difference. Oh, God, Kirk, it still feels like a defeat. But we can't do this anymore. We'll sell what we don't need. Even the house, if worst comes to worst. We can downsize to a smaller house. Sell the RV. It's not like we'll be able to go on vacation anyway."

"Shit, Caro! We'll have to go out and get real jobs," Kirk said, and Carolina began to laugh. Better that than cry. There was no good out of crying.

"We'll just have to start all over again," she replied. Her heart ached for Kirk. He had been the boss of his own company for so long. It had been her notion to get out of Dallas, move back to San Antonio... and that notion had brought economic doom upon them both. She had started all over again many times; the last time being when her friend Alicia told her about the watch company opening, at the mall in Dallas, the job she had walked away from when she married Kirk. "We've got connections, friends. We can work the customer network, if worst comes to worst. We'll always get by."

"Sure thing, Caro," he reached over the desk; another battered DOD surplus item, bought at auction at the Fort Sam Houston DRMO yard. "Look. Whatever our lawyer advises, we hang together as a family, for us and for Jordie. This place is an albatross around our necks, no kidding. We can get rid of it and start new. I won't mind working for someone else, for a change. Take an anchor off my neck, worrying about how to make payroll, that I gotta bail one of the regular guys out of jail on a Saturday morning after payday for being drunk and disorderly, that I have to hand-hold another unhappy client who might just not pay the overdue bill if they don't like how I suck up to them ... let some other poor bastard worry about all that. I'm tired, too."

"I know," Carolina took his hand in hers; her poor, hardworking, exhausted husband, Jordyn's daddy, who had been all day mowing acres and acres of grass, on a cranky and barely functioning mower, because that was all they could salvage after the flood, and the client had paid for that service in advance anyway. "We'll get through it. Let's get this anchor off our backs, and then ... we regroup."

"OK," Kirk slumped into the chair. "We will."

· · ·

Their personal credit was still good, all the outstanding bills were paid – but filing for the business bankruptcy still hurt. To Carolina, it felt like admitting a failure, killing a bit of their spirits. They had been doing so very well for twenty years and more ... and now they were financially just barely breaking even. They said nothing much about it to Jordyn, but she was an intelligent and observant teenager. When it became obvious that Garden-Grow was no longer theirs, and that Kirk and Carolina both were scanning the job want-ads, filling out applications, and scheduling interviews Jordyn announced that she had started a part-time job at HEB.

"Baby, you're still in school!" Carolina protested. "What about your grades? You simply can't let your grade point average drop."

"It's a summer job" Jordyn explained. "Look, Mom, I can at least save up and pay for books when I hit college. Don't worry. I'm going to apply for every scholarship program that is offered."

"You shouldn't have to worry about money," Carolina said, "We don't want to burden you."

Jordyn gave a theatrical sigh. "Cause that's your job, Mom? Look, I'm not blind. I know that the flood was a disaster, and you and Dad are in a pinch. I can help, you know. I'm not a child anymore."

Carolina got a job as an administrative assistant at a big local bank; basically, she was an executive secretary for one of the upper-tier managers. It was not a particularly difficult or challenging job, given her previous experience as a nurse, store manager, or office manager. She went to work every morning in a tall glass office building just off the 410 Loop North; after fighting the daily commuter traffic morning and afternoon, the only mildly challenging part was having to wear a suit or pant suits, as a certain level of professional appearance was required; no more dressing down for the Garden-Grow office in scruffy jeans, sneakers, and a tee-shirt. At least, she and Jordyn were not required to give up their cars, or Kirk his pickup truck, as part of the business bankruptcy. All that they lost was the acreage on which Garden-Grow had operated, the sheds and office buildings and all the contents. Kirk also found a job almost at once, in the sales office of another landscape services company.

"It keeps the wolf from the door, at least," Kirk observed, and Carolina shook her head. She had been going over the bills for utilities, insurance, the mortgage on the large house, even just gas, and groceries.

"The wolf is just lurking at the end of the driveway," she said. "And looking towards the door, licking his chops. We have to live within our means, the means of an admin assistant and a landscape services salesman. With just the two of us and Jordyn going off to college soon, we can get along in a house a third the size of this. That would slash our living expenses, right there."

"I hate to do it," Kirk said, wistfully, looking around at the living room of the house that they had built, when they had expected to do so very well from Garden-Grow; a large house, almost 4,000 square feet, which seemed even roomier, since a large part of their furniture and household goods intended for it had been ruined or destroyed outright in the flood. "We put a lot of thought into this place, but we don't need the payments."

They put the house on the market, and made back all the construction costs, as well as the few years of equity that they had in it. Carolina found a smaller house, one that was not very much larger than the little house where she and Justin had lived when he was a toddler, and she was a new widow mourning the loss of a husband, and Daddy who had gone away and never returned. While arranging for the sale of the large house and purchase of the smaller one, their realtor mentioned that a local homebuilder was looking to hire motivated sales personnel.

"No salary, but a generous commission on completed sales," the realtor told her. "The housing market is wild just now and the commissions, if you're good at it, make all the difference. You could easily make a mint in commissions. You might want to look into it; you know the area really well, and I think you have the right personality for big-ticket sales. Most home buyers don't want to deal with some punk kid just out of college. They'd rather work with someone who has some maturity on them, who really knows the ropes."

"I'm surprised that you aren't going for it," Carolina said, and their realtor laughed.

"No, I'm doing just fine as I am – the housing market is on an upswing now. My grandfather used to say – that when it's raining porridge, make certain that your bowl is right-side up."

· · ·

Carolina thought about that for a few days. The admin assistant's paycheck was OK, and it was a safe and secure job, but not particularly generous when it came to the salary. With a child going to a good college, and eventually wanting a comfortable retirement for herself, and Kirk, working as an administrative assistant just would not allow that, although it would have been more than adequate if she were still in her twenties. It was a distinct temptation, knowing that with drive and hustle, she might make several times that in commissions. More and more she felt like she ought to take that risk. Before the ink was completely dry on purchase of the smaller house, she was already looking into the possibility of going for the all-commission job, selling new houses. She was offered the job almost immediately. She gave notice to the bank and plunged into the world of selling new homes. It turned out that their realtor was right: Carolina did have the knack for it and the market was booming locally. As their realtor friend said, the market was really wild. It seemed as if most of the newcomers and new couples setting up a household in San Antonio wanted to move into a new house, a new house with all the latest trends incorporated; stainless steel appliances, granite countertops, wall to wall carpeting ... a hilltop site with a view, an outdoor kitchen, a spacious back yard, a walk-in pantry or mudroom, natural limestone siding. It wasn't just fun for Carolina, getting people settled into their dream house, but the stream of commissions paid, and paid very well. This was downright exhilarating after the years of struggle with the landscape business, even before the flood, Mr. Blaine's treachery, and how her lawyer in Dallas had cheated her of the last of Maci's child support. She was able to pay the remainder of Jordyn's tuition at TMI for her senior year there, and for that part of her tuition, additional fees and living expenses at Baylor which Jordyn's scholarship in athletic training didn't cover over the first three years.

"So, I take it that the wolf is banished from the door?" Kirk ventured, at the end of that first year, when Carolina had brought in an income in triple figures.

"The wolf has sorrowfully given up on us, and is actively haunting other doorways," Carolina replied. "God, I'm so glad that I took up that job. If I had stayed at the bank, we'd still be pinching pennies until snot came out Lincoln's nose. You know, you ought to think about selling houses, too. You're already experienced at big-ticket sales."

"I might at that," Kirk agreed. It was a terribly tempting thought. A few good years of selling new houses, and they might be able to retire in considerable comfort. How different their prospects looked now, compared to the hard work and heartache of trying to keep Garden-Grow solvent.

"Real estate and the housing market goes on a seven-year boom and bust cycle," Carolina pointed out. "And right now, it's about two years into the boom. You'd be getting into it just in the nick of time."

FINALE
THE ANNIVERSARY

After the anniversary party was over, Carolina kicked off her shoes and collapsed onto the sofa. The cavernous living room of the big house on the hilltop north of San Antonio was strewn with the aftermath of generous hospitality to many guests. This was the house which Carolina and Kirk had finally built after making more than they had ever dreamed possible in a booming real estate market over twenty years since the flood of '98 had ruined Garden-Grow and driven them into declaring bankruptcy. But the quietly efficient staff from an upscale caterer based in Alamo Heights were making headway clearing away the abandoned plates, silverware, and glasses. Out on the covered lanai which overlooked the city, twenty miles to the south, the buffet table was already wiped clean. The distant lights of San Antonio twinkled on the horizon, and the strings of lights and the paper banners which decorated the lanai and the pool house swayed in the light breeze.

"Whew!" she exclaimed, "What a party! What fun to see everyone, and see how well the children are doing, but honestly, I'm glad it's done. I'm exhausted."

"Forty wonderful years," Kirk remarked. "To us, – time flies when you're having fun. Want some?" He gestured from the wet bar around the corner, with a half-full bottle of champagne. "We might as well finish it off, rather than let it go to waste."

"Waste not, want not," Carolina agreed. Kirk topped off two champagne flutes and handed one to Carolina before settling onto the sofa beside her. "Happy fortieth anniversary, darling."

"Happy anniversary, honey," Kirk put his free arm around Carolina's shoulders, and she laid her head next to his on the tall back of the leather-upholstered sofa. After a moment, Carolina remarked,

"It really doesn't seem as if it has been that long ..."

One of the catering staff appeared in the arched doorway to the formal dining room, with a large tub in her hands. She had a little nametag on her apron – Kari, over the catering company's tasteful logo.

"Is it ok, if I clean up in here now, Mrs. Davis?" she asked, and Carolina replied,

"Sure – I don't think there's much, though. Our daughter's girls were having a contest, seeing how many dirty plates and cups they could collect." She chuckled, "I think they were making a contest of it, like an Easter egg hunt. Jordie and Brianna have raised some darling little girls, haven't they Kirk?"

"They have, indeed," Kirk took her hand which wasn't holding the champagne flute and kissed it. "Just like their grandmother. Indominable – I can hardly believe Jordyn is a doctor now... not a medical doctor," he added hastily to the young woman industriously collecting what the little girls had missed. "A Doctor of Physical Therapy."

"That must be interesting," Kari remarked, gathering up an elusive glass from where it had been abandoned on a bookshelf.

"Yes, it is," Carolina replied with a brief sigh. "And she is good at it. You just never know how your children are going to turn out – and they can surprise you in so many ways."

"How many children do you have, Mrs. Davis?" Kari asked as she worked; idle curiosity, it sounded like – something to cover the awkwardness while cleaning up in front her customers. From upstairs came the sound of children's laughter and the footsteps of a small child running across the guest bedroom floor: Jordyn's daughters appeared to be resisting bath and bedtime. They heard the distant voice of Jordyn threatening not to read the latest chapter of the Harry Potter adventure that was their nightly bedtime treat if they didn't behave. Brianna took her daughter back to the guest house. All was quiet from upstairs after that.

"Four kids for us together in total; I have a son from an early marriage. Justin. He is fifty-six now, very handsome, and he works with men who have substance issues, which he would know about, as he worked through some of them himself. Justin has two sons and is a great father. Then my daughter Maci – from my marriage before Kirk. She married an Army NCO, and they have been stationed all over the States, and to Germany several times." "They have two sons of their own, they are grown, now."

"Brianna is my daughter from my first marriage," Kirk added. "She runs a recovery center in Dallas for women with alcohol and substance abuse problems – and she has two children, a boy, and a girl. Beautiful kids – they're staying in the guest house tonight, before they head back to Dallas in the morning. Jordyn is the youngest, the one child that we have together."

"Wow," said Kari earnestly. "It sounds like you have a wonderful family and to be married for 40 years, that's a long time. You don't look old enough to have a son 56 years old, Mrs. Davis, you must have married when you were a baby" Kati said jokingly.

Carolina winced. "Yes, younger than I would like to admit," That was a teenage marriage, and they have a high divorce rate," she replied. The question still cuts like a knife when the subject comes up about her young marriages. Sensing this, Kirk kissed her hand again.

"But the one that we celebrated tonight," he said grandly, "Is the one that lasted for 40 years! The most important of them all; forty years of ups and downs, but we stuck it out. That is exceptional for our friends and family our age,"

"Congratulations," Kari nodded, solemnly, and gathered up the last stray plate into the tub.

"Thank you" Carolina replied, warmly. "And if you have a chance, tell your boss that his staff did a great job helping us pull off this party."

"I will," Kari beamed happily. She balanced the tub on her hip and did one last survey of the set of shelves on which most of the abandoned plates and glasses had been deposited.

"Well, goodnight, Mrs. Davis ... Mr. Davis."

"Goodnight, and thank you," Carolina said, as Kari vanished into the dining room. Carolina closed her eyes; she was so tired ...

"Bugs you still, doesn't it?" Kirk dropped that question into the silence, a silence broken only by the distant voices of the catering staff, clearing up in the kitchen at the other end of the house.

Kirk could tell that when Carolina talks about her past that it upsets her. He noticed how she winced when she answered the girl about being so young when she had Justin. "Yep," Carolina replied, and rested her head on Kirk's shoulder again.

"That you think people are judging you?" he asked, gently. Yes, it is like my life is an open book, a comic book to some people. They think it is funny and don't take into consideration how I feel or the circumstances of what happened to me during those awful times in my life.

Carolina snorted "They don't have any idea how much it hurts, to know that I had given up friends and family – everything at 16, to marry a guy who used me to prove to himself that he was not gay and then to be tossed aside for another man. They have no idea of what it was like for me, having a child at eighteen, a very sick child, born with multiple birth defects, and never knowing what his future was going to entail. I just thought I was grown, *ha*! I grew up *real* fast. They had no idea of what it was like, living with a violent habitual liar and thief ... never knowing when I was going to say something that would set him off and get hit or punched!" They have no idea what it feels like to lose your husband in a war! It all hurts! But I always feel like I am being judged, about my marriages, that is why I don't talk about them, so it is like my past is a dark secret and it shouldn't be. No one knows what it feels like until they have walked in your shoes. Yeah, I made bad choices, but that's not me now." Carolina felt tears whelping up.

"It's OK, Caro," Kirk pulled her a little closer, and Carolina relaxed a little – but only a little. Kirk was so calm, even-tempered – a very rock to be relied upon, no matter what the situation. In that, she had come to realize, he was very much like Daddy. "All that happened a long time ago. A lifetime ago."

"I know. I suppose I ought to let it all go, by now," Carolina admitted. But there is still another thing that no can ever imagine what it feels like is to have you father leave unexpectedly and never come back and never hear another word about where he had gone or what really happened to him. It is heartbreaking! Sure, you lose a parent, but you have closure. He and I were very close and for him to just disappear is something I will never get over. There was never any closure.... You know Kirk, there is one thing that I wish I could have had at this party ... although I know that it likely wouldn't have been possible ... he'd be in his nineties, at least...."

"What is that Caro?" Kirk asked gently.

"One more dance with Daddy," Carolina replied. "Just one more dance."

ABOUT THE AUTHOR

Constance L. Cooper is a native Texan, raised in San Antonio. Married 41 years with grown children and nine beloved grandchildren. As a Real Estate Broker, she formed a real estate brokerage and loved making dreams come true and dealing transactions with her clients for the last 16 years. But always had a desire to be an author. She and her husband love traveling in their motorcoach and enjoys and meeting people.

NOTE FROM THE AUTHOR

Word-of-mouth is crucial for any author to succeed. If you enjoyed *One More Dance with Daddy*, please leave a review online—anywhere you are able. Even if it's just a sentence or two. It would make all the difference and would be very much appreciated.

    Thanks!
    Constance L. Cooper